THE
SHEPHERD

THE SHEPHERD

DAN BILODEAU

iUniverse, Inc.
Bloomington

THE SHEPHERD

iUniverse books may be ordered through booksellers or by contacting:

iUniverse
1663 Liberty Drive
Bloomington, IN 47403
www.iuniverse.com
1-800-Authors (1-800-288-4677)

ISBN: 978-1-4759-1255-5 (sc)
ISBN: 978-1-4759-1299-9 (ebk)

Library of Congress Control Number: 2012906353

Printed in the United States of America

iUniverse rev. date: 07/11/2012

To Julie, the most loving person I know.

Men never do evil so completely and cheerfully as when they do it from a religious conviction.

—*Blaise Pascal*

ACKNOWLEDGEMENTS

A special thanks to Marie-Lynn Hammond for her editorial guidance, honesty and patience.

PROLOGUE

During a period of my life which I'd rather forget, I became relatively close to someone who has caused me many sleepless nights in the course of my subsequent life and in the lives of countless others—a monster that walked among us.

His name was Roland King and although his corpse has been rotting six feet under for twenty years, I still cringe and shiver at the mere recollection of his face and of his name. Roland King: the self-professed New Prophet of God, the martyr, the self-righteous bastard.

Roland King, a.k.a. King Cobra, came from somewhere out west but no one ever knew exactly where. My best guess would be the Seattle-Vancouver corridor, but that's just a guess—and not even an educated one at that. To be perfectly honest, I never wanted to know, nor did I care to. The fact is, the more I knew about Roland and his minions, the more I became a part of the madness.

From what I heard, Roland was a loner who, one day, just like the prophets David or Abraham or Moses himself, experienced a sudden revelation passed on by an angel. This angel, according to Roland, had descended from the heavens to relay a new message from God. The message: to amass an army—holy warriors—in order to wage war upon the forces of darkness led by the Devil, the Antichrist and the Army of the Beast.

While this claim in itself was preposterous, even more absurd and dangerous was what—or who—he and his heinous clan defined as belonging to the Army of the Beast.

For anyone who cared to know or who dug deep enough to uncover the roots of Roland's insanity, one would have to look no further than his very own mother and father. Raised as Presbyterians in the midst of the hippie movement of the 1960's, a teenaged Roger and Janine King had suddenly renounced their faith following Roland's birth in

1966, the reason for which is still being debated today. For whatever reason, they became what are known as Identity Christians, eventually joining the Church of Jesus Christ—Christian, a white supremacist church founded in the late 1940's. From what I understand, Identity Christians believe that white Anglo-Saxons are the true biblical Israelites and that Jews are the spawns of Satan. Plain and simple. They also hold that non-Caucasians have no souls and therefore can never earn God's favor or be saved and that salvation must be achieved through both redemption and race. Through their association with the Church, the young couple met prominent members of various anti-Semitic organizations, including the Aryan Nations, which they would ultimately join in the late 1970's.

As members of the Aryan Nations, the couple attended numerous meetings, lectures, and sessions, becoming more radicalized as time went on. They often travelled to the group's headquarters in Hayden Lake, Idaho, to attend gatherings and ceremonies. They read hate literature such as *The Turner Diaries* as well as *The White Man's Bible*. They passed out flyers and leaflets encouraging the population to "fight back against the Zionist blood-sucking pigs" and to join the resistance against what they considered the "mongrelization of the nation" and "International Communism." They went to protest rallies during Jewish holidays. They desecrated Jewish establishments with Nazi symbols. They took part in assaults against prominent Jewish members of society. They even established their own anti-Semitic hate line and newspaper.

Jews were not their only targets, however. They also targeted African-Americans, homosexuals, Natives, immigrants and anyone else who didn't fit the mold of the stereotypical Anglo-Saxon Caucasian Christian.

This is the world in which Roland was raised. A world of hate. A world of intolerance. A world of racial and religious prejudice. And as the old saying goes, the apple didn't fall far from the tree.

In the midst of his parents' madness, a teenaged Roland ran away from home and became another one of those street kids seen every day, begging for change, cleaning windshields, holding up a sign or a thumb in hopes of getting somewhere—anywhere.

During Roland's years on skid row, his father was murdered— allegedly at the hands of a Jewish activist in the U.S. It happened on June 17, 1983. Roland, then a resident of Calgary, only learned of his father's murder several years later. After learning the news, he attempted to locate his mother, who had not been heard from in years and who was thought to have been murdered as well. During his quest, he came upon a man by the name of Reverend Wyman Hunt, then a minister at the Central Presbyterian Church in Vancouver. Although there's still much speculation and disagreement surrounding their first encounter, it's widely believed that the two met during the summer of 1986 when Roland presented himself at the church to collect used articles of clothing or other donations.

Hunt was no ordinary pastor, however. He had made quite a name for himself as an extreme traditionalist whose personal convictions didn't always reflect the doctrine of his faith. As far as politics and religion went, Reverend Hunt not only tended to lean to the far right end of the spectrum, but transcended it with a quiet and contagious fury. As fate would have it, Hunt managed to track down and inform a destitute Roland that his father had left him his estate: a small farm in a rural area just outside Kelowna.

Not questioning why his parents—who had disowned him following his alienation from the family—had left him the family farm, Roland returned to his home town in early 1987 and took up residence in his father's farmhouse. There he discovered a plethora of hate literature in the form of magazines, books, leaflets, pamphlets, and newspapers. Never taking more than a passing interest in them, Roland had originally set them aside with plans on burning them in the old wood stove he used to heat the small and decrepit structure.

He lived there, in almost complete isolation and destitution, for the next two years. I say "almost complete," had it not been for the occasional trip into town to perform odd jobs or for frequent visits by none other than Reverend Hunt. At first, Hunt's presence at the farm was aimed at helping Roland locate his mother. But unbeknownst to Roland, Hunt had an ulterior motive.

Over the years, Hunt became a father figure to Roland. Together, they talked politics, economics, history and, more importantly, religion, the end of the world and Armageddon. Hunt talked much about Roland's parents, their beliefs, and what they had fought to defend—what his father had died to defend. On numerous occasions, some of the leftover literature was retrieved as a reference to help support an argument. Hunt, often quoting from the *White Man's Bible*, and like a professor to a student, preached a much different version of the Holy Bible and, more specifically, of the descendants of biblical Jews.

Hunt spoke of a British Israelism, a Protestant religious movement whose popularity peaked during the Victorian era. This movement asserted that Europeans, Anglo-Saxons, Germanics and Slavs are the true descendants of the Israelites through the Ten Lost Tribes of Israel. Christian Identity, Hunt explained, was derived from British Israelism. However, what Hunt didn't mention was that British Israelism didn't advocate anti-Semitism.

Instead, Hunt spoke of Anglo-Saxons and Aryans and how it was his parents' belief that they were God's chosen race. He spoke of Eve's seduction by the Serpent, and how together they conceived Cain. According to the literature, Hunt explained, today's self-proclaimed Jews are actually descendents of Cain—and of Satan. He spoke of the United Nations and Communism as tools used by Jews to assume a New World Order.

Hunt frequently spoke of Armageddon, the Second Coming of Christ, and RaHoWa, an inevitable racial holy war during which millions will perish—marking the period of Tribulation. According to Hunt, the Tribulation will be part of a cleansing process, a time during which Jews and their allies will attempt to destroy the white race. Hunt explained that it is the intent of the Jews and their allies to force God's chosen people to wear the Mark of the Beast and that those who refuse will be forbidden from participating in commerce, business and politics and will ultimately be annihilated from the earth. However, as God's chosen people, it's the White Race—the Aryans—who will be victorious. Only after the final battle is over and God's kingdom is established on earth will the Aryans be recognized as the true Israelites.

At first, Roland was skeptical. Nevertheless, he enjoyed the discussions and the debates with his only companion. Every now and then, he would pick up a piece of literature and engage in some reading to satisfy a growing curiosity. The more he and Hunt spoke of such things, the more he read. He became so immersed in these teachings that, in the end, he couldn't help but accept this theology as truth. The fine line between fact and fiction was, in Roland's mind, no more. There was only fact—a twisted and terrible one at that.

And thus began Roland's indoctrination into the dark world of racial and religious extremism. For years, he read, studied and listened. Quietly, slowly, in his derelict shack, he metamorphosed into something more sinister than what he had spent countless years trying so desperately to escape.

Unlike the average extremist, Roland didn't join a movement or organization. According to him, these organizations, while on the right path, were limited, flawed and disorganized. Their membership was scant, made up of unworthy rag-tags who knew nothing about their roles and the righteousness of the struggle. Despite this, he became well known among right-wing circles. After all, he read the same literature, participated in the same rallies and lectures, and shared many of the same values. Many had attempted to recruit him as an official member of their so-called organizations.

But Roland never took the bait. Instead, he festered and fermented in his own pool of hate. Then, in 1989, on a cold September day, he disappeared. Vanished. Like a ghost. For the longest time, Hunt and others closest to him believed he had been the victim of an abduction or murder at the hands of the many enemies he had made. Many feared he suffered the same fate his parents had.

Sometime during the summer of 1996, in the midst of a heat wave, Roland suddenly reemerged from his seven-year hiatus and revealed his divine experience to Hunt and to the few that cared to listen. Word on the street spread quickly about a lunatic claiming to be God's newest prophet and Roland soon became the butt of ridicule and scorn—not to mention death threats and other abuses.

However, it didn't take long for Roland to find weak and fertile minds to influence and manipulate. By the end of the summer of 1996, Roland had recruited and radicalized the initial numbers he desired. The result was the birth of one of the most wicked and violent cults the world had ever seen. There were twelve official members in total, with many more supporters, and they called themselves the Dominion of God.

CHAPTER 1

The shiny brass number on the door reads 1114. *Well, this is it,* I tell myself after verifying it corresponds with the number I'd written down on a slip the day before. *It's now or never.*

Instead of knocking, I take a step back to collect my thoughts. It suddenly dawns on me that despite having spent many nights of debauchery in the city, I've never been at the Hilton in Niagara Falls until now.

Poised to make that first rap on the door, many thoughts and emotions flood through me like a tsunami ready to swallow everything in its path, including my sanity. To be perfectly honest, a part of me desperately wants to turn around and walk away—for my own sake. That'd be the sensible thing to do. But there's this other side of me, one I've yet to tame, that insists on staying for reasons that seem to have been brought on by fate and other extenuating circumstances.

I still have no idea why I've been summoned here. Everything will be revealed to me in due time, I was told. Naturally, I feel suspicious. The first thing that springs to mind is the Dominion of God and ultimately, Roland King. Something inside me tells me my presence here at the Hilton likely has something to do with it.

God help me if it does.

I can't help but place a hand on my chest, cringing at the mere thought of the Dominion—or DOG as it was commonly known—and its sadistic rituals, thankful I'd never taken part in such madness. Even to this day, the mere thought of the Dominion of God sends a cold chill down my spine. I haven't forgotten that somewhere out there are former members of Roland's diabolical little cult, the Devil's true rejects.

My fists naturally clench as I step forward and prepare to knock on the door. From somewhere behind it, voices are heard. I take a step back and recoil, as I'm only expecting one entity. Maybe it's just the television, but something tells me it's not. I step forward again. I rap on the door four times.

Not three.

Not five.

Four times—two pairs in rapid succession.

The voices go silent. I can hear footsteps approaching. From behind the door, a chain is removed. The bolt-lock is unhinged. The handle to room 1114 twists and turns.

The door slowly opens. I step inside.

The room is dimly lit, the lamp sitting on a fancy desk denying the room of complete darkness. The shades are drawn and a half-smoked cigar rests in an otherwise empty astray.

I was right, the television set *is* off.

The chain and bolt lock are secured behind me by Frank Drumlin, a man who I haven't seen in nearly twenty years. So long ago that I barely recognize him at first. He greets me with a firm handshake and escorts me into the room.

On one of the two queen-size beds sits a man I've never met before. Much younger than Frank, he looks at me curiously, seemingly unsure as how to introduce himself. He's dressed in a snappy navy-blue suit with a beige shirt and a diagonally striped tie. His short brown hair is messed with a bit of pomade or gel. He stands up as though to greet me as I pass by. With things still brewing inside my head, I don't even acknowledge his presence. After all, I wasn't expecting this—him, I mean.

Frank follows behind me and takes a seat on the fancy chair before the desk. I turn to face him under the light and notice he's aged terribly since our last encounter. As I struggle to remember exactly how many years have passed since our last exchange, he opens a briefcase sitting on the desk.

"Long time no see, old friend," he says, pulling out some files. His eyes sift through the pages. "How long has it been? Fifteen? Twenty years?"

"Yeah, twenty sounds about right."

"Twenty years . . . God, how time flies," he answers, staring aimlessly at the ceiling. "How have you been?"

"I've been good," I say, but that's a complete lie.

"A few gray hairs, I see?"

It's true, I've begun to gray. Only along the sides, though. I mean, nothing that would warrant Hair Club for Men. Still, I can't believe he points this out. I stare back, making it obvious I'm looking at the crown of grey around his balding head.

"Yeah, I know," he continues, "Father Time has caught up to me too."

Twenty years, I remind myself. Hell, he must be well into his late fifties now—perhaps older. It's a wonder he's not retired already. But it's morbidly true—age has caught up to him. Probably too many late nights like this over his lifetime, I figure.

"This is Agent Jacob Hoffman," he says, motioning to the younger man in the dark blue suit. "Jacob, this is Liam."

Our eyes finally meet and we shake hands and I notice his firm grip. Tall, fit, well-dressed, and fairly attractive by the standards of most women I'm sure, he looks as though he just stepped out of the pages of GQ magazine. I can't help but wonder whether Jacob Hoffman is his real name. After all, these people tend to go by aliases.

"Nice to meet you, Liam. Or do you prefer Mr. Sheehan?"

"Liam is fine."

"Jacob is one of our newest and finest recruits," Frank offers. "I hope you don't mind him being here. He'll be taking over my portfolio in a few weeks."

Taking over his portfolio?

"I'm retiring in September," Frank reveals. "The wife and I have talked about it for quite some time. I think it's about time I hang 'em up. God knows I'm too old for this."

"Congratulations, Frank," I say. "Well deserved, I'm sure."

Frank Drumlin has spent his entire working life in security and intelligence. I know this because he told me, and because I've worked for him for a good part of that time. He began his career with the Royal Canadian Mounted Police—the RCMP—and then transferred to the Canadian Security Intelligence Service when the latter was created in 1984. Although I don't know the specifics of his postings or operations, I know he's worked on various files and in various regions. Twice he was seconded to the FBI, once to the Australian Security Intelligence Organization and once to Scotland Yard. He has extensive experience in domestic terrorism and radical right-wing groups. As a young RCMP recruit, he was heavily involved in the *Front de libération du Québec* debacle—more commonly known as the FLQ crisis—back in the 1970s. He's a nice guy, but he tends to lose himself in his work and forgets that there's more to life than dealing with shit like this.

An old-school type of guy, he was what they call in the intelligence field my "handler" during the Dominion of God fiasco that erupted in late 1996. I can't wait to hear why my presence is requested here today.

But first, queue the small talk.

"You still follow baseball, Liam?" Frank queries, grabbing the remote control. He turns on the TV and scrolls through the channels. After much scrambling, he finds the local sports channel, which is airing a baseball game between the New York Yankees and Toronto Blue Jays. He then raises the volume slightly to equal our conversation level. They do this to drown out anything we say in the event we're being watched—or, more importantly, listened to. Not that it'd really matter, as anyone with the proper equipment could easily isolate electronic noise from real noise.

"So what have you been up to all these years?" Frank asks.

"Nothing special. I work at a local deli during the day and I used to bartend at O'Reilly's Pub before it burnt down." I say this with little humility as I know he wasn't expecting any different. I'm not exactly high up there on the food chain. I can barely make ends meet and my girlfriend is actually the one supporting us.

"Still with Sarah?"

"Yeah, still with Sarah."

"You finally get married? I mean, after all these years?"

I shake my head.

"I always thought she was a nice girl. You should marry her someday, Liam. Make an honest girl out of her. She'd make a good wife," Frank offers, then picks up the extinguished cigar in the ashtray and lights it anew. His thin, chapped lips begin to suck on it voraciously.

"I know she would," I reply, "but I'm not interested in marriage anymore."

Truth is I lost all interest in the institution of marriage, and church in general, during the days of the Dominion of God. Hanging out with religious fanatics kinda does that to a man after awhile, especially when these fanatics become extremists, and even more so when they become terrorists. Once a devout Catholic, I became agnostic shortly following the whole Dominion debacle. Nowadays, I'm leaning toward atheism. But the jury is still out on that.

Frank shakes his head. "Don't let a few wing nuts dictate your faith. If you do, they win. They control you. You should go back to church. Get married. Make an honest woman out of her."

I say nothing. I know that he knows my financial situation and my thoughts on organized religion and the institution of marriage, and I know he'll use it to his advantage.

"Jacob here got married himself just a few months ago, ain't that right, partner?" he says, turning to his younger counterpart, who is nodding in agreement. "A spring wedding—it cuts costs. It wasn't anything too fancy. Plain and simple. Like the good old days. Weddings don't have to be so expensive, you know. Right, Jacob?"

"That's right."

"Congratulations," I tell him.

"Thanks."

Frank pulls out some more files from his briefcase. "Just so you know, Jacob knows the history of our relationship and the things we've worked on. He's well aware of the good work you've done and your loyalty."

I nod.

"Look, I'll cut to the chase," Frank says, dropping the files onto the desk. "I think you know why you're here, don't you?"

I don't answer. Instead, I let them think that I'm unsure, that I have no idea. Truth is, I have a pretty good idea. They look at one another and wait for my response, like two scientists waiting for a lab rat to react.

"It wouldn't have anything to do with the bombings last week now, would it?" I finally reply.

They both nod in sync.

"What the hell do you want from me?" I ask.

Frank takes another drag from his cigar. "Nothing much. Just your insight. Your thoughts on the situation. We were wondering—well, hoping really—if you had any input . . . any suspicions as to who may be behind them, even if it's just a hunch."

"What makes you think I might know something?" I reply, annoyed.

"Nothing makes us think you know anything," Frank replies, crushing his cigar. "Truth is, we don't have anyone else we can turn to for insight, and with such connections. We've got nothing. Neither do the police. This whole thing came out of the blue."

"Connections to what? For Pete's sake, Frank! Are you actually referring to the Dominion? They're dead, remember?" I spit angrily, not realizing the tone of my voice. "What connections do you think I still have? And why would the Dominion attack a bunch of mosques? Besides, you don't think that—"

"Liam, just calm down," Frank says, retrieving a folder from his briefcase. "We have no expectations. I know it's been twenty years since we severed ties and there likely aren't any connections, but we just thought we'd give it a try."

From the folder, Frank pulls numerous glossy photographs of what appears to be a crime scene along with several recent newspaper clippings. Handing them over, he requests that I go through them in hopes of stirring some distant memories. Most contain demolished mosques. Others reveal people running and crying, body parts and blood. I take one quick look and then simply disregard them. Although not in such vivid color, I've seen them all before.

"Let me guess, you think they have something to do with Black Friday?" I ask.

The two men nod in unison.

Black Friday has gone down in history as being the deadliest terrorist attack the world has ever witnessed. It happened just over a year ago on July 1st, otherwise known as Canada Day, a national holiday and the equivalent to Independence Day in the U.S. Over five thousand people lost their lives that day, nearly twice the toll of the infamous attacks of 9/11. On July 1st, nearly a million people flood the streets surrounding the Parliament buildings and the grounds around them and partake in various festivities, outdoor concerts, air shows and fireworks—just to name a few. A million people. No one saw it coming, despite all the indications that the country was on al-Qaeda's radar. The intelligence community had warned them . . . had warned us. No one took it seriously.

Then it happened.

An eighteen-wheeler with its cargo packed full of explosives. Remember the Oklahoma City bombing in 1995? Well, the Ryder truck used was packed with roughly 2,300 kilograms of ammonium nitrate and nitromethane. That bomb was enough to destroy most of the Alfred P. Murrah Federal Building, killing 168 people. The Black Friday truck driven by Islamic extremists was packed with over 6,000 kilograms of the same components, nearly three times the amount in the Oklahoma City bombing. Now, mix this stuff with tens of thousands of nails, nuts, bolts or whatever can make a good projectile. Then, take a million people packed tight like sardines in a can and plow an eighteen-wheel truck at over 130 kilometers per hour through them and detonate that 6,000-kilogram explosive.

Although the blast occurred some three hundred yards away from the Parliament buildings themselves, it was enough to shatter every single window pane directly exposed to the blast. The other buildings along Wellington were either completely obliterated or had collapsed due to the intensity of the blast. Five thousand and seventy-three people dead. Nearly fifty thousand injured, most seriously and permanently.

That was a year ago last week.

The U.S. was also targeted, with attacks planned for Independence Day only a few days later. However, due to a heightened security and threat level, several attacks were foiled, with the exception of one that claimed the lives of 150 people in Philadelphia.

As it turned out, the group responsible was not al-Qaeda, but a similar group of homegrown terrorists who were influenced by the al-Qaeda ideology. In Canada, four people have been arrested in connection and are awaiting trial. In the U.S., six were arrested in connection to the attack in Philadelphia and the planned attacks in Washington, Chicago and Los Angeles.

I remember Black Friday quite vividly, although I wasn't in Canada at the time. I was actually in New York, where I grew up, to visit some relatives. I have dual citizenship and consider both countries my home. Black Friday struck a very deep chord, as did 9/11 before it.

"What? You think the mosque bombings were some type of retaliation for Black Friday?" I ask.

"Maybe in part," Frank replies. "Think about it . . . three Canadian mosques were hit: Ottawa. Montreal. Toronto. The explosions all within ten minutes of each other—all on the eve of the anniversary of Black Friday. Then, a fourth one in New York."

"In part? What would be the other part?"

Frank glances over to Jacob and back to me. "I'm sure by now you've heard of the comprehensive peace plan that will be proposed by the European Union and presented to the Israeli government and the Palestinian Authority in late October. A series of peace talks has already been scheduled in Rome and will be hosted and mediated by the EU over the next several months. The League of Arab States has also been invited to observe the talks, which are anticipated to build upon the *Arab Peace Initiative* that was first proposed by the league in 2002 and on the *Roadmap for Peace* plan that was presented by the quartet of the U.S., Russia, the UN and the EU in 2003."

"So what?" I reply, skeptical about any settlement to the conflicts in the Middle East. "I mean, nothing has ever worked before. What makes this newest plan any different?"

"I don't know," Frank replies. "Something tells me there may be more interest and motivation from all parties this time around. The EU really wants to put an end to the Israeli-Palestinian conflict once and for all—for both economic and security purposes. The fact that the League of Arab States has been invited to observe the talks and perhaps even be involved in the discussions is unprecedented."

I don't respond to this, still unconvinced and unimpressed. Instead, I decide to take a second look at the newspaper articles that were handed to me. Photographs of the carnage fill the pages. No one saw it coming. The only solace was that the death toll was much lower than first thought: a total of 346 for all three mosques in Canada and 91 for the mosque in New York. It was definitely well planned, with the attacks taking place during the noon prayer on the last Friday of Ramadan.

"Do you have any idea who might be behind the bombings?" Jacob asks, speaking up for the first time. Although eager, he seems to respect Frank's seniority and knowledge, letting his older counterpart take the lead in the questioning.

"Not a bloody clue," I reply.

"Are you sure, Liam?" Frank resumes. "Have you heard anything? Even the slightest whisper? Do you suspect or know of anyone who might know something?"

"Sorry, Frank. I'm afraid I can't help you . . ."

He leans back in his chair, discouraged.

"I'm sorry, Frank. I know what you're thinking, but I don't associate with those types anymore. I've distanced myself on purpose. I'm as clueless as you are."

"Are you surprised by the bombings?"

"Well, yes and no," I reply. "I suppose I'm not surprised that someone out there had the thought of retaliating in one way or another. There are lots of radicals out there on both sides, you know that. And a growing number of anti-Islamist groups. But I have to say I'm surprised that there were absolutely no warning signs. You must have *some* leads, don't you? The police must have some people on their hit list—"

"The RCMP is investigating every possible lead," Frank says. "So are we. We're looking at any and every criminal, thug, white supremacist or religious fanatic out there with a known propensity for violence. And for any anti-Islamic groups. But we're not aware of any operating in the country."

"But it's clearly not the work of petty criminals or a group of rag-tag renegades," I say.

"Right. But we don't know of any group with the resources or capabilities to carry out such coordinated attacks. So we may even be looking at an international ring, given the U.S. attack." He pauses for a while to reflect. "Do you know what materials were used in the bombings?"

"Enlighten me."

"The explosive used in the U.S. blast was RDX—you know, a C-4 component. Thankfully, there were markers. We've traced the source back to an explosives manufacturer in Tennessee."

"Plastic explosive?"

"That's right," Frank replies. "The same type used in demolitions. You know, general blasting. Packs one hell of a punch. The military uses it in their operations. However . . ."

"What?"

"What concerns us more, Liam, is the type of explosives used in the blasts here at home. Ever heard of TATP?"

"Can't say I have."

"It's the acronym for triacetone triperoxide. Its street name is 'The Mother of Satan,' at least in the terrorist underworld," Frank says with a smirk. "Fitting, isn't it?"

I nod.

"It's one of the most powerful non-nitrogen-based explosives, if not the most," Frank notes. "Remember the shoe bomber? Well, it's this shit he attempted to use to blow up an airliner. You can make it out of household items, namely acetone, hydrogen peroxide of a high concentration—not exactly the stuff we use for wounds—and some type of acid like battery acid. A trip to your local hardware store or pharmacy is all it takes. Hell, it's probably the cheapest explosive out there."

"So what's your point, Frank?"

"My point is this: someone out there, likely in our own back yard and likely right here in the city, is producing this stuff—and in dangerously large quantities. Home grown. Probably right out of their basement or makeshift lab. It's simply too dangerous to travel with this stuff. It can be set off by the slightest temperature change, friction or impact. Trust me, you don't want to keep this shit around for too long—or at least not a large quantity of it—let alone travel with it for an extended period. Also, while you can make it from readily available materials, it's a pretty meticulous and dangerous process. You need the right equipment and know-how. Your average Joe would simply blow himself up trying to make it, as have numerous would-be terrorists around the world, hence its street name."

"I see . . ."

"The finished product is a white powder or small crystals—virtually untraceable and undetectable," Frank continues. "For the amount needed for the three blasts, someone really skilled had to produce it. We're talking kilograms of this stuff. We're thinking someone with a background in chemistry or biology. We need to get to the bottom of this before more of this shit shows up. Is there anyone from the days of the Dominion that fits this description?"

"Not that I can think of."

Frank gets up from his chair and makes his way over to the mini-bar. He pulls out two cans of ginger ale, scoops ice from a plastic bucket on the counter and drops a few cubes in three glasses.

"You still like your Jack and ginger?" he asks.

I hesitate. "Sure."

He mixes three drinks and hands both Jacob and I a glass.

I turn to the television. The Yankees have just hit a three-run home run.

Damn.

Frank walks back to his chair by the desk and retrieves some files from his briefcase. He then hands them to me. "You remember these three fellas?" he asks.

I open up the files one at a time. I'm not surprised at what I find inside: old surveillance photos of three former acquaintances of mine, likely taken during the days of the Dominion and the investigation that ensued.

Still, it's enough to make the hairs on the back of my neck stand up. "What about them?"

"You think they have anything to do with it?" Frank probes, taking a lengthy sip from his drink.

One by one, I look at the photos of Conrad French, Miroslav Milenkovic and Derek Devlin. Their whereabouts unknown since the 1997 standoff at the King Farmhouse and the disbanding of the Dominion that resulted, I can't help but wonder what the hell ever became of them. I hope for humanity's sake they're all resting cozy in wooden boxes.

"Have you heard from any of them over the past twenty years? Or even heard *of* them?" Frank asks, rather impatiently.

"No, never."

"Do you know of their whereabouts?"

"Nope."

"Do you think they would be capable of something this big?"

"No, I don't."

"And why not?"

I take a moment to reflect and taste my drink. "Because they're nothing more than skinheads, petty criminals and religious fanatics . . . nothing more than a bunch of followers. I don't think they have the brains or the know-how to pull it off. Why the hell would they even want to blow up some mosques anyway?"

Frank leans back and pulls out yet another file from his briefcase. He stares at it long and hard. "Do you know who or what the Black Mamba's supposed to be?"

I think about it. "No, I can't say I do."

Frank sighs, then hands me a single sheet of paper. It's a photocopy of some type of hand-written letter or communiqué. It reads:

July 2nd, 2016

To whom it may concern:

The Dominion of God is reborn! It is time for us to fight back against foreign aggression and counter the forces that seek to destroy us! The spawns of Satan are among us! The government, the Courts and the laws of man have failed us. Make no mistake about it. This is only the beginning. The War has begun. The time of Tribulation is upon us. We must engage and prepare for the Rapture and the Second Coming. Only the righteous will be left standing at the End Times. Let the Dominion of God be your shepherd. The time has come for us to claim back the world of God's Dominion and offer it to Him.

Black Mamba

"The Dominion of God," I mumble to myself, dumbfounded. "It can't be . . ."

"The Doomsday Cult . . ." Jacob murmurs, sounding distracted.

"That's right," Frank says. "The Dominion of God a.k.a. the DOG a.k.a. the Doomsday Cult. As far as we know, it became defunct when Roland went down in ninety-seven," Frank adds, looking to Jacob for his attention. "It hasn't come up on our radar since—until now." Frank frowns. "Black Mamba . . . isn't that a spider or something? Are you sure you've never heard of this?"

"Yeah, I'm positive." I hand back the letter. "When did you get this? Why hasn't this come out in the papers?"

"It was faxed to the federal police just yesterday," Jacob replies.

"Do you know anyone who could help us?" says Frank. "Anyone who might know the whereabouts of the remaining three?"

"No. I'm sorry, Frank, I can't help this time. And to be honest, I really doubt it has anything to do with them. I mean, why would they claim responsibility? It's probably a bunch of wannabe cultists or anarchists—imposters—claiming to be the Dominion."

"That's possible. But if you hear anything, Liam, let us know. As you saw in the letter, they're promising more to come, whatever that might be. So if anything comes to mind, let us know. It may save lives."

I finish my drink and stand up abruptly as though I'm about to leave. I make it seem that way, but I really have no intention of leaving, even though leaving would be in my best interest. "Look, Frank, I'm not interested in being your rat anymore. I'm done with that. I've moved on with my life. You agreed to cut me loose, remember?"

"Yeah, I do remember, *Liam*. I'm not—"

"So whatever it is you're thinking of, forget about it! I'm not interested in putting my ass on the line and messing up my life more than it already is! Do you understand me?"

Frank sighs and looks over to Jacob. "Liam, we're not asking you to do anything. All we're saying is if you happen to hear anything or have any insight to share, we'd be happy to listen, OK? If it truly *is* the DOG . . . if it has resurfaced, I wouldn't be surprised if it plans to call upon some of its old supporters."

"I was never a supporter, Frank."

"You know what I mean."

We fall silent. The only sound is the ball game on TV. Eventually Frank places everything back inside his briefcase and locks it up. "You still like to gamble, don't you, Liam?" he says in a snide kind of way.

Son-of-a-bitch! I can't believe he's using this card.

"We helped you get out of debt, remember?" he says, looking away toward the drapes. "Just think about it."

I bite my tongue and say nothing. Sure, Frank did help me with my debts. Cash in exchange for information, that's how it works. They prey and take advantage of people's weaknesses, like mine. Gambling. My only vice. OK, so that's not entirely true. I have to admit, I do like my J.D.

"We can help you again," he says, turning away from the drapes. "If you come up with anything, just let us know."

"I doubt I will," I reply defiantly, although secretly wishing I had something to offer. Fact is, I'm more in debt now than I've ever been before—$100,000 to be exact. It may not seem that much, but when considering my credit rating and my $35,000 yearly salary while living in downtown Toronto, it takes an awfully long time to pay it back. It's even worse when owing such a debt to individuals like the ones I owe. Let's just say they aren't exactly a friendly neighborhood credit union.

For one thing, their interest rates are much higher.

It's no coincidence we're at the Hilton in Niagara Falls, just steps away from the casino, I'm sure. I'll bet my left nut 'ol Frank here has taken a quick look at my bank account or perhaps my lender's accounts before summoning me here. He's come armed and with a game plan. I wouldn't expect anything less.

"Like I said before," Frank continues, "I'm heading for retirement in just a few weeks. I won't be able to help you anymore, but Jacob here will. He can help you in a very big way. He's a smart kid and has my full confidence."

Jacob steps forward and politely hands me a business card. "I may not be as suave as 'ol Frankie boy here, but I'll do my best."

"Thanks," I reply, reading the card, which is nothing but a phony business card with his alias—Jake Hartman, Legal Assistant, Williams & McAllister Law Firm—along with his contact information. Without much thought, I slip it in my wallet. "Hope you fellas don't mind but I'd prefer not to be contacted," I say emphatically. "Neither at home or on my cell phone. If I ever have something, *I'll* call *you*."

As though expecting this, the two investigators nod.

"I'll be around for the next few weeks to help out." Frank slaps Jacob on the back. "But Jacob will gradually take the lead in all my files. Did I mention he was top of his class?"

I look at Jacob, but just momentarily. "Is that so?"

"Yeah, he's a pretty smart lad. He'll do just fine. Maybe one day, just maybe, he'll be able to fill these shoes." Frank grins.

"Oh, I don't know—those are pretty big shoes to fill!" Jacob replies in a brown-nosing kind of way.

"Hey, you know what they say about guys with big feet . . ."

Both Jacob and I laugh.

We spend the rest of the night in small talk while watching the rest of the ball game. The Yankees end up beating the Jays 6-4, taking over first place in the American League. Even though I'm originally from New York, I hate the Yankees. I always preferred the underdogs, I guess.

After the game, we each down one more drink and I begin to feel the alcohol coursing through my veins. I love my whiskey, but I know I shouldn't drink it. I made a promise a while ago to someone I care a lot about. I really have to work on keeping my promises.

I bid goodnight to the two investigators and leave the room. I've booked myself into a different hotel just down the street—on their tab, of course. While I'm skeptical as to why they chose Niagara Falls as our meeting point, I have to admit I feel more comfortable here than in Toronto, where I know just too many people.

As I'm heading down the elevator en route for a light snack and then maybe a game or two of poker, a million things go through my head. However, I can't think very straight on account of the whiskey. Instead on ruminating on what just happened, I decide to follow the overhead signs in the hotel lobby that eventually lead to the indoor glass walkway and straight to the casino.

CHAPTER 2

My heart's pounding heavily and I start to feel nauseous as I hang up the phone in the kitchen of our apartment. Sarah looks at me as though I'm about to keel over, but there's something else as well in her expression. I'm not quite sure what that is, but what I do know is that she doesn't seem impressed.

"What's wrong? Who the hell was that?" she probes.

"Nothing . . . no one . . . it wasn't important."

"It wasn't important, huh? So why do you look like you've just seen a ghost?" she continues, following me out of the kitchen.

A ghost.

How ironic.

"Jesus Christ, Liam! What are you hiding from me?" she hollers, tailgating me so close a cop would pull her over.

"For the love of God, Sarah! It was no one! Quit hounding me already!" I make my way into the bedroom. Naturally, she follows me and scrutinizes my every move. She's a good girl, really. But she can be a little over-bearing at times—especially when she feels I'm keeping something from her.

"It was those creeps Omar and Raoul again, wasn't it?"

I ignore her and look for my wallet. After much scrambling, I find it in the pockets of the jeans I wore the day before. Sarah's still standing in the doorway like a bouncer at a nightclub. I know I can't leave unless I come up with something.

"You want to know who it was? Huh?" I say, formulating my excuses as I go on. "An old friend who told me that one of our childhood friends has just been killed in a car accident. You happy?"

She stands there and says nothing at first, arms crossed.

"One of my best friends growing up. I hadn't seen him in years."

"Oh, well then . . . I'm sorry to hear that," she says sincerely, almost ashamedly. She instantly softens and abandons her post at the door. "Who was it? Do I know him?"

"No, you don't! Now do you mind? I need to get some air. I just need to be alone right now." I walk up to her and kiss her on the forehead.

"Of course . . ."

"I won't be long," I assure her as she abandons her blockade, letting me out of the room. "I'll do the dishes as soon as I get back, OK?"

"Don't worry about it, I'll do them," she offers, but I insist I'll do them. I feel too guilty not to do them. I feel guilty for making her feel guilty. But I don't know what else to do or say. I can't possibly tell her the truth. Let's just say that would be disastrous to our relationship. I should've let her think it was Omar and Raoul, the lesser of two evils.

God how I wish it had been Omar and Raoul . . .

I slip on my shoes and leave. I take the stairwell and exit through the side door. As I walk away, I can see Sarah through the window of our second-floor apartment. She's doing the dishes, wearing one of her tank tops that really accentuates her features. Pale skin. Auburn hair tied up in a pony tail. Looking sad and regretful. Damn, now I feel really guilty. I make a mental note to make it up to her later.

I immediately make my way down Dufferin Street and round the corner in the heart of Little Portugal. Once on Dundas—or Rua Açores in this part of town—I trek several blocks past numerous shabby and weathered Portuguese storefronts with the odd Asian market every now and then. Made mostly of gray or brown brick, or a shade thereof, most buildings in the area don't go beyond two or three floors, the first usually being the shop with the upper floors being rented out as apartments. Something I hadn't noticed until now is the near complete absence of trees or other vegetation along the sidewalk. Nothing but asphalt, concrete and brick in the midst of which streetcars carve their way from one end of town to the other. Kind of depressing now that I think about it. Whatever. This has been our neighborhood now for the past year and I don't foresee a move any time soon.

I continue down Dundas until I come to a 7-Eleven, where a phone booth stands unoccupied at the very corner of the Dovercourt Road intersection. Although I'd planned to call Jacob with my cell, the phone booth is probably better.

I weigh my options for a minute or so and ultimately opt for the booth. Scanning the area for any onlookers, I enter the booth and take out my wallet. I flip through a million discount cards and the few banking cards that I own and other personal I.D. I eventually find Jacob Hoffman's phony business card and dial the number.

"Jake here," he answers.

"Jacob . . . I mean, Jake . . . it's Liam . . . Liam Sheehan. Remember? We spoke a few days ago in Niagara Falls."

Jacob takes a few seconds to respond to finish chewing whatever it is he's eating. "Of course I remember! What can I do for you?"

"I need to speak to Frank. Is he around?"

"No, sorry. Is there anything I can help you with?" In the background, I hear the humming of an engine and the sound of traffic.

"I don't know," I reply, scoping the area for onlookers. "You'll never guess what just happened. Some fuckin' coincidence . . ."

"What?"

I take a moment to collect myself. "Get this. I get a phone call from this guy called Mario, Mario Martel. Frank would recognize the name. Ever heard of him?"

"No, can't say I have."

"Well, this is a guy I haven't heard from in years . . . maybe fifteen or twenty. He was a supporter of the Dominion of God."

I hear Jacob give a low whistle of surprise.

"Mario was a supporter, not a member," I specify, not sure if Jacob really understands the difference—or if there's even a difference, for that matter. "Anyway, he calls me just a few minutes ago at home. At my freakin' home! How the hell he got my number is beyond me. I'm unlisted. Anyway, he calls me up and shoots the shit, reminiscing about old times. Then, he says *our* presence is requested for a meeting tonight in a couple of hours at an undisclosed location. He said he'll only tell me the location in person. He's on his way to pick me up as we speak!"

The noise of traffic in the background at Jacob's end ceases. "A meeting? Organized by who?"

"I don't know. I asked, but all he replied was that *all the king's men* would be there. Like some type of royal ascension or something."

"All the king's men?" Jacob repeats as though not having heard correctly.

"Yeah, *all the king's men . . .*"

"Shit, do you think that refers to—"

I pause to think about it. "You mean Devlin, French and Milenkovic? No way. There's just no way. No one's seen or heard from them since the fall of the Dominion. Hell knows if they're even still alive."

"What did you tell him?"

"I told him I'd meet him at the 7-Eleven on Dundas in an hour or so. That was a half-hour ago. That's where I'm at now. I'm really not keen on getting involved with these guys again. I don't have a good feeling about this. Whatever's going on, Mario sure is keeping a tight lip about it."

"No kidding."

"I don't know what to do, Jacob. I need to talk to Frank," I insist, not because I don't have faith in the guy, but because Frank is much more experienced and more familiar with the case—and with me.

"Listen, sit tight. I'll talk to Frank. When did you say this was going to go down?"

"I don't know exactly . . . but within an hour maybe."

"Shit. That doesn't give us much time. I'll try to get a hold of Frank. Look, if our boys happen to be there, try and get as much information as you can. Where they live. Where they work. What they've been up to for the past twenty years. Anything. Again, they're not suspects in the bombings—at least not yet."

"What? You want me to go to this meeting and ask questions and then have you show up at their front door? Are you kidding me? You might as well put a bullet in my head right now!"

"OK, OK. Take it easy," Jacob says softly. "You know it's not going to go down like that. We're not going to put you at risk—never have and never will. You know that's not how we do business. If you're able to deliver any information that'll lead us to them, you know we'll cover. Besides, Devlin, French, and Milenkovic's past involvement with the Dominion is public. So the fact that authorities are looking for them should be no big surprise, especially to them. We've released the letter admitting the Dominion's involvement in the bombings."

I get temporarily distracted by a few shady-looking men loitering in front of the 7-Eleven. I watch as they approach each new patron, seemingly begging for change. My heart begins to pace as one of them suddenly approaches the phone booth. I'm asked if I have a light, to which I reply that I don't. And just like that, he retreats back to his pack and bothers me no more.

"You have?" I finally reply.

"Yes. It's just gone to several newspapers and media outlets," Jacob admits. "The Dominion of God will now be front and center in the media. Nosy reporters and investigative journalists will salivate over this, digging deep to find info on the missing members. The RCMP is heavily engaged in this investigation, as is the FBI. So whatever you might find out tonight, the Dominion's got no way of knowing where the information—"

"I don't buy that for a second," I tell him. "I'm not twenty-one anymore, Jacob. Look, if I'm going to do this, it won't be for free. I expect compensation or an allowance—just like before and nothing less."

"OK, I'll talk to Frank," Jacob replies, almost whispering. "I'm sure we can arrange something. In the meantime, hang tight. Call me as soon as you can once it's over."

"Is there any possibility of having a tail? I'd feel much better."

"I'll do my best. There isn't much time," Jacob replies, in a matter-of-fact kind of way. "And we don't even have an exact time or a location. I can see if we can get a team at the 7-Eleven pronto, but that's highly unlikely. How are you getting to this meeting again?"

"Mario is picking me up in less than a half hour," I reply, remembering only bits and pieces of our conversation.

"Any idea what he's driving?"

"None."

"OK, hang tight. I'll see what we can do," Jacob replies, as the sound of traffic can once again be heard from his end. "I'm heading back to work as we speak. I'll make some calls."

"Sounds good," I say, still uncertain about my decision. I have no interest in doing this. Not for me. Not for them. Not for anyone. The only comfort I can find—the motivating factor—is the money that could be in it for me. If this meeting turns out to be nothing more than a bloody birthday party, I may not get anything. However, if it turns out to be more, it could mean a lot of dough—and my ticket out of debt.

I hang up but stay in the phone booth, glancing around to see if there's anyone nearby who might be listening or if my ride's already arrived. Thankfully, all that remains are a few teenagers loitering in the

---

parking lot. I step out of the booth and make my way into the store. Inside, I buy a couple of energy drinks and a snack.

This could be a long night.

All the king's men. The words play over and over in my mind like a broken record. After stepping back outside, I look up at the evening sky and hope to God *all the king's men* aren't who I think they may be.

CHAPTER 3

Being the lone man in the back of Mario's rusty Sentra makes me a hell of a lot less nervous than sitting in front with one man back, I have to admit. I've seen enough gangster movies to know that.

I've been in the car for only five minutes and I can't help wonder whether this death trap on wheels will make it to the next mile—the odometer's now approaching 350,000 kilometers. The brakes squeal and grind as what were once brake pads dig into the rotors. The shocks are shot. How this car ever passed any safety inspection or air quality test is beyond me. The exhaust coming from its rattling tailpipe fills the interior, and the thought of carbon monoxide poisoning crosses my mind.

I listen carefully as the two men sitting in front engage in small talk. The driver, Mario Martel, reveals he's been living in the Montreal area for the past several years. The passenger, a man known as Roch Dorion, has also been floating around the same area as well. I haven't seen either man since the days of the Dominion.

As I mentioned earlier to Jacob, Mario was never a full-fledged member of the group. Neither was Roch. Both were simply low-level grunts, as I was—just pawns in Roland's chess match. I became well acquainted with them, Mario in particular. I knew Mario even before the days of the Dominion as he used to go to the same church I did in Vancouver. That was before he converted to Christian Identity and ultimately to the DOG. It was through Mario that I was able to infiltrate the Dominion, which ultimately led to its demise.

Mario is actually a personable guy—at least when compared to those traditionally affiliated with the group. The problem with Mario is that he's easily influenced by ideas that offer an explanation for his miserable existence and justify his contempt for what he believes are the causes of his miseries. He's a follower, not a leader. He's also a wanderer and never seems to have a fixed address. I suppose that's how he originally got caught up with Roland and the rest of his crew.

Roch is a different story. From what I remember, Mario and Roch are good friends and, according to what I'm hearing, have kept in touch over the years. While Mario's perfectly bilingual, Roch can barely speak English and has a very strong French accent when he does. He gets frustrated trying to speak English and often ends up having Mario translate. Most of the time, he just mutters to himself, usually French curse words, which tend to be religious in nature. He was reprimanded on several occasions by members of the Dominion for using the Lord's name in vain.

Roch is one guy I'll never trust. He hates everybody. I don't think there's any rhyme or reason. He just does. I never know what mood he'll be in, and his moods tend to shift dramatically from one second to the next. If he's not bipolar, then I'm not Irish. Anything can set him off. That's probably why he's got such an extensive criminal background and been in and out of prison and juvenile detention since his early teens. Breaking and entering. Theft. Armed robbery. Assault. Assault with a deadly weapon. Uttering death threats. All part of his dossier. His criminal affiliations also extend to one of the motorcycle gangs in the Montreal area—the Hell's Angels, I think, but to what degree I'm not sure.

By anyone's standards, Roch had one messed-up childhood. His father used to beat the crap out of him while his mom used their tiny apartment in Montreal as some type of brothel where she'd prostitute herself and get high on crack with her clientele. This usually happened while Roch's father worked the nightshift. The night he found out, he took a twelve-gauge shotgun and blew her head apart and then his own—all this in front of Roch, who was only eight years old at the time.

Talk about one messed up childhood.

"So where are we going?" I ask, breaking up the chit-chat between the two.

Roch looks back and grins. "Some church, I *tink* . . . hey, Mario? *Calisse!* What's da fuckin' name of it again?"

"Not a church, you moron," Mario replies, keeping his eyes on the road.

"What da hell is it den?"

"It's not a church!" Mario scoffs, curiously annoyed. "It's just a meeting place in a basement somewhere." He looks at me in the rear view mirror. "Liam, you remember Reverend Hunt?"

I think for a moment. "Wyman Hunt? Yeah, I remember him. What about him?"

"Well, he's a clergyman over at St. Andrew's now. He was reinstated a few years ago. Can you believe it? Anyway, he rents this place out downtown. He's letting us use his basement for the night."

I can't believe my ears. "What? Are you kidding me? He got reinstated? I didn't even know he was still alive! God, he must well be in his eighties!"

"Eighty-one," Mario says, keeping his eyes on the road. "I don't know how long he's been there though. He's moved around quite a bit. I know he was in Winnipeg for awhile, even spent some time in the States. Good 'ol Reverend Hunt. Thank God we have him on our side."

"Um . . . yeah," I reply, but I don't mean it. Not that I have a beef with Hunt personally. But he's dangerous. Not in the physical sense. No, his poison is much more infectious. Very old-school, extremely conservative and puritanical in his views, Hunt was the only pastor to allow Roland and his clan to organize and pray in his church before his excommunication. Neither a member nor exactly a supporter, the old Reverend was a symbolic icon, I guess—a figurehead of sorts. For Hunt, the Dominion became a vehicle to express his extreme views and his hate. Following Roland's return from his exile in the mountains, he wrote *The Last Testament*, a six-hundred-page volume of Roland's account, including a new message from God. In the end, the scriptures were nothing more than a radical and altered version of the Old Testament with selected readings from the New Testament, in particular the Book of Revelations. I still can't believe he was reinstated.

"Yeah, good old Reverend Hunt . . ." Mario repeats, his eyes looking back to me in the mirror.

A few rain drops begin to hit the windshield and Mario activates the windshield wipers. The weathered rubber stripping of both wiper blades slithers across the glass like cooked spaghetti, rendering the blades completely useless.

"How do you know all this?" I ask.

"Relax man," Roch replies, "We don't know any more 'dan you, OK?"

"Yeah, well, I beg to differ. I still have no damn clue as to who we're meeting—or why! Who the hell told you about it, anyway?"

Roch turns around and for the first time faces me. "Cyril told us."

"Cyril?" I reply, dumbstruck. "Cyril? Are you bloody kidding me? What the hell is this? Some kind of high-school reunion? Who the hell are we meeting?"

"We told you, we don't know," Mario replies, a little irritated by my line of questioning. "All we were told was that we'll be meeting all the king's men, just like I told you. No one knows anything, certainly not Cyril. Cyril was told to get in touch with Roch and I, and I was told to get in touch with you. That's it. Now chill, alright?"

This does little to soothe my apprehension. "I'm not going to fuckin' chill, Mario! If it's who I think it is, I don't want anything to do with them. I'm done with that shit!"

"Hey man, like I said, chill. Let's just see what this is all about, OK?"

"Fine."

I sit back, angrily cross my arms, and say nothing more. I suddenly feel like a child in the back seat who's just been scolded by his parents. Roch looks back at me and smirks. How I'd love to sock him one.

We cruise for another five minutes or so and then turn onto Winchester Street. At this point I begin to wonder whether or not we have a tail, but it may have been too late for Jacob to assemble a surveillance team.

Mario parks the vehicle and we dash across the street to avoid as much downpour as possible. A few houses down, we dart up a set of concrete steps as Mario rummages in his pockets to find the key. He unlocks the front door and we disappear inside.

The main floor of the unit is very modest. The floor is all carpet, grey and dirty. The walls are a yellowed white, likely from cigarette smoke. From what I recall, the old pastor was a chain smoker. The front door leads us immediately to the living room area, where two old sofas sit perpendicular to each other. In the corner stands an old bubble-screen television set. A coffee table sits in the center of the room, overlooking a picture window concealed behind brown drapes. A few paintings hang on the walls, one a depiction of the U.S. Civil War and the other what appears to be a depiction of Armageddon—angels and cherubs warring with fallen angels in reddened and fiery skies. Past the living room is a short corridor leading into the kitchen. A set of rug-covered stairs ascends to the unit's second floor. But we don't go into either of these areas. Instead, we remove our shoes and open a door just beneath the staircase that leads to the basement. Mario peeks in and motions for Roch and me to follow. As we make our way down the creaky wooden steps, we can hear chatter and soft whispers coming from below.

Unlike the main floor, the basement is only partially finished. Thin carpet and cheap imitation wood paneling. The ceiling is unfinished, leaving wooden beams and electrical components exposed. There are a few doorways—minus any doors—leading to smaller rooms whose concrete floors are left uncovered.

What really catches my eye however, are several posters pinned to the walls in the main area. Some appear to be authentic propaganda posters for the Nazi Party during World War II. One is a painting of Hitler holding a red Nazi flag in front of an army of soldiers carrying similar flags. In the center of the piece is some type of bird descending from the heavens. There is writing in German, but I can't read German. Another poster bears a Nazi symbol above a chess board over which hovers an eagle. More German writing. A Confederate flag hangs on a wall above a dirty green sofa, with a banner of the Othala Rune just next to it. Across the room from the green sofa is another sofa, over which hangs a British National Party flag and a second Confederate flag. On a coffee table sitting between both sofas are old newsletters and pamphlets for the Dove World Outreach Center, some inciting readers to burn the Koran in commemoration of the attacks on 9/11. Other newsletters from groups such as Stop the Islamization of Europe and Stop the Islamization of America are spread across several end tables, recliners and other chairs as though a round-table discussion is about to occur.

At the entrance to this living area I spot a bookshelf, which I scan as I pass by. I instantly recognize the spines of several of the volumes, *The White Man's Bible* being one of them. At the far end of the room are four men, one of whom I recognize as Cyril. I don't immediately recognize the other three. After all, it's been twenty years. All four cease their conversation and greet us with handshakes and nervous smiles. After chit-chatting for a few minutes, we realize that none of us have any idea why we're here.

One guy, who introduces himself as Nash, says he came all the way from New York City in someone's stead just for this meeting. The others, as I soon learn, are Canadian but from various parts of the country. Most of us, including me, are originally from the west coast and have relocated elsewhere following the disbanding of the Dominion.

I eventually learn that Cyril had since taken up residence somewhere in Saskatoon, where he's working as a non-licensed mechanic at some wrecking yard. From what he's wearing, I'd swear he's in the middle of a job. Dirt and oil stain his faded jeans. His dirty white t-shirt reeks of sweat and smoke and God knows what else. Always unshaven. I really don't know what to make of him. He never says much. A skinny and slimy type of guy, either he's always clueless or knows a lot more than he leads to believe.

The other two men, who I've only met on one previous occasion, introduce themselves as Shane and Vladimir. Both are originally from Vancouver and are now living somewhere in Toronto, which makes three of us now living in the GTA.

Outside, a storm approaches. Flashes of lightning can be seen through the small, curtain-covered windows just below the ceiling. Thunder erupts, growing more intense by the minute. The lights flicker and go off for a second, then come back on again.

After waiting around for nearly a half hour, we consider leaving, but then hear footsteps creeping down the stairs leading to the basement. Shadows soon emerge, growing larger as they make their way down. When the shadows are no longer and three familiar figures are finally revealed, I feel, almost instantly, as though my world has come to a crashing halt. I just stand there in denial, unable to come to terms with what I'm witnessing and what I can only figure is about to happen.

CHAPTER 4

It feels as though all the air has been instantly sucked out of the room by a giant vacuum. Although I'll never know for sure, I'd be willing to bet that the blood pressure of every one of us has just gone up a few notches. No one dares to say a word as we watch the newcomers make their way across the room.

Lightning and thunder erupts and the lights go off again.

Back on.

"Glad to see you've all made it," says one of the men, setting aside the duffel bag he's carrying and removing the dark hood that covers his head. I immediately recognize him as Derek Devlin and his companions as Conrad French and Miroslav Milenkovic. All three are wearing dark hooded cloaks. "I'd like to thank you all for coming, and a special thanks to you, Nash, for having come all the way from the Big Apple," he finishes, then retrieves strange, paddled-shaped wands from the duffel bag, handing Miroslav and Conrad each their own. "I hope you don't mind, but before we begin we'd like to perform a quick scan."

"A scan for what?" Mario asks.

"They're metal detectors. We can never be too careful, you know."

"Metal detectors?" I ask in turn. "For what?"

"We can't take the chance of being bugged," Derek replies. "Please, this will only take a minute."

One by one, we line up as though going through airport security. More like a herd of cows being led to the slaughter. At least that's what it feels like anyway. The three share the duties of scanning us from head to toe, asking us to remove any metal from on our person. Watches, keys, change, rings and other items are placed onto the coffee table. Once a man is cleared, he's asked to take a seat on one of the many chairs or sofas around the room.

"I'm sure you're all wondering why you're here," Derek says, sitting down on one of the recliners after having scanned the last man. Although he's aged, he appears as menacing as ever. "You're here because you've been asked to be here. Not by us, but by someone else—someone who thinks very highly of you and is inviting you to be part of a very exclusive union."

We all look at one another, utterly bewildered.

"It's been a while, we know," Derek continues, "but we're all a little older and a little wiser. Gentlemen, we're here to announce that the Second Coming—the White Horse—is upon us. The New Prophet has arrived, just as Roland had foretold. He has come to warn us that the Antichrist is among us and will soon foster a peace treaty with Israel which will mark the beginning of the Tribulation. He has come to continue the work we started nearly twenty years ago—the work that was left unfinished."

Derek pauses as Miroslav hands him what appears to be the Holy Bible. He then opens the book to a pre-determined page. "Gentlemen, a war is upon us. The Tribulation is upon us. Many signs and many prophecies have already been fulfilled with another soon to be fulfilled. I'm sure you recall Matthew 24 wherein he speaks of these signs. In case your minds forget, I will remind you of them. In his book, Matthew states: 'And as he sat upon the mount of Olives, the disciples came unto him privately, saying, Tell us, when shall these things be? And what shall be the sign of thy coming, and of the end of the world? And Jesus answered and said unto them, Take heed that no man deceive you. For many shall come in my name, saying, I am Christ; and shall deceive many. And ye shall hear of wars and rumors of wars: see that ye be not troubled: for all *these things* must come to pass, but the end is not yet. For nation shall rise against nation, and kingdom against kingdom: and there shall be famines, and pestilences, and earthquakes, in divers places. All these *are* the beginning of sorrows. Then shall they deliver you up to be afflicted, and shall kill you: and ye shall be hated of all nations for my name's sake.'"

Derek pauses to let this sink in.

No one says a word.

"Gentlemen," Derek resumes, "We're here because these signs are occurring or have already occurred. There are many false prophets out there, many false Christs. And they have deceived many, but not us."

More silence.

"And wars? Are we not already at war?" Derek shouts, becoming more agitated. "Since we last crossed paths, we have witnessed numerous acts of war. They have increased in severity, frequency and destructiveness. There have been ideological wars. There have been territorial wars. But the wars I'm talking about, gentlemen—the ones Matthew speaks of—is of a spiritual war, pitting nations against nations, kingdoms against kingdoms. A global war! And it is *we*, the followers of Christ—God's *true* people—who are being afflicted, hated and persecuted in a growing number of nations! It is *we* who are under attack!"

Again, Derek pauses to gage the reaction of every man.

I turn to Mario who nods in agreement.

"There are more famines now, more epidemic diseases and more earthquakes and tsunamis and natural disasters than at any point in time! If you watch the news, read the newspaper or surf the web, you'll know the proof is out there! The End Times are upon us!"

Derek hands the Holy Bible to Conrad and steps aside.

"Gentlemen," Conrad begins, his voice coarse and deep. "These are just some of the signs that the End Times are drawing near. Matthew also speaks of the gospel being preached throughout the world for a witness to all the nations. Thanks to advances in travel and telecommunications in the 20th century and the creation and advances in the World Wide Web in more recent years, this has already been accomplished. We're also witnessing a dire and unprecedented godlessness and apostasy in the world today as explained in 1 and 2 Timothy. And of course, there's the fulfillment of many biblical prophecies which I won't get into at the moment."

Conrad sifts through the pages of the bible until finding the passage he's looking for. He raises his eyes to us. "But for God's *true* people, there will be nothing to fear of the End Times or of the Tribulation before them. I refer you to Matthew 24:29-31 where it says: 'Immediately after the tribulation of those days shall the sun be darkened, and the moon shall not give her light, and the stars shall fall from heaven, and the powers of the heavens shall be shaken: And then shall appear the sign of the Son of man in heaven: and then shall all the tribes of the earth mourn, and they shall see the Son of man coming in the clouds of heaven with power and great glory. And he shall send his angels with a great sound of a trumpet, and they shall gather together his elect from the four winds, from one end of heaven to the other.'"

He flips pages yet again: "1 Thessalonians 4:15-18 also speaks of our redemption. It says: 'For this we say unto you by the word of the Lord, that we which are alive and remain unto the coming of the Lord shall not prevent them which are asleep. For the Lord himself shall descend from heaven with a shout, with the voice of the archangel, and with the trump of God: and the dead in Christ shall rise first: Then we which are alive and remain shall be caught up together with them in the clouds, to meet the Lord in the air: and so shall we ever be with the Lord. Wherefore comfort one another with these words.'"

Conrad closes the Bible and hands it back to Derek. "Gentlemen, this is what the New Prophet has come to do. He has come to comfort us with these words. This is what we have come to do on this night, to comfort *you* with these words."

Miroslav, who's also wearing a dark hooded cloak, steps forward and continues the speech. "Gentlemen, the days of Tribulation and End Times are upon us. As Roland had written, days of Tribulation will take form of brutal war that will destroy most of mankind and bring forth extraordinary suffering. Some call it Holy War. Some call it World War III. Others call it Armageddon. But do not fear! For God has called us to war before and has given us great victory!"

I have to admit, while it isn't the greatest, Miroslav's English has much improved over the years. He still sounds rather robotic and monotone, as do most from the Balkans, and speaks with a thick, Russian-like accent. At least it sounds Russian, if you ask me. He also tends to omit most articles in his speech, such as "the" or "a", which only accentuates his accent.

"Now, we're being again called to war—the biggest and final war! A war to end all wars! The Army of the Beast has gathered in preparation for this war and has grown stronger! Their onslaught has already begun! We must prepare for period of Tribulation . . . and for Great Tribulation and for Second Coming of Christ and for Rapture that will ensue because *we* are the elect! *We* are being called upon to fulfill our duties as good Christians and as God's true people! As good Christians, *we* have to reclaim God's Kingdom and offer it back to him!"

As I listen carefully to Miroslav's intense sermon, I can't help but feel I'm already in way over my head. I should've followed my instincts and refused to participate in this clandestine meeting. Nothing good is going to come of this.

Nothing.

"In case your memory is failing you, my name is Miroslav and with me here are Derek and Conrad. We've come a long way since the days of the Dominion. The Dominion of God died with the Prophet Roland. But now it is reborn!"

I listen to Miroslav's deep, lifeless voice. My eyes shift to the man next to him, Conrad French, a.k.a. Frenchy. He's one mean looking son of a bitch and age has done nothing to soften his image. Also wearing the Dominion's traditional ceremonial robe, he looks more like he belongs in a bike gang than a religious cult. Likely in his mid-forties by now, his entire face is marked with scars, the origins of which I can't even imagine. His graying hair is still curly—frizzy even—despite being soaked. Instead of the thick, Elvis-type sideburns he used to sport, even thicker and fuzzier mutton-chops now grow along the sides of his face. His fat, crooked nose looks like it's been broken a few times, likely during some of his infamous brawls. And Conrad is built like an ox. Standing six feet tall and weighing well over 220 pounds, he's one of the last men I'd ever want to piss off or challenge to a fist fight.

A former member of the Western Guard, Conrad was Roland's muscle during the Dominion's short but deadly campaign. In and out of prison since his late teens, he was well known among white supremacist circles, often acting as an enforcer for several groups during gatherings and rallies. He often took his role too far, however. Among his numerous arrests was one for the beating of a Jewish demonstrator in Montreal; he served two years in prison for that. Though Conrad was once one of the most feared supremacists of his time, he wasn't the smartest of the crew.

No, I'd have to give that title to the man on his left, Miroslav Milenkovic. Also known as "Miro" or "Money Man" during the years of the Dominion, Miroslav was likely Roland's most prized asset. After all, he has a degree in economics from the University of Belgrade, I think, and was the Dominion's treasurer, so to speak. Hence the alias "Money Man." All monies directed toward the cause were handled by Miroslav and no one else. He once held, and may still hold, several bank accounts under many names in the U.S. and Canada as well as in Europe. He used to have—and probably still has—major connections in the Balkans. I'm talking drug dealers and weapons procurers and smugglers. He also owned or co-owned a few small businesses he'd use for money laundering purposes. Of course, none of them were in his name. He was never registered as a partner either. He was more like a silent partner.

A true warlord, Miroslav's indoctrination in anti-Islamism came at an early age. His father and most of his uncles were decorated army commanders in the former Yugoslavia. When the republics of Croatia and Slovenia declared independence from Yugoslavia in 1991, a young Miroslav was recruited into the army to perform his mandatory military service. After completing basic training, he was stationed with his uncle in Bosnia-Herzegovina where tensions were rising and talks of independence were also taking place. His uncle, commander of his brigade and a self-admitted racist, painted a rather dark picture of the Muslim population and its violent history towards Serbs. When Bosnia-Herzegovina finally declared independence in 1992, Serbia, the largest and most powerful of the republics, refused to let it go as it did with Croatia and Slovenia. As a result, Miroslav and his brigade, along with many others, were summoned to Sarajevo in order to gain control of the city. Thus began the longest military siege in the post world war era.

When the Bosnian Serb Army came into being, a young Miroslav was assigned to a brigade that fell under the Sarajevo Romanija Corps. For the next forty-four months, units under the corps settled in the hills and areas surrounding the city, implementing a military strategy aimed at terrorizing and killing residents with a specific attention to its Muslim population. From the hills, Miroslav and his brigade assaulted the city by shelling and sniping basically anyone who came in their sights. Women. Children. The elderly. It didn't matter. After it was all said and done, tens of thousands of people in the city were killed or went missing with quadruple the number of wounded. As for Miroslav, he once told me that he and his fellow soldiers kept tabs and placed bets on who would kill the most civilians in one day, week or month. According to him, he was the unanimous winner with nineteen kills in one day and forty-eight in one week.

When the war was over, many of the senior army officials responsible for the Sarajevo Romanija Corps and the siege of Sarajevo were eventually arrested and convicted of crimes against humanity. As word spread of the sweeping arrests of those having committed such atrocities, many, including Miroslav, his father and his uncle, fled the Balkans. With the help of some of their many contacts, they obtained fraudulent documents and flew to Canada separately where they claimed refugee status. While his father and uncle were ultimately discovered and extradited back to Serbia a year later, Miroslav, a mere private in the Bosnian Serb Army, flew under the radar and was given status as a protected person. He later applied for permanent residence which was also granted. For all I know, he could have obtained his citizenship by now.

As I scrutinize Miroslav, I realize he hasn't changed much since the time I last laid eyes on him. Tall and lean, he appears exceptionally fit for a man in his early forties. Although a little thinner, his light brown hair shows no signs of graying. His skin is thick and leathery, marked with a few lines and creases around the eyes and forehead. His face is also marked with a couple of scars, one just under his chin and another above his left eye, splitting his eyebrow in two. Both likely obtained during the war. He has a perpetual frown. The man just never smiles. But there's actually a shred of intelligence behind this hostile exterior. He's a tactician, probably due to his military background. Everything he does is coldly calculated. Out of the three remaining members of the DOG, Miroslav's the one I trust the most because he isn't completely insane and is much less volatile than his counterparts, which brings me to Derek Devlin, a.k.a. Red Devil.

If there was such a thing as a poster boy for hatred, prejudice and intolerance, Derek would be it. Derek hates absolutely everybody. Jews. Sikhs. Muslims. Hindus. Even Christians, depending on the denomination. Blacks. Asians. Natives. Homosexuals. Transvestites. Whatever. It'd be fair to say Derek hates everyone under the sun who doesn't fall under the stereotypical Caucasian, heterosexual, Anglo-Saxon category and who doesn't share his views.

Derek was the youngest of the twelve original Dominion members and was recruited at the tender age of sixteen. A street kid and skinhead, he was the first to fall under Roland's wing and was likely the Dominion's most radical member aside from Roland himself. All it takes is one look at this guy to see what he's all about. His entire body is literally covered in tattoos. But not just any tattoos. I'm talking swastikas, emblems and logos from various hate groups, scriptures and quotes from various

Books of the Bible, biblical symbols such as the tree of the knowledge of good and evil as well as Adam and Eve, the forbidden fruit and the serpent, and passages from Roland's *Last Testament*. I never knew whether to look at him or read him.

Fairly tall and slender, Derek is also dressed in a ceremonial robe. Being a skinhead, his head is shaved to the scalp. He's easily one of the most volatile people I've ever met, a real loose cannon. But a smart one, as he's quite well read. To be honest, he scares the shit out of me and is one of few people walking this planet that's caused me many sleepless nights. He likely would've been Roland's successor if he wasn't so insane and unpredictable. I pray for the sake of mankind that he's softened up over the years.

As I stare into Derek's intense brown eyes, he resumes the sermon.

"Gentlemen, Black Friday was a sign. A wake up call. As was 9/11 and all other attacks perpetrated by the Army of the Beast. It was a sign that the forces of evil have begun their assault on the Kingdom of God and that the Tribulation is upon us. We, God's *true* people, are being targeted for annihilation! It is a silent and invisible genocide! A spiritual cleansing! And we've only witnessed the beginning! Slowly, we're growing smaller in numbers while they are multiplying, like a deadly virus. Like an endangered species, we're becoming extinct."

I look around the room and notice several heads nodding ever so slightly as they soak up every word being spat out of Derek's putrid mouth.

"You see, the goodness of the Christian heart has allowed this to happen. But our goodness has bred naivety. We've allowed the false prophets to spread their filth and infect otherwise good Christians! By the goodness of our hearts we've allowed them to build their places of devil worship so they can congregate and organize their takeover and our annihilation."

This gets a particularly loud reaction out of the group.

"The Armies of the Beast are expanding their empire. Their tactics are twofold! They're flushing us from *their* lands while slowly infiltrating themselves into ours and spreading their seed. They claim the City of God—our city—as their own! They fight each other to claim ownership when the City of God belongs to God's true people—the true Israelites!"

Derek takes a breather and simmers for a moment.

"There are many of us out there—many who feel the same way as you and I. They're frightened. They know that a great evil is upon them, but they can't see, hear or feel it. They seek answers, but don't know where to turn. They seek help, but don't know who to turn to."

At this point, Derek pauses and appears to assess who is listening and who is in agreement. He studies us one by one. So do Conrad and Miroslav. Since everyone else is nodding his head, I nod in turn.

"As *The Last Testament* has foretold, there is now someone to turn to. The New Prophet is here. He has come to unite us, God's people. I, for one, have sworn my allegiance, as have my brothers Conrad and Miroslav. We've been called upon to resurrect the Dominion of God. To be the voice of the voiceless. To be the power of the powerless. To be the shepherds to the lambs! The Dominion of God is to be God's army that'll lead his people through the valley of darkness!"

I notice that by this point the others seem to be almost mesmerized by Derek's rant, as though under a spell. Glossy eyes. Mouths wide open. I try my best to look mesmerized as well.

"And as *The Last Testament* has foretold, Revelations seven and fourteen of the Bible which refer to God's one hundred and forty-four thousand servants who are to be sealed with his name on their foreheads is to be the Dominion of God. Do you know what this means? It means the Dominion of God is to be God's servants. God's Army. *We* are of the Twelve Tribes of Israel! *We* will be protected from all harm and devastation at the time of the Tribulation! At the end of the age! *We* have an ultimate destiny!"

"Gentlemen, you've all been summoned here tonight by the New Prophet himself. He has witnessed what Roland had witnessed. He has touched the hand of God. He is seeking his shepherds and calling for your allegiance to the Dominion of God once again. He knows you are strong. He knows your convictions. He loves you as brothers. And he is here to save you."

The room goes silent as the storm outside rages on.

Finally, Mario asks the question that has been lingering in everyone's mind. "So who is the New Prophet? What's his name?"

The three surviving members of the Dominion of God look to one another in quick consultation. "His Christian name is unimportant," Derek finally replies.

"Then what do we call him?"

"He'll be known to you only as Black Mamba."

Again, the room goes silent. From what I recall, Black Mamba was the name used to sign the letter Frank showed me. But *Black Mamba* as the New Prophet? It's hardly what one would expect as the name for such a figure. Whoever Black Mamba is, he has a real name. Just like Roland did. However, it seems Derek and the boys may have learned from their past mistakes. Unlike with Roland, they're protecting him.

Protecting him from someone like me.

Derek's eyes lock with mine, digging into my very soul. "Gentlemen, you have been chosen to undertake the work of God—to defend and restore His kingdom," he intones, now looking at the others. "By pledging your allegiance to the Dominion of God, you'll become privy to many extraordinary revelations and instructions through the New Prophet. We are the chosen ones. If you accept this invitation, each and every one of you will have a very important role to play. When all is over, they'll make us saints. We'll be gathered by the angels and take our place with Christ our savior at the right hand of the Father."

"Is Black Mamba behind the bombings?" Mario asks hesitantly, obviously unsure about the timing of his question. "I mean, what type of role or what type of work will we be expected to do?"

"Only Black Mamba knows who was behind the bombings," Conrad replies sharply. "It's a need-to-know principle. That's the nature of the work. There are too many forces out there willing to conspire against the righteous. If you accept the invitation, then in time, as you prove yourselves worthy, you'll come to know. We'll all be in it together. But we'll also be operating individually, in cells. No one will know what the other is doing. It's the only way to effectively operate without compromising the Lord's work."

Cyril leans forward in his chair. "Were the bombings in retaliation for Black Friday? Were they—"

"Don't ask such questions," Derek replies sharply, visibly annoyed.

Silence ensues.

"We'll leave you alone for a few minutes to discuss among yourselves," Miroslav says, placing his hood back over his head. "Those who choose to leave may do so without any condemnation. But should you decline the invitation, you're never to speak about this gathering to anyone for as long as you walk the earth. You're never to speak about the Dominion or Black Mamba. If you do, you'll be punished severely in this life and the next. With that said, we hope you join us in our most honorable and sacred brotherhood. We're in need of men like you to not only follow, but to lead a new generation of warriors. We trust you'll make the right decision."

With that, all three men leave the room and make their way upstairs.

The room falls silent, leaving the rest of us to brood over the opportunity that's been presented—this seemingly most generous and exclusive proposition. If only one man chooses to leave, just one, I'll be out that door like a bat out of hell. But no one does and I can't afford to be the only dissident.

Besides, we all know what would happen to those who left.

The fact that they all remain seated doesn't surprise me. These guys aren't exactly average citizens. For as long as any of them can remember, their hearts have been filled with fear, ignorance and hate. Fear of the unknown. Fear of the unfamiliar. Fear of what is different. For the past twenty years, this fear and this hate has been repressed. Sleeping, like an ancient relic, waiting for the perfect opportunity to surface once again.

I fear that opportunity has just presented itself.

Slowly, they begin to encourage one another, like a quiet uprising. A storm of hate and prejudice starts to brew, and soon a hurricane erupts. They egg each other on as though they're the last line of defense for Christianity—or at least *their* version of Christianity. It's now *us* versus *them*. Good versus evil. Their minds are fertile ground and have been for quite some time. Their beliefs are very real: that the end is near, that a war is upon us and that the white horse will arrive and destroy the Beast; that many parts of the Holy Bible are inaccurate and corrupt; that they're God's true people, and that they'll be saved at the time of the Rapture, when only God's elect will be taken by his Son into the clouds and gathered as an army to destroy the Army of the Beast and establish God's Kingdom. Their sole purpose in life is about to come to fruition. Their indoctrination and radicalization has already begun.

And God knows there are many more weak and fertile minds out there.

Listening to their talk, I begin to feel very nervous. Before my very eyes, a demon is reborn.

Fifteen minutes fly by and Conrad, Miroslav and Derek re-enter the room. This time, however, they're unrecognizable. With their hoods draped over their heads, each man is now wearing something I haven't seen in twenty years. Silver and metallic, the ceremonial masks that conceal their faces can only mean one thing: a ritual is about to take place.

These are the faces that have haunted my dreams. Expressionless, cold, haunting and devoid of humanity, these are the last faces the victims of their diabolical rituals saw before being sacrificed. I've only ever seen them once before, from afar. I had hoped to never see them again.

So many terrifying memories I thought I had suppressed come flooding back. I can see them now—these insane rituals that made Opus Dei look like the Mickey Mouse Club. One of their most heinous practices came in the form of self-sacrifices, or "Purifications" as they'd call it.

The Purification was a ritual performed somewhere in the mountains. There were two types of Purifications: one to anoint new members, the other to offer a sacrifice to God. During an anointment, three deep gashes were carved into the chest of each new member. The cuts basically looked like a triangle with its apex pointing to the right. Some said it was simply the letter "D" to represent "Dominion." Some said it had a higher significance, like the Holy Trinity or something of that nature. During the ritual, members wore black hooded robes and eerie, expressionless silver masks. Once every member had begun bleeding, strange prayers were recited and hymns from *The Last Testament* would be sung. Each member's blood would be collected in a chalice and offered to God.

But the anointments were nothing compared to the brutality of the sacrifices. During these Purifications, a victim, called a "sufferer", was presented before a formation of the clan and tied to a cross, hands and feet bound and mouth gagged. The sufferer was chosen by Roland weeks in advance, and it was usually a prominent member of a religious community. The cross was raised. More prayers were recited. Roland would then take a dagger and offer it to the sufferer, who would then be given the option of opening their own jugular before the lighting of the fire.

I've spent many nights thanking the good Lord that I had never taken part in this ritual. But, from what I heard, most victims were simply too distraught or terrified to open themselves up—even after a fire was lit at their feet. This was meant to represent the Lake of Fire in which they would ultimately burn. Some, as their bodies became consumed in flames, would manage the courage to put an end to their suffering. Others just burned to death, uttering muffled shrieks through their gagged mouths.

Any blood that was spilled from a sufferer was collected in the chalice and offered to God. As the victim bled and burned, more prayers and more hymns were recited. The ritual was over. The charred remains were left hanging on the cross, for as long as it managed to stand erect.

The sufferer was usually a priest, rabbi, imam, or any religious cleric. Basically, anyone who embodied, according to Roland, false prophecy. They were sacrificed and offered to God so their souls—their very life forces—were forever extinguished. The Dominion believed that those who had been so terribly corrupted by the forces of evil were unable to repent and save themselves. These offerings were made to weaken the Army of the Beast and to return balance and order to God's Kingdom.

With every last ounce of strength and will, I wrestle with the urge to jump out of my chair and bolt for the stairs. From the nervous glances around the room, I can see I'm not the only one feeling such apprehension.

One of the three is carrying a golden chalice, which he carefully places on the coffee table. Another is carrying a thick book which I recognize as a copy of *The Last Testament*. The third man, Derek I believe, is carrying a dagger in a leathery sheath. All three men stand before us, silent, until Derek speaks.

"I'm pleased to see you're all still here." His voice is slightly muffled by the mask. "Our leader, Black Mamba, will also be very pleased. And we'll all be rewarded, in time."

"But first things first," Derek continues. "You'll now be asked to swear an oath, an allegiance to the Dominion of God—which is an allegiance to God himself." He retracts a silver dagger with a slender but long blade from the sheath.

I turn to Mario, who looks back to me, each of us knowing what the other is thinking.

We've seen this blade before.

"As you swear this oath, a slit will be carved into your chest with this blade. Through this wound, you'll release the impurities and sins that infest your body and your soul. You'll ask for forgiveness and for absolution. The blood that is shed will be collected into this chalice and presented to the Lord so that it can be cleansed. You are not to cleanse your wound or to attempt to stop the bleeding, for it will stop when you're free from sin."

Then, Derek, Conrad and Miroslav stand up and head to the first man to their right, who happens to be Cyril. They ask him to stand up. Nervously, Cyril does and is then asked to remove his shirt. One of the masked men, Conrad I believe, opens the tome he's carrying to a predetermined page. He begins to recite the oath and instructs Cyril to repeat it after him. As Cyril recites the oath, Derek slides the dagger's blade along Cyril's left breast. A large gash immediately slices his skin. Another two gashes follow. He is asked to lean forward. The man carrying the chalice, which by deduction appears to be Miroslav, places the cup beneath the wound, catching the blood spilling from it. Cyril is then asked to get to his knees. A collective prayer is said in the name of Roland and the Dominion of God. With his own blood, a cross is painted on his forehead. Cyril is then given a white cloth to wipe his abdomen as blood continues to trickle from his wound and into the cup. Once the bleeding has subsided, he's offered a cloth to soak up the remaining blood. A final prayer is read.

Then, onto the next man.

As I approach my turn, I again fight the urge to flee, wanting no part of this insane ritual. But it's too late. By having agreed to attend this gathering, I'm already a part of it—whether I want to be or not. It feels like I'm being compelled to stay by some ungodly force, some power stronger than my own.

I'd better get a damn good commission for this.

As though the scene has been perfectly scripted, I'm the last to pledge the oath. I watch as the silver faces finish up with Mario and then make their way over. My mind races as I uselessly try to come up with an excuse not to perform the pledge.

I have to get out of here . . . I have to get out of here . . .

Do it now, Liam!

Derek instructs me to remove my shirt. Reluctantly, I do so. He then begins to recite the oath. I repeat after him. I bite my lower lip and wince as he slices my chest open just above the left nipple. It hurts like a bitch. I wasn't expecting it to hurt this much. Miroslav then places the chalice beneath my breast as blood drips into the dark red mixture. More prayers from *The Last Testament* are recited.

After it's all over, Derek, Conrad and Miroslav return to their seats but don't sit down. Derek then instructs everyone to rise. Holy water and wine is added to the chalice, which Miroslav then raises high above his head. Derek leads the group in another prayer.

"This cup represents the cup of Christ, which contains your lifeline, your bloodline, your impurities and your sins. From this day on, and in the eyes of the Lord, you are forever cleansed of sin. You are forever a part of one another and a part of Jesus Christ our savior. Your covenant is complete, thus commencing your sacred journey as one of God's most trusted and esteemed servants."

After the ritual, we each take our seats. At this point, I start to feel nauseous—sick to my stomach as though I'm about to vomit.

"Welcome, gentlemen," Conrad announces. "Welcome to the brotherhood and your new family. You're now defenders of our faith and part of the Dominion of God—the last line of defense against the Army of the Beast."

For the next hour or so, Conrad, Miroslav and Derek give instructions to the group, handing out general assignments that are to be completed by every man. Then, we're asked to return to the upper floor, after which we're summoned, one by one, to meet with them privately. It's during this private conversation that I'm handed a specific assignment that is to remain unknown to the others. Then blessings are given all around and we're invited to join the trio in prayer downstairs. Thunder continues to rumble as we pray in silence. Once the storm passes, we leave quietly into the night.

CHAPTER 5

I don't bother to drive to Niagara Falls this time. Instead, I agree to meet Jacob at the Holiday Inn, suite 1438, in downtown Toronto. He's dressed casually this time, with dark blue jeans and a white polo shirt, seemingly more relaxed as well. In his possession is a briefcase, much like the one Frank had on our previous encounter.

"Where's Frank?" I ask, made a little leery by his absence.

Jacob pours me a drink. "He's busy tying up loose ends."

Although I shouldn't be drinking so early in the afternoon, or at all for that matter, I accept the offer and he hands me a Scotch on the rocks. "Yeah, well, tell him I want to talk to him the next time you see him."

"Sure thing."

Jacob turns on the television. He then flips through his notes. "So, let's revisit what you told me last night. You said—"

"Hold on just a minute," I interrupt. "Before I spill the beans, I want to know what the hell's in it for me."

"Frank has made a request for a payment, but that will all depend on what you have to say and on the credibility of the information," Jacob replies cautiously. "It's completely out of my control. It's up to the powers that be. If we see that you're in a good position to provide valuable information and be of help, you'll get what you're looking for—and then some. I guarantee it."

"Yeah, well, you have no idea what I had to go through last night." I stretch my collar to expose my wounds.

"What the hell happened to you?" he says, his eyes widening.

I mull things over for a minute. "Alright, I'll tell you about last night, but that'll be it. I won't be assisting any further unless I get a guarantee of an allowance and protection or immunity. I won't say anything more until I get paid. I'm not doing this shit for free. I guarantee you, after I'm finished what I have to say, you're gonna want me on your payroll."

"I'll take your word for it," Jacob responds calmly. "Now, what the hell happened last night and what happened to your chest?"

"You remember when I told you that *all the king's men* were to be in attendance?" I say, taking a sip from my drink.

"Of course."

"Yeah, well, it turns out that it was in reference to none other than the three surviving members of the Dominion of God—Derek Devlin, Conrad French and Miroslav Milenkovic."

"Holy shit." Jacob drops his head and scribbles something.

"As I mentioned yesterday, the man who picked me up was Mario Martel. He had Roch Dorion already with him. They're former supporters of the Dominion. I'm sure they came up on your radar many moons ago. They were never part of the inner circles or ever involved in any decision making, much like myself. As far as I know, they may have donated a few times to the cause and may even have been involved in its propaganda campaign near the very end—maybe some recruiting."

I pause to let Jacob catch up on his notes.

"Go on."

"Anyway, I'm driven to—get this—Wyman Hunt's residence."

"You'll have to refresh my memory."

"Reverend Wyman Hunt. The pastor who was excommunicated after the fall of the Dominion. He was never a member nor was he ever involved in its activities. But he was a figurehead and a very influential person in Roland's life. I'd say he was the soil to Roland's seed."

"Ah yes, I remember reading that. He's in Toronto now?"

"Yeah. Apparently he was reinstated by the Presbyterian Church. He's now the minister-in-association over at St. Andrew's. Don't know how long he's been in town though. Anyway, so we meet at his house on Winchester. The others in attendance I know only as Cyril, Shane and Vladimir. There was another man there by the name of Nash. He said he came all the way from New York just for the meeting. But I don't believe he's a high-ranking member. He said he came in someone's stead. With the exception of Nash, whom I'd never met before or even heard of, everyone present was a former supporter of the Dominion. I believe it was Conrad, Derek and Miroslav who scheduled the meeting, which turned out to be some type of recruitment and initiation into the Dominion."

From an envelope, Jacob pulls out a copy of the letter from the group claiming responsibility for the mosques attacks, along with some photos. "The missing three . . . they're still alive and kicking? Could this be them?" he enquires, handing me the photos.

I stare at what appears to be surveillance photos of three hooded men at Wyman's front steps amid a downpour. "So you did have surveillance after all?" I ask.

Jacob nods.

"Yeah, that's them. They were wearing the Dominion's ceremonial robes. They also had their masks. As far as I know, they only wore them during their rituals—like the Purification. Man, when I saw those masks I nearly fainted."

"Holy shit . . ."

I can't help but smirk. "Holy Shit is right—and an understatement." I then explain the course of the meeting and the ritual performed. I try to slow down as Jacob jots the information onto his notepad. I then remove my shirt to reveal the full extent of my wounds.

"My God. You should get stitches for that!" he exclaims.

I slip my shirt back on. "Back in the days of Roland and the Dominion, they used to perform a ritual called the Purification. They called it the "Lost Sacrament." A human sacrifice. A "Sufferer", as they liked to call it. The Purification was meant to cleanse them through bleedings, as Roland had been purified in the mountains by the angel," I explain. "Anyway, as a victim bled, a ritual was performed and prayers were recited until the bleeding had subsided, marking the end of the Purification and thus the offering to God. That's essentially what happened last night—a Purification. Only it wasn't a sacrifice, but an anointment. One I was not very keen on being a part of."

"Shit."

"Yeah, shit is right."

Jacob looks to be mulling something. "So would it be fair to say that Derek, Conrad and Miroslav are leaders of this new group?" he eventually asks.

I think it over. "No, not exactly."

"They're not? Then who?"

"Black Mamba," I reply, "just like in the letter." Jacob begins to scribble again on his notepad. "They call him the New Prophet, and his arrival had apparently been prophesized by Roland before his death. You know, kinda like the return of Jesus Christ. They believe in Roland's World War III prophecy, a Holy War, which is really nothing more than a regurgitation of a Nostradamus prophecy. I'm telling you, they actually believe this war has already begun."

"They sound like they're all out of their minds."

"Definitely. Their only purpose is to bring about the end of the world. To initiate the Tribulation, a period during which man will have one last chance to obey the true word of God. This period'll be marked by war and extraordinary suffering. At the end of this period, the Rapture will take place, where all those who followed the word of the Lord, whether they're dead or alive, will be gathered into the clouds by the angels in order to meet Christ upon his Second Coming. Roland and his supporters believed that only those who serve the Dominion of God will be gathered at the time of the Rapture."

"I see . . ."

"The Dominion also believes that with Christ, they'll then descend onto the earth and vanquish the Army of the Beast and establish his Kingdom for the next one thousand years. At the end of this millennium, Satan and his forces will be released for the final battle—Armageddon. Upon defeat, the dark Lord and his spawns are to be cast into the Lake of Fire. Only then will God's Kingdom be fully achieved in the form of a new heaven and a new earth."

Jacob leans back into his chair to let this all sink in, seemingly overwhelmed. He remains still for a minute, lost in thought. "So what makes them think the End Times are upon us?"

I explain to Jacob the signs described in Matthew 24: the wars, the famine, the epidemics, the earthquakes, the tribulations and the globalization of the word of God. Like a good student, he jots everything down.

"What about this godlessness and apostasy you mentioned?" Jacob asks.

I ask Jacob to hand me a copy of the bible he brought for the purpose of our debriefing. "This can be found in 1 and 2 Timothy, which discuss the character of men in the last days." I scour the pages for the relevant passage. "For example, 2 Timothy 3 says: 'This know also, that in the last days perilous times shall come. For men shall be lovers of their own selves, covetous, boasters, proud, blasphemers, disobedient to parents, unthankful, unholy, without natural affection, trucebreakers, false accusers, incontinent, fierce, despisers of those that are good, traitors, heady, high-minded, lovers of pleasures more than lovers of God; having a form of godliness, but denying the power thereof: from such turn away. For of this sort are they which creep into houses, and lead captive silly women laden with sins, led away with divers lusts, ever learning, and never able to come to the knowledge of the truth.'"

"So what's it supposed to mean?"

"Well, the Dominion believes this has been fulfilled by recent generations. That men are lovers of themselves and not lovers of God. That we live in immoral times, made obvious by the things we've allowed on TV, the radio, the Internet and so on. That our political and economical leaders and systems—even democratic one—are corrupt. That a growing number of people are turning away from God, be them Atheists or New Age doctrines, believing he doesn't exist or that he is not omnipotent. That mankind is behaving as though it is God while denying his power."

"This is the godlessness they speak of?"

"That's right." I reply, sifting through the pages for another passage. "As for apostasy, 1 Timothy 4 states: 'Now the Spirit speaketh expressly, that in the latter times some shall depart from the faith, giving heed to seducing spirits, and doctrines of devils; Speaking lies in hypocrisy; having their conscience seared with a hot iron; Forbidding to marry, and commanding to abstain from meats, which God hath created to be received with thanksgiving of them which believe and know the truth.'"

"Again, you'll have to enlighten me . . ."

"Basically, the Dominion believes the church nowadays is making too many concessions in order to please New Age thinking or to keep up with modern times defined by immoral men. Accepting homosexuality or alternate lifestyles. Worshipping mother earth instead of God. Reincarnation. Karma. The belief in past lives. Denying Christ as the only way to salvation. The Dominion believes these are the symptoms of apostasy. It also believes that Judaism and Islam, among many others, are what is referred to as doctrines of devils."

Jacob soaks this in, taking many notes along the way. He pauses as though trying to remember something. "Back in Niagara Falls," he finally says, "Frank mentioned the mosque bombings being perhaps linked with the announcement of a European Union-brokered peace plan that will be presented to Israel and the Palestinian Authority. Why is this relevant?"

I take a moment to reflect in turn, trying my damndest to remember the details and the doctrines the Dominion used to carve into the minds of its followers. And so, I tell him about Babylonian King Nebuchadnezzar's dream of a giant statue and of the Last Days as interpreted by Daniel in Daniel 2. I tell him about the statue's head made of gold, chest and arms of silver, belly and thighs of bronze, legs of iron, and feet of iron and clay, which some end times prophecy fanatics, including the Dominion, believe correspond to the Babylonian Kingdom, the Medo-Persian Empire, the Greek Empire, the Roman Empire and a fifth empire that will be a revived model of the Roman Empire—hence the feet of iron *and* clay. I tell him that it is the Dominion's belief that the European Union is *the* revival of the Roman Empire. I also tell him about the Dominion's belief that the first day of Tribulation will take place when the Antichrist, who will rise out of the reemergence of the Roman Empire, fashions a peace agreement—a seven year peace treaty—with Israel; the covenant that is also mentioned in Daniel.

"So they think the Antichrist will rise out of the European Union??"

"Yeah, something like that. Or that the EU *is* the Antichrist who has falsely come to act as a peacemaker and will foster a peace treaty with Israel. That's why Frank mentioned the upcoming peace plan and ensuing negotiations."

"So this Tribulation," Jacob says, recapitulating, "Is a seven year period, correct? Two three and a half year periods?"

"That's right. Twelve hundred and sixty days—or three and a half years—after the peace treaty is signed with the Antichrist and half way into the seven year Tribulation, the Antichrist is to rebuild the Jewish Temple on the Temple Mount in Jerusalem and declare himself the one to bring peace to the Jewish People. The Antichrist then sets up an image of himself in the Jewish Temple, stops the daily offerings to God and declares himself their leader. This is called the "Abomination

of Desolation" in the Bible. The Jewish people, who the Dominion believes are those who follow the Dominion of God and who are therefore the true biblical Israelites, will then see Antichrist's true colors and realize he is a fraud. Remember now, the Dominion, along with many anti-Semitic groups, believe that the Jewish nation and the Jewish people we know today are imposters and that they are not the Israelites—God's people—that are mentioned in the Holy Bible. Anyway, the second half of the Tribulation, the latter three and a half years, is called the "Great Tribulation" and will be marked with the wrath of God unto the Antichrist and the unbelievers."

"So if the Dominion considers the Jewish nation to be its enemy, why did it go after mosques? Why the mosque bombings?"

"The Dominion considers all doctrines and all faiths to be its enemies," I reply. "Only those who follow its own doctrine and come to see the deception of the Beast and of the false prophets are to be offered salvation and redemption. As for the mosque bombings, they were simply in retaliation to what it considers is today's biggest threat to God's kingdom."

"Hmm . . ." Jacob ruminates this for awhile. "So when is the Second Coming of Christ supposed to take place?"

"The Dominion believes the Second Coming and the Rapture will take place at the end of the seven year Tribulation period when Christ will gather his elect into the clouds and wage Armageddon against Satan and his followers."

"Man, that's fucked up shit . . ."

"Yeah, well, it's all a matter of interpretation I suppose."

I can tell Jacob has had enough of Bible 101 for one day. Hell, I've had enough myself. Fact is, I've just surprised myself how well I remember all this stuff. And perhaps 'surprised' isn't even the right word. 'Scared' or 'freaked out' would be more appropriate.

We sit still for awhile, lost in our own thoughts.

"Black Mamba," Jacob eventually says, breaking the silence. "I looked it up on the Net, turns out it's a snake, not a spider. Frank was wrong. I'll have to rub it in."

"A snake?"

"Yeah. Think there's any significance?"

"The hell if I know."

Jacob shakes his head. "Does this person have a name?"

"I'm sure he does, but they wouldn't reveal it," I reply, finishing my Scotch. I watch as Jacob pours me another one. "They said only *they* will ever know his true identity. I say *they* as in Conrad, Derek and Miroslav, of course."

"Do you have any further information on this person? A telephone number? Address? Date of birth? What about Derek, Miroslav, and Conrad? Any coordinates for them?"

I shake my head.

"Why Black Mamba?"

"How am I supposed to know?" I retort. "I'm telling you, they told us nothing about this new leader—this prophet—other than the fact that there are big plans in store for us and that there's a lot of work to be done. Man, you should have seen the group. They all bought into it—each and every one of them. They actually believe that this is a sign from God, that Roland's prophecies are being fulfilled."

Jacob looks up from his notes and frowns. "How so?"

"Well, Roland once said if his efforts failed, a war would be waged by foreign elements in retaliation. He said the enemy would first seek to ostracize and banish God's people from their lands and then seek control of foreign soil by way of undermining and overthrowing the very foundation of their faith and of their societies. He said democracies would fail and would fall only to be replaced by a new and final form of governance. He also said it would be a slow process of infiltration and subversion. This would come by way of violence—major attacks aimed at destabilizing and wreaking havoc on democratic governments and their populations. His prophecies are just that: in the forms of 9/11 and Black Friday and all other attacks in the past decade or two, and of course the coming of the New Prophet, who they believe to be Black Mamba."

"Big deal," Jacob replies. "Nostradamus predicted a holy war five hundred years before. Just like you said, World War III. Other organizations, like the Creativity Movement and the White Crusaders of the RaHoWa, have also predicted a racial holy war. So what Roland had to say was nothing new."

"Perhaps," I reply, "but these guys believe the prophecies have come true and they're intent on fighting back!" I realize I've got goose bumps all over me as I say this. "Jacob, I was there and let me tell you it was a scary, disturbing sight. I'm telling you, something big is going to happen. I don't know what. I don't know when and I don't know where. But it'll end up in lives being lost—that I can guarantee."

"And the mosque attacks are likely just the beginning . . . just as the letter said." Jacob scrambles through his notes. "Jesus, this is big. Did they say anything about the attacks?"

"Not much. Only that Black Mamba knows who was involved. I strongly doubt that Conrad, Derek or Miroslav were the masterminds. They may have had a part in executing the attacks, though. But that's just a hunch. If you ask me, Black Mamba—whoever this is—is behind them."

"Are there any others involved?" Jacob asks, pouring himself another Scotch.

"I don't know—not to my knowledge. However . . ."

"What?"

"They've already begun a recruitment campaign—they call this Phase I."

"Phase I? Recruiting? How? Where?"

"Via the Internet, mostly," I reply, remembering Conrad's instructions to the group before calling it a night. "Religious and racist websites, chat groups, blogs, tweets. We've all been given an assignment to scour the Web for religious extremists, former white supremacists and other radicals like neo-Nazis. The plan is to convert them to the Dominion of God."

"How many are they looking to recruit?"

"I don't know. No numbers were given. However . . ."

"However?"

"I wouldn't be surprised if their ultimate goal is to recruit one hundred and forty-four thousand members."

"What makes you say that?"

"Well, that was Roland's ultimate goal back then. They believe God's one hundred and forty-four thousand servants as mentioned in the book of Revelations will ultimately be those who adhere to the Dominion of God."

Jacob looks at me as though in disbelief. "Huh. You'll have to excuse my ignorance but I have no idea what you're talking about."

Again, almost reluctantly, I pick up the Bible and flip through the pages until I find what I'm looking for. "Revelations 7 says: 'After these things I saw four angels standing at the four corners of the earth, holding the four winds of the earth, that the wind should not blow on the earth, on the sea, or on any tree. Then I saw another angel ascending from the east, having the seal of the living God. And he cried with a loud voice to the four angels to whom it was granted to harm the earth and the sea, saying, 'Do not harm the earth, the sea, or the trees till we have sealed the servants of our God on their foreheads.' And I heard the number of those who were sealed. One hundred *and* forty-four thousand of all the tribes of the children of Israel *were* sealed.'"

I then flip to the next page. "Revelations 14 says: 'And I looked, and, lo, a Lamb stood on the mount Zion, and with him an hundred forty and four thousand, having his Father's name written in their foreheads. And I heard a voice from heaven, as the voice of many waters, and as the voice of a great thunder: and I heard the voice of harpers harping with their harps: And they sung as it were a new song before the throne, and before the four beasts, and the elders: and no man could learn that song but the hundred and forty-four thousand, which were redeemed from the earth.'"

"So what does this all mean?" Jacob asks.

I have to sit and think for a bit, struggling to remember the details of Roland and the Dominion I've long sought to forget. "Well, in the seventh year of his exile, Roland claimed he was released and sent to assemble an army in order to initiate the Tribulation—basically, the beginning of the end of the world. Roland recruited them personally: anarchists, skinheads, rebellious teenagers, outcasts, the homeless, ex-cons, petty criminals, the weak, the hopeless—or anyone with a penchant toward religious extremism. He'd take them all into his fold, reform them and purge them from their sins. He'd promise them eternal life and power and bliss. All would pledge an allegiance to the Dominion of God and vow to battle the forces of evil in preparation for the Second Coming of Christ and the End Times. There were twelve original members in all, including Roland, along with numerous supporters. Roland called it his Twelve Tribes. Together, they were to recruit an army of one hundred and forty-four thousand."

"Go on . . ."

"You see, according Roland, his Dominion of God was to be those one hundred and forty-four thousand servants of God that are mentioned in Revelations seven and fourteen—those who are to be sealed with the name of God on their foreheads so they would be protected from devastation at the time of the Tribulation and at the end of the age. Roland believed he and his Dominion of God were given an ultimate destiny and a distinct role: to annihilate anyone deemed ungodly or to bring them before Jesus Christ upon his return at the time of the Rapture."

Jacob jots down more notes. "That's crazy shit. One hundred and forty-four thousand people? That's pretty ambitious."

"It's never gonna happen." I offer, not overly confident.

"So these websites . . . did they mention any in particular?"

"As a matter of fact," I say, pulling out a slip of paper from my wallet, "I was assigned to a couple of sites, one being the CUG, the Christian Unity Group. The other is called The Word of God." I hand him the sheet containing the URLs, login IDs, passwords and other pertinent info.

"Perfect! This is going to help a lot."

"We were told never to identify ourselves by our real names online or to speak about the DOG or of any other members. However, we were encouraged to mention Black Friday and the mosque bombings to elicit reactions and opinions. We were told to initiate conversations and try to draw out the *faithful* or *God's people*, as they like to put it. We've also been given electronic files to upload or to forward to interested parties—readings and passages from *The Last Testament*, *The White Man's Bible* and even the Holy Bible. Once we've identified potential supporters or sympathizers, we're to schedule future conversations or private chat sessions with them and ultimately hand them over to Conrad."

"Hand them over? What do you mean?"

Again, I reach for my pocket. This time, I retrieve a black and slender memory stick. "With these," I say, handing over the stick for his scrutiny. "We're to save all our conversations on these flash drives and hand them over to Conrad once a potential candidate is identified."

Jacob examines the stick. "Looks pretty basic . . ."

"They're apparently encrypted with this software. I think I can save stuff on it, but can't retrieve or access anything. It takes a password or encryption keys or something."

"Hmm . . ."

I can tell the wheels are spinning deep inside my handler's head. I already know what he's going to ask next. Something tells me encryption is the least of his concerns. I bet he and his agency have all the technical experts to crack any type of encryption known to man.

"Listen," he says, "is there any chance of you handing over a stick before delivering to the Dominion? I'd need just a day or two. I'd love to put our tech guys up to the task. If not, I could provide you with a second stick."

"I suppose that's do-able," I reply, "I just don't want to be caught with my pants down without it, you know what I mean?"

"Understood."

Jacob hands me back the flash drive and jots down more notes. He agrees to provide me an extra memory stick as soon as possible. As with the Dominion, I'm to save all conversations and any other information I receive before handing it over to Jacob and his agency.

"So," he continues, "is this something you're each to do on your own time?"

"Yeah. We were cautioned never to use our own personal computers and to use public Internet cafés or other public terminals. You don't need to open an account in these cafés. You don't even need to present any ID. All you do is walk in, write your name and telephone number down on a sheet and your start time. Once you're done, you pay for the time spent and that's it. These guys are incredibly security-conscious. Several protocols were established and we're never to break them under any circumstances."

"Such as?"

"Well, the Internet thing for starters. We're to open email accounts using Gmail or Hotmail, using false information of course. We're to verify our accounts regularly—weekly, actually—for any instructions or upcoming meetings. We're not to communicate using any home computer or home telephones or cell phones—anything under our real names."

"Have you opened an account yet?"

"No, I haven't."

"OK, when you do," he replies, "and when you start receiving messages from the Dominion, save any and all messages on the same flash drive that I'll provide for your IM chats or whatnot. This'll put us in a great position to trace the origins of any delivered messages."

"No problem."

Jacob scribbles more notes. "So no residential lines? No cell phones? Is email the only method the Dominion plans to use for communications?"

"No."

"What else then?"

"Pay phones."

"Pay phones?"

"Yeah, pay phones," I repeat. "Only pay phones are to be used should a member need to contact another member. Satellite phones are out too. In time, we'll be given a cell phone, but only for specific purposes or operations. I don't know the cell phone provider or the subscriber of the account—or accounts. I don't have any more information on that. Like I said, we're never to use our own cell phones. That's fine with me as I'd rather not be using my cell to connect with those freaks. I'm telling you, they're extremely security-conscious. They're doing whatever it takes to avoid being detected."

"I'll say."

"You haven't heard the best part," I say, chuckling, "Last night they show up with these portable metal detectors. Like the ones they use in airports. They scan our bodies from head to toe, getting us to remove our belts, rings or whatever piece of metal we're carrying. They say it's only a precautionary measure. You know, in case we're bugged."

"Metal detectors?"

"Also, we're forbidden to use our own vehicles and taxi cabs to get to gatherings or for any DOG purposes. Instead, we've been instructed to use the public transportation. Subway. Bus. Trolley. Whatever."

"Have they scheduled another meeting?"

"Yeah, they have," I reply, taking a sip from my Scotch. "But like the last one, it'll only be confirmed at the last minute. All I know is that it likely won't be at Hunt's place again."

"Speaking of Hunt," Jacob says, "was he present at this meeting?"

"Oddly enough, no."

"How did you get in?"

"Mario had a set of keys. I'm assuming some of the others also had a set. Cyril, Shane, Vladimir and Nash were already there when we got there."

"Interesting . . ."

"I'll say."

We sit quietly for a moment while Jacob catches up on his notes. "Anything else?" he asks, pressing on the tip of his ball-point pen.

"Huh?"

"Is there anything else you'd like to add?"

"Yes, actually there is," I say, as something suddenly springs to mind. "Along with recruitment strategies, we've all been assigned specific areas in our respective cities."

Jacob raises an eyebrow. "Oh?"

"Well, you see, we've each been assigned a geographic area in a particular city. For example, I've been assigned to Toronto's east end—everything east of the 404, including Scarborough and Markham. I don't know who has Toronto's other areas. Nash was told to have New York separated into four areas, so I'm assuming there are more people involved in the States—or at least in New York."

Jacob presses his ball-point pen anew and begins to write. I give him the exact geographic breakdown for each member.

"So what's the purpose of this allocation?"

"Well, aside from recruiting purposes, each member is to seek possible areas of refuge and gathering. Any real estate. Also, we've all been told to scope out and gather as much information as we can on places of worship in our respective areas."

Jacob abruptly looks up. "Like mosques?"

"Mosques, synagogues, temples . . . just to name a few."

"What for?"

"I'm not sure," I reply, taking another drink. "We've been told to collect information on their addresses, size, surrounding neighborhood, doorways and exit ways, streets and routes leading to them, prayer times and approximate number of members."

Jacob seems to be transcribing everything I've just said word for word.

"That's not all," I continue. "We've also been told to gather information on prominent members of religious communities: imams, sheiks, rabbis, and so on."

"What kind of information?"

"You know, home addresses, family members, other occupations and daily routines."

"This doesn't sound good."

"You're telling me!" I reply and I can tell that Jacob is thinking exactly what I'm thinking. "I figure—"

"Another bombing may be in the works."

"Yeah, or maybe even an assassination or a kidnapping," I offer.

We exchange looks. Jacob's eyes flutter from left to right; he's obviously lost in thought. He eventually gets up and pours himself yet another Scotch.

"Anything else?" he queries.

"Just one more thing," I reply, finishing my drink. "We're to have this info collected by late September."

"Late September?" Jacob looks at his watch. "That's in just over a month. Did they give you any indication as to what this information will be used for—or even better, when exactly?"

I shake my head.

Jacob takes a deep breath. "OK. This is already much bigger and much more serious than I thought—than what *we* thought. A month doesn't give us a lot of time. I'm gonna make sure we get you on board and that you receive an allowance. Not just a one-time payment. I don't see it being rejected by the big men upstairs. You're in a very sensitive and unique position to provide valuable information—"

"You're damn right I'm in a sensitive position!" I retort. "I'm not doing this unless I know I'm going to be protected and paid. I'm already in way over my head!"

"I understand your concerns and I promise you they'll be addressed. I should have confirmation by tomorrow—perhaps the day after, at the latest. With what you've provided me, it won't take much convincing to have you working for us again."

"I want guarantees, Jacob," I reiterate. "Guarantees that my identity will never be revealed by you or your agency. Guarantees that I'll never have to appear or testify in court. Do you hear me? I want guarantees that my life will never be put in jeopardy."

"Not to worry," Jacob replies, sorting out his notes. "You'll have the same guarantees as before. Nothing's changed. We don't compromise our sources. We never have and never will. All the information you provide will be classified at the highest levels and will never be made public. You know that. Besides, we collect intelligence, not evidence."

"Oh yeah? What about the RCMP? Huh? Or the Americans? I'm sure they'd love to get their hands on information like this, and I strongly doubt you won't be sharing this information." I get up and start pacing around the room. "I'm not an idiot, Jacob. I know it'll ultimately fall into their hands. After all, this is criminal activity we're talking about. We already have a confession from the DOG and now I've confirmed its revival. I know damn well you have no powers of arrest. This is beyond your mandate. Do you figure I'm so naïve as to think you'll just use this information to—what? *Advise* government?"

Jacob sighs and doesn't respond right away. Finally he says, "You're right. There's nothing I can do with the information other than warning government agencies, including appropriate police agencies." He sounds almost regretful. "But, it's still *our* information. We choose what is disseminated, how it's disseminated and to whom. I assure you, we always make certain our sources are never compromised or revealed. Think about it. Human intelligence is our highest priority. It's our *raison-d'être*, if you will. Can you imagine if something ever came out about one of our sources being made public? It'd simply be the end of us."

"Fair enough."

My thoughts then turn to the debt I owe to some very impatient people. I want to hold back and keep these details to myself, but I'm desperate. "Jacob, I'm in trouble. I owe some very shady people a large amount of money."

"How much and to whom?"

"One hundred thousand dollars," I respond, giving him the background on my unfavorable predicament. But something tells me he knows already.

"I'm sorry to hear that, Liam," he replies, seemingly with genuine concern. "I'll try my best to help you out. But right now, that's out of my hands. I'm a man of my word and I don't want to make any promises I may not be able to keep. I'll put forward your request. In the meantime, keep me informed of any new happenings, OK?"

I nod.

"Good. For now, I'll honor your request not to be contacted and will only contact you via your landline if I absolutely need to get a hold of you. If you want this to change, let me know."

I nod again, although feeling somewhat uneasy. Sarah's already suspicious about some of my acquaintances. Having another stranger call me at home would only add to her paranoia.

"Oh, and one more thing," Jacob adds. "Keep in mind the police, including the RCMP and various municipal police forces as well as the FBI, are currently investigating the mosque bombings. Many of them—if not all—are working together on this. We'll do our best so that your name doesn't surface in any investigations. Whatever you do, stay away from any type of criminal activity. If the DOG asks you to do anything criminal, you must emphatically refuse—unless, of course, your life is being threatened. Believe me, you don't want to become involved in anything that would make it hard for us to get you out of. If you do, we may have no other choice but to sever ties with you. Do you understand?"

"Yeah, I hear you."

"Good. Now I'd better get back to the office to write my report and get the paperwork done for your allowance. Also, we managed to get a few plates, including Mario's Sentra. We're running some checks as we speak. I'll let you know if anything comes up."

"Sounds good," I reply, anxious to get out the door.

While Jacob gathers his belongings, our conversation lightens up and we talk about baseball. He says he'll try to get us some tickets for the next home game before the end of the season, between the Blue Jays and the Orioles.

Jacob eventually excuses himself and leaves the room, offering me the room for the night as it's already paid for. I politely decline, knowing full well my return home is expected sooner rather than later.

CHAPTER 6

It's Sarah's night off and by the time I get home, it's already 10:30. The apartment is quiet and dark, and I avoid turning on any lights or making too much noise as I fumble and stumble clumsily down the hallway and into the bedroom. I slip into bed hoping she's sound asleep.

Of course she isn't.

She rolls over as though she's been waiting for me all along. "Where were you?" she asks, forgetting I told her I was at the game—which of course, I wasn't.

"Honey, I was at the game, remember?"

"I know that," she replies, as though having anticipated my response and her ensuing reply. "I meant, where were you all day? Prior to the game?"

"Jesus, Sarah, I was at work—"

"No, you weren't!"

"Huh? Of course I—"

She sits up, towering over me. "Quit fuckin' lying to me, Liam! I know you weren't at work! I went by today and Henrique said you took the afternoon off! So what did you do all afternoon?"

Sarah and I have been together off and on now for over twenty years. I can only think of one other occasion when she visited me at work. That was to pick up my stuff after I'd nearly cut off my left hand with a bone saw.

"I'm sorry, baby!" I reply, engaging in damage control. "I'm really sorry. I should've told you. It was quiet at the shop so Henrique gave me the afternoon off. I met up with some old friends that were in town for the day."

"Old friends? Who?"

My mind scrolls through an infinite list of people I know until landing on a few plausible choices. "Nick and Greg . . . they were passing through on their way to Windsor. You know, to the casino."

She becomes even more agitated. "Nick and Greg? You mean Nick and Greg from Carol's wedding?" Nick and Greg aren't exactly her two favorite people in the world. She's convinced that it was Nick and Greg who precipitated my eventual downward spiral into the world of booze and gambling. They were a bad influence, I'll give her that. Neither man ever held a steady job and they'd both usually end up drinking their social assistance checks at the end of every month. As part of my recovery and promise to her that I'd get sober, I agreed to quit associating with people like them.

"I actually just ran into them during lunch. They insisted I have a drink with them. I declined, but they wouldn't accept no for an answer. You know how they are."

"Yeah, I know," she barks, returning to her pillow. "I'm sure they asked you to join them in Windsor too!"

"No, of course not."

"Bullshit!"

"Baby, I'm telling you the truth!" I reply which, in theory, is true.

"Well, I don't believe you."

"Why did you come to my work anyway?" I ask, cunningly turning the tables on her. "You never visit me at work! What gives?"

"I came to pick up your keys. I was at Starbucks this morning getting a coffee and I think I forgot them there. I must've left them on the counter or something. When I went back, they were gone. So I was locked out of the apartment."

"So how did you end up getting in?"

"I was able to get a hold of Ruben and he gave me a spare key," she replies, now snuggling comfortably next to me.

Ruben is our superintendent—a real sleaze.

"I'm sorry I wasn't there, honey," I say, sincerely. "Why didn't you call beforehand? I had my cell with me—"

"I tried! You weren't answering!" she whines, clearly annoyed.

"I'm sorry, baby."

"How's your chest?" she asks, pulling my shirt to ensure my wound is still properly bandaged. "Is it healing OK?"

I told her I sliced my chest on a few sharp rib bones after dropping a quarter of beef that I was unloading from a truck at the deli. Perplexed as to why I hadn't gone to the hospital to receive stitches, she'd insisted on treating the wound herself.

"Yeah, it's coming along just fine."

"My poor baby . . ." she says, kissing me softly. She continues caressing me, all the way up to my neck and lips. Her silky smooth skin. The smell of her hair. The taste of her lips. It's enough to drive a man insane.

We embrace passionately and soon become intimate. God, how I love being intimate with this woman. She's without a doubt the most passionate lover I've ever had—not that I've had that many. Without ever knowing, she has the power to make me forget all my worries, all the evils of the world and the insanity that surrounds me. I'm in bliss. She's like an angel without wings, my own personal savior.

In the midst of our passion, the thought of marriage crosses my mind, as it has many times before. But there's something holding me back. I still can't grasp what it is. Somewhere along the way, I seem to have lost my faith.

But my faith in what?

Marriage?

Religion?

God?

Once the ecstasy and the euphoria have passed, I ponder this for a while. I've lost my faith in *something*, I'll be the first to admit. But the way I see it, we're comfortable now—happy, even—and that's all that matters.

CHAPTER 7

For the next few weeks, I don't hear from anyone. Not Conrad. Not Derek. Not Miroslav, or anyone else from the Dominion of God. I begin to think I dreamed the whole thing up. Despite this lull, I busy myself with collecting information on mosques, synagogues and temples, as well as on the homes of imams, sheiks and rabbis, among others, much to my discomfort. With every religious institution I hit, I can't help but feel guilty. I fear that the information I provide will ultimately lead to terrible things—things that go against everything I believe in. But I have to engage. I simply can't present them with bogus information. I have to engage to remain credible in the eyes of the Dominion of God—those snake eyes, always watchful, dubious and evaluating.

Although I feel I may be putting lives in danger, I remind myself of the bigger picture. By remaining credible, I'll be saving lives and not endangering them. Hopefully.

During the day, I work my regular schedule at Henrique's Meats & Deli. When I'm not working, I'm doing recon for the Dominion. The area I was assigned has over fifteen mosques and Islamic associations. An intricate map that was given to me highlighting my area is now covered in dots and indicators of their location. I take notes, as requested by the Dominion leaders. I do this for approximately two hours a day in between shifts and my time at home with Sarah. I explained to her that Henrique has altered my shifts so that I start later in the mornings and finish later in the evenings. She isn't very fond of this arrangement as it means we get even less "together" time before she leaves for her night shift at ten o'clock as shift supervisor for Sani-Pro, a large cleaning company responsible for many of the city's downtown office buildings.

I end up gathering all the information that was requested. Doorways and entryways. Security systems. Names of leaders and approximate number of worshipers. Descriptions of neighborhoods surrounding the mosques and dwellings. Schedules or special events. Everything.

I also conduct regular Internet searches and engage in conversations with people whose real identities are still unknown to me. My preferred establishment is an Internet café just down the street from our apartment called Net Chase. Sometimes I'll alternate and head downtown where there's a plethora of cafés, most along Yonge Street. I do this mainly because I'm paranoid and think it unwise to use the same place repeatedly—especially one so close to home.

Most websites I visit, including numerous chat rooms, end up yielding very few results. However, one site has presented several potential candidates. This is the one I told Jacob about, the Christian Unity Group, or CUG. It can't be accessed by using Google or Yahoo—or any other search engine for that matter. To find it, one has to first know it exists. To know it exists, well, one needs to know the right people. Having been estranged from the World Wide Web of white supremacy and Christian extremism many moons ago, I lack the contacts to find such a site. Conrad, Derek, Miroslav and Black Mamba, however, do not.

To access the site, I need an ID and password. These change regularly. Enter the wrong ID or password, and the IP address attempting to connect to it will be permanently blocked. Thankfully, I've been handed the various IDs and passwords that'll change over the course of the next month or so.

I've been keeping a close eye on a user who goes by the alias "Angelic," usually found in Cherubs' Den, one of the CUG's numerous forums and chat rooms. He and several others regularly partake in cryptic anti-Semitic and anti-Islamic discussions. I've been observing their discussions for a while without ever hitting a single key. It's clear that whoever these people are, they're pretty contemptuous of a wide range of individuals and groups, particularly those of Middle Eastern origins.

Out of curiosity, I sometimes browse through the site's various instant chat rooms, some centered around geographic region, others around denomination or biblical topic. The more I observe and follow the various discussions of each particular forum, the more I feel as though I've entered a world in which I don't belong—a dark and sinister world that I could've never imagined, not even in my worst nightmares.

Take the most hateful, the most accursed, the most illiberal, intolerant, bigoted and racist souls on the face of the planet and bring them all together. Wherever they are in the world, they all gather there, in Cherub's Den.

On one occasion, I find myself scrolling back into Cherub's Den and I focus on the ramblings of Angelic, who seems to be the group's antagonist and by far the most vocal member. Highly opinionated, he—or she for all I know—is very well versed with respect to the Bible, often quoting certain passages to support his biases. He rambles on and on about the "mongrelization of America" and of western society as a whole as well as about the necessary destruction of all Islamic and Jewish states for what he called "the restoration of the Kingdom of God."

Of course, everyone participating in the discussion is in agreement. But it's Angelic who is both fuel and fire.

The mongrelization of America is discussed for what seems to be an eternity. Most of the chatter comes in the form of short, somewhat discombobulated statements and mindless gibes. The more I read, the more I realize how most of the conversation lacks flow, not to mention reason and morality. Then, finally, comes the topic of the mosque bombings and the Dominion of God. That's when I jump in.

I quickly learn that Angelic is writing from somewhere in Canada, contrary to my suspicion that he's American. He goes on and on about how the mosques bombings were justified and were an appropriate and necessary response to the series of terrorist attacks against western targets over the past decade. According to Angelic, it's about time someone stood up to foreign aggression. A few others in the chat room also share this sentiment.

I ultimately invite Angelic to a private conversation, which he accepts. During our chat, it's clear he reveres the Dominion of God, and he expresses his wish that more action be taken against Islamic targets. When I tell him his bark is likely bigger than his bite, he adamantly stresses his support for the Dominion or anyone else who has enough balls to stand up and speak out against foreign aggression without fear of being labeled a racist or a bigot. In fact, he even indicates that he'd love to have been the one to detonate one—or all—of the bombs that day. I ask him if he'd ever consider joining a group like the Dominion of God. His answer: *When do I join?*

I suggest we talk again. We agree on a time and date and end up engaging in numerous conversations over the course of the next few weeks, all of which I end up saving on two flash drives: one provided by the Dominion, the other by Jacob, to whom I've managed to return the device following most of my online conversations.

The more I chat with this fellow, the more convinced I become of his unfaltering views and his hatred toward ethnic minorities and all non-Christian religious communities in general.

At times I encourage Angelic. Other times I challenge him. But he's relentless and doesn't break or soften his stance—ever. I don't ever mention my affiliation with the Dominion of God. I don't need to. That's why I remain somewhat skeptical throughout our interactions. It seems almost too easy. I can never be too careful. Cops have been known to scour these sites. Ironically, I pray this is the case. I'd feel much more comfortable knowing I've been interacting with an undercover cop. On the flip side, if he is in fact an undercover agent, I'd no doubt be one of his subjects of investigation. Whatever the outcome, I've done my homework. I've found my guy.

CHAPTER 8

I'm lying in bed with my eyes wide open when the sound of my latest ringtone can be heard in another room. Forgetting Sarah's just left for work, I let it ring until the caller decides to hang up. A floor above me, a fight breaks out, marked by loud crashes and heavy thumping mixed with shouting and cursing and more shouting. I wrap a pillow around my head in a futile attempt to drown out the noise.

Again the cell phone rings.

I quickly jump out of bed and locate the tiny device in the living room. Before answering, I wait for the ruckus upstairs to subside. "Hello?" I answer, as the sound of something heavy crashing to the floor above fills the room.

"Is this Liam?" the voice asks, clearly on a pay phone.

"Yes."

"Liam, it's Cyril. Are you alone?"

"Yeah, why?"

"I have a message for you, from Miroslav." A long pause. "Do you have a pen or pencil handy?"

"Just a sec," I reply, searching for a notepad and pen. "Got it. What's up?"

"Miroslav wants you to meet with Vladimir tomorrow at four thirty."

"Vladimir? Tomorrow? What the hell for?"

"I don't know."

"Where?"

"At . . ." he begins, followed by the sound of crinkled paper being smoothed out. "1973 Finch Avenue. At the Norfinch Shopping Centre, I think. Ask for Farm Boy."

"Farm Boy? Are you kidding me?"

"Nope."

"Why all the way out there?" I ask, not overly keen on that part of town.

"Like I said, I don't know," Cyril answers sharply. "I was just asked to pass the message. I was told to tell you it's important and not to be late."

Damn it! I'm working tomorrow!

"Liam?"

"What?"

"You got that?"

"Cyril, I'm working tomorrow! I can't make it!"

"That's not my problem," Cyril replies, his tone indifferent. "Take the afternoon off. Go home sick. Do whatever it takes. Much emphasis was placed on you not being late. So if I were you, I wouldn't be late. *Capice?*"

"I'll see what I can do," I reply, fuming inside. More time off means less money in the bank. My mind momentarily shifts to Jacob, who I pray has good news for me as far as a payment is concerned.

"Remember, 1973 Finch Avenue at four thirty. Be there."

The sound of a dial tone suddenly fills my ear. Annoyed, I hang up and tear the sheet from the notepad. I then make my way to the bedroom where I place it on the dresser, next to my wallet and keys so I don't forget it in the morning. I set my alarm clock for 6:00 a.m. and turn off the lamp on the night table next to Sarah's side of the bed. Falling flat on the mattress, I lie there for the next twenty minutes or so and contemplate calling Jacob to bring him up to date. The red digits floating in the darkness indicate it's already 10:30 p.m. Although Jacob did mention he could be reached at all times of the day and night, whatever it is, I figure, it's nothing that can't wait till tomorrow—or until I get my allowance.

CHAPTER 9

I often dream of being in a garden. It's been recurrent for as long as I can remember. In this dream, the sun is out without a cloud in the sky. It's warm but comfortable. An ocean breeze fills my lungs and the lungs of others in the garden. The garden appears endless, limitless. Fruits and flowers as far as the eye can see.

A deep sense of serenity and peace engulfs my soul. This feeling. This energy. It is inescapable. Never in my life have I felt so vibrant and so alive. And I can tell that everybody else in the garden feels that way too. Every being in the garden, either human or animal, seems to radiate love and joy.

Although I don't recognize everyone around me, it's as if I've known them all since the beginning of time. There are people from all backgrounds and walks of life—all unfamiliar, yet strangely familiar. There is no prejudice and no judgment. Everyone is equal. There is no hurt and no hate and no pain. Suffering is nothing more than a myth—something that seems to have never been.

Almost aimlessly, I wander through the garden, admiring the exuberant life it contains. Everyone I pass, from the smallest child to the elderly—waves and smiles and greets me as royalty. As though I'm their own flesh and blood. More striking, however, is this warm flow of energy—this feeling—that emanates from each and every soul, which in turn resonates in my own.

As it always does, my path leads me to a large and majestic fountain that can be seen from miles away. There are simply no words and no language to describe its splendor and beauty. It seems to be alive. Breathing. Calling. Its essence drawing me to it. And I'm not alone, for all around me an endless stream of beings is being summoned as well. The closer I get, the more powerful its essence becomes and the more alive I feel.

Upon reaching the magnificent springs, some enter the fountain's realm and become completely immersed, as though entering a city with translucent and permeable walls. Others simply douse themselves in its freshness. Others drink from it. Some simply make the trek to admire it and to bask in its glory. As for me, I'm not quite sure what I want to do—or what I'm supposed to do.

I just stand there, in awe of this kingdom. But when I think about taking a step forward toward the fountain, I become suddenly paralyzed. From the horizon, something horrible approaches. A sound. A sensation. Its roar becomes louder as it draws near. The skies become dark. The peace and serenity and love that was felt just a moment ago slowly fades. Screams begin to fill the garden. At a distance, a fire rages, consuming everything and everyone in its path. Those close enough to the fountain seek its shelter. Still only a step away, I cannot move.

I watch helplessly as all the beauty of the garden burns and is reduced to ashes. Unfortunate souls burning, burning. The flames grow bigger and brighter with every soul the fire consumes. The heat becomes unbearable. Nothing but fear and terror. From the angry flames emerges an army of ghosts—silver faces reflecting the flames that surround them. I pray for a miracle but the fire rages on. If I could only take that last step . . .

CHAPTER 10

Henrique is a good guy. A Portuguese immigrant, he settled in the area in the late seventies and is one of the most respected men in his community. I like to call him the Portuguese Godfather—minus all the crime and stuff. Most refer to him as "The Butcher". Despite his rough and tumble exterior, which is usually accentuated by his blood-stained apron, he has a pretty soft heart. I could've told him I felt sick. I could've told him any other lie. Instead, I simply tell him that things haven't been going well between Sarah and me and that I wanted to take the afternoon off to spend some much needed time with her. Aware that she and I are working opposite shifts and rarely have any time together, the old butcher generously excuses me from my duties for the rest of the day, despite already being short-staffed.

Instead of heading home, however, I make my way to Dufferin Street and take the next bus heading north. Twenty minutes or so and a couple of transfers later, I get off at the corner of Jane Street and Finch Avenue. After crossing the street en route to the Norfinch Shopping Centre, I take the slip with the address out of my pocket to make certain I'm in the right area.

I continue walking past the strip mall's numerous stores until I come across storefront at the very end with a subtle sign saying "E-Z Grocery".

I cautiously make my way inside. It's a small convenience store with a healthy selection of fresh fruits and vegetables. Most, if not all, are imported, including plums, pears, apples, apricots, cherries, peaches, grapes and a variety of berries. Amid the fresh fruit at the front of the store is the counter which is unmanned. Noticing someone at the back, I make my way past the fresh fruit section and head down one of several aisles whose shelves are stocked with countless cans and jars of fruit, juice products, purees, jams and other non-perishable items. I stop to inspect some along the way but am unable to read their labels which appear to be printed in a foreign language—either Serbian, Bosnian or Hungarian. It could be Russian for all I know. It all looks the same to me.

I stop in front of a display case where a variety of baked goods are displayed. Pies. Cakes. Tarts. Cookies. Behind the display is an elderly woman who appears to be of Eastern European descent. She doesn't notice me right away, her attention focused on preparing some type of pastry. On the counter next to the display case, there's a bell with a sign: "Please ring for service." I tap lightly on the bell.

"How can I help you?" she says in a thick eastern European accent.

"Hi there, I'm looking for Vladimir."

She shakes her head and leans forward, cupping her ear. "Who?"

"Vladimir."

"I'm sorry . . . no Vladimir here."

I'm about to turn away when I remember Cyril's instructions. "Is Farm Boy here?"

"Ah, Farm Boy? You find him in 'da back," she replies, pointing toward the back of the room. "But you go from outside. Around 'da building. In 'da back."

"Outside?"

"Yes, around 'da back," she repeats.

I exit the small grocery store and make my way toward the back of the building. There's a sign on the brick wall that says "E-Z Travel at the back." A surveillance camera is mounted on the upper corner facing the parking area.

Upon reaching the back, I find exactly what I suspected: nothing but rows of back doors and loading areas for the mall's numerous shops. At least, that's what it seems at first glance. The door behind E-Z Grocery isn't like the rest. It's a glass door protected with steel bars. Hanging on the inside of the door is a "Sorry, we're closed" sign. Above it is another sign that reads "E-Z Travel". Next to the door there's a doorbell with a small sign above it saying "Please ring." Above it is an alarm system that appears to be disabled.

Stepping up to the door, I shade my eyes and peek inside. While the reception area is dark and vacant, a light emanates from a back room.

I ring the doorbell and wait. A shadow appears, and then Vladimir unlocks the front door. "You're late," he says.

I look at my watch. It's 4:35 p.m. "Sorry, I was at the front. Didn't see the sign on the side—"

"That's OK. Come in."

I step inside and Vladimir immediately locks the door behind us. "Follow me," he instructs, waving me over to the back room. "Had a hard time finding the place, huh?"

"Not really."

As I enter the room, I'm taken aback by the sight of Miroslav sitting in a chair in front of a large desk. He stands up and greets me, then directs me to take a seat on an old chair next to his. Vladimir takes his place behind the desk, facing Miroslav and me. Several stacks of papers, envelopes and stationery along with an old desktop computer cover the desk's entire surface. The room, much like the desk, is in total disarray. Documents are lying around everywhere. Some are travel documents, some not. There are documents on the floor, some atop an opened filing cabinet and some on the seat of another chair next to mine. More documents on several shelves of a cheap bookcase along with many binders. On the floor behind the desk sits a safe.

"How have you been, Liam?" Miroslav asks, lighting a cigarette.

"Not too bad, I guess."

"How's Father MacLean these days?"

"I wouldn't know," I reply nervously, surprised by Miroslav's knowledge of the priest at my former church. "I heard he had cancer, though."

"Yeah, I heard that too."

"Colon cancer, I think."

"I've been praying for him," Miroslav says. "He's good man."

"Yes, he is."

Miroslav sucks on his cigarette. "Listen, I know you haven't been going to church."

"Is that so?"

"Yes, it is," he replies. "Why is that?"

"No particular reason . . ."

"Well, you should go back to church, comrade. Pray for all of Christianity. Pray for battle we're about to engage in and success of the Dominion. Get married. Have many Christian babies. We need more. The Devil is multiplying before our eyes. We need to grow in numbers."

"So, how have you been?" I ask, to deflect him. "What have you been up to all these years?"

"I've been good. Been all over the place—Europe, mostly. You know, running a few businesses here and there. Trying to earn decent living."

"So this is your new venture?" I query, doing my best not to appear overly inquisitive or curious. "Fruits and travel?"

"This? No. I just help out around here sometimes. Accounting and stuff. Vladimir is main man here," he says. "I help finance place. Let's just say I'm silent partner."

I take a good look at Vladimir who does nothing but stare me down. A slender man with a large forehead and protruding brow, dark hair, and cold blue eyes sucked back into his skull, he also appears to be of eastern European descent—likely one of Miroslav's business partners. Whoever he is, he sure doesn't say much.

"Good for you." I finally say.

Miroslav looks at me curiously and leans back in his chair. "Look, the reason I asked you here is because we need favor. Actually, it may be several favors, but all the same . . ."

Favors. Great. That's all I need—to be doing favors for the DOG.

"You've got dual citizenship, correct?" he asks, his knowledge of the fact no surprise to me.

"That's right."

"You're also Nexus member, correct?"

I think I know where this is going. Nexus is a program for those who travel frequently between Canada and the U.S. It's simply a matter of applying and passing security screening checks. Once approved, one is considered a low-risk traveler and is given a Nexus card. Having one of these cards gives a member the privilege of using lanes and kiosks designated to expedite the border clearing process, generally undergoing a less rigorous inspection, if any.

I simply nod in response.

"Good. Listen, the reason I ask is because I need you to courier a parcel—a briefcase, to be precise—to New York in a week or two. You up for that, my friend?"

I take a moment to mull this over, shifting my gaze back and forth from Miroslav to Vladimir. "I don't know, Miroslav. It depends what

I'm carrying. I'm not crossing any border with a shitload of drugs or contraband cigarettes or anything that can put me behind bars. You know what I'm saying?"

Miroslav almost cracks a smile, as though slightly amused. "Of course no drugs and no contraband anything. We're not in trafficking business here. Are we Vladimir?" he continues, looking over to Vladimir, who's grinning. "No, all you'll be carrying is correspondence, notes from meetings and instructions to and from our members in the States—nothing more."

"Correspondence? Can't you just call or email them instead? Or why not send it via regular mail?"

"Those documents you'll be carrying, we can't afford to have them lost in mail. Or tracked or intercepted. Same goes for email. That's why we need courier."

"Great, so I'm a fuckin' mailman now?" I scoff, annoyed by the task I'm being assigned. "You know—"

"Mailman." Miroslav repeats, signaling Vladimir to punch something into his computer. "I like it. I like it a lot. I was going to give you Gopher as your alias, but I like Mailman more. Mailman it is, comrade."

"Miroslav, wait," I say. "I'm not sure I'm comfortable with this. I mean, I may still be referred to secondary inspection. If—no, *when*—they find the briefcase, they'll want to open it. What the hell do I tell them? Huh? That I'm on official Dominion of God business?"

"Relax, my friend. We have it covered," Vladimir says, breaking his silence. I quickly notice his English is much better than Miroslav's, with only a slight noticeable accent. "When the time comes, we'll tell you exactly what day, what time and what crossing to use. The briefcase will be locked with a key and combination. It's virtually impenetrable. If you're asked to pull over for further inspection or something, ask to speak with the shift supervisor whose name we'll provide—in time. If worse comes to worse and you're asked to open the briefcase, or if they threaten to break it open, you'll have a remote, like this one here," he says, showing me a tiny plastic gadget that resembles a remote car starter. "At the push of a button, you can incinerate everything inside. Some type of acid and dissolving paper. At the push of another, you can activate an electric shock, eighty to one hundred volts I think, if it's ever stolen or falls into the wrong hands. Anyone who touches it would be in for a big surprise. Needless to say, there'll be no documents inside identifying you or linking you to the DOG. If you're slapped with a fine, We've got it covered."

"So what the hell do I tell them I'm carrying?"

"You tell them that you've been asked to transport documents on behalf of Father Xavier from St. Paul's Basilica," Miroslav replies. "The alleged recipient will be Father Fernandez at the Basilica of Our Lady of Perpetual Help in Brooklyn." He hands me a sheet of paper with the coordinates for the basilica and Father Fernandez. "Of course, this is just alibi. But don't worry, it won't ever get to that. I promise."

"So who am I really delivering to then?"

"One of our guys below border," Miroslav replies. "Vladimir will give you his name and exact location when the time comes."

I frown and remain silent.

"I can tell you're skeptical," Miroslav offers, crushing his cigarette in an ashtray. "I assure you, you've got nothing to worry about, comrade. Along with briefcase, Vladimir will give you cell phone and my contact number. You call me if things don't run so smoothly. Use this cell phone only, not your own. Worst case scenario, they detain you for few hours, slap you with fine, and send you back to Canada."

"Yeah, I hope so."

"You'll be doing a great service for the group. It won't go unnoticed. We'll be with you. More importantly, God will be with you."

"Where will I be picking up this briefcase?"

"Right here, my friend. Vladimir will give you key and code for alarm," he says, as Vladimir hands me another sheet of paper and a key. "The instructions are clear. Just remember to lock up and reset alarm when you leave. Again, Vladimir will give you more specifics when the time comes. Expect phone call within a week or two. Be prepared to go on short notice, likely during weekend. And use Nexus lane."

Although I haven't yet agreed to do this, I suddenly realize that Miroslav's talking as though I had. "Don't worry, I plan to."

"Excellent." he says, rising to his feet and extending his hand. "I'm very grateful for this. Black Mamba is very grateful for this. Vladimir will be in touch with you. Is there any way to reach you other than at home?"

"Yeah, I'd prefer if you try me at Henrique's Meats & Deli first," I reply, shaking his hand. I offer him my work hours and the telephone number and watch as Vladimir jots them down on a notepad. "Outside my working hours, you can try my cell."

"Perfect. Well, you'll have to excuse me, gentlemen, but I have to get going," Miroslav says, slipping on an old leather jacket. "We'll be scheduling another meeting in the near future. Peace be with you, comrades."

Miroslav exits the room, leaving Vladimir and me in awkward silence.

"Liam, if ever you have any problem with the key, go see Dragana at E-Z Grocery," Vladimir finally says. "She has an extra one. But remember, you're only to come to this office when asked to do so. Trust me, Miroslav verifies the alarm registry once in a while to see when the office was accessed, got it?"

"Yeah, I got it."

"Good, well, I guess we better get going." We exit the building and I watch as Vladimir locks up and shows me how to set and reset the alarm. We then make our way back to the front of the building, where Vladimir reminds me that he'll be in touch within a week or two. I watch as he walks through the front door of E-Z Grocery and disappears from sight. As I head back toward the bus stop, I plan how I'll use this latest piece of intelligence as leverage for an allowance from Jacob.

CHAPTER 11

The moment I get home, I call Jacob, who's more than eager to meet with me after I'm done giving him the gist of the events at E-Z Travel. As Sarah is currently sleeping and isn't due to leave for her shift until nine-thirty, I tell him I can only meet with him after this time. Jacob tells me this isn't a problem and so we aim for ten o'clock. We agree to meet at another hotel, this time the Delta on Gerrard Street.

At the hotel, I give him everything. Cherub's Den. Angelic. All the stuff I've gathered on mosques and imams. I also hand over the latest memory stick he had given me which now contains more recent conversations. I decide to hang on to the Dominion's flash drive. I'm just not comfortable not having it in my possession—at least for now. It may be tamper-sensitive and that could get me in a lot of trouble.

I describe my rendezvous at E-Z Travel and E-Z Grocery. I give him the alarm code, my new alias, the planned trip down south and the instructions handed to me, including details of the high-tech briefcase I'm to deliver.

Despite all this, I can tell Jacob is frustrated by the missed opportunity to track Miroslav. "I'm sorry, Jacob," I say. "I didn't know Miroslav was going to be there. It kinda took me by surprise. Had I known, I would've contacted you ASAP."

"That's OK," Jacob responds, shaking the numbness from his hand. "At least we know there's a connection between Miroslav and the E-Z businesses. We can go from there. You've done good. Anything else on this Vladimir guy?"

I take a moment to reflect. "Sorry. I don't even know his last name."

"No worries, maybe he'll come up in the business registry."

"So now what?"

Jacob says nothing and leans back into his chair. For the next while, we contemplate possible courses of action. The obvious scenario would be for me to access the businesses during off hours—particularly in the middle of the night—and scour the place for any information that might be useful. Maybe plant a bug. However, there's just one small problem: the surveillance camera and the fact that Miroslav keeps track of the alarm system's registry. Therefore, showing up in the early hours of the morning and disabling it wouldn't be a viable option. My *associates*—and I use the term loosely—would immediately know that someone with the code entered the premises, whether the camera is operational or not.

Jacob and I also discuss a staged break-in, but this doesn't solve our camera issues nor does it really solve our alarm dilemma. While I'm sure Jacob and his team could arrange that the security company respond unusually slowly to an activated alarm, or that the alarm is never received, this could create problems for the security agency as well as more suspicion on the part of the Dominion of God.

And I'm not comfortable with either scenario. There'd simply be too much heat on me. It wouldn't take long before they put two and two together. In the end, it's agreed that a surveillance team be put on 24/7 watch at the E-Z businesses until we figure out how to bypass the alarm and camera systems. Considering the fact that I'll eventually be returning to E-Z Travel legitimately, there's no point compromising my position. *When* and *if* the opportunity presents itself, I'm to gather as much information as I can. This includes making copies of any pertinent documents by using the photocopy machine in their back room. It also includes taking snapshots of the premises using a small digital camera that Jacob will give me. Of course, this can only be done if I'm lucky enough to be alone there. The window of opportunity becomes even smaller given that I'm only supposed to be there for a pickup, meaning I can only be there for a brief period of time.

As for my visit to our neighbors down south, Jacob and I agree that there may be a connection between the Dominion and a U.S. Customs and Border Protection official. So Jacob insists that I follow Miroslav's instructions if any problems arise. That way, the more I can learn, the more I can report. If things escalate and Miroslav's plans to bail me out fail, or if I'm left hanging high and dry, Jacob assures me that he'll get me out of trouble. If anything goes terribly wrong, I'm to contact him immediately. But I have to be careful. If the Dominion does in fact have a contact within the CBP, the last thing I'd want them to discover is that I've just made a phone call to an intelligence officer.

"I don't care what they do or what they say." Jacob hands me another one of his phony business cards. "Ask to speak with Jake Hartman. Tell them he works for your lawyer and that you'll only speak with Jake. Got it?"

"Got it."

"Good. If you can, call me as soon as you find out when or where you're scheduled to make this delivery, or for anything else for that matter. Hopefully we'll be able to get a surveillance team to follow you. In the meantime, I'm going to see what can be done about our CBP situation. Report back as soon as you can, especially if you get the names of any border officials you've dealt with. If there's a right-wing element within the ranks of the CPB, this could really get complicated. Get me everything. Names of who you've met. License plates. Everything."

"Gotcha."

Then he adds, "We we're thinking of placing a bug on you. Would you be comfortable with that? And do you think there'd be a chance to place a GPS on any—"

"Hell no," I reply without a moment's hesitation. "Not in a million years! Do you not remember the metal detectors? There's no way in hell I'm having anything on me!"

"Damn, that's right," Jacob replies, slightly defeated. "OK, we'll stick with a surveillance unit. As far as your conversations with Angelic and some of the others go, we've managed to pinpoint a few IP addresses and service providers. We're keeping a close eye on them." He pauses while he shuffles through his files and retrieves a large paper envelope. "Now, the moment you've been waiting for . . . your allowance has been approved. You'll get $3,000 every two weeks—after taxes. Congratulations! You're officially working for us now."

For the first time in a long time, a sense of relief washes over me. I can't help but smile.

"In addition," he continues, "you're getting $6,000 up front for the information you've already provided."

"Nice."

"Of course, there'll be bonuses depending on the quality and accuracy of your reporting. That'll be assessed on a monthly basis. I can't say exactly how much, but I guarantee you it'll be worth your time."

"I'm good with that."

"Now, what I'll need from you is your account information. We'll be depositing your payments directly into your bank account every two weeks. We prefer a paperless environment."

For a moment, I freeze. "Crap, I completely forgot! Sarah and I have a joint bank account. I can't have payments deposited there!" I think it's fair to say that Sarah will notice an extra six thousand dollars accumulating monthly.

"What about opening up another bank account?"

"What? With my credit?" I reply, remembering all my previous rejections and why I got involved with loan sharks in the first place.

"Sure, why not? I've come prepared. Everything you need is here." Jacob hands me some forms. "We'd prefer you select either one of these two banks—for administrative reasons, but that's totally up to you."

"TD Canada Trust or RBC?"

"Yeah. Once you start getting paid, use that money to pay off your debts," Jacob says. His eyes narrow. "I mean it. I don't care how much you owe or to who. Pay 'em off. Be careful how you spend the rest so as not to arouse suspicion. And please, Liam, for the love of God, don't use this on alcohol or gambling."

"I don't gamble anymore, Jacob."

"I'm glad to hear it," he replies, packing his briefcase. "In the meantime, keep me posted. If you have any difficulties opening up a bank account, let me know."

Before leaving, we chit-chat for a bit, turning things to a lighter side. We talk about baseball again, the season winding down. We also discuss marriage and religion. While he tells me he got married this past April and that he and his wife are trying to get pregnant, he never reveals her name. Nor does he ever say much about her or his family. I suppose that's normal. I wouldn't expect a spy to reveal too much about his personal life.

I, on the other hand, am not so guarded. I tell him Sarah and I met in high-school but only started dating after graduating. I tell him we've been off and on in the past twenty years but that we're currently going through our longest "together" streak—five years and counting. Naturally, he enquires why all the break-ups. I tell him it usually had to do with the subject of marriage, which I've promised but not delivered on a few occasions. I explain to him that Sarah absolutely wants a religious ceremony but that ever since my infiltrating the Dominion twenty years ago, my faith and belief in religious institutions have been tenuous at best.

Like Frank did, Jacob gives me the spiel on how I shouldn't let a bunch of fanatics and extremists give religion a bad name and scare me away from my faith. Easier said than done, I tell him.

On this last note, Jacob bids me goodnight and leaves me alone to wrestle with my thoughts. An unsettling feeling begins to develop in the pit of my stomach. Guilt. I think it's guilt. Not just guilt about Sarah and marriage, but the guilt of having to deceive and lie and keep secrets from her, the only person who's ever really trusted me. I've kept so many secrets in the past. I'll have to keep many more in the coming days, weeks and months, but hopefully nothing beyond that. It doesn't feel good. But I'm the one who's got us into this mess and I'm the one who's got to get us out. I hate the irony of my situation. By wanting to provide a better life for Sarah, I've managed to ruin us and send us spiraling down the path of poverty. I've prayed countless nights for things to change. Maybe for once, my prayers have been answered.

CHAPTER 12

Mario is the first member I hear from in quite a long time. It's late on a Thursday night and Sarah has already left for work. Out of the blue, he calls and instructs me to meet him at the Union Subway Station in twenty minutes. He tells me to bring everything I've been able to gather so far with respect to my assignments.

Thank God I held onto that memory key. I tell myself, making a mental note to *always* trust my instincts.

I immediately call Jacob. He tells me to go along with whatever's going down and to call him as soon as it's over. Once again, he explains that the possibility of having a tail depends entirely on the availability of his staff and their ability to assemble a team on such short notice.

Then I retrieve all my files and the Dominion's memory key that I've kept hidden beneath the bottom shelf of our entertainment unit in the living room—the only piece of furniture in our apartment that falls under my jurisdiction and which Sarah would never bother disturbing. I stuff the files, maps, notepads, and memory key into a duffel bag and head out the door.

When I finally get to Union Station, the platform is relatively quiet, with a minimum amount of activity at the designated waiting areas. Newspaper, litter and other remnants of the day's activity cover the floor. A handful of people wait impatiently for the next train to arrive. Strange folk loiter in the shadows in almost every corner. A beggar is wandering erratically across the floor, asking for change or anything else that can be spared. It's Mario who ultimately finds me, grabbing me by the arm.

"Hey man, over here . . ."

I follow him back to a bench by the wall. We sit down in the shadows. "So, what's up? What's going on?" I ask.

"We have a meeting in less than an hour—"

"A meeting? Where?"

"St. Andrew's." He looks around nervously. "Keep your eye open for Shane, Cyril and Roch. Also, keep an eye open for suspicious individuals. I've been here scoping the place out for awhile. So far, so good."

"St. Andrew's? The church?"

"No, the fuckin' golf course," Mario answers sarcastically. "Of course the church!"

"Why St. Andrew's?"

"How the hell should I know?"

"Why didn't we just meet there instead?"

"Hey, I don't give the orders. Now keep an eye open for suspicious individuals."

"Suspicious individuals?" I scoff. "What? You gone paranoid now?"

"Never assume you're not being followed," he says in a rather condescending way. "You can never be too careful. I mean, I know we have no reason to be paranoid, but you have to be attuned to shit like this. How do you know you weren't followed?"

"Followed by who?"

"Cops. Spies. Who the hell knows? Anyone investigating the bombings, I guess. Do you think they're not out there looking for Derek, Conrad and Miroslav? Haven't you seen the newspapers? I'm telling you, man. This is serious shit we're in."

"Tell me about it," I reply, unsure as to Mario's feelings about the whole situation. "Are you really up for this? I mean, being part of the Dominion and whatever they're up to—whether or not they were involved in the bombings?"

"Hell yeah," Mario whispers, looking around. "Aren't you?"

"Of course, but—"

"You know, it's true what Derek said. We're under attack. Every day, they're using our rights and freedoms to get away with planning, funding and executing their terrorist operations! This is a war. It's about time someone stands up to them. Who do you think will do that? The government? The military? The cops? The courts? Are you kidding me? We're losing the war. Our laws are flawed, man. You know as well as I do the courts protect their rights more than they do ours! The Toronto

Four—you know, those four bastards sitting in jail awaiting trial—do you think they'll ever get convicted?"

"I sure as hell hope so . . ."

"Wishful thinking, man," Mario replies, lowering his voice. "I bet you they're out walking the streets by the end of the year. No matter how much evidence you have on these guys, they always end up walking."

I say nothing more in hopes of ending the discussion. From the corner of my eye, I spot Roch, Cyril and Shane approaching. We exchange greetings and engage in chit-chat. It turns out that none of us have a clue as to the purpose of the meeting or those expected to attend. According to Mario and Shane, it was Vladimir who got in touch with them and informed them of the gathering. Mario was instructed to inform Roch and me, while Shane was told to get a hold of Cyril. Evidently, there appears to be some type of hierarchy, with me at the very bottom of the pecking order.

The roar of an oncoming train echoes throughout the tunnel, erupting into a full blown thunder as it enters the terminal. We all watch in anticipation as it comes screaming to a halt.

"This is it," Mario says, darting toward the open doors. "Let's get going!"

"What? We're taking the subway? Why don't we just walk there?" I ask, perplexed as to why we don't just walk two blocks to the old church. My questions simply go unanswered as I follow closely behind my associates.

Like foot soldiers, we dash toward the train before the doors close. We take a short ride and get off at the St. Andrews stop. There, we resurface, walk half a block and make our way up the steps and to the front doors of St. Andrew's Presbyterian Church.

The church itself is a large, grey and medieval-looking structure with a distinct architectural style. With two square tower turrets complete with pointed roofs at the front corners of the building and an even bigger tower at the rear along Simcoe Street, it resembles almost as much a fortress as it does a church. The senior minister is Reverend Alan Maitland, a popular local figure who's appeared on several television broadcasts on Sunday mornings. He's a tall and slender man with dark hair and intense, dark eyes. From what I've heard, he's a passionate and influential man. So is his minister-in-association, Wyman Hunt. I can't help but wonder whether Reverend Maitland is aware of Hunt's renewed involvement in Christian Identity and the Dominion of God.

The moment I step inside, I'm overcome by a strange and unusual sensation, as though an infinite number of eyes are staring down on me from somewhere up above. Judging. Shaming. Scorning. That's when I realize that it's been nearly twenty years since I've step foot inside a church—or any place of religious worship for that matter.

Upon approaching the first set of pews, I stop and take a good look around. The first thing I notice is the chancel at the far end, its dome-like ceiling and walls painted in patterns of gold, green and blue. Majestic multi-colored stained glass windows, Union Jacks and other flags surround it. At the back of the chancel just below the stained windows and overhanging flags is the communion table before a row of pews to each side. Above each set of pews stand two dozen organ pipes arranged in a semi-circle and mounted on a rounded platform. Before the chancel is the main floor sanctuary; numerous rows of pews divided by a middle isle and two side isles. Here, the walls are coated a rosy-beige. Above these pews is an upper gallery decorated with more stained glass windows. At the very back of the sanctuary—in the upper gallery—rests a large organ, the church's true gem. A few parishioners are spotted praying in the first set of pews near the front. Our presence goes unnoticed.

Like ghosts, we wander quietly through the open doorway leading to the church basement. Upon reaching the final steps, a small group of men appear at the far end of the hall. Among them are Derek and Conrad, who are engaged in discussions with several individuals that I don't recognize. Our arrival prompts them to pause in and look over our way.

"Good evening, gentlemen. Glad to see you made it," Derek says, motioning to a room to his left. "Please, take a seat inside. We'll begin shortly."

One by one, we stream into a room where Nash and another unidentified man appear to be getting acquainted. Nash excuses himself from the conversation and greets us with a handshake. He introduces the other man as Zack, who stands up and greets us in turn. Zack appears to be younger than the rest of us, I'd say in his late twenties, maybe early thirties. He has a lean and solid build with short blond hair. He has a strange, rather robotic demeanor. Partially visible on the left side of his neck is a tattoo of a Nazi swastika within an Iron Cross. A scar stretches across his neck. Nash reveals that Zack is also American, and has been invited by Derek and the others to this meeting.

The first thing that occurs to me is that Zack must be a new recruit, perhaps discovered through the Internet. The thought of Zack being Angelic also crosses my mind, but Angelic stated he was from Canada, which disproves that theory, not to mention the fact that I have yet to disclose any of our conversations to the Dominion.

We wait another fifteen minutes or so until we hear Miroslav's deep voice from down the hall. He eventually appears, followed by Vladimir and the others, with Derek and Conrad at the tail end. The door is closed and everyone takes a seat, forming a near-perfect circle.

Derek is the first to address the group. He thanks everyone for coming and introduces several individuals. One by one, they identify themselves as Chris, Craig, Sonny, Hal and Zack. I make a mental note to remember their names. With the exception of Zack and Nash, all are from Canada. In my head, the wheels begin to turn. *Who are these guys? Are they all new recruits? If so, who recruited them?* The thought of the Dominion being able to recruit so soon is quite disconcerting and leaves me with an unsettled feeling in the pit of my stomach.

For the first half of the meeting, this is exactly what's discussed: recruiting. Together, we participate in a brainstorming session—what has worked, and what has not. We also discuss developing relationships with other like-minded groups and individuals—religious fanatics or nut cases, as I prefer to think of them. There's even mention of approaching white supremacist groups such as the Aryan Nations, the Klu Klux Klan, the Northern Alliance or even former members of defunct groups such as the Heritage Front and the Silent Brotherhood, in hopes of luring those who are more religiously inclined and who are more likely to convert to the Dominion of God. Much emphasis is placed on the importance of recruiting down in the U.S., most notably in areas known for religious conservative views and where militias and right-leaning groups are known to operate. We're also encouraged to look for potential candidates among those who've been personally affected by 9/11 or Black Friday—or any other act of terrorism for that matter.

In general, the consensus is that the Internet provides the easiest and safest means to recruit not only on a national scale, but on a global one as well. On the Internet, it's easy to go unnoticed and undetected. It's easy to be anonymous. Ironically, it's agreed that churches or other religious sanctuaries are off-limits, primarily because they attract and house too many moderates or liberals, which presents too many potential dangers to the group. According to Derek and the others, such Christians are weak and naïve and not worthy of the Dominion of God.

We also talk about the goals of the Dominion, which are still ambiguous to most of us, with perhaps the exception of Derek, Miroslav and Conrad. An open discussion ensues where each of us has a chance to speak up and voice our desires and opinions on how to improve what the group considers a weak and fragile system of governance defined by gross liberal policies and legislations.

"For too long," Derek proclaims, "We've let the forces of evil live among us, protected by our laws, our rights and our freedoms! These very laws and rights that were conceived for you and I and our Christian ancestors are now being abused and altered to fit their mold. Don't be fooled, they now have more rights than you and I! It is *we* who are being assimilated! It is *we* who are forced to adapt! This is only a part of the Devil's tactics! He has sent false prophets to deceive us and to weaken us! Because of their poison, our government no longer represents us! Our courts no longer protect us! Gentlemen, we must ask: How has this happened? Where is our shepherd guiding us through the valley of the shadow of death?"

Some shake their heads and grumble in disgust, others nod.

"I'll tell you where," Derek continues, "Right here. The Dominion of God is the shepherd. Gentlemen, *we* are the shepherds. Together, we will go where no one else dares to go. We will do what no one else wants to do. We will do it in the name of Jesus Christ our savior who will lead us in the eradication of the forces of evil and the restoration of God's kingdom. Just like our ancestors the Israelites, God is commanding us to battle against our enemies. He is commanding us to destroy everything that belongs to our enemy. He is commanding us to not spare them: to put to death men and women, children and infants. Nothing about the enemy is to be spared. Their history and their memory must forever be wiped from the face of our consciousness."

A collective *Amen* echoes throughout the church cellar.

"That is our mission! The Dominion of God will protect good Christians, whether they have found the path of the Dominion or are on their way, and all those who have renounced the words of the false prophets. Together, we will annihilate the Army of the Beast! We will put an end to these germs that infect our Kingdom!"

Again, this draws another loud reaction from the crowd.

"But sadly," Derek continues, his voice deepening, "The only way to accomplish this is through war. It is the way the enemy has chosen to engage. It is what has been foretold. Dialogue and democracy has gotten us nowhere and will continue to get us nowhere. You cannot negotiate with the enemy—with non-believers. We do not speak the same language. Their minds and their souls are infected. Those who say you *can* are both naïve and gutless. They are idealists, not realists. It is because of their naïve and bleeding hearts that we, God's people, suffer today." He pauses, his eyes growing in intensity. "Alas, there will be those who oppose us. Those who will doubt us. Even those of our own kind. Make no mistake about it, there will be resistance."

In this light, Derek assures us that the mosque bombings were just the beginning; the possibility of more attacks on mosques and other religious institutions is explored. The abduction of influential religious figures for ransom or to obtain certain demands is also proposed. The purpose of this? To divide the population. To draw out the righteous and weed out the weak. To instill fear and doubt among the citizens of the world. To initiate a breakdown in foreign relations with non-secular states. To create chaos. All this to identify God's elect and to initiate the Tribulation and the End Times.

The issue of fundraising is item number two on the night's agenda. Although there are some objections, it's agreed that a monthly fee of twenty-five dollars per member be implemented to help fund the group's activities. This will be in addition to funds provided by Reverend Hunt, who has agreed to smuggle out a percentage of the offerings received at St. Andrew's Church. And there's the promise of more contributions from several Christian Identity churches south of the border. While no one bothers to question the relative insignificance of these funds, I believe I already have the answer to what will be the Dominion's principal source of funding.

For that, I'll have to be patient and wait for the opportunity to present itself.

The latter half of the night we end up discussing current events and politics, including the existence of Islamic and Jewish states and the need for a state based on the fundamental principles of the Dominion of God in order to counter the spread of the false prophets and for the preservation of God's "true" people—a base from which to operate and launch an all-out assault against the Army of the Beast. This leads me to believe the Dominion is envisioning something much bigger than simple bombings or abductions.

We also discuss something that I haven't put much thought into lately, that is, the upcoming peace talks in Rome between Israel and the Palestinian National Authority. According to Derek and the others, the comprehensive peace plan, titled *Israel–Palestine Action Plan for Lasting Peace*, was presented to both parties earlier today and talks will commence shortly in the hopes of bringing peace in the Middle East. Interestingly, the talks are to be held in secret with representatives of the League of Arab States and the European Union in attendance. When considering the Dominion's belief that the period of Tribulation is to commence when a peace treaty with Israel is signed, this stands to be very, very significant.

On a local level, we discuss the trials set to start for the Toronto Four, that is, the young men accused of participating in the terrorist attacks of Black Friday, three of which are currently being held at the Toronto West Detention Centre while the fourth—and the youngest—is being detained in a separate institution. This sparks a heated debate on past trials of accused terrorists both in Canada and the U.S. as well as abroad, and the ensuing lack of justice. The two Americans among us express their emphatic discontent with Canadian lawmakers and policies, claiming that Canada is much too lenient and naïve a society to adequately deal with the evil-doers. As expected, all the others in attendance—except me—agree with this philosophy. Both Nash and Zack also remind us that the trials are being closely monitored in the U.S. and will be a testimony as to Canada's stance on extremism and terrorism.

Needless to say, everyone in the room is confident—no, convinced—that the Toronto Four will walk. There's simply no faith in the system. None. The more they brood over this, the more irate they become.

As for me, I offer nothing but inauthentic support to everything that they spew from their hateful mouths. I don't dare say anything to contradict anyone or to create suspicion.

After nearly three hours of discussion, we prepare for the anointment of Zack and the other newcomers into the Dominion of God. As on the night of my own initiation, Derek, Miroslav and Conrad garb themselves in silver masks and dark robes and preside over the ritual. Together, we recite prayers from *The Last Testament* and sing a few hymns. One by one, the men are sliced open and their blood collected in a chalice. More prayers are recited, more hymns are sung.

After the rituals are complete, each man is invited to a one-on-one meeting with one of the leaders. The first three men to be summoned are Shane, Vladimir, and Zack. I watch as they're each escorted to a separate room. The rest of us simply end up loitering silently in the large empty hall, waiting for our turn.

A lifetime seems to go by before the first man emerges from his meeting. Cyril is summoned next. Then it's Mario, followed by Roch, Nash, Chris, Craig, Sonny, and Hal.

Patiently, I wait for my turn. I watch as the only other man left is summoned to the room occupied by Miroslav, who I had hoped to be paired with. Although I'd never admit this to anyone, I utterly dread a one-on-one meeting with Derek. Conrad is a distant second.

Alone, I wait in the church cellar, wishing nothing more than to be far away from the Dominion of God. The more time goes by, the more I regret my decision to become a part of this madness. I become increasingly jittery and nervous, sweat running down my back and covering my palms.

I'm about to make my escape when a door suddenly opens. Out comes Hal, who wishes me goodnight and makes his way up the staircase, the sound of his heavy footsteps echoing throughout the empty church. Then I hear the heavy wooden doors slamming shut.

"Looks like you're the last man standing, Liam," Conrad says with a grin, leaning against the doorframe, "Come, let's talk."

CHAPTER 13

"Miroslav tells me you've agreed to help us with couriering important materials," Conrad begins, taking a seat. "I'm glad to hear that. You're doing us a great favor. Black Mamba is very thankful. Remember, you're doing the Lord's work . . . and that never goes unnoticed in His eyes."

"Whatever I can do to help," I reply, sitting down.

"Last time we met, you were assigned a task. Have you had any success?"

I open my duffel bag and hand over my files and the memory stick. "Everything I was able to gather is in that file," I offer. "Mosques. Imams. Islamic institutions. Security systems. Points of access. Maps. Description of neighborhoods. It's all there. As far as any potential recruits, there are a few."

"Excellent!" Conrad replies, sifting through the material.

"In particular, you might want to get in touch with an individual who identifies himself as Angelic. He's exactly who we're looking for. He's home-grown. I chatted with him over a dozen times. Everything is on the flash drive. This guy's the real deal. He knows his stuff and he's well read. Blames Jews and Muslims for the downfall of western society and believes in a Jewish and Islamic conspiracy to destroy Christianity. He insists the Holocaust is a hoax and praises Hitler for quashing a Jewish uprising that would've spelled the end of Christianity as we know it. He believes that Islam is now the new evil and that it must be dealt with in the way the Nazis dealt with the Jews. He praises those responsible for the mosques bombings and practically worships the DOG."

"Interesting . . ." Conrad replies, eyeing the flash drive. "All your conversations are in here? His email address?"

"Yeah."

"Excellent work, Liam." Conrad stuffs the black memory stick into his pocket and hands me a new one. "Continue doing the same. Keep up the good work."

"Thanks. If you don't mind me asking, what will this information be used for? I mean . . . the information on the mosques and stuff. Another attack I presume?" The moment the words roll from my tongue, I get a feeling that my query may have been too sudden, too forward. I watch as Conrad raises an eyebrow. "Let me guess—need to know, right?"

Conrad simply nods in agreement, never taking his eyes off me.

"That's fine," I reply, searching for something to deflect any suspicion. "I mean, I busted my balls getting this stuff together. I sure as heck hope it'll be used for something—"

"Black Mamba knows exactly what it'll be used for. He has a great vision and a great plan. That's all that matters. That's all you need to know for now."

"I understand."

"The less you know—the less we all know—the safer it is for the Dominion. The more people know, the more dangerous it becomes and the more vulnerable the Dominion becomes. When people know too much, that's when mistakes are made. Everyone's a part in the machine that is the Dominion. It doesn't matter whether one part knows what the other is doing. As long as each part does its job, the machine will work as it was meant to work."

I nod.

"But I'll tell you this," Conrad continues, changing his tone. "Something is about to go down . . . and you *will* be called upon."

"OK, but can you give me any indication as to when I may be called upon? I mean, I do have a life here. I have a job and other obligations and kinda need to know in advance sometimes—a heads-up, you know? I won't always be able to get up and go at the last minute like this."

Conrad smirks as though it wasn't the first time he's heard this complaint. "Early January. Be available at night. And no, we won't be setting off any bombs. Black Mamba assures us that is not what the Lord wants. The innocent will not suffer. The blood of the innocent will not be shed."

"January?"

"That's right. Is that good enough advance for you?"

"Yeah, thanks."

"Remember, you're not to discuss with others what you've been tasked with. Don't tell anyone about your trips down south, you hear? They don't need to know, just as you don't need to know what they've been tasked with. If you hear of anyone discussing their tasks to others or if anyone discusses their task to you, I'd appreciate you letting either myself, Derek or Miroslav know."

"No problem."

"I believe in you, Liam," he says, placing a hand on my shoulder. "Black Mamba believes in you. The Lord believes in you. Miroslav tells me you've abandoned your faith. Please, go to mass and pray for the Lord's guidance and protection. Pray for your brothers. Pray for the Dominion and repent your sins."

"I don't believe I need to—"

"Don't be a fool!" Conrad sneers. "You don't have to be a practicing Catholic to be in a Catholic church, just as long as you act like one. Get my drift? Go pray for the Dominion."

"Doesn't Hunt have his own Church of Jesus Christ Christian?" I say. "Doesn't he hold meetings or masses or something? Why haven't I been invited yet?"

"Never mind Hunt, he's not part of the Dominion. But he does need our protection. We can't risk losing him. You hear?"

"Yeah."

Conrad suddenly jerks to his left and reaches into his pocket. "Oh, and one more thing," he says, pulling out what appears to be a deck of plastic cards. "Everyone is getting their own ID—a membership card, I guess you can say."

I take the flimsy white plastic card that he hands to me. I flip it over several times to inspect it. There's nothing on it but a black magnetic strip and a series of numbers.

"You won't find anything on it," Conrad says, "other than that number, I mean. That's your personal identification number or PIN. You may want to write it down somewhere in case you ever lose it. You'll need it for future gatherings."

"Is there anything *in* it? I mean, like my name or personal info?"

"The only thing it contains is your ID number, your name, place and date of birth. There's nothing linking you to the Dominion of God. Even better, there's nothing that can read them other than our own reader. Thank Miroslav for that. God knows where he comes up with these."

"Why the need?" I ask, unable to understand its utility.

"As our great organization grows bigger and stronger," Conrad replies, sounding much like a proud father speaking of his children, "we'll need them to keep track of everyone. We'll need to have everyone accounted for and be accountable."

"Fair enough," I offer, slipping the card in my wallet.

"Good. Now please, go to church and pray for our success," Conrad says, getting up from his seat and opening the door. "We'll be in touch. There'll be more meetings in the coming weeks. Please, go in peace."

I nod and slip quietly past Conrad and ultimately Derek and Miroslav, who are the only members left in the church's empty basement. I don't bother to engage in further discussion and neither do they. Instead, I hastily make my way back up the staircase leading to the church's front entrance and disappear into the night.

CHAPTER 14

October blows by in the blink of an eye. Baseball season is over. The Yankees are World Series champions—again. Now, it's hockey and basketball season. And in Toronto, this can be a very painful experience. On another note, my meetings with Jacob have increased, averaging one or two a week. I show him the ID card that was assigned to me. Although it'd be beneficial for Jacob to take it in and have it analyzed at his headquarters, we both agree that I shouldn't be caught without it. So, on a few occasions, Jacob brings along a technical expert who uses his equipment to try to read the card.

All attempts so far have failed miserably.

Also during this time, I manage to set up a checking account with TD Canada Trust without much hassle—to my surprise. The first installment of six thousand dollars comes in mid-October and covers the first month and a half of my work as an informant. Since then, I've been receiving payments every two weeks, as promised. For the first time in a very long time, the stress caused by my financial burden has subsided—at least somewhat. Things are finally starting to look up.

As far as my dealings with the Dominion of God go, three more gatherings have taken place within the past month. And for the first time, the messages were relayed to me via email. These messages I've saved onto Jacob's flash drives which I've handed back to my handler on every occasion. The sender of these messages shows only as "The Prophet" using the email address theprophet@vica.net. While Jacob has intimated that he is not familiar with this host, he guarantees they'll get to the bottom of this.

To my—and Jacob's—dismay, none of these meetings are held at St. Andrew's or at Wyman Hunt's residence. Like the elusive serpent, the Dominion manages to slip through the cracks, never holding a meeting in the same place twice.

I have to hand it to them—to Derek, Miroslav, Conrad or whoever is really in charge. No matter what our scheme is, no matter what the plan, the Dominion of God is always one step ahead of us. It has proved very efficient in the practice of misinformation in order to avoid any kind of detection. Where it says it'll be one minute, it's somewhere else the next. Apparently, Jacob's surveillance team has grown tired of waiting several hours at bogus meeting points. Around-the-clock surveillance has been established at Wyman's residence, St. Andrew's and the E-Z businesses. Of course, no further gatherings have been held at these locations, nor have any members of the Dominion been seen entering or exiting these premises.

The Dominion's counter-surveillance aptitudes go well beyond this. Even when a tail is established, it's short-lived. Twice, a surveillance team managed to follow me from home only to lose me and my companions somewhere in the underground corridors beneath the city. On one of those occasions, the team's position had been compromised after Mario noticed we were being followed at the Queen subway station. A confrontation ensued between Mario, Roch, and members of the surveillance team, who insisted they weren't following anyone. Its cover blown, there wasn't much the team could do other than watch us board the train and disappear from sight. Of course, this didn't happen in view of any of the subway system's security cameras.

Rarely have any members of the Dominion been caught on camera. And when they are, they're facing away, as though knowing full well the positioning of every single recording device in the city.

When we finally reach our rendezvous points, we're all scanned for metal or whatnot—again with those paddle-like wands, every single time and with no exceptions. It goes without saying that the effectiveness and the security-consciousness of the Dominion have remained impeccable.

With every gathering, new members are anointed. So much so that I've begun to lose track of everyone. Most are only introduced as and referred to by their aliases. This goes for everyone: I'm known to the others as the Mailman, Miroslav as the Moneyman, Shane as the Milkman, Conrad as Frenchy, Derek as Red Devil or simply Red, Cyril as the Mechanic, Mario as the Iceman, Roch as the Rocket Man, Vladimir as Farm Boy—to name a few. Last I counted, there were sixteen new members in all, not including those south of the border, whose numbers are unknown to me. With the initiation of every new member, I can't help wonder whether Angelic is one of our newest investments. I've come to accept the fact that I'll likely never know.

One thing that's becoming clearer, as I've related to Jacob, is that the Dominion is preparing for a strike in the New Year—likely in the form of a kidnapping. What remains unclear, however, is the purpose of this act. Jacob and I have discussed this for hours. Though a ransom remains possible, my gut tells me it's unlikely. Money doesn't appear to be an issue with the Dominion—at least not yet anyway. While Jacob and I have considered the possibility that kidnapping a member of a religious community could be done simply for the sheer purpose of killing in the name of sensationalism, we figure that a more likely scenario would include that certain demands be met—demands which I can't even begin to fathom.

Jacob and I also spend large amounts of time discussing the scheduled peace talks between Israel and the Palestinian National Authority, which are now set to begin in a matter of days. I remind him of the Dominion's interest in these talks and of the prophecies relating to a peace treaty—a covenant—between Israel and the Antichrist and the commencement of the Tribulation. While he agrees as to the significance of these events, he is of the opinion that these new peace talks will be no more successful than all previous attempts to bring peace to the area. Regardless, this is something we both agree we should keep our eyes on. In this vein, Jacob requests that I relate to him strategies, if any, the Dominion may formulate with respect to developments in the peace process.

Other than that, I have absolutely no idea what's going on at Jacob's end. That's just another downside to being an informant. I have no idea how my information is being or will be used. I know we've had a tail on several occasions. I know because I was able to spot them and because Jacob has admitted this. However, Jacob tells me his surveillance unit has had an unusually difficult time keeping track of our movements. Beyond this, I'm left completely in the dark.

In the meantime, Jacob is preparing me for my anticipated visit to E-Z Travel and subsequent trip to the U.S., a call I'm still waiting for. He's given me a tiny digital camera that looks and works exactly like a ball-point pen. Under no circumstances am I to take any pictures with the use of my cell phone. Should I happen to be alone at the E-Z office,

I'm to take as many pictures of the interior as possible to illustrate the layout. I've also been tasked with taking snapshots of any documents in plain view or that may be of interest. There's also a photocopy machine in the back that's at my disposal.

I've also been asked to pay close attention to the security systems installed at the facility, and to check whether the camera is actually functional and whether a monitor and recording device are running inside. I'm also to report the name of the security company that the E-Z businesses use. My time inside is to be kept at a minimum in order to avoid suspicion. Five minutes, tops.

Sometime during the first week of November, I get the call. I'm alone working my shift at Henrique's when the phone rings.

"Henrique's Meats & Deli," I say. "Liam speaking, how can I help you?"

"I'm looking for the Mailman," says a deep and unfamiliar voice.

Taken aback, I pause for a moment. "Yes, this is him."

"There's a special delivery to New York for 5 p.m. tomorrow. Everything you need to know is at E-Z. Pick up your parcel there at 6 a.m. sharp. You know what I'm talking about?"

"Yeah, I know."

"OK, orders are from the big man. He trusts you. Do not disappoint him."

"No worries."

"God bless."

The caller hangs up, but I remain frozen with the phone to my ear and anger growing inside. Soon my head hurts so much it feels like it's going to explode. The thing is, tomorrow is Saturday and I'm scheduled to work. Even worse, tomorrow night is Sarah's night off and we have plans to go out for dinner. We rarely have time off together. I can't even remember the last time we went out for dinner. Then again, if it wasn't for this extra cash I'm secretly making and masking it as overtime money, we wouldn't be going out for dinner in the first place.

Defeated, I reach for my cell phone and make a call. A groggy voice answers.

I bite my lower lip. "Hi, honey . . . I've got some bad news . . ."

CHAPTER 15

It's early morning and the door is locked and the security system is activated upon my arrival at E-Z Travel. From the corner of my eye, I can see the security camera's tiny red light blinking steadily overhead. Without paying it too much attention, I turn my focus on the access panel for the alarm system. The label reads SafeTech. A tiny digital screen indicates the time and date. Reading the instructions from the slip Vladimir gave me, I punch the code and watch as the panel's lights flicker from red to green. I then take the key and unlock the door.

Inside, all the lights are off and the heating is kept to a bare minimum. Looking at my watch, I note the time. I then quickly make my way toward Vladimir's office in the back. The blinds are drawn; all is dark inside. Although the area is still complete chaos, it's been somewhat tidied up since my last visit. There are no more papers lying on the floor. Binders and books sit on their shelves and the desk area has been cleared of documents, except for a large black briefcase, the accompanying remote and key, and a cell phone. On the briefcase is a note. It reads:

> Going to: Our Lady of Perpetual Help, Brooklyn, NY 526
> 59th Street. Take Whirlpool Bridge anytime between 07h00
> to 09h00. Use Nexus lane. Ask for Wes Sanderson, shift
> supervisor, if you encounter any trouble at the border. Tell
> him you have a delivery for Father Fernandez at OLPH. Be
> at the OLPH school parking lot at the back for 17h00. Look
> for a black Lincoln Navigator. You can always reach me at
> 905-692-668. Take this cell phone with you. Please return it
> here after delivery. God bless.

I immediately grab the cell phone and inspect it. A tiny black device, it's rather basic and unsophisticated when compared to some of the fancier models out there. After fidgeting with it for a moment, I realize it's a pay-as-you-go device—a Nokia 2720. There's no call history and nothing in its contacts list. While it appears to be capable of sending and receiving texts, there are no messages in its logs. It's like it's never been used before.

The briefcase is a Mezzi, as indicated on its front panel. It has two combination locks and two draw-catch key locks. It's made of solid aluminum with chrome handles. It appears to have been altered, likely to accommodate its self-destructing mechanism. It suddenly dawns on me that I was never given any code for this contraption. I search around, futilely, for a code and I shake my head in frustration and disgust. This could get me in a lot of trouble at the border. But there's no time to worry about that now as I've got business to take care of.

From my jacket's interior pocket, I retrieve the ball-point pen Jacob gave me. I take a quick look around for any interior cameras, monitors or recording devices, then begin by taking snapshots of the office by pressing on the pen's clip. I take them from every possible angle. The desk. The bookshelf. The computer. The photocopy machine. The window. The whole room. Nothing is spared. I do this all in record time. Every now and then, I stop to look over my shoulder or to listen for any signs of life.

Nothing.

I then make my way toward the front area and look out the door. The only vehicle in the parking lot is my own. I take more snapshots. I then make my way back to the office. There, I perform a quick visual scan of the various binders and books and documents that have been left in plain view.

Examining the bookshelf, my eyes wander to the bottom shelf and, ultimately, to the safe sitting on the floor next to it. To my complete surprise and disbelief, the door's been left ajar. I get down on my knees and take a quick peek inside. Instead of money, which I expected to find, the vault appears to hold numerous documents contained in several folders.

Carefully, I open the door wide enough to reach inside and retrieve some of the files. The first folder to strike me as curious bears a label indicating "Invoices" plastered across its front cover. Most of the documents inside are unbound. As I sift through the numerous invoices, I realize that none of the purchases or transactions appear to reflect anything one would expect from a travel agency. It soon dawns on me that these are records for E-Z Grocery. Most of the transactions are with foreign produce companies, the bulk of which are from the Balkans, with Serbian farming companies the primary exporters. That's not so odd given that E-Z Grocery sells fruits and vegetables, but what strikes me as curious are the amounts of the transactions, some suggesting that E-Z Grocery purchases $50,000 worth of plums and peaches on a monthly basis. I strongly doubt that store is capable of holding and selling such a large inventory. I also can't help feel there's something else I'm missing about these files . . . some type of subliminal message that hasn't yet been unraveled by my conscious mind.

I place the folder aside and grab another volume labeled "Balances." Unlike the previous collection of invoices, this registry is completely intact, much like an agenda or notebook. I flip through the pages, which reveal countless rows and columns of names and numbers. While some of the columns appear to be dollar amounts—minus any dollar signs—others remain meaningless to me. Some of the names in the columns seem to be names of individuals while others appear to be name of companies, some of which coincide with names on the invoices. In all, there are five or six columns of numbers and a couple of columns of names. Although this means absolutely nothing to me, it may mean something to Jacob and his agency. As for the rest of the numerous books and documents lying around, nothing has yet to pique my interest.

I look at my watch to assess the time. I've been here just over four minutes. Not bad. I can still afford several more without raising too much suspicion. If ever I'm questioned, I decide that my alibi will be that I needed to use the washroom.

Quietly, I take the invoices and the notebook to the photocopy machine. After feeding the machine as many invoices it can take at one time, I then have to manually copy the open pages of the notebook, one spread at a time. I do this with extreme vigilance, listening between prints and occasionally peering out into the hall and reception area.

I then put everything back, leaving the safe ajar as I found it, and stuff the copies into my jacket. I grab the aluminum briefcase, the remote device, the key and the cell phone, stowing the latter three in my pockets. I'm taken aback by the weight of the briefcase, which increases my doubts as to its contents. I take one last look around, exit the building, reactivate the alarm and return to my vehicle, where I store the briefcase in the space where a spare tire used to rest beneath the floor of the trunk. Before slipping behind the steering wheel, I take a quick look up and down the street. A few blocks away is a surveillance unit—a dark Trailblazer—just as Jacob had promised. If it indeed followed me from home, I hadn't noticed it. Regardless, the sight of the truck reassures me. I climb into my vehicle and begin my long and risky journey to Brooklyn.

CHAPTER 16

Traffic heading across Whirlpool Bridge is relatively light as I enter a designated Nexus lane. Still, I'm quite annoyed by the detour I was instructed to take. The Queenston-Lewiston Bridge further north would've enabled me to hit I-190 much sooner, shaving a half hour or more off my time. I'm sure the surveillance team, which has consistently trailed a few vehicles behind, must be wondering why on earth I've taken such a route.

It's now 7:45 a.m. As usual, I scan my Nexus membership card in the card reader—which also pays my toll—and cross the bridge. Once across, I proceed to the inspection booth, where I'm greeted by a U.S. Customs and Border Protection officer. Sitting like a rat in a cage in his booth, his eyes are hidden behind smoke colored sunglasses with reflective lenses. He appears quite young, perhaps in his early to mid-twenties; he wears the typical navy blue uniform, with all its badges and insignias sewn or pinned onto it, with a name tag that reads "D. Charlton" pinned on his chest.

"Good morning sir," he says, staring at me through the smoky lenses of his aviator sunglasses. "May I ask your destination?"

"Brooklyn, New York. Sir."

"And what's the purpose of your visit?"

"To visit an old friend of mine," I reply. "I'm originally from the area."

"Really? So you're an American citizen?"

"Yeah, I have dual citizenship," I explain, pulling out my I.D. cards from my wallet. "See? Oh, and here's my U.S. pass—"

"That won't be necessary, sir," he says, scanning the interior of my vehicle. "How long do you plan on staying in New York?"

"Oh, just for the day—likely coming back later tonight."

"Uh-huh," he replies, not really listening. "Bringing anything with you? Luggage? Or anything like that?"

"Nope."

He then grabs a pen and writes something on a slip of paper. Handing me the slip, he points to a parking area near the office. "Please pull your vehicle over to the designated area so we can take a quick look around."

At first, I'm taken aback by this request. I mean, I've been through these lanes many times before without being subjected to any further inspection. "Umm . . . sure, no problem," I reply and make my way to the inspection area. There, I'm greeted by yet another border officer whose name tag reads "P. Mancini" and who requests that I exit my vehicle and hand over the slip. I do so without protest and watch as he quickly makes his way around the vehicle, looking through the windows. Upon reaching the back, he stops and looks at me through the rear window. "You mind popping open your trunk, sir?"

Hesitant, I reach for the remote and release the lock. From my position at the front of the vehicle, I watch as the officer disappears behind the ascending deck lid. My palms begin to feel cold and clammy. My mind races.

The vehicle suddenly begins to shake followed by a loud *thud*! The officer reappears and makes his way back toward the front of the vehicle. "Not carrying anything with you, huh?" he barks.

At first, I'm at a loss for words. I can't help but feel like a child with his hand caught in the cookie jar. "I'm sorry?" I say, playing innocent. I look around and spot the black Trailblazer clearing customs and continuing on its way.

"You know exactly what I'm talking about!" he snaps, spitting on the ground. "The briefcase—what's in it?"

"Oh, um . . . it contains important documents destined for Father Fernandez at the Basilica of Our Lady of Perpetual Help in Brooklyn." I slide my hands into my jacket pockets in search of the remote. "I . . . I'm on official business for—"

"Sir, please open the briefcase," he orders sternly, then communicates with someone through his two-way radio.

Shit.

Another officer suddenly appears and is briefed by Officer Mancini. Together, they return to the vehicle's storage compartment and tell me to follow. The first officer instructs me to open the floor cover which I do, revealing the aluminum briefcase.

"What's in the briefcase?" he asks.

"Documents belonging to Father Fernandez at the Basilica of Our—"

"Documents? What kind of documents?"

"I'm not quite sure, to be honest with you. I was asked to deliver it to him."

"Asked by whom?"

"Father Xavier in Toronto—"

"Documents, huh?" barks the second officer. "If it's just documents, why bother concealing it?"

My lips move, but they don't say a word. The officers convene and summon yet another officer, apparently of a higher rank. I suddenly remember Miroslav's instructions. "I'd like to speak to the shift supervisor, please. I want to speak with Wes Sanderson. I believe he's on duty?"

"Hey, buddy, *we* call the shots here!" hollers the third officer.

"Look," I say, lowering my tone, "this is a matter of business of the Catholic Church. I insist on speaking with Wes Sanderson."

Again, the officers deliberate and beckon yet another party to the scene. A tall, rugged-looking man joins the trio. Judging by the stripes across the shoulders of his uniform, it's my guess he's the most senior of the group. He's also older, with a salt-and-pepper mustache to match his full head of hair. After being briefed by his colleagues, he turns his gaze to me. "Why do you want to talk to Wes Sanderson?" he queries, chewing gum as he speaks.

"This is a highly sensitive matter. I must speak with Wes Sanderson—"

"Well that'd be me," he replies, "so what the hell is so sensitive here and who the hell are you?"

"I really don't know, to be quite honest," I reply, my hand cradling the briefcase's remote inside my pocket. "My name is Liam Sheehan. I'm just on my way to Brooklyn to deliver a briefcase to Father Fernandez at—"

"Yeah, yeah, I heard all that," he interjects, spitting out his gum. He then dismisses his younger colleagues and orders them back in the office. "Come on, show me this briefcase."

I guide him to the vehicle's storage compartment. He eyes the briefcase with keen interest. He then picks it up and studies the locking mechanism. "Wow, nice fuckin' briefcase. They sure make these things secure nowadays, huh? Can you open it for me?"

At this point, I'm about to press a button—any button—on the remote. Buried deep inside my pocket, I have no idea which is which. I could either disintegrate everything inside, or give Wes Sanderson quite a jolt. I doubt he'd appreciate the latter. But at this point, I couldn't care less if the damn thing explodes.

"Um, well, I have the keys, but not the combination," I explain. "But I do have a contact number for the person who does—"

"You know, normally, I'd have to have one of these scanned for its contents. I could confiscate it. I could seize your vehicle. Request a full body search and all that. Hell, I could detain you for this," he warns, handing me back the briefcase. "But, you seem like a decent fella to me. Church business you say? Alright, I'll take your word for it. I don't need to speak to no one. Go on, get out of my sight—and don't you let no one know I gave you a freebie or else next time there won't be no freebie . . . got it?"

"You got it."

"Go on, get out of here!"

I don't say another word as I deposit the briefcase back into the trunk—only this time, in the actual luggage compartment and not the spare wheel hold. I then get back into my car and attempt to catch up with Jacob's men. In the rearview mirror, I can see the shrinking image of Wes Sanderson staring back at me for several minutes until I'm finally out of range.

I spend the next hour or so attempting to locate the black Trailblazer and thinking about the events that transpired at Whirlpool Bridge and, ultimately, about Wes Sanderson. There was definitely something peculiar about him and about the preferential treatment I received. Something doesn't add up. I should've been questioned thoroughly and detained back there. The briefcase and even my crappy old car should have been seized, scanned and sniffed for explosive materials. I should've been searched and fined and returned to Canada. I got none of that. How Miroslav knew to request the assistance of Wes Sanderson is beyond me. Evidently, there's a connection. Whatever it is, I sure don't like it.

The thought of contacting Jacob during my ordeal at the border crossed my mind. But the more I think about it, the more relieved I am that I didn't. After all, if Wes is in any way connected to the Dominion, asking him to contact a lawyer and not Miroslav as instructed would've completely blown my cover and would likely have been my death sentence. I try not to think about that for the rest of the trip.

CHAPTER 17

The Basilica of Our Lady of Perpetual Help is a massive grey stone structure that's visible from several blocks away, towering above all surrounding edifices. Along with the rectory and ancillary buildings, it occupies a full square block, extending all the way back to Sixth Avenue between Fifty-Ninth and Sixtieth Street where the red bricked OLPH elementary school is located. Like many basilicas, it has no steeple. Instead, two large turret towers stand before arched entryways at the front of the building. Between the towers is a cross sitting atop the front peak of the basilica's triangular roof. It suddenly occurs to me that, in many ways, it resembles St. Andrew's Church back in Toronto.

As I approach it along Fifth Avenue, my mind becomes inundated with youthful memories of midnight masses and other occasions celebrated with my mother's side of the family. My parents, bless their souls, were married in the old basilica. I was baptized there. My First Communion was also celebrated there, as was my Confirmation. It was also the site of my mother's funeral, which was when I last stepped foot inside.

My eyes begin to water as I struggle to hold back tears. If there's one good thing the church reminds me of, it's my mother—the kindest person I've ever known. I don't know how to explain it, but faith for her came naturally. She wasn't the typical churchgoer. She wasn't simply *religious*. She was spiritual. She explained to me once that being religious and being spiritual weren't necessarily one and the same. One could attend mass every week and every holiday, sing all the hymns, recite all the prayers, receive all the sacraments and believe in Jesus as the Son of God and in God our Father. While it does make one religious, my mother would say, it doesn't automatically make one truly at one with God.

Still, to this day, I'm not quite sure what that means.

She always gave me good advice, though. She'd tell me to look beyond the walls of the church—or any other place of holy worship—in order to be at one with God. To look beyond shrines and symbols, as God does. To see everyone as one and the same. She'd warn me never to use my faith as a reason to differentiate myself from another or to look down on others who do not share the same views. Never to use it to turn against another. She'd often say typical phrases like: "judge not lest ye be judged" or "love thy neighbor as thyself" or "the Lord works in mysterious ways". But I knew that with my mother, it wasn't just something she said. She lived by those words. It was as though she knew or understood things most of us don't. She loved everyone. Unconditionally.

God how I miss her.

The vehicle's digital clock reads 5:45 by the time I veer into the school parking lot along Sixtieth Street. The Trailblazer hasn't resurfaced since I spotted it at the border, but I know it can't be very far. Or perhaps Jacob's men have relinquished their pursuit and handed over the reins to their American counterparts. Whatever the case, I just hope whoever has taken the lead in surveillance can get close enough to take decent snapshots—or whatever else it is that they do.

As indicated on the note Miroslav left, a black Lincoln Navigator sits idly in one of the empty spaces, awaiting my arrival. Its windows are tinted black, making it impossible to identify those inside. I station my own vehicle a few empty spots from it, kill the engine and step outside. With the sun setting, the air is cool so I zip my jacket up to my neck. Without paying too much attention to the Navigator, I make my way toward the rear of my vehicle and lean against its frame. My arms crossed, I wait for signs of life from the large SUV. Several minutes go by before the Navigator's passenger door opens.

"Hey Liam, how was the trip?" Nash asks, disembarking from the vehicle.

"Not bad . . . I was intercepted at the border, though."

"Really?"

"Yeah. Funny thing, though," I respond in a matter-of-fact way, "they found the briefcase, but the border guard in charge just let me go through without putting up much of a fuss. He didn't even ask to see its contents. I wasn't frisked or questioned or identified or charged or anything—even after I lied about it."

"Well, that's good news!"

"No shit," I reply, going along with it. "It's almost as though he's one of our guys. Wes Sanderson was his name—ever heard of him?"

Nash stops to reflect. "Nope, can't say I have."

From the Navigator's driver side door, Zack emerges. In the midst of a heated discussion with another party on his cell phone, he excuses himself for a minute. I try my best to eavesdrop on his conversation, but to no avail.

"So you got the briefcase?" Nash asks, walking over to the rear of the vehicle.

"Yeah, it's in the trunk." I pop open the compartment. "I hope you have the combination for it 'cause I sure don't."

"Actually, I don't!" Nash replies from somewhere behind the vehicle.

"So who the hell does? Who is this going to?"

Nash emerges with the briefcase in hand. "I'm not quite sure, to be honest. All I know is I have to deliver it to Tennessee. Do you have the keys and remote?"

I hand him the keys. "Tennessee?"

"Yeah."

"We have people in Tennessee?" I ask, stupefied.

"I don't know . . ."

"Do you know what's inside?"

"Nope."

At this point I realize that Nash knows just as little about the contents of the briefcase as I do. And I doubt Zack knows any more. Whoever this briefcase is going to obviously is more important than all of us combined. *Derek talked about expanding the Dominion down south,* I remind myself. *I'm sure an old Confederate State like Tennessee offers a lot of potential.*

Zack returns after ending his call. He greets me and we end up chatting for a while. But despite my attempts to get them to talk about the Dominion, it becomes evident they have no interest in discussing it. I'd even go as far as to say they seem uncomfortable talking about the Dominion, as though it's some kind of taboo. Evidently, they're buying into this need-to-know principle. In order not to raise suspicion, I abandon my quest for information.

As we're about to say goodbye, Nash retreats to the Navigator and returns with another briefcase. "Here, I almost forgot . . ."

"What the hell is this?" I ask, baffled.

"You're supposed to bring this back to Miroslav," Nash explains, handing me the much larger and heavier briefcase. "Didn't he tell you?"

"No, he didn't bloody tell me!" I retort. "Damn it, I can't risk getting caught again!"

"I wouldn't worry about it if I were you," Nash responds, pulling out a folded sheet of paper. "Here's some instructions in case you get into trouble. Relax, man. It's a piece of cake!"

I take a few moments to read the instructions. Essentially, they're the same as the ones I followed previously. *Use Whirlpool Bridge . . . use Nexus Lane . . . anytime between 11 p.m. and 5 a.m.* There's only one notable difference: instead of requesting to speak with Wes Sanderson of the CBP, I'm to ask for Brent Weiss of the Canada Border Services Agency.

This revelation leaves me feeling very uneasy and anxious.

What the hell is going on here?

"You see?" Nash says. "Miroslav has got it all taken care of!"

I shake my head in disbelief. "Is he paying these guys off?"

"You ask too many questions, man," Zack interjects, his eyes narrowing suspiciously. "Remember what our leaders said—don't ask questions. There are things we don't need to know or aren't supposed to know. As long as things get done according to plan, there'll be nothing to worry about. Have some faith!"

"He's right, Liam," Nash says, placing a hand on my shoulder. "No one will let you hang high and dry. We don't do that to our brothers. And the good Lord will protect you. We're doing His work. This is His plan. You know that, don't you?"

The more I listen to Nash and Zack, the more I realize how they're slowly being—or have already been—brainwashed by the fanaticism that is the Dominion of God. There's something eerily mechanical about their speech, their tone and their words. The empty look in their eyes says it all. They're being programmed, their thoughts becoming automated. It suddenly strikes me how Nash and Zack and Mario and the others are morphing into something even they hadn't expected and don't even recognize. Witnessing this transformation first hand leaves me with a sickening feeling deep down in the bottom of my gut.

"Of course I know that," I eventually respond.

"Good—then we'll be seeing you soon," Nash says. "I think another general meeting is being planned for the end of the month. Until then, take care of yourself. And God bless."

"God bless," I reply.

I watch Zack and Nash get into the Navigator and disappear behind the tinted windows. The engine starts. I wave goodbye as they exit the parking lot. Eventually, the large SUV disappears somewhere down Fifth Avenue while the street lights flicker to brighten the darkness that is slowly creeping up and chasing the daylight to the other side of the globe.

I stand there for several minutes staring at the old basilica. A part of me longs for nothing more than to relive all the celebrations and joys this structure once afforded me and my family. Bringing people together in the name of love: that's its intended purpose. I can't help wonder how something as sinister as the Dominion of God could've been born out of such good intentions. But I guess that's the frightening irony of it: that the heart of man is capable of harboring such good and then turn it into something so evil.

After scanning the area for any signs of a surveillance unit, I contemplate entering the basilica to spark more distant memories, maybe even kneel for a moment of prayer. As it has many times before, I'm invaded by a relentless feeling of guilt for having abandoned my faith. It's true what Frank said—I've let evil win. I've let the Dominion win. For over twenty years, it's had a hold on the better part of my soul and has hung onto it like a keepsake. Yet no matter how hard I try, I can't break free. Although I realize that interpretation is the root of the problem and not any creed per se, I fear that I'll once again become one of them if I return to any form of organized worship.

Instead of entering the basilica, I go back to my vehicle, knowing that time is not on my side. I'll need to cross the border yet again with a suspicious package during a designated time frame. Back home, I have a co-conspirator, a handler and a significant other waiting for my return—all of whom I have no intentions of disappointing.

CHAPTER 18

Instead of meeting at a hotel this time, Jacob and I meet at a safe house. It sounds like James Bond type stuff, I know. Like some type of secret lair. But in reality, all it turns out to be is a third floor apartment in an old brown brick building in the city's east end. As for the bottom floors, I haven't the slightest clue what they're used for or who's renting them. There's absolutely nothing fancy about the place. It's just an outdated structure in an even more mundane neighborhood. But I suppose unassuming is exactly what Jacob is looking for in a place like this.

The apartment itself consists of the bare minimum. A small living area with an even smaller kitchen and dining area. Two old sofas in the living room. A coffee table. End tables with lamps. TV set on a stand. In the kitchen, a cheap-looking kitchenette set, and a back door leading to a fire escape. Just before the kitchen, there's a corridor hanging left that leads to the bathroom and two bedrooms. In each bedroom there's a twin-size bed. With the exception of a clock radio and the television set, there are no electronics or any other common luxuries anywhere. The walls are completely bare—no pictures or any other decorative items. The shades are drawn at every window, the only source of light stemming from a light fixture with a ceiling fan rotating slowly above our heads.

There, I debrief Jacob on my escapade down south. I hand him the slip of paper that was left on the briefcase in Vladimir's office. I also hand over the camera-pen and the numerous photocopies of invoices and spreadsheets. For the first half hour or so, Jacob studies the sheets carefully.

"You see these columns," he says, sliding his finger down one of the spreadsheets. "This first one here appears to be transaction dates. This next one's likely to who the transaction was made with. This one here seems to be an amount owed, and this one's likely an exchange rate.

Here we have the value of the transaction in dollars. I'm not sure about this last one . . . the numbers appear to be account numbers or banking transaction numbers."

I pour myself another glass of whiskey. "Why does he bother doing this?" I ask. "It doesn't seem very professional—everything's sloppy and handwritten."

"That's because I don't think these transactions are legit. Or at least not anything he wants to keep on official record. See these names?" he says, reading some aloud. "Dimitri, Milan, Zeljko, Mr. J . . . these aren't exchanges between businesses. They appear to be exchanges between individuals."

"What the hell for?"

"That's what I'd like to know," Jacob replies, taking a sip from his own drink. "I'm no expert in transnational criminal activity or terrorist financing, but there are people I work with who are. My best guess is that these are hawala transactions."

"What?"

Jacob puts his glass down. "Hawala—it's an ancient informal remittance system that originated in Southeast Asia. It's actually still being used today in many countries as an alternative to traditional banking systems. While it was intended for legitimate transactions, somewhere along the way it began to be used for illegitimate ones as well. It's often used by criminals, mafias and terrorists for money laundering purposes."

"How is it different from funneling money through a bank?"

"Well, its most attractive feature is that it's practically untraceable, or very hard to detect. You see, it's a way of transferring money without actually ever having to move it."

"I don't follow . . ."

"OK, here's how it's done. Say Miroslav wants to purchase something over in the Balkans, for example, weapons. Now, in the traditional banking system, Miroslav would have to send funds via a wire transfer from one bank account to another or by writing a check or physically moving actual money overseas. Either way, Miroslav risks getting caught because there's either an electronic or paper trail left behind. Everything is recorded and would be traceable. Even the money itself being couriered overseas—it risks being intercepted. If it's an especially large sum, a sudden withdrawal from or deposit to a bank account might attract the attention of banking officials and the authorities."

"OK, go on . . ."

"So instead, what Miroslav would do is approach an individual or business that's a known hawala dealer. In this case, let's say that's E-Z Grocery or E-Z Travel. And let's say Miroslav wants to purchase $10,000 dollars worth of weapons from back home. Miroslav would give Vladimir at E-Z Travel the $10,000 in person. Vladimir, in turn, calls up one of his close associates in the Balkans or maybe even Russia—someone he does regular business with. So, in this case, say he calls Dimitri in Serbia, who's owner of a small farming business, and he says to Dimitri, 'I need you to give $10,000 to Mr. X,' who's an arms dealer, from whom Miroslav plans on buying weapons. So Dimitri agrees. What Dimitri does next is he writes down the date, the amount, Vladimir's name, the exchange rate, the total value in dollars and so on. Dimitri then arranges to have his own money personally couriered to Mr. X. So, in the end, all that happens as far as the movement of money goes is that Miroslav has given Vladimir $10,000 and Dimitri has given Mr. X that same amount—in dinars or whatever currency—over in Serbia. No money was physically moved between Vladimir and Dimitri or between Miroslav and Mr. X. Get it? It's all paperless and very hard to trace."

"OK, but why would Dimitri agree to use some of his own money for Miroslav to buy arms? How does Vladimir pay him back?"

"Good question. That depends. You see, maybe Dimitri already owes Vladimir some money and is repaying a debt. These pages right here," Jacob explains, waving the copies, "are likely Vladimir's or Miroslav's records of who owes what to whom. So, if that's the case, then Vladimir has nothing to send Dimitri. He doesn't need to pay him back. But if, on the other hand, Dimitri doesn't owe Vladimir any money, then Vladimir can repay him through legitimate—and I use that term loosely—business transactions. Example: if Vladimir wants to order something from Dimitri's farming business in Serbia for E-Z Grocery, then Dimitri could 'over invoice' Vladimir. So in our case, Dimitri would be charging Vladimir $20,000—complete with invoice and receipt—while only sending $10,000 worth of merchandise. That way, Vladimir is repaying Dimitri the $10,000 that is owed. Or, if Vladimir is also in the business of exporting products to Dimitri, he could 'under invoice' Dimitri, meaning Vladimir would be sending Dimitri $20,000 of merchandise while only charging him $10,000. These are just the common scenarios. It can get much more complicated than that. But you see how hard it would be to trace? The illegitimate transactions are masked within legitimate ones."

"I see . . ." I say, trying my best to understand.

"With hawala, you don't have to disclose any pieces of identification to open a bank account, you're offered a lower exchange rate instead of the official exchange rate, and the transfer is done instantly instead of taking several days or weeks to get from one individual to another, minus many other service fees and charges a bank would normally issue. The only profit a hawala dealer will make is a small commission for handling the money. In the end, hawala is much cheaper, faster and safer for anyone wanting to secretly transfer money."

"So the invoices," I remind him, picking up the stack of copies of the various receipts and invoices. "I mean, you're telling me that these fruit and vegetable companies are over-charging E-Z Grocery for their products?"

Jacob leans back into his chair, looking up at the ceiling fan. "Well, that's what it looks like to me. I think the invoices correspond with these charts. Do you think E-Z Grocery can afford to buy, let alone stock thirty, forty and fifty thousand dollars worth of merchandise on a monthly basis??"

"Nope."

"So, then we have to ask ourselves, if E-Z Grocery isn't actually buying fifty thousand dollars worth of peaches and plums, what is it buying? And if it is purchasing something else, how is it getting into the country?"

I let this sink in.

"This is what we need to find out. And as far as E-Z Travel goes," Jacob continues, "It could be serving to advertise where or what countries the E-Z businesses have hawala contacts. This is speculative, of course. But I've seen it before with so-called travel agencies."

I remain quiet, but my mind is spinning with questions.

"Again, it's all speculation," Jacob repeats. "I'm no expert in this stuff. But I know people who are. You don't mind if I take these copies for further analysis?"

"No, of course not."

"Perfect. And we'll also take a close look at those pictures. You've done well, Liam. Very well. The FBI's surveillance unit was able to take great snapshots of the exchange and all those involved. Same goes for the Navigator and its license plate. As for Wes Sanderson and Brent Weiss and the border situation, leave it up to me. But if ever you're asked to cross the border again and things go bad, you're to contact me and me only. Under my alias, of course. Until we figure out what's going on there and if there are connections to the Dominion, it's too risky for you to trust any border officer no matter their rank."

"Wait a second . . . did you say the FBI?"

"Yeah, we had no choice," Jacob explains. "We don't conduct surveillance on U.S. soil. But don't worry about a thing. They don't know you're one of ours. No one else knows this but me and my superiors."

"So you're telling me I'm now one of their subjects of investigation?" I retort. "What if they decide to arrest me? To detain me at the border? Huh? Then what?"

"Take it easy," Jacob replies. "If they were ever to arrest you, we'd get them to extradite you back to Canada. We'd also approach the FBI and inform them of your status as an informant. Until that time comes, if it comes, I don't want any foreign element knowing of your involvement with us. You have to appear as a legitimate member of the Dominion, even if it means arrest in the U.S. We'll take care of the rest."

"What about the border situation? Won't I be identified in their systems and intercepted whenever I cross?"

"Not necessarily. They may just let you go through in order to track your movement—"

"I don't like this one bit," I bark, shaking my head.

"You have nothing to worry about, I promise," Jacob responds. "We've done this before, trust me. We have our contacts who'll make sure you're protected and returned to Canada should you get arrested or detained."

"Fine," I reply, realizing there's not much more that can be done at this point. I'm relieved and grateful that Jacob didn't divulge my affiliation with his agency to the Americans. The fewer that know the better. Still, I certainly don't like the prospects of being picked up by U.S. authorities.

"You good?" he asks.

"Yeah."

"Good," he replies, aligning the numerous sheets by tapping them on the table. "As for these invoices, there's something odd about them . . . it's like there's something blatantly obvious we're missing."

"Funny, I was thinking the same thing earlier."

"Some of these companies appear to be the same as the ones in Miroslav's notes. Some of the names on the invoices are maybe the same as well. See here?" he says, dropping the pages onto the table and pointing to a particular area on an invoice. "The seller here is Milan Mitrovic, likely the same as Mil M. on the balance sheets. On this next invoice, we have Zeljko Gorkic—could be Z.G. on the balance sheet. Here, we have Aleksandar Mitic—possibly the same as Alex over here. You see the pattern?"

I nod, but somehow still feel as though we're missing something. We continue to study the invoices, comparing the recipients to the names on the alleged hawala transactions. Turns out our attention was focused on the wrong end of the transactions. It catches my eye even before it catches Jacobs's. On every invoice, the buyer is identified as "Marcus Stephen Black" of E-Z Inc.

Jacob and I exchange stares.

"Holy shit," I finally say, "You don't think this could be . . ."

Silence.

"Black Mamba," we say simultaneously.

More silence ensues as we ponder the implications.

Black Mamba. It makes perfect sense. The Dominion's founder, Roland King, was generally known by clan members as King Cobra. In my opinion, it's more than a mere coincidence that we suddenly have a Marcus Stephen Black associated with E-Z Grocery, and this mysterious Black Mamba character.

"This is good," Jacob exclaims, pointing to the invoice. "Not only do we have a name, but banking information to go with it. Bank account number. Branch number. Transit number. It's all here."

"So now what?"

"Do you have any idea who Marcus Black could be?"

"None . . . never heard of him."

"OK, well, just leave it to me. I'll look into it ASAP."

For the next half hour or so, we go over the invoices and the balance sheets again. We explore many possible scenarios as Jacob bombards me with a ton of questions, including questions about the cell phone that the DOG gave me—the same one I was told to return following my arrival back in Canada. I give him the make and model of the device, as well as the number and the service provider. However, that's as much information as I can give him. While I'm no telecommunication expert, I reckon it's enough to enable Jacob and his agency to intercept its communications, which I assume—and hope—is what's being done on any telephone accounts belonging to the E-Z businesses and maybe even Reverend Hunt. Whatever the case, Jacob tells me he'll try and identify the cell phone's registered user as well as the user for the emergency contact number I was to call had things gone hairy at the border.

Jacob gives me some last-minute instructions before we head out the door. I'm left feeling pretty good about myself and about the headway we've made. My handler has proven to be very reliable, courteous and, the nature of our association aside, a good friend. Which reminds me of Frank, who I haven't heard from since our first encounter in Niagara Falls. With every passing day, I begin to accept the fact that I'll likely never see or hear from him again. There's nothing much I can do about it. That's just the name of the game and nature of the beast.

CHAPTER 19

For the next few weeks, the Dominion keeps me very, very busy. I'm asked to go to New York again on several occasions, couriering a variety of items ranging from briefcases to a single sealed envelope. Go figure. But what bothers me the most—what's most frustrating—is that every time, I'm only given a day's notice. On one occasion I'm given only ten hours' notice. Ten hours. It takes about nine to get to New York.

To this day, I still have no idea as to the nature of the contents sealed inside the myriad envelopes, boxes, booby-trapped briefcases and other parcels I've delivered.

To no surprise, my encounters at the border are with Wes Sanderson of the U.S. Border Patrol and Brent Weiss of the Canada Border Services Agency. We're now on a first-name basis. It's become obvious the Dominion is timing my trips to match their shifts. Forget about any vehicle inspection. Forget about typical questioning. Forget about detention. All I get is a "Hey Liam! Off to New York again? Yeah? Well, have a nice day!"

To test them, at times, I leave the briefcases and parcels in plain view. They never even bother to ask—or even look.

With every delivery I make down south, there's another one going back up north. Some parcels are light, some are heavy. Yet I'm always told they contain nothing more than documents. Meeting notes. Yeah, right.

With every delivery but one, I've managed to take advantage of my time alone at E-Z Travel. I've taken more pictures and copied more files and more books. I've also managed to find a recent record of the security system's registry, including times when the system was enabled and disabled. Evidently, and to no surprise, access to E-Z Travel and E-Z Grocery is being monitored. What does surprise me, however, is that there appear to be others who have also accessed the office in the wee hours of the morning.

Could it be Jacob and co.?

I quickly put this theory to bed. Had anyone accessed any of the E-Z businesses without authorization, I would've heard about it. There would've been rumblings within the Dominion. Besides, Jacob has assured me that *they*—or SafeTech security company—have been unsuccessful in overriding the system and the security camera. There's no way to disable the system and make it look as though it had never been disabled. So, this leads me to believe there are possibly others engaged in similar nocturnal activities on behalf of the Dominion of God. In this respect, Jacob is going to show me some still images taken from E-Z's security camera and provided by SafeTech in hopes that I can identify the individuals involved.

From what Jacob has related, the SafeTech account is under the name of Marcus Black. This is also the case for the cell phones that are assigned to me—and which I've never had to use—during my expeditions across the border. Oddly enough, it's never the same phone or the same number. Even more bizarre is the fact that every cell phone number I've reported becomes discontinued before Jacob and his agency have a chance to intercept their communications. It goes without saying that Mr. Black is becoming a more central figure in the investigation into the Dominion of God. Despite this, I have yet to encounter anyone by that name—or any name remotely close to it.

Only a few new gatherings have taken place, all of which have required the presentation of an ID card or PIN number. As before, I'm only told via email—from The Prophet—where and when to meet my associates, not where the meetings will actually take place. This makes it impossible for Jacob and his men to bug a location in advance. While surveillance units have been mobilized in our pursuit, Mario and the boys have proven to be even more apt at countering these tactics. The Dominion is not only highly alert and paranoid, but extremely well disciplined and organized.

For the most part, the Dominion's gatherings are held in the basements of Presbyterian churches—be it the Knox, Calvin or Rosedale. I can only assume they were booked and secured by Reverend Hunt. What catches me by surprise on a few occasions is the use of Baptist and Catholic churches. This leads me to wonder whether or not our little group is simply one cell in a larger and expanding network.

Regardless, it appears the Dominion's web of support has now gone interfaith.

One of our gatherings was described as a general meeting, where everybody was in attendance—an ever growing number at that. These, we were told, are to take place about once a month. In this particular case, over thirty individuals were present, including two women. I'm left completely in the dark as to the status of these newcomers and their true identities, including whether or not we're all a part of the same cell. With the exception of our very first meetings at Reverend Hunt's residence and at St. Andrew's, I've yet to witness any further indoctrination or initiation. Still, something tells me everyone present during these sessions has already undergone the rite of passage.

From what Jacob has told me, his agency continues to conduct surveillance on E-Z Travel and E-Z Grocery as well as on some of the churches I've been able to identify—except these are random surveillance and spot checks and not around-the-clock like before. This, I figure, is likely due to a lack of resources. The results are numerous pictures of individuals frequenting these establishments, most of whom have nothing to do with the Dominion of God—at least not that I'm aware of.

Some DOG members have been spotted, however. Vladimir, who has been identified as Vladimir Mladic, is seen coming and going from E-Z Travel several times a day. Same goes for Dragana, who I've learned is Dragana Lazarov and Vladimir's aunt. But so what? I mean, they work there. Customers go in and out of E-Z Grocery and E-Z Travel every day, none of whom Jacob and his agency, including myself, has been able to identify. Needless to say, the main prizes are Derek, Miroslav and Conrad, who've gotten a lot of publicity since the release of the letter in which the Dominion claimed responsibility for the mosque bombings. Numerous media sources report that they're hiding out somewhere in the northwestern U.S. or British Columbia. God only knows where they're getting their information. Whatever the case, up to this point, Derek and company have managed to escape detection.

Even less successful are the stakeouts at the churches or at locations where the Dominion has hosted past councils. The Dominion never goes to the same meeting point twice. That seems to be its *modus operandi*. And usually, by the time I'm made aware of a location, it's much too late in the game to advise Jacob. In fact, I can't think of one instance where I wasn't in the presence of another member when being made aware. When Jacob's men finally do manage to stake out an anticipated location, the Dominion ends up at the other end of town. I can understand their frustration. Time is a luxury that the Dominion has yet to afford us.

What's been happening beyond that I've no idea. So far, no one from the Dominion has been approached for questioning. Not Vladimir. Not anyone. There's no point—it would jeopardize the whole operation. The Dominion would likely disappear and go further underground, not to mention be extremely suspicious of its members. Not good for me. There are no grounds to arrest anyone in relation to the mosque bombings as there is very little, if any, evidence against them. Nor is there any evidence against the E-Z businesses. There just hasn't been an opening yet, and my information is to remain information and not evidence. Still, I've got lingering doubts as to Jacob's ultimate use of the information I've provided. I mean, he's already admitted to passing some on to the FBI, though I've yet to hear any fallout as a result of this.

According to Jacob, the investigation into the mosque bombings is moving at a snail's pace. There are very few leads. From what I'm told, dozens of pharmaceutical companies, and acetone and peroxide producers and distributors, as well as chemical and industrial products wholesalers, have been approached both north and south of the border. I can only assume the authorities are looking for suspicious, irregular or frequent purchasers of these products. So far, they've come up with nothing. I can only reckon they're looking for a needle in a haystack.

The investigation itself has been a regular topic of discussion in the House of Commons, with the prime minister being heavily criticized by the opposition for not having done enough to reassure Canadians that the government is doing everything it can to keep them safe and to discourage hate crimes. While a special commission has been established to look into the attacks, federal agencies have been criticized for not allocating enough resources to the investigation. Much of this criticism has stemmed from prominent Islamic leaders and organizations as well as foreign governments, particularly those of Islamic states such as Saudi Arabia and Iran. Needless to say, both the U.S. and Canadian governments are under immense pressure to find those accountable so they can be brought to justice.

Along with the investigation of the mosque bombings, not a day goes by without the mention of the trials of the Toronto Four—those accused in the Black Friday massacre—whose preliminary hearings have finally started. It's all over the papers, and on the Internet and the airwaves. The accused, Abdil al-Zahhari, Mahmood Al-Mahak, Youssef Khan, and Amer Khazami, face a combined total of forty-three charges under the Canadian Criminal Code, including charges of financing and facilitating terrorism and conspiracy to commit a terrorist act. All four remain in detention, with al-Zahhari held in a separate institution. I can guarantee the Dominion is also keeping a close eye on the matter.

Meanwhile, in Rome, the first round of peace talks between Israel and the Palestinian National Authority have already concluded, which is also monopolizing the news. While very little is being disclosed to the media, the most contentious issues, it is being reported, are those surrounding security and borders, as well as Israeli settlements and the battle for ownership of *the* holy city of Jerusalem. On one hand, the PNA is seeking the establishment of a Palestinian state within specific boundaries and the removal of Jewish settlements in the Palestinian territories. Israel, on the other hand, is seeking security, recognition and acceptance by their Middle Eastern neighbors as a legitimate Jewish state. Despite this, both sides have admitted that much progress has been made which they're hoping to build on during the next round of talks scheduled in December. Although there have been protests and demonstrations throughout the world because of the secrecy of the negotiations, most have been unusually peaceful. Even radical and terrorist groups traditionally opposed to any agreement with Israel have remained remarkably still—at least for the time being. Likewise, I have yet to hear any rumblings coming from the inner circles of the Dominion of God.

The hunt for Black Mamba—or should I say, Marcus Black—has also heated up. The bank accounts belonging to Mr. Black have been linked to several financial institutions in and around Toronto. Whoever this Mr. Black is, he has over twenty million dollars in assets at his disposal—at least that we know of. For someone who's managed to garner a small fortune, Mr. Black's existence and whereabouts are virtually unknown by anyone formerly associated with him. According to Jacob, the Financial Transactions Reports Analysis Centre of Canada is having a field day with this. Apparently, it'll take weeks, if not months, to sift through, sort, track and analyze all the raw data. Mr. Black was last known to have been working for a large financial institution located in Kanata, Ontario. His employer, or former employer, The Fleisschman & Reid Group, reported Mr. Black as being M.I.A. shortly after Black Friday.

Interesting coincidence.

As for me, the extra money I've been earning for my services to Canada's intelligence community continues to provide me with some relief from what has been a very problematic situation for Sarah and me.

I figure it'll only be a month or so before I can make a substantial payment to my lenders. For the first time in a long time, I can sleep relatively well at night.

CHAPTER 20

The inferno approaches. There is fear and chaos. Desperate souls seek shelter, some finding it within the fountain. I, on the other hand, am paralyzed. I watch helplessly as the once luscious garden withers and turns to dust before my eyes. Those who have not found shelter are consumed by the flames, their cries echoing in the nothingness that is left.

In the air, a foul smell is spreading. It grows stronger and stronger as the wall of fire draws near. It ultimately dawns on me that it is the smell of death. With every breath I take, I become weaker and emptier inside.

In the distance, from the farthest reaches of existence, an unworldly roar erupts. The sound alone brings instant death to those too weak to withstand it. It's a harsh and deafening howl, from which issues a series of ungodly shrieks and shrill screams. With every soul that perishes, the sound grows stronger, louder, seemingly fueled by the suffering and death that surrounds me. The flames too grow in intensity.

From the great wall of fire, the source of the deafening shrieks emerges: An army of ghosts on horseback, their silver faces reflecting nothing but the fires from which they were born. In their eyes, nothing but darkness and death. The giant steeds on which they ride, both monstrous and grotesque, trample everything and everyone that is left standing in the decaying garden.

The stench is now unbearable and I can no longer breathe. My legs begin to tremble, but still I can't move. The wall of fire is closing in on me, as is the Army of the Beast. My skin begins to sear under the intense heat.

I'm finally able to overcome my paralysis. The fountain is just in reach. I take a step forward, but not toward the shelter that I seek. There is something I must do. There is something I can do . . .

My eyes open to the sound of heavy footsteps rushing toward me. Two large shadows loom over me as I lie paralyzed beneath the covers.

Before I can react, two large hands wrap themselves around my neck and begin to squeeze. I attempt to escape the grip, but am overpowered. I gasp for air, but nothing comes in or out. But instead of letting me succumb from a lack of oxygen, I'm thrown across the room. I slam hard against the dresser, my head taking the brunt of the blow. The ceramic lamp sitting on the unit falls over and shatters against the floor. Again, I'm lifted completely off my feet and shoved against the wall, where I receive a barrage of heavy blows to the stomach until my insides are nearly liquefied.

Dazed, I stumble and fall to my knees. I try to throw up, but can't. I heave and cough. A steady stream of saliva and bile pools on the floor. The two shadows argue with one another, but everything is inaudible to me. Another blow, this time to the head. A kick to the ribs forces whatever remaining air out from my lungs. I gasp for breath, pleading for the assault to stop.

Again, the larger of the two shadows reaches for my neck. I fight back, but to no avail. I'm raised from my bloody mess and pinned against the wall. "You think we wouldn't find you?" shouts one of the voices, which I recognize instantly. "You think you can hide from me? Huh?"

"No, Omar, it's not like that," I beg, attempting to squirm my way out of his grasp. More pressure is placed on my throat until not a sound or breath can escape. I abandon any form of resistance, knowing full well I'm no match for this mountain of a man, who probably outweighs me by a hundred pounds or more.

"Shut the hell up!" Omar rages, spitting as he speaks. "We've come for what's ours. Where's the fuckin' money?"

Still, I can't respond.

"You know, Liam," the smaller of the two shadows begins, "we've been pretty patient with you. We've been patient because we like you. And how do you repay us? You test our patience. But our patience has worn thin."

"I ought to break every fuckin' tooth in your mouth," Omar spits, swinging his arm back with a clenched fist. "I ought to break every bone in your—"

"Don't bother," says Raoul. "He's no good to us with dental bills." He takes another step closer, and I hear the sound of a switchblade flicking open. Omar loosens his grip. I gasp for air. "But maybe we should leave him with a little reminder."

Omar's thick hand is immediately replaced by the cool steel of the blade. Raoul grabs me by the hair and pins my head to the wall. The sharp edge of the blade pressed firmly against my neck, I freeze. I don't dare make any sudden movement. "Raoul, please, stop! Give me another month!" I say through my clenched jaw. "I'll have half the money by then . . . you have to believe—"

"That's what you said last time!"

"I mean it this time. I'll have the money. I'm working on—"

"I say waste him!" Omar growls, his breath warm against my neck. "Where's the money, Liam?"

"It's coming . . . I promise . . . just give me a little more time."

Raoul slides the very tip of the blade along my neck, teasing and taunting. "More time you say? You must think time is all we got! Time is not on your side, my friend. No, time right now is your enemy."

"On my mother's grave, give me a month . . ."

"You're up to a hundred K now. Pretty soon it'll be one twenty," Raoul says. "You see? Time, my friend, is not yours. You don't want more time." He runs the blade up and over my chin. Behind him, Omar grins.

In one quick motion, Raoul swipes the blade across my left cheek, slicing it wide open. Although I can't see it, I can feel warm blood trickling down to my jaw. "Next time it'll be your tongue, or maybe your eyes." He releases his handful of my hair and thrusts his knee into my groin. The immense pain cripples me as I fall to the floor. "You know, I just had an idea. Maybe the next time we come here, it won't be for you . . ."

"Yeah, I'm sure we'd manage to get our return out of that pretty little girl of yours," Omar sneers, grabbing his crotch. "I know a lot of people who'd pay good money for a piece of ass like that."

"Christmas," Raoul continues. "If nothing by then, we come back. And it won't be to deliver presents. Half by Christmas. The rest by the New Year. You know how to reach me. I'll have to insist you pay me in person. You got that?"

I nod, spitting blood out from my mouth.

"Good."

As quickly and as quietly as they arrived, they're gone. For several minutes, I simply lie there, crumpled in a fetal position. I wait for the pain to subside before attempting to stand. I then stumble my way to the bedroom door and turn the lights on. The room is a mess, with the bed, night table and dresser displaced. Blood stains the floor and the wall behind me. Numerous items, including the shattered lamp, are sprawled across the floor.

I slowly make my way to the bathroom to assess the damage. A deep gash beneath my left eye—it'll need stitches. Blood running from my nose and my mouth. Left eye slightly swollen. After treating my wounds and applying a few bandages, I quickly get dressed and make my way to the nearest hospital. Along the way, a single thought reigns over all others. Somehow, I'll have to come up with fifty thousand dollars in the next month. I refuse to think about the consequences if I fail.

CHAPTER 21

Sarah is there waiting for me upon my return home. "Jesus Christ, Liam!" she shouts. "What the hell happened here?"

I don't respond and turn the lights on.

"Oh my God! My poor baby! What happened to you? Are you OK?"

"I'm fine . . . it's just a scratch."

"Just a scratch? Just a scratch?" she shouts, running over to me. She runs her fingers ever so lightly down my face. "Jesus, Liam . . . your eye! You're all stitched up! What the hell happened here?"

She begins to cry. I can't even look her in the eye.

"It's those creeps again, isn't it?" she correctly assumes, tears running down her cheeks. "Omar and Raoul? Don't lie to me—"

"I'm not—"

"They were here?"

"Yeah."

"Jesus Christ! How did they get in? Did you let them in?"

"No, I didn't," I reply, mulling over how they managed to enter the premises. "Does it really matter? I mean, they would've gotten to me one way or another, here or somewhere else."

"My keys!" she exclaims. "You remember? I lost them over a month ago! You don't think that—"

"No, I don't think they have your keys, Sarah. What are the odds?"

"I'd say the odds are pretty damn good!" she says, her voice now trembling as she becomes more distraught. "God damn it, Liam! What if they were following me? What if they were following me that day and stole my keys! I told you that day I had a funny feeling that—"

"OK, just calm down!"

"Don't tell me to fuckin' calm down! I get home and our apartment looks like a hurricane just went through it, there's blood on the floor, my boyfriend is missing, and you're telling me to calm down? Don't you dare tell me to calm down!"

"I'm sorry, baby," I say gently, hugging her tightly and rubbing my hand through her smooth auburn hair. "I'm sorry. Everything'll be alright. I promise."

Her whole body is now trembling. "Jesus, Liam. What have you done? What have you done to us? We don't have the money! Where are we ever going to come up with the money?"

"Everything will be fine . . ."

"We need to call the police!"

"No! No we don't," I answer sharply. "The police'll just make things worse. You think Raoul and Omar are upset now? Just wait till we call the police. The police will have nothing on them and they'll be set free. And then I'm dead."

"What are we going to do?"

"We're . . . I mean *I'm* going to pay them back shortly. You'll see. Everything will be fine."

"Pay them back?" she hollers, pushing me away, "Huh? With what money are you going to pay them back?"

"Just leave it to me," I reply trying to sound confident and self-assured.

"Leave it to you? That's what I've been doing for the past twenty years! And look at where we are now!"

"Look, I—"

"How are you going to come up with . . . what is it now? A hundred thousand dollars? What sort of scheme are you planning now?" She pauses as though a light bulb just went on inside her head. "Your trips to New York! Of course! It all makes perfect sense! Tell me, what have you been doing there? What—or who—the hell are you involved with in New York?"

"I told you, it's family business. My cousin Lana—"

"Stop, it Liam! Stop it! You goddamn liar!" she shouts while weeping. "I called your aunt the other day and she told me your cousin is fine! She had no idea what I was talking about! So what the fuck is going on in New York, huh? The way I see it, you're either having an affair or you're involved with some of your old acquaintances again! So which is it? Huh? Are you cheating on me or selling drugs?"

"Jesus, Sarah! You know I've never cheated on you and never will! How can you even think that? You have no reason ever to be worried about anything like that!"

"So you're selling drugs to repay your debt? I knew it!"

"Of course not!"

"Then what? What? What's happening in New York? Tell me the truth, goddamn it!" The floodgates are open. The tears are really coming down now as she collapses on the bed, elbows on her knees and hands gripping the back of her head. "I don't know who you are anymore . . ."

"Sarah, I promise you, this time I'll make things better. Please, you have to trust me. Please don't give up on me—on us."

I wait for a reaction, but get none. I watch helplessly as the tears continue fall onto the floor, her sobs the only sound. A long and lonely silence ensues. For the first time since my involvement with the Dominion and with Jacob, I contemplate telling her the entire truth and dealing with whatever consequences may result from it. I think about the possible fallouts of telling her, the worse of which would be having her let slip my status as an informant at the wrong place and the wrong time—and to the wrong people. I think about it long and hard and come to the realization that I'm being a big hypocrite. I want her to trust me when I've never given her any reason that she should, while at the same time I'm concerned about trusting her when she's never given me a reason not to.

I decide it's time to spill the beans.

Just as I get ready to set the truth free, my cell phone rings. I ignore the first few rings. "I'll get it," I finally offer, leaving the bedroom. I make my way to the living room and retrieve the phone, which is buried between the sofa's cushions.

"Hello?" I say.

"Yes . . . is this the Mailman?"

"This is. May I ask who's speaking?"

"It's the Mechanic. Are you alone?"

"Not really—"

"Doesn't matter. Your services are needed."

"When?"

"Sometime within the next several days," Cyril a.k.a. the Mechanic replies. "It hasn't been confirmed yet. Could be tonight, could be tomorrow night or later this week."

Inside me, an inferno is born. "No! No, goddamn it!" I whisper angrily through my teeth. "You listen to me. You tell *Moneyman* that I'm unavailable tonight! And this week too! What am I supposed to do? Just sit around for a week? I'm not going back to New York! I'm in enough shit already—"

"New York? Who said anything about New York?"

"Then what?"

"I can't tell you right now," he says. "Just be available and be ready. I'll explain everything later."

"Where? When?"

"You're going to be picked up somewhere. I don't know where exactly. You'll get a confirmation call in the very near future. You'll need to go to E-Z within the next 24 hours. A cell phone is there ready for pickup. You understand?"

"Damn it! I have better things to do than drag my ass all the way across town to E-Z! Do you hear me?"

"I understand. You're not alone. We're all in this together," Cyril says in an attempt to calm me down. "I don't know what you've been up to nor do I want to know. All I know is that you'll be needed soon. I've been told to tell you to keep your evenings and nights free this week no matter what the cost."

"I'll see what I can do. I can't make any promises."

"For now, just worry about picking up that phone. Someone'll be in touch with you. It's imperative that you get that phone no later than tomorrow and keep it on you at all times. A charger will also be provided."

"Alright."

"Good. God bless. Talk to you later."

"Yeah, see ya."

I sit motionless for a minute. My head is spinning, as are my thoughts. It takes a while before I can collect them again. I know I have to call Jacob, but that'll have to wait—at least for now. There are far more important matters for me to resolve at the moment.

I return to the bedroom, where Sarah is still weeping. I quietly make my way over and sit next to her on the bed. I wrap my arms around her and kiss her on the temple. I don't say a word. I just want her to know that I'm there for her and that I'll always be there for her. That I'll make things better. That I'll protect her from any harm. That together, we can overcome adversity no matter how insurmountable it may seem. I want to tell her all this, but I know that talk is cheap and that I've done a lot of talking over the years. For now, I know that caressing and embracing her will be far more comforting and reassuring than any words will ever be.

CHAPTER 22

I'm sound asleep and in the realms of the garden when an unfamiliar ring wakes me from my slumber. Confused, I look around blindly into the darkness. Another ring. The flickering of light. Then I remember the cell phone I picked up the night before. A quick glance at the alarm clock tells me that it's 3:00 a.m. Another ring. I quickly get up and fetch the device from the dresser.

"Hello?" I answer.

"Yes, is this the Mailman?"

"This is."

"This morning—soon—you're needed."

"Who is this?" I say, letting my eyes adjust to the darkness.

"That's none of your concern. You were told to be prepared for anything within the next several days, were you not?"

"Yeah, I was told to be prepared, but I wasn't told *what* to be prepared for!"

"It'll be explained shortly. First you need to get to Union Station. Be there for 3:30. Familiar faces will find you there. You'll only be needed for a few hours. You'll be back in bed by sunrise. Got it?"

"Union Station at 3:30. Got it."

"Good. Bring the cell with you."

"Sure."

"Goodbye and God bless."

The caller hangs up before I get a chance to utter another word. I bolt to the kitchen and pick up my own cell phone, which is being charged on the counter. I scroll through my contacts list until I get to Jacob's—or should I say, Jake Hartman's—name. Several rings later, he answers.

"Jacob, it's Liam. Something's going down tonight. I don't know what it is. I've been told to be at Union Station for 3:30. Apparently, I'm supposed to meet other members there."

"Union Station? Meeting who?" Jacob replies, his voice somewhat groggy.

"I don't know. They said they'd tell me later. I'm not sure I'm keen on this, you know? I have no idea what's going on here! I'd feel a lot more comfortable knowing you had a tail . . . you know what I mean?"

"Stay cool," Jacob replies, his voice becoming crisper. "I have a team already on standby. Just go with the flow, alright?"

"Yeah, I got it."

"If anything changes, let me know. Good luck."

"Thanks, I'll need it," I reply and end the call. I then make my way back to the bedroom and slip on a pair of jeans and a beige hoodie. I bury my keys, wallet and cell phone deep inside my pockets. Slipping on a baseball cap, I make a pit stop in the bathroom, where the image of my battered face reminds me of the events of only a few nights ago. Staring long and hard into the mirror, I douse my face with cold water, wondering how I got myself into this.

There's a knock on the apartment door.

What the f . . .

I exit the bathroom and stare at the door at the end of the hall. Someone's pounding on it. My heart begins to beat heavily and adrenaline courses through my veins. I creep quietly to the kitchen and slide a butcher's knife from its wooden base. Slowly, I make my way to the door and look through the peephole. On the other side are two men who I don't immediately recognize.

More knocking.

I unlock the dead bolt but leave the chain attached, opening the door as far as the chain will let me. "Who is it?" I ask, peering through the opening.

"It's Frenchy. We decided to come pick you up instead."

What?

"Let's get going," he whispers.

I unfasten the chain and swing the door open. Waiting with Conrad is Shane. Both are dressed in black from head to toe. "I was told to meet at Union Station," I say. "Who was I supposed to—"

"You were supposed to meet with us," Conrad explains, speaking softly. "We changed our minds. Come on, we don't have much time—and wear something dark." He stares at my face. "What the hell happened to you? And why the are you holding a knife?"

"Long story . . ." I reply and excuse myself for a second. I return to the bedroom where I slip on a darker shirt and darker pants. I then grab my darkest jacket—a black polyester ski jacket—and follow my visitors out into the hallway, locking the door behind me. We make our way down the stairwell and head out the side exit. Idling at the curb is a dark blue commercial van whose side door slides open to let us in. One by one, we embark and take a seat. There, I'm briefed on what will be taking place in just a matter of minutes.

CHAPTER 23

The inside of the van carries a scent much like that of the cellar of a turn-of-the-century home—musty, damp and clammy. Once all our tasks are assigned, we play musical chairs and swap seats. Having been given the task of driving, I take the wheel. I don't protest. I'd much rather be the driver than any of the other roles Conrad has assigned.

Following Conrad's instructions, I drive away. At one point he becomes suspicious and is convinced we're being followed. To counter this, he alters our route and gets me to take unnecessary turns and exits all the way west of the city and back. Sitting quietly in the back seat are Shane and Cyril, who appear unbothered by Conrad's paranoia. I wonder whether both are as clueless as I am about what's going on. Judging by their calm and stoic demeanor, I'm guessing they know a lot more than I do.

The Macdonald-Cartier Freeway is as uncongested as it'll ever be and we speed eastbound at 120 kilometers per hour. Along the way, I recount the events of the night before, explaining my cuts and bruises. While Conrad offers assistance in dealing with the matter, no one seems overly concerned.

I think about it long and hard. *The Dominion taking care of my problems*, I repeat to myself. I have no doubt Conrad and company could dispatch Raoul and Omar quite easily. But Raoul and Omar aren't at the top of the food chain—that I'm almost certain. The money I owe likely belongs to someone higher up in the criminal underground—someone much more powerful and with a lot more clout than anyone in the Dominion of God. Basically, someone I'd rather not have to deal with.

So I dismiss the idea.

We eventually find ourselves in a sketchy neighborhood in Scarborough, one of the suburbs at the eastern end of the city. There, Conrad instructs me to take a right onto Ellesmere and then a left onto

Bellamy. Shortly after, he orders me to turn left into a narrow alleyway that's bordered by trees and dying hedges. I drive to the back of an apartment complex where a dark parking lot awaits us.

That's when it strikes me. I've been here before, as part of the Dominion's recon assignment. This is my area. This is the apartment complex where an important member of the Muslim community in Scarborough—and in the Greater Toronto Area—resides. Suddenly, I feel as though I'm about to throw up my own heart.

Conrad tells me to station the van in the alleyway, where it's well concealed. The narrow laneway is very dark, the glow from the nearest street light barely breaking through the shrubbery and trees. We wait there for nearly a half hour while Conrad keeps a close eye on his watch.

It's now 4:15 a.m. and most of the city is still sound asleep. We wait another five minutes before Conrad gives Shane and Cyril a signal to quietly exit the van.

"We're just doing some recon, so wait here till we get back," Conrad orders in his deep, coarse voice. "Keep an eye out for us in your rearview mirror. When we get back, we're heading straight to the Marshalling Yard. You got that?"

I nod nervously.

"Whatever happens, do not leave without us. We'll be right back." He shuts the passenger door before swinging it back open. "And if you see a car or someone coming by out front, just press on the brake. The brake light will serve as a warning sign. We won't be coming back to the van if we see the brake lights are on. You got that?"

"Got it."

Conrad closes the van door very lightly and takes off with his co-conspirators. In the rearview mirror I watch as they head toward the back of the apartment complex and then disappear quickly into the dark.

I wait for what seems to be an eternity, my mind racing and my body infected with guilt. I know exactly what's about to go down. I also know that I shouldn't be here, that I should've refused to go along. Even more so, I should've refused to take part in the initial recon assignment. *This is all your fault,* I remind myself, the guilt becoming unbearable. *Whatever happens tonight, you bear sole responsibility . . .*

My thoughts ultimately return to Jacob and his team and whether they're still needlessly waiting at Union Station. I pray that Conrad's earlier paranoia was justified and that we were indeed being followed. I consider contacting Jacob with my cell but fear getting caught red-handed. For all I know, they could be in and out in a matter of minutes or even seconds.

I wait impatiently and wrestle with my thoughts, keeping a steady eye on the rearview and side view mirrors, hoping for my associates' imminent return. The longer I wait, the more fidgety I become. My nerves are shot and I soon begin to tremble. The thought of leaving without them crosses my mind, but I know I'd be a dead man if I did.

It's not until 4:50 a.m. that I spot four shadows emerging from around the corner of the complex. *Four shadows?* I look ahead toward Bellamy for any vehicles or signs of life, but there are none.

The back doors of the van swing wide open and I watch as Shane and Cyril throw an unidentified man in the back, hopping in afterward and slamming the doors behind them. My heart nearly skips a beat when I see that the man's hands are bound with thin metal wire and his mouth is sealed with gray duct tape. His attempts to scream are futile, the sounds nothing more than low grunts as he struggles to set himself free. Cyril and Shane immediately jump him, pinning him to the cold metal floor and choking him to obstruct his airway. They then fit a black haversack over his head, tightening the strap firmly around his neck.

To my right, the passenger door swings open. Conrad, wearing a black ski mask, quickly gets in. "Drive," he says, removing the mask.

"Jesus Christ!" I bark, shifting the van into drive. In a matter of seconds, we're heading back down Bellamy and Ellesmere. I'm fuming inside, but I'm also petrified. "What the fuck is going on, Frenchy? Why didn't you tell me we were kidnapping someone!"

"Settle down," Conrad replies, then turns around. Moans and grunts are coming from the rear. "Hey you two, keep him quiet—and keep your heads down!"

With the exception of the driver and passenger side windows at the front, the rear windows, and of course the windshield, the van has no other windows. I watch in the rearview as Cyril and Shane lower their heads until they're no longer in sight.

"Why didn't you tell me we were kidnapping someone?" I ask again, much more vigorously. "Do you have any idea what kind of trouble we've just gotten ourselves in?"

"Calm down," he says, turning his attention back to the road ahead. "We have a mission to accomplish. God's work. And for that to happen, we're going to have to get our hands a little dirty and ruffle a few feathers. You knew that when you joined. Black Mamba wants us to operate on a need-to-know basis. You didn't need to know. That's it, that's all. *Capice?*"

"No, I don't *capice!*" I retort. *Need to know? Need to know? You're damn right I need to know!* I'm livid inside, but I try hard to restrain myself. The last thing I want is for Conrad to get suspicious and brand me as a dissident.

"Look, Black Mamba knows what he's doing, trust me," Conrad says, softening his tone. "He knows the errors Roland made in the early days. Too many people knew too much. That's what led to his downfall and that of all the others. That's how the cops knew about his operation. There was a snitch among us. A Judas. Someone had to have tipped the cops. Just like Jesus our Savior, Roland was betrayed."

"So what you're saying is that Black Mamba doesn't trust any of us?" I ask, realizing the irony of the situation. "Don't you think we should all be on the same page here?"

"Look at it this way," Conrad says. "Our organization is much like a living organism. Now, an organism needs all its parts to function. The lungs. The liver. The heart. The kidneys. You get the picture. All the parts function independently from one another, but yet are still dependent on each other to keep the body going, to survive."

He pauses to peer out his side window and says, "Turn left, next street." Then he continues his lecture while I bite my tongue.

"The heart doesn't know the purpose of the kidneys. The lungs don't know the purpose of the heart. Only one organ in the entire system knows what all the parts are doing—and that's the brain." He then turns to me to see if I'm paying attention. I can feel him staring at me. "Black Mamba is the brain."

What does that make me, then? I ask myself.

Conrad turns away and tells me to take a right on McCowan. We eventually reach the Canadian Pacific's Agincourt Marshalling Yard, an industrial and derelict section of Scarborough. It's just past 5:00

a.m. The train yard is quiet, with few people around and little activity. Even the homeless are scarce as it's an unusually cold night, even for late November, and I can only assume most have found their way to a shelter or some form of refuge.

The clearing sky is cold and grey as vapors rise from the sewers and from the chimneys of the yard's numerous shops. The access lanes are worn and weathered, full of potholes. As we pass a large building under renovation, I notice a lone vehicle—another van—parked up ahead near two sets of train tracks, atop of which several train cars lie dormant. Smoke rises from the van's exhaust pipe. There are no other vehicles around and no other signs of life.

Several tracks deeper into the train yard I see numerous empty cargo stocks, caravans and other carriage wagons, but the area looks abandoned and forgotten.

"Pull up next to the van," Conrad instructs.

The van appears identical to our own. Two men disembark from it and head for the rear. I follow their movement from my side mirror until they disappear from sight. I then direct my attention to the rearview mirror and watch as the back doors swing wide open. Conrad then orders Shane and Cyril to hand over the captive.

"Wait here for just a second," Conrad tells me before joining the others in the back.

I turn around to get a better glimpse of those involved and of the helpless man in their custody. Although his head is still covered by the black haversack, I can tell by his hands and his body that he's an older man, likely in his sixties or seventies. He's thin and feeble and the others have no difficulty handling him. He's dressed in a light garment that looks much like a night gown.

I eventually recognize one of the two other men as Derek. He's wearing a black toque drawn all the way down to his eyebrows. From his head to his feet, he's dressed in black. He appears to be all business as he instructs Shane and Cyril and a third handler, who I can't identify. The old man is viciously manhandled, beaten, and thrown into the back of the other van.

My eyes drop down to the van's license plate and I make a mental note of the number. The transfer takes no longer than a minute. Shane and Cyril enter the second van and don't return.

I wait nervously until Conrad emerges from the back of the other vehicle. I roll down my window as he approaches.

"OK, everything's going according to plan." He opens the driver door. "Move over. I'll take it from here."

I scoot over to the passenger seat as Conrad hops in and slams the door shut. The other van has already left the compound.

"Where the hell are they taking him?" I manage to ask.

"Again, that's need-to-know," he responds. It sounds almost rehearsed. "Hell, I don't even know myself," he adds with a smirk, but I'm hardly amused.

Truth is, I don't believe him—not for one second.

We don't converse much on the drive back. I've never found Conrad very pleasant to talk to. He can be quite intimidating and moody. Everything seems to offend or annoy him or make him suspicious. Still, I'd much rather be riding with Conrad than with Derek.

"Who was he?" I ask, unable to remember the man's name from many on whom I had conducted recon.

"Ibrahim Hassan Falat," Conrad replies. "One of your guys. Remember? You did some good recon on this place."

"Why him?"

"As you *should* recall, he's the imam at the mosque on Eglinton." Conrad sounds annoyed. "He's also head of the Canadian Islamic Institute. He's the one who led protests against the government a few years back, saying Muslims were being discriminated against by law enforcement and immigration agencies. He regularly sponsors the immigration of suspected Islamic extremists. More recently, he's been lobbying for the release of the Black Friday conspirators. He also wants to introduce an all-Muslim political party and Sharia law into the country."

"What's going to happen to him?"

"I don't know. That'll all depend . . ."

"On what?"

"Look, I'm not too sure myself, OK?" he barks irritably. "All I know is that Black Mamba wants to speak to him. Don't worry. Everything will be fine."

I keep my mouth shut for the rest of the ride. A few blocks from my apartment, Conrad pulls over to the curb.

"Sit tight and keep a lid on it," he says. "This'll be all over the news in a matter of hours. So don't react or say anything stupid to anyone, you hear? Oh, and I'll need that cell phone back."

I hand him the cell phone.

"OK, we'll be in touch. There'll be a gathering again, maybe in a few weeks when this all blows over. You'll be available, right?"

Although unsure, I nod.

"Good. Have you gone back to church?"

"No."

"What's the matter with you?" he snaps. "Look, if you don't want to go to mass, try St. Andrew's. I hear Reverend Hunt gives one hell of a sermon. I, of course, can't be seen there."

I nod again.

"Whatever you do, pray for the success of the DOG. We're doing the Lord's work. I want you to go to church this Sunday."

"Fine."

I exit the van and Conrad speeds away. I take one last look at the license plate, and when I get inside I scribble it down onto a piece of paper along with the other one I've memorized.

It's now 6:15 a.m. The apartment is quiet and empty. Sarah hasn't returned from work yet, thank God. I hop in the shower and get a change of clothes. I'm tired as hell. My eyes are burning and I feel like I could fall asleep standing. But I can't afford to. I have to be at work in another hour. My mind races, filled with dreadful thoughts. I think about the helpless man who's somewhere in the custody of Derek Devlin and the Dominion of God. I know whatever is to become of him, it can't be good and I'm responsible for it. Then I begin to worry about my own plight: I'm now an accomplice in the kidnapping of a prominent religious leader.

Just when I think things can't get any worse, I turn on the television and flip through the channels only to find the same thing everywhere. NBC. CBS. ABC. CTV. CBC. BBC. CNN. Just to name a few.

According to the reports, the Saudi ambassador to Canada, Aarzam Khalid Hussain, and his sixteen-year-old son are missing and believed to have been abducted late last evening near their place of residence in the nation's capital.

Sweat is coming out of my pores. I don't know for sure, but I get the feeling this event is related to our kidnapping of Ibrahim Hassan Falat. It can't be just a coincidence.

Can it?

Now, kidnapping a religious leader and Canadian citizen is one thing. Kidnapping a foreign national and diplomat is a whole different ball game. The stakes have been significantly raised and the consequences will be that much greater. I can't even imagine the possible fallout. I may be in big trouble. After all, Jacob cautioned me not to engage in the Dominion's criminal activities.

I contemplate not telling Jacob about my involvement in the kidnapping. But he knows something went down last night and that we didn't end up at Union Station. I pace around my apartment as though I'm about to have a nervous breakdown. It dawns on me that I'm in way over my head. It feels like I've lost total control of my ship and I've veered directly into an iceberg, the bulk of which I've yet to uncover. I'm sinking fast. The world around me slowly darkens until I'm left with only one option.

I have to get in touch with Jacob—now.

CHAPTER 24

Despite my scheduled shift at the deli, I agree to meet Jacob right away at the Holiday Inn on Bloor Street. As usual, he's already waiting for me by the time I get there. This time, he's sporting a dark suit with a dark blue shirt and a grayish tie. He appears fatigued and drained.

He takes one look at me and freezes. "What the hell happened to you?"

I explain the incident with Raoul and Omar. I tell him that I need to come up with fifty thousand dollars by Christmas and the rest by the New Year or else I'm a dead man—meaning no more intelligence for him. He explores the possibility of going to the cops, but we both know the likely outcome: A bit of jail time, if any. Perhaps thirty days for breaking and entering—at most. Perhaps a little more for assault or any prior convictions. They'll be out in no time with a much bigger grudge. As for their loan enterprise, forget about it. The cops will have nothing on 'em.

So instead I push for a cash advance in exchange for the information I possess about the abductions. I know it sounds devious and selfish, but I can't help it. I'm desperate.

And so is he.

Jacob collapses on a comfortable-looking chair in the corner of the room. Quietly, he mulls over my proposal. I can sense his frustration, but also his desperation.

"I can't promise anything, but if what you have to tell me is worthwhile, then I'm sure the powers that be will consider a cash advance or a bonus instead of your biweekly salary." He opens his briefcase and sorts through numerous documents. "But first things first. Tell me what you have on the kidnappings. Shit has hit the fan. Saudi officials are hounding the prime minister and the government, including Foreign Affairs, for answers. And the PM, the Privy Council, the Minister of

Public Safety—they're all knocking on our doors. A lot of heads are rolling but we have nothing to tell them. So, I'm hoping you can give me something."

My nerves are shot and all I can do is nod.

"What happened last night? We waited around forever at Union Station! Where did you go?"

I remain silent, unsure as to what to divulge. I was warned not to get involved in any criminal activity, and I'm afraid if I admit my part in the abduction of the imam, that'll be the end of my relationship with the agency—and of any further payments. And then I might as well just offer my head to Raoul and Omar on a platter.

"What's wrong?" Jacob eventually asks.

"The missing imam," I manage to muster, "They took him . . ."

Jacob's eyes immediately light up. "Who took him? Took him where?"

"The Dominion," I reply, feeling guiltier by the minute. "Early this morning . . . at dawn . . . they took him from his residence as he was leaving for morning prayer."

Jacob begins to jot down the information. "Do you know exactly who was involved?"

I hesitate. "Conrad, Derek, Shane, Cyril and . . ."

"And?"

"I was their driver."

Jacob looks up sharply, but doesn't comment.

"Do you know where they took him?" he says.

"No. I don't even know why they took him."

Jacob flips through his notes. "A month or so ago you told me the Dominion was preparing for a strike, but only in the New Year. This has caught all of us off-guard. Why the drastic change in plans? Were you aware of this?"

"No, I wasn't aware of any change of plans. Nor was I aware of an actual target."

Jacob then riffles through what appear to be transcripts of a television or radio broadcast. "Aarzam Khalid Hussain and his son Faisal were believed to have been taken between 12:00 and 12:30 this morning as they were returning from an event hosted by the Ottawa Muslim Association. According to eye witnesses, a dark van was seen driving in the area during the course of the evening. Hussain and his son were being driven in a black Cadillac when it's believed they were swarmed by a group of men at a quiet intersection in the city's west end. The Cadillac was found abandoned in a remote parking lot in the city's south end. Hussain's driver, who's also his bodyguard, was found dead at the scene." He looks up at me. "Does any of this sound familiar to you?"

"Not really."

"Not really? That isn't exactly a resounding *no*."

"Look, I don't know anything about the ambassador's abduction," I reply. "But I do know that the imam was taken in a dark van and transferred to yet another, just like the one spotted in Ottawa."

"Can you elaborate?" He sounds frustrated. "I need details."

"Conrad picked me up at home. In a dark blue commercial van," I begin. "It was shortly after 3 a.m., just after I called you. He told me they changed their minds about Union Station. Shane was with him and Cyril was waiting in the van."

"And then what?"

"Conrad told me to drive and so I drove." I then proceed to tell him what happened, about the old man, and getting him to the train yard and into the other van.

I pause to let Jacob catch up on his notes.

"And?"

"And then everyone left in the other van, with the exception of Conrad and me," I reply. "Conrad took over at the wheel and drove me home."

"And that's it?"

"That's it."

Jacob jots down more notes. "Where the hell did they take the imam?"

"I told you I don't know. Conrad wouldn't tell me."

"Where was Conrad heading after he dropped you off?"

"I don't know, but I did manage to take down the license plates." I fish in my pockets for the crumpled piece of paper with the information and hand it to him. "I couldn't find a V.I.N. anywhere. Not on the door or the dashboard. They must've been removed."

He takes a long hard look at the slip. "BIJS 541. Ontario marker. BFWL 298. Also an Ontario marker. Good. This is good. This is a good start. Do you know what makes? What models?"

"They were both Ford Econolines," I reply, trying to remember any other bit of information about the vehicles. "Like I said, commercial vans—with no windows on the sides. The one I was in was completely stripped inside. It was quite old, probably late eighties or early nineties. Rust on the sides above the wheel wells. Cracked windshield."

Jacob sits back in the cushion chair and digests everything I've just told him. I'm beginning to think he's prepared to overlook what I did. But after a moment's reflection, he sits upright again and frowns.

"Liam, do you understand what you did? You're now an accomplice to a kidnapping, forcible confinement and God knows what else! Damn it, what did I tell you about being involved in criminal activity?"

"I know—but I really didn't have a choice!" I retort.

"You always have a choice!" he barks. "I specifically told you not to get involved in any criminal matter! You understand I have no choice but to report this to my superiors, which will most likely mean we have to suspend our relationship with you!"

"What? Are you bloody kidding me?"

"I warned you," he says, trying to collect himself. "We can't be dealing with persons engaged in criminal and terrorist activities! Your assignment is to collect information on those activities—not to participate in them! How would it look if it ever came out that we're not only doing business with persons involved in criminal or terrorist activities, but funding them as well?"

"But I had no other choice!" I shout, my blood boiling. "Do you want me to lose credibility? Do you want the Dominion to start suspecting me? Hell, if it wasn't for me, you'd have nothing. Nothing!"

Jacob stands up. He begins to pace back and forth across the room. "I have to report this to my superiors. They'll probably tell me to pass this along to the RCMP. Granted, we don't have to divulge the source of the information—"

"Fine! You do what you have to do," I interject. "But I'm never going to testify in court, I can guarantee you. I'm under no obligation. You even assured me that—"

"Relax, I never said you'll have to testify," Jacob says. "But you do know that the RCMP and the FBI are actively investigating this. They have a joint taskforce set up to investigate the mosque bombings and I'm sure they'll make the link. They're working around the clock. They have their lists of suspects and it's just a matter of time before arrests are made. They're currently looking for several of your friends, who are wanted for questioning—"

"They're not my friends, Jacob!"

"The point is," he continues, "they have many leads and many names on their list, including yours. They don't have enough information for an arrest just yet, but your name will definitely come up on their radar. As I said, we'll likely have no choice but to suspend our relationship with you—at least temporarily—until we have a better handle of the situation."

"Damn it, Jacob!" I shout, slamming my fist against the table. "I'm in this because of you! If you let me hanging high and dry, I'm going straight to the cops—no, the press—myself!"

"We're not going to let you hang high and dry," Jacob says, trying to alleviate the tension. "I'll talk to my superiors and see what can be done. If the RCMP is actively investigating you, we may have to let them know you're one of our guys. We're meeting with them tomorrow. We'll go from there."

"I'm not taking the fall for this," I mutter. "Do you hear me?"

"You're not going to take the fall for anything, I promise you," Jacob says smoothly. "We have ways to protect you." His pager, clipped to his belt, begins to vibrate. He takes a quick look and says, "I have to go. Do you still have that cell phone they lent you?"

"No, Conrad took it back."

"Did you manage to take down any of the numbers? You must have been contacted, right?"

"I was, but 'unknown caller' was all that was indicated. As for the cell, it was a different number and provider—again. Telus this time."

Jacob jots this down along with the telephone number I provide him. Understandably, he doesn't appear very enthusiastic. "This cell phone situation is becoming very frustrating. As I already told you, we haven't been able to put a single trace on any of the numbers you've provided. They become discontinued the moment we begin the intercepts. It's like they know they're being tapped. Some of the numbers are only active for a few days. As some go out of service, new ones are popping up. All registered to E-Z Travel or E-Z Grocery under the name of Marcus Black."

"That's strange . . ."

"Anyway, we're still looking into it with local cell phone companies." He puts his papers in his briefcase. "As for Conrad and the others, do you have anything as to where they're currently hiding out?"

"No, still nothing."

"OK, then, sit tight. We're working on it. I'll look into those license plates. Which reminds me, we checked Mario's plate. It's linked to an old address of his in Montreal. He hasn't lived there in ten years. So we have no current address for Mr. Martel, but we're still looking."

"Something tells me he's no longer residing in Montreal," I offer.

"Yeah, that's what I was thinking," Jacob replies. "Also, I'll enquire about the train yard as I believe there are security cameras throughout the compound. Hopefully, someone saw something. Same goes for Falat's neighborhood." He stands up and smooths out the creases in his trousers. "Do you have anything else to tell me?"

I shake my head.

"If you do, you know how to get a hold of me," he says, heading for the door. "I'll be in touch—probably sooner rather than later."

"Any luck with tracking The Prophet's email address? Or Vica.net?"

Jacob freezes in mid-stride. He shakes his head and turns to me. "Apparently, this isn't going to be as easy as I thought. But hey, I'm no techie. Turns out whoever is hosting Vica.net is using a rather sophisticated firewall and I.P. blocker unlike anything we've ever seen before. Every new message leads us to a different I.P. address, mimicking some poor schmuck's somewhere across the world. But I'm confident my guys will get to the bottom of this and break through that firewall. Mark my words. For now, just keep getting me those messages until I receive direction from my headquarters."

"Will do."

Jacob excuses himself and quickly exits the room, leaving me to stew in utter confusion. I feel as though the world is turning rapidly beneath me, spinning out of control. I suddenly feel sick and run for the bathroom, but nothing but long strands of thick phlegm and saliva ooze out of me. I run the tap and splash cold water on my face, hoping it'll wake me from this awful nightmare.

But of course it doesn't.

The image in the mirror before me reflects nothing more than the angry yet terrified look in my eyes, eerily reminiscent of an image I haven't seen in over twenty years. Something is hemorrhaging deep inside me. Perhaps it's my soul. Whatever it is, I can't seem to find a way to stop the bleeding.

This isn't worth it, Liam. Get out now while you still can, I tell myself, although unconvincingly. In the end, my own stubbornness and my need to repay those debts will be the death of me. *Jacob won't abandon you. Everything will be fine. Pay your debts, and that's it.*

After that, it'll all be over.

After that, you're getting out of the Dominion of God and away from this mad world of cat and mouse for good . . .

CHAPTER 25

A few days fly by without even a whisper from Derek, Conrad, Miroslav or any other member of the Dominion of God. The abductions of the imam and the ambassador and his son have flooded virtually all media channels on a daily basis. The early morning news. The early evening news. The nightly news. The newspapers. The radio. The Internet. The *New York Times*. The *Globe and Mail*. The BBC. CBC. CNN. Al Jazeera. One would have to be blind *and* deaf not to know about it.

The Saudi embassy has already criticized federal law enforcement officials for their failure to apprehend those responsible for the mosque bombings. The consensus among most Saudi officials is that the government hasn't done enough—that it's not taking the threat against Muslims seriously. This latest incident has only exacerbated the sentiment, adding salt to the wounds. While no one has yet to claim responsibility, there have been rumors of the Dominion being involved.

The Saudi Arabian government has called for swift justice as well as for its participation in the investigation. Of course, Parliament has refused any Saudi involvement but has assured the Saudi government that progress has been made and that the perpetrators will be brought to justice imminently. It has urged the Saudis not to let this latest setback undermine the Middle East peace process that is set to resume in Rome in a matter of weeks.

From the few conversations I've had with Jacob over the past few days, my guess is they've made very little headway in their investigations. Whether there's any progress or not, he and I both know the Saudis likely have their own men—their own spies—operating within the country and actively conducting their own investigation.

The more I hear about this, the more it makes me very nervous. Although the incident falls under the jurisdiction of domestic agencies, I can't help but wonder what measures the Saudis might secretly be taking to enhance their own investigation and who their efforts will lead them to. Although the rules of engagement generally dictate that a government is not to conduct intelligence activities on ally soil without permission, cooperation or the knowledge of the host country, most do nonetheless. They do it secretly and clandestinely. The last thing I want is for my name to surface in a foreign investigation, especially one by a state with a very different philosophy of justice than our own.

Jacob has assured me that my name won't be mentioned in any investigations, at least not on his side. He also told me that he's informed the RCMP that he has a man on the inside with information. He's admitted to passing along some information to the RCMP. I wasn't pleased to say the least. However, he has also assured me that whatever is to transpire, I'll be given immunity. According to him, the RCMP has asked to speak with me, a request I've refused thus far.

I'm playing hard to get for a few reasons, the most important being the fact that I haven't yet received a response to my request for a cash advance. The clock is ticking. I don't have much time left before Raoul and Omar return. The RCMP's desperation to meet with me and crack this investigation wide open is my leverage. Jacob knows this, and he'd be a fool to let his only gateway into the Dominion fall at the hands of two lowly loan sharks. Should Jacob—or the RCMP for that matter—come up with the money, then maybe I'll talk.

But for the time being, all is quiet.

A week after the kidnapping, I get a phone call.

It's 4:30 p.m.

"Are you watching TV?" Jacob asks without even a "hello."

I was watching an old *Seinfeld* re-run, but I don't tell him that. "Yeah, why do you ask?"

"Turn to channel three," he says, sounding rather excitable and distraught. "Or channel four or six, seven, or eight . . . or sixteen, seventeen or eighteen . . . take your pic."

I scramble for the remote and tap through the buttons several times before getting a response. I make a mental note to replace the batteries—again. The first thing that comes to mind is that they found the old imam's body in a field somewhere on the outskirts of the city or at the bottom of Lake Ontario. Or, even worse, they found the bodies of all three abductees. In either case, I become an accomplice to a murder. I can kiss that bonus goodbye.

In a perfect world, they would've found the abductees and arrested the kidnappers. I imagine Conrad, Derek, Miroslav and the others being led to the police precinct in handcuffs. I pray for this.

When I finally scroll down to channel eighteen, my worst fears are confirmed. For a fraction of a second, my insides feel as though they've imploded, leaving nothing but a void—a deep void that quickly fills with fear, anxiety and, worst of all, guilt. Although I feel as though I'm about to pass out, I remain focused on the images onscreen.

"You see it?" Jacob asks, following a moment of silence.

"Yeah, I see it."

"It appeared on the Internet just under ten minutes ago," he explains, his voice sounding faint and distant. "It's currently posted on various sites, including YouTube."

I can barely register Jacob's words, even less muster a reply.

"Liam, you there?"

"Yeah . . ."

"We have to talk about this," Jacob insists, his voice sounding as though it's coming from another world or a distant dream. "Liam, I have a copy of the recording in its entirety. I need you to take a look at it, pronto."

I sit still, frozen in horror.

"Liam!" he yells, his voice snapping me back to reality. "Every second counts! Do you hear me? This is important. This is—"

"I hear you," I finally reply, "What do you want from me?"

"Just come take a look at the clip—in full length and full audio. We've managed to enhance all the background noises. My people are currently analyzing the feed. We—I mean I, have a few questions for you."

It sounds like he let slip something he shouldn't have.

"We?"

"Liam, please," Jacob begs. "Lives are at stake here. We need all the help we can get."

He explains to me that Sergeant Louis Kipling, a senior investigator for the Royal Canadian Mounted Police's National Security Criminal

Investigations unit, is with him. Evidently, *"we"* includes Sergeant Kipling. Given that I'm actually complicit in the initial crime, the sudden involvement of a federal police officer puts me even more on edge and it feels like Jacob has betrayed me. Who knows what he's told Kipling.

Despite my apprehension, I agree to meet with them—not so much because of a desire to cooperate, but to appease my deep sense of guilt and responsibility. I owe it to the missing men. And, before I can ask another question or say another word, Jacob reveals that my request for a cash advance was approved—even better, approved as a bonus. He instructs me to meet them on Front Street across from Union Station in exactly fifteen minutes.

Then he hangs up.

I stare at the receiver and hang up in turn. I take one last glance at the screen before me as the reporter and anchorman wrap up their special report. I turn off the television but the images remain etched in my mind. Even as I exit the apartment complex and begin my walk down to the nearest station, the images of dark robes and silver masks continue to haunt me.

CHAPTER 26

A beige Camry is already waiting for me across from Union Station. In the front passenger seat is Jacob and at the wheel is a man I can only assume is Sergeant Kipling. Both are dressed casually, wearing jeans and leather jackets along with dark sunglasses despite the setting sun.

Without even a word, I'm directed into the vehicle. Inside, there's a particular scent of leather and vinyl. One quick look around and it becomes evident this is a brand-new vehicle—likely leased by the agency.

"Nice wheels," I say, a little out of nervousness.

Sergeant Kipling pays no attention to me and immediately puts the car in drive, struggling to evade a sea of pedestrians: the average citizen finishing a hard day's work and heading back to the sanctuary of home. Many disappear below the concrete and asphalt surface underfoot to catch the subway, like ancient ghosts summoned to the underworld.

Nearly ten minutes pass before Jacob finally breaks the silence. "Sorry for the lack of introduction," he says, staring back at me through his sunglasses. "We were kinda in counter-surveillance mode. You know, for your own protection. You can never be too careful."

I nod but this somehow fails to reassure me.

"This is Sergeant Kipling who I mentioned on the phone," Jacob continues, facing forward once again. He pauses for a moment, likely expecting the Sergeant to respond. Although Kipling turns his head slightly to peer in the rearview mirror, he doesn't say a word. I stare back at the reflection in the mirror and into the dark shades that conceal his eyes. He stares at me long and hard before finally nodding his head and removing his glasses.

After a mere ten minutes in his presence, I don't know what to make of Kipling. He's already established himself as not being very personable. *Must be old-school,* I tell myself, *like those bad-ass cops you see in movies.* I can tell by his stature he was once a very formidable officer—someone I wouldn't have wanted to mess with. However, time doesn't appear to have been a good friend to the old sergeant. Likely only in his fifties, he appears more like he's in his sixties: grey hair, withered and yellowish skin, creases in his upper lip as though he's sucked on a few cigarettes in his day. Dark circles beneath his eyes. Someone who's led a hard life, it would seem.

"Not a big talker," Jacob explains, half-heartedly poking fun at the sergeant's expense. "But someone you want on your side, Liam. You know what I mean?"

"If you say so . . ."

"Listen, Liam," Jacob says, taking off his sunglasses. "I've briefed Sergeant Kipling on your situation. I know you said you weren't open to it, but I really had no choice—Headquarters' direction. But I want you to know you've got nothing to worry about. Only Sergeant Kipling and I—along with our supervisors at HQ, of course—are aware of this. And I suggest we keep it that way."

"And what does that mean for me?" I ask.

While I was initially annoyed that Jacob spoke with Kipling before telling me, after putting more thought into it, I'm a little relieved. Fact of the matter is, I'd much rather the RCMP find out about my involvement with the Dominion of God through Jacob and his clones rather than through their own investigations. *At least Jacob didn't leave me hanging high and dry,* I tell myself in order to feel reassured.

But still, something tells me I'm not off the hook.

It can't be that easy.

We drive out of the downtown core via the Gardiner Expressway and ultimately veer north onto the Don Valley Parkway. However, instead of remaining on the parkway, which would've eventually brought us to highway 401, Kipling takes the Don Mills exit and heads into an old East York neighborhood that is very unfamiliar to me.

"Where are we going?" I ask, totally perplexed.

Jacob turns around, repositioning his sunglasses. "Somewhere confidential," he answers, and I notice Kipling staring back at me through the rearview mirror once again. They both stare at me for a few seconds before turning their attention back to the road.

After a few minutes of driving around the suburbs, we head into a commercial stretch riddled with small businesses including pawn shops, international grocers and takeout joints. At one point, Kipling reaches for a small black contraption clipped to the sun visor. Shortly after, he veers into a parking lot that leads to a small commercial building.

The edifice itself is very plain and sits inconspicuously among other small and unremarkable establishments. Like most of the buildings around it, it's made of dark brick, some of which has begun to crumble. A seemingly perfect cube, it sports no signs and no visible address. From the street, it's virtually unnoticeable thanks in large part to a row of evergreens at the front.

Kipling rounds the building, bringing us to the rear and to a downward ramp leading below ground. We enter the passage, which leads to a small underground garage. At first, I'm a little skeptical about Kipling making a clean entry into the narrow tunnel, but it becomes evident the old cop has been here before. Without incident, he manages to swerve around tight corners and other obstacles until he finds a place to park. Jacob then tells me to exit the vehicle and wait for further instruction.

Both Kipling and Jacob remain in the car for a few minutes, so I look around. The parking area is poorly lit and unkempt. I can see mold growing along the concrete walls and ceiling, which is likely responsible for the strong, musty odor. There appear to be two stairwells, one at each end of the garage.

I watch as Kipling and Jacob finally get out of the car and begin to make their way toward the stairs. I follow closely behind my handlers, who disappear into the nearest stairwell just below a faded exit sign. We quickly make our way up three flights of stairs, where Kipling swipes an access card through a reader, unlocking the stairwell door. We then find ourselves in a short corridor with a door at the end. There are other doors along the way, but they're all unmarked. Beside each door is a black card reader with a glowing red light. As we pass by, Kipling checks every door to make sure they're secured. The corridor walls are painted a plain white, with various scratches and chips in the drywall. There are no pictures or paintings—or anything decorative, for that matter.

"Where are we?" I ask, following closely behind Jacob.

"One of our secure office spaces," Kipling replies.

Upon reaching the far end of the corridor, we enter a boardroom, which is the only room that isn't locked or secured with an access system. In the middle of the room there's a large conference table with several leather chairs around it. There are two large windows, each hidden behind heavy blinds. In one corner, by one of these windows, is a chair and coffee table. On the table sits a telephone and a blank note pad. At the opposite end of the room, a lone television set sits on a stand, the words "No Signal" flashing across its blank screen. On a shelf beneath the television are numerous devices, including a VCR and a Blu-ray player, and several others that, for the life of me, I can't seem to identify.

Jacob invites me to have a seat directly in front of the screen and pulls up a chair beside me. "So how are you doing?" he asks, seemingly genuinely concerned.

"Could be better . . ."

"I hear you," he says. "Listen, like I said, there are very few people within our organizations other than Kipling and I who are aware of your situation." He looks over to Kipling, who's fiddling with the electronic equipment beneath the TV. "And only Kipling and I are aware of your real identity. I want you to know you have nothing to worry about and nothing to fear. You're in no real trouble as far as your involvement is concerned with the kidnappings—"

"I acted on your behalf—"

"I know," Jacob replies, nodding slightly. "And believe me, you've been a real valuable asset. We appreciate everything you've done. Kipling is impressed, isn't that right, Lou?"

"Uh-huh," Kipling replies, his attention still focused on the equipment.

"Fact of the matter is, we're close," Jacob reveals. "We know some of the players involved and their methods. However, we don't know where to find them and we don't yet have enough hard evidence to prosecute. Like Frank mentioned before, we know that the explosives used for U.S. bombings were C-4 explosives. Thanks to the DMDNB marker that was identified, we believe we've located their source. That's on the U.S. side. Over on our side, it's a whole different ball game. Other than a typewritten letter and TATP residue, we have nothing."

"Liam," Kipling interrupts, turning to look at me, "do you know of a wrecking yard that's being used by any of your friends?"

"They're not my friends," I reply abruptly.

Kipling stares at me long and hard with a smirk on his face. "Well then, are you aware of any wrecking yard being used by your . . . what . . . associates?"

"No."

"Liam," Jacob says, trying to deflect my attention away from the sergeant. "Every day brings us another piece of the puzzle. The footage that you saw on TV is another piece. But that was just a fourteen-second fragment of what was posted on the Net. The footage you're about to see is about ten minutes in its entirety."

"I see . . ."

Kipling removes himself from the front of the television screen, revealing a blank image. A few seconds later, the image of three men suddenly appears. In a large room, each man is tied to a cross. Black sacks cover their heads. Other than their undergarments, their bodies are naked. The room is bare. Nothing but white walls surround them.

Although their identities are concealed, I know exactly who they are. And so do Jacob and Kipling.

On the bottom right of the screen, the date and time glow green. The recording was done only a day after the abduction. For the first few minutes, nothing happens. Then, three men armed with what appear to be semi-automatic rifles appear and make their way behind the abductees. All three wear hooded robes and it isn't until they turn to face the camera that their silver masks are exposed.

Those metallic silver faces. Like ghosts, they have returned. Intense, the eyes behind them stare wildly into the camera. Looking back into them, all I see is emptiness—lifeless spheres devoid of whatever humanity they once held. Despite their empty glares, a fury in them remains. It takes just one second to see it . . . to feel it.

From the corner of my eye, I can see both Jacob and Kipling taking turns staring me down, hoping to get some type of reaction out of me. I can sense their anticipation. But I'm so nervous and anxious and terrified I can't even blink.

With the use of a remote control, Kipling pauses the video. "OK, although we don't know with certainty, let's just say it's safe to assume that the captives are the imam, the ambassador and his son," he says. "The imam on the left," he continues, pointing to the tall, slender figure, "the ambassador in the middle, and his son on the right," he finishes, pointing to the smallest captive, then looking at me.

"I'd say that's a fair guess."

"So who the hell are these three fellows behind them?" asks Kipling, as he and Jacob turn to me.

"I don't know."

"Bullshit!" Kipling bellows. "You know exactly who they are!"

"I'm sorry, are you calling me a liar?"

Jacob motions for the Sergeant to stand back. "Liam, look for clues. Their voices are somewhat muffled by their masks, so listen carefully." He motions for Kipling to resume the video.

As we continue to watch the recording, another thirty seconds or so elapse before the silence is broken by the tallest of the hooded figures. After only a few words, I recognize the voice instantly—it's unmistakable. I say nothing and continue to listen to his monologue.

"We are the righteous," he intones. "We are the resistance against a war that has been waged against us. A war that no state can quell. The enemy calls this war *Jihad*, and we, the infidels." He goes on in the vein I've heard so often, about how God's true people are under siege, how humanity has been misled by false prophets, how the Tribulation, the Rapture and the Second Coming of Christ is upon us, and how our governments have done nothing in response to 9/11 or Black Friday. And so on.

Then the speaker pauses for a brief moment and nods to the men standing to his side. Almost simultaneously, all three captors reach for the necks of the three hostages. The sacks on their heads are removed, revealing the imam, the ambassador and his son.

All three appear extremely weak and exhausted, no doubt the result of sleep deprivation and starvation. Bruises cover their bodies. Sweat is pouring down their foreheads. All are gagged with dirty cloths stuffed deep inside their throats.

The masked men then direct their firearms to the heads of their victims. The speaker resumes his speech.

"Here is your enemy!" he shouts angrily. "The imam who preaches hate at his place of worship! The ambassador who covertly schemes to destroy us while overtly promoting peaceful international relations! And his seed who has been bred to hate and trained in warfare in order to continue their so-called *jihad*! People, their hate for you is strong! Do not be fooled by their cries of persecution!"

In the background, a strange humming sound commences like that of an air conditioning or ventilation system.

"We are the Dominion of God. We are here to ensure that your government is held accountable for the harm that has been done to you! We are here to ensure that there will never again be a Black Friday, a 9/11 or any other form of aggression against God's *true* people! And our mission has just begun."

The speaker pauses for another brief moment and then pulls out a small scroll from his robe. He unravels it and begins to read.

"Prime Minister, on the twenty-fifth day of the twelfth month of this year, the infidels you see before you will be executed should our demands not be met. Our demands are threefold. One, your government is to sever all diplomatic ties with non-secular states. Two, your government is to institute a new regime—one that is governed by, and adheres to, strict Christian principles in accordance with the Dominion of God. Three, you are to close down the borders and legislate a mass exodus of all non-Christians from this land. These are our demands. This is your only warning. While the lives of these three sinners are in your hands, this will be the least of your concerns should our demands not be met."

End of taping. The screen goes black.

Sergeant Kipling shakes his head as he fidgets with the video equipment. "Are they out of their fuckin' minds? They can't possibly believe that anyone will even consider any of these ridiculous demands!"

"Of course not," Jacob replies, still staring at the screen. "They'd have to be complete idiots to believe that such demands would be taken seriously. And something tells me they aren't idiots. These demands are too outrageous, which I think is exactly what they want. I think this is very calculated."

"That's what I was thinking." Kipling is browsing through the video, apparently looking for a particular point in the clip. "It's like it's been purposefully orchestrated so that their demands *aren't* met. Man, this is going to cause the government a lot of headaches and embarrassment."

"Liam," Jacob says, "does this have anything to do with the upcoming peace talks in Italy? Is this the Dominion's attempt at undermining the process?"

"I . . . I don't know . . ." I reply, unable to make any sense of it. "I haven't heard anything about such a goal. I mean, it wouldn't make much sense. More than anything, the Dominion would want the peace process not only to go on, but conclude in the signing of a treaty. It would mean the beginning of Tribulation, something it has been waiting for since the time of Roland. Why would it seek to undermine it?"

"Good question and good point." Jacob replies, turning to the Sergeant. "Lou? What are your thoughts? Any ideas?"

The old sergeant simply raises his shoulders and shakes his head.

"Why on Christmas?" Jacob asks. "Out of all the days in the year, they had to pick Christmas!"

Both Kipling and Jacob look at me. But I don't have any answers to give them. All I can do is stare back in confusion and denial.

"Christmas," Jacob repeats. "That gives us just under a month. In the world of kidnappings and ransoms, that's like an eternity. In reality, however, it's very little time." He then turns to me. "Liam, do you recognize any of these men?"

"Yeah, I think so . . ."

"Well?"

"The speaker, that's Derek Devlin. I'm almost positive. His voice. His height. I can't think of anyone else it could be."

"How positive are you?" Jacob asks, "Like eighty, ninety percent positive?"

"Yeah, I'd say about ninety percent positive."

"What about the others?"

"It's definitely not Miroslav or Frenchy. Frenchy's too broad and Miroslav's too tall to be the other two fellas. I'm completely stumped."

"OK, so, if that's Devlin," Jacob mumbles, flipping through his notes, "And Devlin is six two, about one-ninety pounds . . . that would make the other two approximately five ten or five eleven, about one-eighty pounds . . . does that sound about right?"

Kipling nods. "Yeah, I'd say that's a fair guess."

"So we have two unidentified males, five ten or five eleven, about one-eighty pounds, give or take," Jacob mutters, grabbing a large panel that's wired to the television. On the panel are several push buttons, a dial and a directional stick. By turning the dial, he rewinds the footage and pauses at the three masked men. With the directional stick and the push of a button, he's able to zoom in to their masks and adjust the image to near high-definition quality. "OK. As you can see, both appear to be Caucasians. You can see the skin around their eyes, their eyelids. One with blue eyes, the other with brown—"

"What about Martel or Dorion . . . or what about Cyril?" Kipling interrupts.

"No, not Mario or Roch. I don't think I know these two guys," I reply, impressed by Kipling's knowledge of the file. I try to refresh my memory of the faces of our newest recruits. *Could it be Hal? Zack? Are there other recruits I'm not aware of?*

"So you're saying there's a possibility that you've never met these two fellas?" Kipling continues.

"That's a possibility, yeah."

Jacob picks up his notes and looks through the pages. "Liam, are you aware of any new recruits? Has the Dominion spoken about having recruited new people?"

"No . . . I mean, not since the last time we spoke, but it's possible," I reply, remembering my interactions with the mysterious Angelic. "The Dominion is continuously recruiting. Mostly through the Internet, like I told you."

"Have you heard from any of them lately?"

"No."

"When was the last time?"

"The night of the kidnapping," I reply, slightly annoyed. I know Kipling knows the answer. And I can sense that he knows that I know that he knows. He's just testing me. That's why I'm annoyed.

"Are you expecting to hear from them or meet with them soon?"

"I don't know."

Kipling then points to the frozen picture on the screen. "The Saudi embassy has confirmed that this is indeed the ambassador and his son." He then points to the third captive. "Can you confirm that this is indeed the man *you* abducted on the morning of November twenty-seventh?"

"*I* abducted?" I scoff. "I was forced into this! I had no idea that—"

"Is this or is this not the man?"

"Yeah, that's him." I'm growing more irritated by the minute. "I mean, I didn't get a very good look. After all, he was gagged and bagged, but I'm almost positive it's him."

"What about weapons?" Jacob jumps in, "Those look like AK-47s. How the hell did they get their hands on AK-47s? Not much of them going around in this country. Do you know who their supplier might be?"

"No idea."

"Have they talked about acquiring weapons?" Jacob asks, reassuming his position as lead investigator.

"No! Hell, I would've told you!"

"I'd put my money on Milenkovic," Kipling offers, "I mean, isn't he from the former Yugoslavia or something? It's no secret there are a fair share of arms that are unaccounted for in the area—not to mention in the former USSR. He must still have a contact or two out there."

"It's possible—"

"You're damn right it's possible! Hell, I'd say it's probable!"

"Liam," Jacob resumes, "Do you have any idea where the Dominion may have gotten its hands on those AK-47s?"

"No, I don't."

"Heard anything more about dealings with companies overseas?"

"I'm sorry, I haven't . . ."

"I suppose they could've come in from south of the border," Jacob proposes, massaging his brow. "With our border situation, everything's possible."

The room goes silent and I can feel the tension mounting in Kipling and my handler. There must be a million questions racing through their minds. A million questions they desperately need answers for—and fast.

The silence is eventually broken by the sound of Jacob's pager. He excuses himself and makes a call using the telephone at the other end of the room. His conversation is short, mostly responses to a barrage of questions I can only assume are coming from his superiors. He returns shortly afterward and begins to flip through more files. He comes to an abrupt halt and looks me straight in the eye.

"Have you ever heard of Dino & Sons Wrecking Yard?"

"Can't say I have."

"Those two vans you say were driven that night," he continues. "Dark blue Econolines. The plates you gave me, BIJS 541 and BFWL 298, are stolen plates. They belong to two separate elderly couples who hadn't noticed they were missing. Hell knows when they were taken, could've been a week before the abduction or even the very night of. But that's beside the point. We have witnesses who say they saw two dark commercial vans with Ontario plates heading into the demolition area at Dino & Sons the morning of the kidnappings. Do you know of any DOG member with connections at Dino's?"

"No, I don't."

"We paid a visit to ol' Dino just the other day," Kipling adds. "Odd fella . . . said he knows nothing about commercial vans being scheduled for demolition. He became quite testy when asked to see any records. After reviewing his files, it was quite obvious why. Turns out he keeps a very poor record of his inventory and of his sales. Everything on paper. No computers. Not everything listed in his inventory matches his actual stock either. Dino & Sons have long been suspected of taking in stolen vehicles, disassembling them for parts, and selling them under the table and splitting the profit with those involved in theft rings. But that's a whole other story. Needless to say, we insisted on seeing his entire inventory. Not just parts, but chassis and other scrap metal. There were numerous auto parts that fit the bill, but no commercial van chassis."

"Liam, if ever you hear anything concerning Dino & Sons, we need to know immediately," Jacobs adds, handing me photographs of Dino and his staff. "This is him, along with his eldest, Chuck, his younger son Fred, and his other mechanics Sean, Geoff and Quentin. If you see any of them, you let us know. Got it?"

I nod.

Jacob and Kipling exchange glances. "We also recently paid Reverend Hunt a visit," Jacob says, "under the pretext of his past relationship with the group, of course. We went to St. Andrew's. He gave us a tour of the church, including the basement. He said the basement hasn't been rented or used by anyone in quite some time—nor has he had anyone ask to use the facilities. When we showed him the pictures of Devlin, Milenkovic and French, he became strangely agitated."

Inside, I'm fuming. I can't believe they went to Hunt before speaking with me. This could've placed me in a very difficult situation had the Dominion confronted me or anyone about this. In fact, I'm quite surprised I haven't heard any rumblings about this. Perhaps Hunt's past association with Roland and the Dominion of God alone was enough to avoid suspicion.

"He tried to turn the tables on us," Kipling interjects. "Reminded us that he's been forgiven for his sins and that he was reinstated as a minister of the Presbyterian Church. Began to question our motives and agenda. Insisted the group is dead and that these new *sickos*, as he put it, are imposters. Said he hasn't heard of anyone formerly associated with the group and wants nothing to do with them."

"We also paid him a surprise visit at home a few days later." It's back to Jacob now. "Told him we had more questions for him. He invited us in and gave us a quick tour of the place, including the basement."

I raise my eyebrows "And? Didn't you see all the racist propaganda? The posters? The Nazi symbols? White power and all that? All the literature?"

Kipling and Jacob look at one another, then back at me. In unison, they shake their heads. "Nothing," Jacob replies. "The place was clean. Are you sure you were at his residence on Winchester that night?"

"Positive!"

Jacob shrugs. "Well, obviously he's not talking. But we're gonna keep trying. He's definitely hiding something. I can feel it."

"So what now?" I ask.

Jacob sits down and leans back into his chair, dropping his head back. He sighs deeply and stares at the ceiling. Then he leans forward and rests both elbows on his knees. "Is there any way you can get in touch with any of them? Mario maybe?"

"Nope. I'm at the bottom of the food chain. They don't give us contact information. It's kinda like a policy of theirs. I've never been given any numbers, other than the E-Z numbers."

"But Mario had your number," Jacob reminds me, somewhat suspicious.

"Yeah, he did. I don't know how he got it, we're unlisted, Sarah and I. So's my cell. I'll have to ask him how he got it when I see him."

"Well, Lou and I are going to keep working on some leads," Jacob says, getting to his feet, "As Lou said to me earlier, those assault rifles were obviously bought off the black market and likely smuggled from the Balkans or the U.S.—the U.S. being more likely given our little problem at Whirlpool Bridge. We're currently looking into that, with the cooperation of our U.S counterparts."

"What about the E-Z bank accounts?" I ask.

"We're still working on that," Jacob assures me, looking over to Kipling, "We've traced some transactions back to Serbia and Montenegro. But things don't run so smoothly over there. Let's just say some agencies are more cooperative than others. We have to be extra careful. God knows there are a lot of corrupt government officials in the former Yugoslavia. But we're making headway."

"What about Black Mamba?" I'm surprised that neither Kipling nor Jacob have thought to ask.

"I was just about to get to him," Jacob replies in a matter-of-fact kind of way. "We're still running checks on Marcus Black. We've gotten several hits and we're exploring some leads," he says and hands me various photographs. Some mug shots. Surveillance pictures.

I'm instructed to look at each picture. I stare at them long and hard. *Strange faces in stranger places,* I say to myself, wondering how on earth Kipling and Jacob ever came up with such an odd assortment of souls. Despite my best efforts, I'm unable to identify any of them—or even come close.

We decide to view the recording a few more times in hopes there's something we may have missed earlier. With the use of his sophisticated control panel, Jacob knocks out the voices and amplifies background noises. We listen carefully to the humming that begins in the middle of Derek's speech and agree that it appears to be the sound of a ventilation system, which suggests the taping may have taken place in a commercial establishment. Jacob also does the opposite, that is, drowning out all background noises and amplifying foreground noise. Nothing much comes out of this.

Both Kipling and Jacob bombard me with more questions, most of them having to do with the events that transpired the night of the abduction and the possible whereabouts of the hostages. However, by the time we're done, we're nowhere closer to any answers than we were an hour ago.

In the end, they tell me to study the photos one more time and to keep an eye open for the faces I see there. I'm also reminded to keep an ear open for anyone with the family name or alias "Black" or any derivative thereof. Blackie. Blackbeard. Blackjack. Whatever.

Kipling eventually removes the media and stores it in one of those cheap plastic cases. Both he and Jacob then lock their briefcases and escort me back down into the stairwell and into the underground parking. Within a matter of minutes, we're back on the Gardiner Expressway heading westbound. Along the way, Jacob reveals that he's been ordered to maintain our relationship despite my involvement in the abductions. This is something that had completely escaped my mind. The catch is, however, that Kipling must now be involved in my handling. According to Kipling, I flew onto the RCMP's radar screens after the FBI reported my license plate following my very first delivery across the border. Both Kipling and Jacob insist that the FBI knows nothing of my role as an informant. They reassure me that the RCMP's involvement in my handling and the FBI's lack of knowledge is for my protection and benefit. After mulling it over for a bit, I figure this is indeed the best scenario and agree to this entente.

At my request, I'm dropped off exactly where they picked me up. It's now dark out, the usual commotion of Union Station having somewhat subsided. A cold wind is blowing from the north, forcing those left wandering about to zip their jackets as far they can go or cover their ears with a hat or their hands.

Before we part, Jacob reminds me of what or who to look out for. To do whatever I can to find out the location of the abducted. I assure him I'll be in touch the moment I hear anything—if I ever do hear from the Dominion again.

CHAPTER 27

It's early December and I've barely heard a word from the Dominion of God. My only contact with the group has come in the form of brisk encounters with Mario, who I'm convinced has taken up residence somewhere in the city. Not coincidentally I'm sure, he just happens to bump into me at the most random of places. I ask about the hostages, but he knows as little as I do. I believe him too. He wouldn't be privy to that kind of information. Neither would Roch or Cyril or Shane—or any other bottom feeders like me.

During our encounters, Mario passes along instructions handed down by the Dominion's higher ranks. I'm to continue my recruitment efforts by quietly sifting through the darker channels of the World Wide Web. I get a handful of new websites with every encounter, along with a login ID and password to gain access. I don't know how the Dominion comes up with these. I don't ever bother to ask. The lifespan of such sites, so far, has been rather short. While new ones are born, others simply vanish into thin air. This happens weekly, almost daily. Those running the show—the site administrators—are both cunning and devious. A particular site can be the main point of contact for numerous days or weeks for a plethora of like-minded religious fanatics, white supremacists, nihilists and would-be extremists, only to disappear the next. Then it reemerges under a completely new domain name. Whatever the ultimate path or destination, its members and adherents always manage to regroup and find themselves under its new name. There are dozens—no, hundreds—of these sites.

To avoid any heat or suspicion from the Dominion, I end up spending an hour or so every now and then at local Internet cafés—just to say I'm doing my part. I manage to converse online with a few individuals who would definitely fit the mold of a right-wing religious fanatic and even more so of the Dominion. This time around, someone by the alias

Naziboy is my most intriguing contact. I end up chatting with this guy, who says he's local, on several occasions. Says he's a Holocaust denier and supporter of several anti-Semitic and anti-Islamic organizations. Says he's also an admirer of the Dominion of God and that the group has brought him new hope in the fight against Zionism and Islamism, which he insists is the Devil's new incarnation. Whatever. Anyway, whenever I come across fellas like Naziboy, and after I've obtained their trust, I do my best to obtain their contact information. Email addresses. Telephone numbers. Whatever works. As before, I save everything on the flash drives provided by the Dominion. Then, I simply forward them to Derek, Conrad or Miroslav through Mario. In exchange, Mario passes me new Web addresses, login IDs and passwords, which I then hand over to Jacob—along with the flash drives he has provided me containing all my conversations—during our now biweekly debriefings.

My rendezvous across the border have become less frequent, at least for the time being. While I've welcomed this much needed respite, it has greatly reduced the amount of cross-border intelligence I've been able to collect for my handler. In fact, aside from sharing information about fleeting and soon-to-be defunct websites, the amount of intelligence I've managed to produce over the past few weeks has been, well, scant to say the least. This is especially frustrating given the turbulent times.

With every day that passes, an unmistakable tension and apprehension can be seen in the eyes of those with whom I cross paths: of complete strangers in the street, and of those closest to me, including Sarah. As expected, none of the Dominion's demands have been met. In fact, not only have they been flat-out rejected by our members of Parliament, they've been scorned and ridiculed by academics and the media alike. Among the most vocal, and rightly so, the Minister of Public Safety himself has issued several statements, describing the demands as "ludicrous" and "reflective of everything that constitutes an immoral, undemocratic and unconstitutional society." Columns in the *Globe and Mail* and the *National Post*, among others, have described the Dominion, and I quote, as "a rag-tag cult of wannabe terrorists" who are "nothing more than a motley crew of misguided, un-evolved and uneducated members of society" whose demands "would only send us back to the Stone Age where these Neanderthals belong" and which are "so outrageous, idiotic, and undeserving of any shred of contemplation and further thought."

For the most part, these words are reflective of the thoughts and opinions of the average person. However, there are those less liberal and lurking in the shadows who have quietly and secretly expressed support for the Dominion—or at least some of its demands. I know because I've been chatting with them. And they appear to be growing in number.

Thankfully, the rise of the Dominion and its attacks have had little impact on the second round of peace talks that have resumed in Rome. In fact, media outlets have been reporting that much progress has been made, with all sides agreeing to do whatever it takes to achieve regional stability. This is significant. Perhaps it's a sign that the rest of the world has seen enough violence and conflicts and wars and the suffering that comes as a result of them. Perhaps it's a sign that even the most bitter enemies can forgive mistakes of past generations and work together at building a better future for their children—and for everyone.

As Christmas approaches, the Government becomes more desperate and introduces a ten-million-dollar reward for any information leading to the identification, arrest and conviction of those responsible for the kidnappings—or any member of the Dominion of God for that matter. This is an extraordinary opportunity, as Jacob has assured me that I'd be eligible for such a reward should my information lead to the desired results. Ten million dollars. The largest reward ever handed out by a federal law enforcement agency. *Ten million dollars . . .*

The end of my troubles.

Forever.

CHAPTER 28

With a little under a week left before Christmas, my every waking hour becomes consumed by the fear of letting a fortune slip away between my fingers. I can't sleep at night. My thoughts become increasingly disconnected and erratic. I even catch myself laughing at the irony of my situation. With a stroke of luck, I could be a multi-millionaire over night. Without it, I could be a dead man with nothing to his name but a large debt. As the clock winds down, I begin to sense that my luck is not the type I'd hoped for.

This year, Sarah and I have agreed to spend Christmas in Pickering with her mother, who's been ill of late. Sarah has already left via Greyhound, having taken a few days off from work. Paid vacation days are not a luxury I have at Henrique's Deli. In fact, I've been asked to work until three o'clock in the afternoon on Christmas Eve, a request I've agreed to considering my frequent absences from work over the course of the past several months. I'm to meet up with Sarah and her mother on Christmas day and then spend a few days with her side of the family. I insisted on this because something tells me I'll need to be available to either Jacob or Raoul—or both—when the clock strikes twelve on Christmas morning.

Since the offer of the reward, I've neither heard from nor come in contact with Mario in any way. Same goes for the rest of Dominion. All is still and all is quiet. So much so that I've become convinced that Jacob and Kipling's surprise visits to St. Andrew's and Hunt's residence were counter-productive. There's no doubt in my mind the old man reported these encounters to the group. Strangely enough, I've yet to hear of any fallout. *Has the Dominion gone more underground? Is it suspecting some of its members?* These are the questions, along with hundreds more, that have obsessed me for the past several weeks.

So many questions, so few answers . . .

Desperately, I've tried everything Jacob and Kipling have suggested—and then some. I've even attended a few services at St. Andrew's, hoping to run into—or at least catch a glimpse—of Dominion members or Reverend Hunt. As it turns out, Hunt no longer conducts regular services.

I've also increased my visits to local Internet cafés, probing my fellow chatters for any information they may have on the Dominion. I've tried to connect with Mario and Roch via their covert email addresses but to no avail. I've also paid several visits to E-Z Grocery and E-Z Travel and have come up with nothing. There've been no signs of Miroslav or even Vladimir. I've done this both overtly and covertly, as I expect Jacob's men have done too. However, in the end, and like everyone else on the planet, I can do nothing more but sit and wait for the Dominion's next move.

My rendezvous with Jacob and Kipling have increased and I'm now meeting with them every other day. Nearly every time, I'm presented with more photographs of suspects, names, addresses, telephone numbers and so on. They advise that they've identified another bank account belonging to Marcus Black as well as tracked down several transactions, many of which lead back to E-Z Grocery and ultimately Serbia and Montenegro. As for Marcus Black himself, he's still a mystery. But both Jacob and Kipling continue to suspect he may be hiding out on the west coast. Perhaps Roland's old stomping grounds. Who knows.

In Rome, the second round of peace talks has come and gone with a third round scheduled to resume in the New Year. Again, very little is divulged to the media. However, there are rumors of an apparent breakthrough thought to be centered around an agreement on borders, the destructions of Jewish settlements in Palestinian territories, and the establishment of a Palestinian State. There are also leaks that many members of the League of Arab States are ready to recognize Israel as a state and ensure regional security should such an agreement be reached. While I have yet to hear from the Dominion with respect to these latest developments, something tells me the group is more than aware of the situation.

On Christmas Eve, I decide to suspend my twenty-year boycott of the Catholic Church and end up attending midnight mass at St. Paul's Basilica. Ironically, this is where I am when the Dominion's deadline finally passes. I sit there, staring into the eyes of Jesus Christ on the cross, thinking selfishly of nothing but the Dominion's next move and the fortune I'm losing. Every now and then, I take a quick peek at my cell phone hoping I've missed a text or a call revealing the captives have been found safe and sound. I pray for their well-being along with the well-being of others whose lives could potentially be lost should the Dominion's goals be achieved.

To be quite honest, I don't like Christmas. It's the time of year I miss my parents the most—especially my mother. She never missed midnight mass, the sole exception being the year she became sick. When I was young, it was my father who babysat me and my cousins while my mother and some aunts and uncles were off to mass. We were usually allowed to stay up pretty late on Christmas eve, but were always sent to bed before their return from the church. My mother would invite everyone over afterwards for drinks and a small feast. I remember my cousins and me being unable to sleep. We'd stay up listening to my father and my uncle's drunken ramblings, pretending to sleep whenever someone would check up on us. Of course, it wasn't the chatter keeping us up—it was the anticipation of hearing sleigh bells ringing or the jolly laughter of someone we were dying to catch a glimpse of.

When I became old enough, I'd attend mass with them. There was something about it—about Christmas—that made my mother glow. I could see it in her eyes. Hear it in her voice. I'd often look up to her as she sang some of her favorite Christmas hymns along with the choir. She had an amazing voice, like that of an angel. My father and I weren't much for singing, but boy did we love hearing my mother.

It was never the same after my father passed away. We'd continue our yearly tradition, my mother and me. Some years we were accompanied by my aunt Rita and uncle Gary. Most years though, it was just the two of us. While she still sang with great joy and passion, there was something missing. There never was quite the same twinkle in her eye, the same spirit in her voice. When she became sick, I attended midnight mass alone while she rested at home and at the hospital in her final years. She was simply too sick and too weak, the chemotherapy having taken its toll. I felt guilty for not remaining with her and I had never felt so alone and empty—even during mass. But I did it for her. I knew that there was nothing on this earth that would make her happier than to know her only child would not abandon his faith after she was gone.

The year she passed away was the last time I went to midnight mass.

Sitting in the back row of St. Paul's Basilica reminds me how unfaithful I've been. I feel like such a hypocrite. An imposter. How disappointed she must be, my poor mother.

I try my best to enjoy the celebration, singing quietly within myself. As I do so, I get this funny feeling as though she's sitting right next to me. As though she never left my side. I swear I can still hear her voice echoing throughout the sanctuary. God, how I miss her.

At the end of mass, the choir engages in an impressive rendition of *O Come All Ye Faithful* as parishioners exit the basilica. It's just before 2:00 a.m. Stepping outside, I exchange greetings with the few who approach me. The night is cold. A soft and quiet snow is falling from the skies above. All around me, merry faces laugh and cheer. Young and old, they leave peacefully, many in large groups. I, on the other hand, am left by myself. My thoughts turn to Sarah, who's likely sound asleep in her mother's house in Pickering. I wish nothing more than to be there with her. But there would be no peace of mind tonight.

Not for me.

Tonight, there's more than one deadline that passes. For one of them, at least, there's good news. I'm to meet with Raoul and Omar in a matter of hours to deliver $50,000 in cash that Jacob is to give me. Raoul has told me to get in touch with him on Christmas morning so he can let me know where we'll meet. For now, however, this is secondary to the plight of the imam and the other captives.

As I cross the street to make my way home, a dark vehicle pulls up next to me. The driver's tinted window comes down. "Liam, get in," Jacob says very softly, his face showing signs of exhaustion.

Confused, I step inside, taking the empty seat next to his. We drive a good distance from the basilica before exchanging a word. A million questions float around in my head.

"I thought I'd find you there," he finally says, his eyes focused on the road and the pedestrians scattered about. "We found the imam, the ambassador and his son."

At first, I'm ecstatic. "You did? Where? When?"

"Riverdale Park. Not too long ago. Maybe twenty minutes or so . . ."

After driving a good distance on Bayview, Jacob reduces his speed. Up ahead, there's a roadblock. The flashing lights of numerous police cruisers and fire trucks soon fill the night sky. Blue. Red. Yellow. Everywhere. Paramedics are also on scene. So are news crews from several local stations. A few police officers are redirecting traffic onto Rosedale Valley Road. I can see smoke rising slowly above a copse and into the night sky about fifty yards past the road block.

Jacob makes his way to the first police officer and rolls down his window. "I was told Sergeant Kipling of the RCMP would be here," he informs the young officer, introducing himself and flashing his badge. The officer peers over his shoulder. He grabs his radio and talks with a supervising officer. He then removes a barricade.

"What's going on here?" I fear the worst.

Jacob drives past the first set of police cruisers that are partially blocking the road ahead. Half a block down to our right, the wooded area is cordoned off with yellow police tape. Firefighters are scouring the area, having apparently quelled a small blaze. Two paramedics stand by, speaking with police officers. No one is being attended to.

"We found them, Liam," Jacob says, bringing the car to a halt. He lowers his window and points to a clearing past the trees. A cold chill runs down my spine. Almost instantly, my fragile world collapses. There's nothing left. Not even hope. I've failed.

My eyes remain transfixed by the remnants of three large crosses that have been erected in a secluded section of the park just past the railway. Each stands well over eight feet. From them hang what I can only assume are the charred remains of the missing men. Smoke and ashes continue to ascend into the night.

Frozen, I remain speechless.

"Whoever put them there," Jacob murmurs, his breath making steam as he rolls up his window, "did so without leaving a trace. Not a single trace . . ."

"Well, that answers one of my questions," I finally say.

"Which is?"

"Whether or not you've caught those responsible."

Jacob shakes his head, looking away. "What a mess. Some Christmas, huh? Merry Christmas, by the way," he finishes glumly, offering me his hand.

I extend my hand. "Not so merry . . ."

My comment goes unnoticed and we continue past the park and toward the next assembly of police officers. Among them, dressed in civilian clothes and conversing with uniformed officers is Sergeant Kipling. Jacob pulls over to the curb. "Stay here for a minute. I need to speak with Kipling."

I nod and watch as Jacob exits the vehicle and joins Kipling and a few officers. Their conversation goes back and forth, with both Jacob and Kipling taking notes. At one point, Jacob takes Kipling aside. As they converse privately, Kipling nods and glances in my direction. He does this several times. They eventually shake hands before parting.

"Alright," Jacob says, reentering the vehicle. "We gotta go."

"Go? Go where?"

"Home base."

"Home base? What the bloody hell is home base?"

"The safe house, sorry. Spy lingo."

"Now? It's Christmas!"

"Yes, now."

"Why?"

"I have some questions for you . . . and some new info."

"Can't this wait?"

"No, it can't."

I say nothing more the rest of the way. On the radio, there are Christmas carols playing. We listen to them quietly. Outside, the parkway and the city streets have never been so bare. A thin layer of snow covers everything. White everywhere. Everything seems so serene. *It's strange how the world can appear so peaceful,* I tell myself, *yet be so full of turmoil and pain.* I lose myself in such thoughts for awhile.

CHAPTER 29

By the time I snap out of it, we're at the safe house. I step out of the vehicle and am overtaken by a deep chill. The snow has ceased and the mercury is dropping faster by the minute. The amount of steam rising from the gutters and chimneys all around us is proof of that. In an effort to escape the cold, we dart for the front door then make our way up two flights of stairs and disappear inside the tiny unit.

"Eggnog?" Jacob offers, retrieving a carton from the refrigerator.

"No thanks."

"Come on—it's Christmas."

"Fine."

Jacob fills two glasses of eggnog mixed with Canadian whiskey. We raise our glasses and say a brief prayer for the recently departed and in hopes of better days. We take some quick sips and then it's down to business.

"Kipling would've liked to be here for this," says Jacob, "but he's tied up for the time being. So, first things first." He opens a few envelopes and sifts through some papers. "I'm happy to announce we're hot on the trail of Marcus Black a.k.a. Black Mamba. He apparently relocated from Ottawa to Toronto after Black Friday. He never reported back to work. No one knows why. Change of scenery maybe. After only a few months in the GTA, he gets arrested for assaulting a waitress in a small neighborhood diner. This is his first encounter ever with the law."

"Strange . . ."

"It gets stranger," Jacob warns. "The charges were withdrawn by the complainant. A month after that, he gets arrested for causing a public disturbance, public intoxication and uttering death threats to a group of university students. According to police records, his behavior was bizarre. Following this last arrest, he was taken to the Centre for Addiction and Mental Health where he was evaluated but eventually released. That was the last time he was heard of in Toronto." Jacob pauses to drain his glass. "It's believed he may have headed west. There are several police reports in Winnipeg, Calgary and Edmonton of a man fitting his description. Nothing too serious. Uttering death threats. More public disturbance. Assaulting a man he suspected of following him. He apparently had no ID on him. It's believed he may have made his way to British Columbia. Do you know of any connections the Dominion might have in these cities?"

"No, I mean . . . perhaps Vancouver. But that was a long time ago. Threats? Assault? Public disturbance? This hardly sounds like the actions of a multi-millionaire."

Jacob looks thoughtful. "Well, he lost his family on Black Friday—his wife, daughter and unborn son. A tragedy like that can unhinge a man. He may have snapped . . . flown off the deep end. And maybe he wanted vengeance."

"I'd say. So why would he head west?"

"God only knows. Frankly, I was hoping you could shed some light. Know anyone in the Dominion who has family?"

I think about it. "No one I can think of. Most of the guys are loners. Single. Lonely. And have been for quite some time. Some, like Shane and Cyril, are said to have girlfriends. Roch apparently has several whores floating around. I doubt any are involved in—or are even aware of—their activities."

"Darn."

"Do you think he's in B.C.?" I ask.

"We have reason to believe B.C. may have been his ultimate destination . . . most likely the Vancouver area." He pauses. "Have you heard of anything coming out of Vancouver?"

"Nope."

"Ever been asked to deliver something to Vancouver?"

"Never."

"Has anyone else? Another member?"

"Not that I'm aware of."

"Is the Dominion active in Vancouver?"

"I don't know."

Jacob rubs his brow in frustration. "Are any of the members from Vancouver or do they have contacts in Vancouver?"

"Reverend Hunt was originally from Vancouver, but he relocated many years ago. Roland was also from that area. It's possible either Mario or Cyril or some of the others still have contacts out there, but none that I know of."

"Nothing in Edmonton, Calgary or Winnipeg?"

"Not that I'm aware of."

Jacob goes through each and every member I've identified thus far, repeating the same questions. Do they have family there? Do they have friends there? Any contacts there? Businesses? I can sense his mounting frustration and desperation. I wish I had more information to give him. I keep hoping I'll have an answer to his next question. This doesn't happen, though. With every negative reply, I feel I'm letting him down, that I'm letting the whole country down. I want to contribute. I also want to please and impress, like a dog wanting to please his owner. Like a student wanting to please a teacher. Sometimes, it feels as though I'm being tested, as though he already knows the answer. I know he knows more.

"What about Mr. Black's bank accounts?" I ask, turning the tables.

"I was just about to get to that." He sets aside some documents and pulls up new ones. "You won't believe this. More wire transfers are being done, some as recent as last week. Again, relatively small amounts. A thousand here. A thousand there. Nothing worthy enough to raise suspicion. Most are transfers to E-Z Grocery, some to E-Z Travel. These are being done through the smallest of his accounts, which is down to just under a million. His larger account, now down to 3.4 million, is also showing activity in the form of slightly larger withdrawals. Not wire transfers. Twenty-five K here. Fifty K there. We're not sure where this money is going. We haven't learned anything new, but that's OK. This shows there's still activity. Funny thing though—although there are many indications he's out west, none of the transactions have occurred out there. Most are done right here in southern Ontario, others in the northeastern U.S. Needless to say, we're getting close."

"That's good to hear," I say as Jacob pours us each another drink.

"Which brings me to the E-Z businesses," he continues. "While we contemplated freezing their bank accounts, including Mr. Black's, it was too risky. We—"

"You were going to freeze the bank accounts? Are you out of your—"

"Listen to me," Jacob says. "It was just thrown out there but everyone agreed it would jeopardize the whole operation. Besides, we're still missing some pieces of the puzzle. We know that E-Z Grocery imports fish and produce from Serbia, but we still have doubts that the transactions are legit. We've just approached our Serbian contacts."

I shoot him a puzzled look.

"I know—it took a while. We have to be careful. Anyway, we have people we can trust. They're looking into it at their end. Now we wait."

"Are you sure they can be trusted?"

"Positive. We've used contacts we have a long history with."

"OK."

I watch as Jacob sets aside some documents and retrieves yet another set from his briefcase. "We're still looking into Dino's Wrecking Yard. We've had surveillance on it since learning of the commercial vans. So far, nothing."

"I haven't heard of any connection between Dino's and the Dominion."

"It could've been a bad tip, I suppose," Jacob replies. "But we have to investigate every lead. We're also still looking into Brent Weiss and Wes Sanderson at the border. This is especially tricky. We haven't brought this up with the CBSA nor with the CBP. Not yet. The FBI is looking into it at their end. We're looking into it at ours. We're keeping a close eye on them. So far, we've found no link between the two and the Dominion of God. Have you been asked to deliver anything in the past month or so?"

"No, I haven't."

"OK. Well, the next time you do, we'll be ready."

I say nothing and look on as Jacob shuffles through his documents and notepads. "If you don't mind, I'd just like to pick your brain once again about the mosque bombings," he says. "Keep in mind that, as I mentioned, the explosives used in the U.S. bombings were C-4 while TATP was used over on our side."

"OK."

"Well, the explosives were manufactured at the Milan Army Ammunition Plant in Tennessee. Milan is operated by AO—that's American Ordnance LLC. The U.S. military is the primary purchaser and recipient of its products. Up until this point, there were no reports of stolen explosives. However, there appears to be a discrepancy between the line of production numbers for M112 demolition charges and the inventory. In all, three hundred M112s—that's three hundred seventy-five pounds of C-4—and approximately three hundred detonators are unaccounted for. Gone. Completely vanished. Obviously, this is serious. This would be one of the biggest—if not *the* biggest—theft of explosive materials in U.S. history. So, the U.S. military and the FBI are currently investigating with the cooperation of AO."

Jacob rubs his temples as if trying to stave off a headache. "This isn't the work of one man. One man alone could not have pulled this off. It had to be an inside job, perhaps even within the military ranks. Our U.S. counterparts have provided us with a list of names and photos of all employees—over one thousand of them—who may have had access to the plant as far back as five years. This includes contractors, military civilians and AO employees." He pauses to retrieve two large envelopes from his briefcase. From them, he pulls out what appears to be countless photocopies of IDs—perhaps access cards of some type. "I was wondering if you'd mind going through these. You never know, maybe you'd recognize some of the faces or names?"

"All of them?" I retort in disbelief. "We could be here all night!"

Jacob looks apologetic. "Yeah, I know. I also have a few pics and info on individuals whose I.P. addresses have led us to Vica.net and The Prophet's email account. We're pretty sure they're victims of a sophisticated system of I.P. masking or rerouting. An old man in Cincinnati. A family in Australia. A government office in Switzerland. Still, we can't overlook anything."

I glance at my watch. It's now 3:00 a.m. I'm tired to the point of exhaustion, but, grumbling, I tell Jacob I'll go through the IDs, though not before making a call to Raoul to assure him I've got the $50,000 I owe him—the $50,000 Jacob says is waiting for me in a secure briefcase in Sergeant Kipling's office.

I make the call with Jacob sitting in the next room. He assures me that the caller ID for the safe house will show up as an unknown number and is untraceable. He also assures me that should anything happen, he and Kipling have my back. According to Jacob, local, regional and provincial police forces have been keeping a close eye on Raoul and Omar for quite some time.

The call lasts no more than a minute. Raoul seldom remains on the phone for too long. He sounds pleased—as pleased as Raoul can sound. He tells me to meet him today at noon out in Scarborough. As expected, he'll accept only cash. What a sleazebag. Loan sharks apparently don't even take breaks on Christmas.

I brief Jacob after hanging up with Raoul. He promises me he'll get in touch with Kipling, who'll then get in touch with Toronto Regional Police, who'll observe the transaction from afar. Should anything go wrong, my back will be covered.

We spend the next hour or so going over the pics of those potentially linked to Vica.net as well as the ammunition plant photo IDs. As suspected, I don't recognized any of the pics drawn from the Vica.net investigation. As for the ammunition plant photos, I study each one carefully. Most are Caucasian males in their thirties or forties. After going through the first few hundred, I freeze at one particular photo. Shaved head. Blue eyes. Pale complexion. Likely in his thirties.

"This guy—he seems very familiar."

Jacob studies the photo. "Hank Mitchell Jr. You know him?"

"No, can't say I do . . . but the face . . ."

"You recognize him?"

No matter how hard I try, I can't pinpoint where I may have seen this man. Or maybe I've never seen him—who knows? Perhaps he simply looks like someone I know. One thing is for certain, I've never met anyone by the name of Hank Mitchell Jr. But that doesn't mean anything given that few in the Dominion go by their real names.

"I'm not sure," I reply. "But he does seem awfully familiar."

"Think good and hard," Jacob coaches, tapping on the picture. "It's very possible he's changed his appearance. He'd also be a few years older too now."

I stare intently, fatigue setting in. "I'm sorry, Jacob. I just can't put a finger on it. My mind is numb and I'm exhausted." I look at my watch. "It's 4:15 in the morning."

In turn, Jacob looks at his watch. "OK. Let's break for the night. I'm exhausted myself. Maybe some rest will help spark something. We should go through them again in the morning. And I'll do a little digging on Mr. Mitchell tomorrow . . . or I guess that's today now. You wanna crash here for the night?"

Although the offer is tempting, I explain to Jacob my need to get back to the apartment to pick some things up before meeting Raoul and Omar, and then leaving for Pickering if all goes well and where I hope to spend some quiet time with Sarah and her mother. I tell him that I'll take a look at the photos again upon my return. He tries desperately to coax me into staying in town. I don't blame him. I want to get to the bottom of this as much as he does, probably even worse. But in the end, understanding familial obligations, he respects my decision.

"We may have more photos to come," he informs me before parting. "The FBI is gathering info on all personnel who would've had direct access to C-4 containment units or bunkers at the plant, including those involved in the shipment and transportation of explosives. Their investigation is ongoing."

"Sounds good."

"Oh, and one more thing," Jacob continues, packing up his briefcase. "What about triacetone triperoxide? You know, the Mother of Satan. Any mention of it within the Dominion's circles? Know of any members involved in fabricating it? Or where it could've been produced?"

"No, sorry."

"What about anyone charged with the purchase of hydrogen peroxide? Or acetone? Or acid?"

"No, no, and no. Look, I've already answered—"

"What about a member of the Dominion with a background in chemistry, or someone well versed in the fabrication of explosives?"

"I'm sorry, I can't think of anyone," I reply, frustrated. I can't help but feel that my value as an informant decreases with every question left unanswered. "There's never been any mention of bomb-making! I've never heard anything about any lab. They don't tell me anything—I'm too low in the food chain! I've delivered mail. Briefcases! That's it!"

At this point, Jacob runs his hands through his already messy hair and exhales. He apologizes for his persistence and slips on his winter jacket. I do the same, and minutes later we're back out into the cold. A light, granular snow has started falling. The streets are even calmer than before.

"Hey, did I tell you my wife and I are pregnant?" he blurts out after settling in the car.

"That's great news." I shake his hand, trying my best to appear enthusiastic. "Congratulations."

"Thanks! We're due in the summer."

"Cool. Boy or girl?"

"We don't know. Actually, we don't want to know. More of a surprise that way . . . my wife just loves surprises."

At my request, Jacob drives me all the way to the other side of downtown, where he drops me off a few blocks away from home. Before we part, he says I'm to call him in the morning an hour before I leave to meet with Raoul. He also reminds me that my services will be needed again when more information becomes available with respect to the investigations into the murders of the three Muslims.

If information becomes available . . .

For now, the only thing that really matters to me is getting the $50,000 into Raoul's hands by noon today. I just hope Jacob and Sergeant Kipling maintain their end of the bargain.

CHAPTER 30

It's 9:00 a.m. when the alarm sounds. Disoriented, I nearly forget where or who I am. When leading a double life with little sleep and a constant diet of stress, my mind tends to do that every now and then. Confusing fantasy with reality. Mixing up stories and roles. Getting caught in lies. Sometimes, I fear losing my sanity altogether. I keep picturing myself in a straitjacket, like in those movies where the conclusion reveals the main character had an alter ego all along and just didn't know it. Too many late nights in strange places are going to be the death of me. Nowadays, if I'm lucky, I may get two hours' sleep per night, three at best.

I manage to drag my ass out of bed and have a quick shower. I wolf down a bowl of milk-less cereal and pack my bags for a short stay in Pickering. Then I call Jacob, who's miraculously already up and about. He tells me that Kipling is on standby with the money. I'm to meet him at 10:45 in a Ryerson University parking lot for pickup. Then I'm to make my way to Scarborough to meet with my so-called lenders.

In my dilapidated Ford Focus I exit the underground parking beneath our apartment complex and head to Ryerson. There, Kipling is waiting patiently for me in a dark Pathfinder. He says nothing more than a "good luck" and hands me a rather worn, black-leather briefcase. Although it's a secure briefcase, it's unlocked. He hands me the key and sends me on my way.

Once in the safety of my vehicle, I open the briefcase. Inside, stacks of one hundred dollar bills are neatly aligned one atop the other. Not that I don't have faith in Jacob or Kipling. I just need to see it for myself. At least I don't bother counting. I trust the math is right.

It's just past noon by the time I reach the specified location in Scarborough. There, Raoul is standing by a pay phone with Omar and a man I don't recognize waiting in a Lexus. I park two spaces away.

Raoul notices me instantly and a large grin spreads across his tanned face, which is plagued with acne scars. "Liam, didn't think you were gonna make it," he says, as Omar and the other large man exit the Lexus.

I quickly scan the area to make sure there aren't any other surprises. I also try to spot any of Kipling's men or undercover cops lurking about, but I don't see any. I sure as hell hope they're around. One can never be too careful around men like Raoul. A verbal agreement and a handshake mean nothing to his kind. On a whim, he could demand the whole amount today, all depending on his mood. Just to be a real ass. His thugs, Omar and this other ninth wonder of the world, would love nothing more than to dispose of troublesome creditors and earn their pay.

"Holy mother of God! Look at you!" Raoul mocks, looking over to his two associates and pointing at the briefcase. "Look at this guy! A briefcase! You're all business today, huh, my friend?"

"You prefer I put it in a garbage bag?" I reply sarcastically.

He ignores the remark. "Give it to me."

I hand him the briefcase. Omar and his partner are now standing beside Raoul, staring menacingly and breathing heavily in their black leather jackets and cheap gold chains and cheap gold rings. Real gangster wannabes. I don't bother looking at them. Not even acknowledging their presence is my best defense. I can tell it's irritating them, but I don't care.

Raoul turns and lays the briefcase flat onto the front hood of the recently waxed Lexus. Unlatching it, he opens it and grabs a stack of one-hundred-dollar bills. He counts them one by one and returns the stack to its original place. He then takes another pile and counts them one by one.

"It's all there, Raoul . . ."

"Mind your fuckin' business, asshole," Omar growls, taking a step forward.

Raoul continues to count. After finishing the second stack, he turns to me. "OK, tell you what. I don't count now. I'll count later. But if there's one dollar missing, one *cent* even, I'll come back for your skin—and your girl's. How about that?"

"You know what? I'd like to see you count it," I say. I just can't trust him. Every dollar could be accounted for and yet he'd turn around and tell me it isn't. In the end, however, he refuses to stand there any longer.

"Hey, looks like I've been a good boy this year," Raoul says, closing the briefcase. "Santa's brought me a nice big present! OK. We're good. I don't know how you came up with this, but you did and that's all that matters to me." He then hands the case over to Omar. "Do you have a key for this thing?"

I give him the key.

"You did good," he says, putting his arm around my shoulders. "To be honest, I thought you were bluffing. I thought you'd skip town. That would've put me in an awfully bad mood. So, you're left with a balance of $50,000. And seeing as I'm in such a good mood, I'll give you a month to come up with it."

"A month?? Raoul I can't—"

"What? You prefer two weeks like I said before?"

"No, no! But I can't possibly come up with that money! It's a miracle I was able to come up with this today! I need more time!"

"Ah yes! Time again. Always more time . . ." he says, thinking. "I don't care what you did to get that money. Prostitute yourself for all I care. Whatever you did, do it again. Have the money by March 1st. Not a day more. That gives you two months now. Happy? But if you're even one day late, you and your girl will be digging each other's grave. *Capice*? Don't disappoint me."

"Fine."

"Good day to you then, my friend," he finishes, retreating to his vehicle, with Omar and his partner following. The car quickly speeds away from the parking lot, leaving me behind in the cold wind.

I head to my own vehicle but not before taking one last look around. The lot is vacant. No signs of Kipling or his team anywhere. Businesses are closed for the holidays. The skies are overcast. A weather system is on the horizon, reminding me I'd better get going before the skies come down.

I veer out the parking area and eventually make my way onto the 401 en route to Pickering and Christmas dinner. I've been looking forward to this for a while. A break. An asylum. A temporary but much needed exile from all this madness.

CHAPTER 31

My days in Pickering with Sarah and her mother pass by in the blink of an eye. For me, there's no real escape there, because news of the execution of the three Muslim men has spread around the globe. Violent protests have finally broken out in many Muslim nations. Locally, tensions between Christians and Muslims are at an all-time high. To make matters worse, Saudi Arabia and other Islamic regimes have threatened to shut down their embassies and consulates until their security can be assured and until the Dominion of God is brought to justice. The tragic outcome of the kidnappings has not only reopened some very recent wounds but has also exacerbated Muslims' searing frustration at the government's inability to apprehend those responsible.

I suspect this is what the Dominion wants, like most extremists: to divide the population, to break down communication and good relations between religious communities, to incite anger and hatred among religious sects, and to provoke the most fundamentalist and extremist members of society. Any riots or protests or threats of breaking diplomatic ties are considered a moral victory for the group.

It's also occurred to me that these attacks—be it the mosque bombings or the kidnappings—may simply be a test: a way for the Dominion to gage the strength and deception of the Devil himself and to measure the arrival and the form of the Antichrist. To the Dominion, the peace talks—let alone the progress made—is a definite sign that the Devil's influence is unfaltering and that the Antichrist, who it believes has taken the form of the heads of the European Union, is on the verge of fostering a peace treaty that will mark the beginning of Tribulation.

And the beginning of the end of the world.

So no peace of mind for me during the holidays. Even Sarah's mother noticed a difference in my behavior. *You seem rather distracted, Liam. Are you OK, Liam? Liam, you seem fidgety.* And on and on it went. When I wasn't being accused of being distracted, I just slept. And before I knew it, I was heading back to my chaotic life in the city.

With her mother not doing so well, Sarah decides to remain in Pickering to care for her and commute to work for the next week or two. It's been really tough on her, seeing her mother deteriorate like that. Though only 73, a series of small strokes have left her struggling to remember how to do simple things, like using an oven or a microwave. She needs to be re-taught such things and to re-learn some motor skills all over again. Sarah's mentioned placing her in a nursing home, but her mom refuses to even entertain the idea. This has also been a contentious issue between Sarah and me, as neither of us have any clue as to where we'd come up with the funds to put her in a decent home. It weighs heavily on my mind the whole trip back to the city. Still, Sarah's absence will at least provide me with an opportunity to do more work for the Dominion—and for Jacob for that matter—without having to pathologically lie my integrity away.

Whether it's out of decency or due to a lack of progress in the case, I don't hear from Jacob during my break. Whatever the reason, I'm sure he and Kipling were kept busy.

I haven't even made it through the door when my cell phone rings. Staggering with my baggage and fumbling to find it, I drop everything once inside and go digging in my pockets. "Hello?" I say, panting slightly.

At the other end, there's silence.

"Hello?" I ask again.

"I'm looking for the Mailman . . ." A rather creepy voice announces.

"This is him."

"You're needed for a delivery ASAP."

"Sorry, no can do—"

"I'm not asking you," says the voice, sternly. "The Warehouse. Be there in an hour."

"Now you listen to me—"

"No, you listen to me! This is a direct order from the highest level. You have no choice but to attend to the matter. Make the delivery or face the consequences."

The caller hangs up and I sit there listening to the dial tone. I instinctively think of calling Jacob. When I do, I get an automated message indicating his mailbox is full. I spend the next several minutes mulling over how I can get myself out of this, but come up with nothing. I even entertain the thought of picking up Sarah and skipping town, but there's no point. It'd only make the Dominion suspicious and God knows that's the last thing I need. Besides, they'd end up finding me anyway. There's no running and there's no hiding—not from the Dominion of God.

The "Warehouse" is actually a code word that Miroslav came up with for E-Z Travel. By the time I get there, Conrad and Derek are there waiting in a black CR-V in the parking area at the back. In the back seat are two men in blindfolds.

"You're late," Conrad scoffs, flicking his cigarette to the ground through the open window.

"What the hell is this all about?" I ask, suddenly apprehensive.

Conrad exits the vehicle holding a dark cloth. "Relax, we have an emergency meeting at a very secret location. We have to blindfold everyone. Boss's orders. We'll take the blindfolds off once we get there."

I look closely into the parked vehicle and am able to identify Mario and Roch as the masked men. "Are you kidding me? Blindfolds?"

"Sorry Liam, boss's orders."

"The boss? You mean Black Mamba? Who the hell is this guy anyway? I swear an oath and pledge to support someone I don't even know! It'd be nice to know who the hell I'm following here and what his intentions are!"

"You will . . . in time," Derek replies calmly, from the front passenger seat.

"When?"

"When it's time for that part of the plan," Conrad says. "Liam, you sound as though you don't trust us. You have to trust us if you want us to trust you. You have to believe in our leader as he believes in you. I assure you, there's nothing to worry about. It's just a little technicality, an inconvenience."

"You wanna talk about trust? We're being blindfolded! So you tell me, who's not trusting who here?"

"It has nothing to do with trust and everything to do with precaution and need-to-know. Ironically, we're inviting those who we trust the most. It's a necessity that you don't know, at least not at this point in time."

"What if I say no?"

Conrad releases a half-hearted laugh. "Then you have something to worry about!"

From the front seat, Derek breaks out in laughter too.

Conrad invites me to turn around and face the car. I hesitate for several seconds, which seem like an eternity. I don't like the looks of this. But I'm afraid that if I refuse to go, I'd only give them a reason to be suspicious or to completely shut me out, which would mean the end of me. The fact that no one knows I'm here—not even Jacob—makes me even less confident. The only consolation I get is the sight of Mario and Roch sitting in their blindfolds. At least I'm not alone in this strange predicament. That, and the fact that this might put me in a unique position to acquire intelligence about this secret location.

Reluctantly, I turn around and let Conrad fasten the blindfold, which darkens my world instantly. I'm then guided into the car, taking a seat next to the middleman—which would be Mario. We exchange nervous greetings. Curiously, neither Mario nor Roch seem fazed. Quite the opposite—they exchange brief pleasantries and crack jokes, perhaps in an effort to lighten the mood.

"So can you at least tell us what this meeting is about?" I ask once Conrad has taken his seat and started the vehicle.

"Relax," he says. "It's just a little recap of our past operation. And preparation for future ones."

Mario and Roch also have their questions. Yet no matter how much we ask, or how much we insist, we get no further answers. It's now clear to me that neither Mario nor Roch has any idea as to what's going on.

In a matter of moments, we're back onto what can only be Finch Avenue. Shortly after, the car swerves in a complete circle clockwise which can only mean we're on a ramp. And judging by the ensuing increase of speed and the absence of stops, we embark on what can only be Highway 400 heading south, I think.

I try to make a mental note of anything and everything I can that would help me retrace my steps. Stops. Turns. Any and all sounds. Even the faintest glow of sunlight peering through the blindfold. Anything that could help me identify the route taken for this protected location.

Less than five minutes on the 400, I get another cue. Total darkness. The sound of our own vehicle reverberating off the walls of a confined space. It only lasts a second or two, but it's obvious: we've just gone under an overpass. The faintest glow of sunlight is back again. This happens another three times as we stay on course for quite sometime without taking any turns or reducing much speed. While its possible we're still on the 400, its more likely we're now on Black Creek Drive which the highway eventually becomes.

We finally end up taking a slight left and continue on this path for several minutes. At some point, we end up taking a hard left followed immediately by our passing under another overpass. Only this time, I can hear the sound of a train roaring overhead. This is followed by another overpass a minute or so later followed by a sharp right. The speed is reduced as we end up turning right one more time until coming to a complete stop. The engine is killed.

The door to my left opens and I'm guided out of the vehicle. Mario and Roch follow behind me. A distinctive sound fills the air—a distant but constant humming sound, like that of high voltage electricity. I make a mental note. One by one, we're escorted up steps—five in all—leading to a concrete platform. I hear the chiming sound of a set of keys. A door is unlocked and opened. We're then guided inside the mystery location, where our blindfolds are removed.

Even without the blindfold, it's very dark inside. A large garage door to my immediate left suggests we're standing in a loading zone of some type. Dusty skids stacked atop one another rest against the opposite wall. Light from another area at the end of a small corridor reveals thick dust floating about. This other area, which I can only see from afar, appears to be the front of the edifice—perhaps a lobby or atrium of some kind. The main space is large and empty, with most of its walls and ceiling gutted. Wires and piping protrude from spaces where ceiling tiles used to be. Boxes, tools, paint cans and various containers are scattered throughout the room.

Whoever the proprietors of the building are, they don't appear interested in keeping it heated. It's as bloody cold inside as it is outdoors. In the air there's a strong scent of some industrial product, like paint—only it's not paint. I've smelled paint before. This smells much stronger than paint. More like paint thinner or nail polish.

"Down here," Conrad beckons from halfway down a staircase leading to the basement level.

Cautiously, we follow him down a narrow stairwell until we reach the lower level, with Derek behind us. The floor and walls here are nothing but concrete. All is dark. Other voices become audible. The further down we go, the stronger and more acrid the scent becomes. The air also becomes damper and mustier.

We eventually make our way down a dark corridor, passing by several unopened doors, until we're greeted by Miroslav, who leads us to the only opened door at the far end of the hall. Already waiting inside and seated side by side on old office chairs are Cyril, Shane, and Vladimir. Standing directly in front of them are four other men I can't identify. Next to Cyril, three empty chairs await us.

Conrad slams the door behind us and quickly gets down to business. "Gentlemen, please have a seat."

I lead the way and take a seat next to Cyril, with Mario and Roch taking the two remaining chairs. Conrad, Miroslav, Derek and the unidentified men remain standing before us.

"Conrad, what's this about?" Mario asks defiantly.

My eyes remain glued on the seven men standing before me. I immediately recognize that something is terribly wrong and that we haven't been invited here for a meeting or to be given instruction for another mission. A cold sweat pours down my forehead, which I hope no one notices.

Distraught, Roch suddenly rises from his chair in protest. With an open hand, Derek motions for him to go no further. Slowly, he drops his hand, guiding Roch back to his seat. "Relax, we're just here to talk—and to get to the bottom of something."

Silence.

"In case you haven't heard," says, Conrad, "a few of Miroslav's business contacts recently received not-so-friendly visits from several police and security agencies over in Serbia and Montenegro. Their businesses were raided and their assets were seized."

A cold chill runs down my spine.

"So what does this have to do with us?" Mario asks angrily.

"Well, Mario, this poses a serious question. Why did the Serbian authorities do such a thing? Why would they suddenly raid each and every business that has regular dealings with Miroslav's enterprise here in Toronto?" He pauses to let the questions sink in. None of us say a word, but we all know what's being implied. "You see, the only place this information can be found is in Miroslav's books. And the only place Miroslav keeps his books is in a safe at E-Z Travel."

Those of us seated exchange nervous glances.

"Gentlemen, you're all the common denominator," Derek says, scowling. "You were the only ones involved in this operation. You were the only ones who were given access to Miroslav's office. Therefore, you were the only ones who could've accessed this information. Thankfully for us, this was bogus information that had been planted for such an eventuality."

Again, silence. I don't even breathe.

"There is a Judas among us," Derek continues, pulling out a pistol from his inner jacket pocket. He points it to each of our foreheads in turn. "A rat. A filthy, scum-sucking rat. Pretending to be one of us. Siding with the Beast. Secretly trying to lead us astray from the path of righteousness . . ."

Again, we exchange glares. In the eyes of my fellow detainees, I see confusion, fear and anger. I also see wonder—and a sudden distrust of the person sitting next to him. I see suspicion and disgust at being betrayed. I can only hope the same can be seen in my eyes.

"So, which one of you will come clean?" Derek asks, studying each of us. "Which one of you will repent and be given a chance for salvation?"

No one makes a sound.

"This is your last chance to be among us when the time of the Rapture is upon us!"

"Jesus Christ, Derek! Put the gun down!" Mario begs, prompting a chorus of pleas from the other men, including me.

My heart pounds heavily within my chest, each beat so powerful that I begin to wonder whether it can be heard by the others. I try my best to control my breathing. I know that if I reveal myself, I'll never again see the light of day. I have no choice but to remain quiet—as long and as best as I can.

"If you think for one second that we don't know who it is," Conrad rages, his voice echoing throughout the ducts, "you sure got something coming to you!"

"Damn it, Conrad! It sure as hell ain't me!" Mario insists, raising his voice to match those of our interrogators.

"Me either!" Roch says, following suit.

"Enough!" Conrad shouts, stepping forward and cocking a pistol of his own. "This is your last chance to come clean! Save yourself now!!"

Again, everybody remains silent. Seconds feel like minutes. Minutes like hours. My mind races. *They're onto me. What do I do? What do I say? Say something, Liam, or you're dead. Say something, say something . . .*

Then, Derek aims his pistol at Cyril and unloads three rounds—two in his chest and one in his forehead. His lifeless body slumps forward, revealing bloody exit wounds through his blood stained shirt. A large, fleshy crater is all that remains at the back of his head. The wall behind him is covered in brain matter and shards of bone.

I stare in horror at the lifeless mess next to me. I nervously wipe away the spray of blood that covers my face. The only thought that remains wedged in my head is that I'm going to be next.

"Let this be a lesson to all of you," Conrad barks, staring us deep in the eyes. "Treason will not go unpunished. This man has chosen his destiny. He has strayed from the path. He now sails into the afterlife, in sin. He has chosen the side of the Beast, the way of the false prophets. His forehead will not bear the seal of God. He will be left behind at the time of the Rapture. He will not be among us in the Kingdom of Heaven."

My eyes return to the limp body as it finally collapses to the floor. *Cyril? They think it was Cyril? How can that be? No, that should be me there. Cyril was not a snitch. He was not working for the feds . . . was he?*

"We have a purpose! We have a destiny! Do you understand? We are doing the Lord's work!" Derek pauses and points to Cyril's body. "This . . . this infidel . . . was no different than one of them. Remember, we are at war! We must be aware and beware of the evil that will try to lead us astray. The Tribulation is nearly upon us, and only the strong and the righteous will survive! Gentlemen, we've all taken an oath! A covenant with God! Do not break that covenant!"

"Damn it, Derek! Was that necessary?" Shane shouts, pointing to Cyril.

"An example must be set," Derek replies, turning away from us. "Chapter 14-1 of *The Last Testament* reveals the Angel before Roland and it said: 'Beware of the Beast and his allies for they will wear two faces and profess to be one of you. Death is to fall upon them in the swiftest of ways so they can find their place with the Beast and await their fate in the lake of fire'!"

"Much damage could have been done," Conrad interjects. "Thankfully, Black Mamba's been looking after us. He's our prophet and our shepherd guiding us through the valley of darkness. He knew of this betrayal. He had foreseen it."

"So the Serbs are investigating the wrong businesses?" Mario asks.

"That's right."

I sit there, pondering the ramifications of giving Jacob bogus information.

"Just to keep you all on your toes, that's all," Derek adds with a smirk, "You're among our best men. We'll need you in the months to come. To provide leadership and guidance to a wave of new followers."

"But we need to be able to do our jobs without worrying about taking a bullet between the eyes!" Mario shouts, visibly upset. "I have a real hard time believing Cyril was a snitch. What proof have you got?"

"Black Mamba has all the proof he needs. All you have to do is be true to the Dominion of God. Be true to yourselves. Do that and you'll never have anything to worry about again," Derek assures us, putting away his pistol. "You are our brothers and we love you as such. Black Mamba loves us as such. Now, let's put this behind us and move forward. The Tribulation is upon us. War—or at least our part in it—will start very soon. It'll be a dark and difficult period. Black Mamba will prepare us for the Rapture and the Second Coming."

Derek directs us out of our chairs and one by one, kisses us on the forehead. Meant as a sign of brotherhood, to me it feels more like the kiss of death. He then heads for the door and motions for us to follow. "Come, we have much work to do . . ."

CHAPTER 32

Those left standing, that is, Mario, Roch, Shane, Vladimir and me, are invited to leave the room in which Cyril's corpse lies in a pool of blood. Without asking further questions, we get up from our chairs and exit the room. We're then guided upstairs by Derek, who leads us into the corridor and across the empty lobby to a room in which sits a large, dusty table. Several chairs surround it. We each take a seat. Conrad, Miroslav and the other interrogators stay behind, likely to clean up the mess and dispose of the body.

I take this time to get over the shock of literally having dodged a bullet that had my name written all over it. It had to be meant for me. *Had they made a mistake? Was Cyril really a snitch?* I doubt that very much. As for the raiding of the Serb companies, I have a bone to pick with Jacob.

"What was that all about, Derek?" Mario asks, finally breaking the silence.

"Cyril was not worthy of the cause. He was a weak link. His loyalty didn't rest with the Dominion of God. He was a traitor."

"Cyril a traitor? That's impossible! He was—"

"Gentlemen, please, we need to move on." Derek retrieves some newspapers and magazine clippings from a briefcase. He then hands them out and invites us to skim through them. "As you may or may not have heard, the case against Abdil al-Zahhari is about to be dismissed. It's anticipated that he'll walk as the federal prosecutors have had to withdraw some key intelligence that was rendered inadmissible by the Court because it was obtained by *torture*."

"Torture my ass . . ." Mario interjects.

"Some believe that the judge is sympathetic to Abdil's position due to his age at the time of his involvement and because of his father's stature and involvement in humanitarian organizations—Doctors

Without Borders being one of them. And the father has ties to several government ministers, who in turn have close ties with Federal Court judges whom they've appointed. As you're probably well aware, this trial has been marked by a manipulation of the very system that is meant to protect innocent Christians like you and I."

Derek pauses to let us catch up on our reading. "Gentlemen, a murderer is about to walk our streets once again. A terrorist. A monster! One of the Devil's own! A crime against good and innocent Christians is about to go unpunished. The system has failed us again. Justice will not been served!"

A loud reaction ensues, the others in full agreement.

"Mark my word, the other three will each walk free as well, and their assault on our way of life, on our spirit, on our morals and principles, will continue."

"So what does this have to do with us?" Mario asks.

"We have to put our foot down and tell the world that terrorists cannot have free rein. And as the sole defenders of God's kingdom, we must defend ourselves! The enemy has many tactics. The total and utter subversion of our legal system is just one of its many methods, and it is but a step toward our annihilation!"

At this point, Conrad and Miroslav enter the room.

"Ah, brothers," Derek greets them. "I was just bringing our fellow disciples up to speed on our next operation. Join us!" Then all three repeat the same rhetoric in order to reinforce their point and to further strengthen the conviction within every man. It's nothing more than a form of brainwashing, a characteristic of the Dominion of God. Us versus them. Good versus evil. And on and on it goes.

Of the three, Derek is by far the most passionate and convincing speaker. He's also the most devout and the most wicked. His conviction is unlike anything I've ever seen before. It's even crossed my mind many times that Derek himself may be this mysterious and elusive Black Mamba. After all, he was Roland's protégé, so to speak, during the early days of the Dominion. Yet no matter how much I try to rationalize this, something tells me he isn't this so-called newest prophet at all.

After force-feeding everyone and providing a convincing yet skewed perception of reality, and after providing sufficient justification as to why action should be taken to correct this reality, they lay the plan out before us.

As with the case of the imam and the ambassador and his son, we discuss several remedial scenarios. This, of course, is assuming al-Zahhari doesn't stand trial. While Mario, Roch and Shane are in a favor of a simple assassination, Derek and the others argue for another kidnapping—this time for a ransom. As much as ten million dollars is proposed. They insist that it's necessary to obtain the cash needed to fund the war.

"It's never going to work, Derek!" Mario shouts in protest. "They'll never pay us! Who are we kidding? They'll just laugh in our faces! How would this happen without it leading the cops straight to us?"

"That's not for you to worry about," Derek replies dismissively. "Besides, this is just an initial discussion. Nothing's been decided yet. Black Mamba will give his orders in due course."

"What would we do with him if we don't get the money?" I ask.

"Then justice and the Lord shall be served," says Derek. "When the time comes, you'll be contacted. A decision is expected in a matter of weeks. Stay abreast of the situation. Stay informed. Read the newspapers. Watch the news. Watch not just for the Toronto Four, but for the peace process overseas."

"I want you all to continue in your recruitment activities," Conrad says, interjecting. "You've all done a great job and we've found some suitable candidates who we've taken under our wing. Some are already among us. You may have met them. Others you likely haven't. Others are soon to come. We're growing stronger and we must keep growing stronger."

Derek takes the lead again. "The goal is for each of you to bring us at least five new potential per month. For these purposes, we'll meet monthly. Things are heating up and you're going to be kept busy. But be careful. Be very, very vigilant. Don't reveal yourselves. You are not to talk about the workings of the Dominion or its membership to anyone. The need-to-know principle is in effect and always will be. Should you deviate from these rules, you will be reprimanded."

"What's our goal, Derek?" I finally ask. "I mean, are we still aiming for Roland's one hundred and forty-four thousand?"

Derek looks to me as though annoyed. "In the end, there will be one hundred and forty-four thousand of us. *The Last Testament* says so, as does the New Testament before it. Roland and the others will be there, as will we. There may not be one hundred and forty-four thousand of us at the start of the Tribulation, but there will be at its end."

I simply nod, as do the others.

"Any other questions?"

We all shake our heads.

As Derek finishes handing out his instructions, a strange but familiar noise is heard overhead. It begins with a distant screech, following by a soft humming sound. I follow the sound up to the ceiling and notice a large ventilation duct left uncovered. That's when it strikes me. I take a quick and inconspicuous look around the room and notice the walls are bare, painted in plain white—just like in the video released by the Dominion in which it claimed responsibility for the kidnappings.

Could this be where they held the imam and company? I ask myself. The more I think about it, the more convinced I am that it is. *Perhaps not in this very room, but somewhere . . .*

We conclude the meeting with a recap of the matters discussed. Then, one by one, we're blindfolded once again. All goes black.

I'm escorted out the same door we came in and led down the steps of the loading dock into a vehicle I can only assume is the same one that got me here—at least it feels and smells the same. I'm then reunited with Mario and Roch as we struggle to make room in the back seat. The others, it seems, are led to another vehicle that I can hear speeding away shortly before we do.

Within twenty minutes or so, after Mario and Roch are dropped off, my blindfold is removed. Only Conrad remains with me in the vehicle. I find myself in the familiar surroundings of Little Portugal. Before we part, Conrad reminds me to avoid any discussions about the Dominion of God and the "sacrifices" that were offered to God on Christmas morning, and also to keep a close eye on the trial of Abdil al-Zahhari. He adds that I can expect further instructions in the weeks to come.

He then expresses appreciation for my recruitment efforts and my cross-border services, which he insists have been invaluable to the movement. He lets me know I'm expected to play a bigger role in the weeks and months to come.

After being dropped off, I quickly make my way home and give Jacob a phone call—and a piece of my mind. I let him know that whatever blunder happened in Serbia hasn't only gotten an "innocent" man killed—I use that term loosely—but has nearly cost me my life. That said, it still boggles my mind why the Dominion would suspect Cyril of being the informant. *Was Jacob running another source that I wasn't aware of? Was any other entity running an informant against the Dominion of God? Or was the Dominion simply mistaken?* I'm not too sure what's going on, but on my mother's grave I plan to get to the bottom of this.

CHAPTER 33

Jacob looks as though he hasn't had a minute's sleep for quite sometime. His clothes are wrinkled and his hair unkempt. His eyes are red with dark bags beneath them. I'd feel bad for him if I didn't look and feel the same.

"Why would they suspect Cyril?" he says, dumbfounded. "Liam, trust me, he was no agent of ours. Nor was he one of Kipling's. And as far as I know, the FBI isn't running anyone up here."

"I don't know why," I say, still fuming. "But they sure had good reason to suspect one of us after your damn contacts down south decided to raid those damn businesses! That could've—no, *should've*—been me with my skull blown apart! You assured me you wouldn't do anything to put my life in danger! You said your so-called *contacts* were reliable!"

Jacob is still standing, pacing back and forth and taking the odd peak out the curtain covered window. Guilt fills his eyes. "OK, calm down. Look, we had nothing to do with it. We had no idea the Serbs planned on raiding those offices. They had given us assurances. Some gung-ho hotshot down there likely went out on his own and took action. We're looking into it. Believe me, we're all very upset over this. I can guarantee you one thing though, it'll really affect our relationship with the Serbian intelligence services. The only thing I can do is apologize profusely on behalf of the agency. We're conducting a risk assessment on the matter to figure out if the investigation—if your position—has been compromised in any way."

"Compromised? I'd sure as hell say it was compromised!"

"Liam, you're currently the agency's most prized asset. We'd be damn stupid if we didn't do everything in our power to protect you."

I say nothing more, brooding.

Jacob's frustration is evident. If I didn't know any better, I'd say his concern lies more in his investigation than my well being. But I can tell he's sincerely regretful.

"Damn it, this really sets us back," he says, shaking his head. "The DOG has sent us on a wild goose chase. They're really screwing with us."

The safe house is our refuge once again. I don't know who pays the bills for this place, but they sure as hell don't care to leave the heat on. It's nearly as cold in here as it is outside, where strong northern winds have picked up. I don't even bother to remove my winter jacket. Nor does Jacob for that matter.

I tell Jacob everything that happened earlier in the day. I try the best I can to identify the area of town where Cyril's murder took place. I give him a description of the building's interior. The sights. The sounds. The smell. I even draw a plan of the main and lower levels. After examining a map in the Yellow Pages of the telephone directory we find in the room, we manage to narrow down the location to a few areas. With the description I've given him, Jacob thinks it may be enough for his surveillance to team to locate the exact whereabouts of the Dominion's secret den. Whatever the case, we both agree that finding this place may be the breakthrough that we need in cracking this investigation wide open.

A piece of information I regrettably can't offer—one that I could've easily obtained—is the vehicle's license plate. I had a chance to look at it when Conrad drove away. I can't believe I forgot that. But, in my defense, I'd just witnessed what should've been my own execution. I was in shock and my nerves were shot. All I can manage to give Jacob is a vague description of the vehicle before it sped away. Not that it really matters as it will likely end up in a million pieces at Dino & Sons or somewhere overseas.

I also tell him about the Dominion's interest in the trials of the Toronto Four—al-Zahhari's in particular—as well as the possibility of another kidnapping should he walk free. As usual, he bombards me with questions, most of which I don't have answers to.

Although he jots everything down in detail, what Jacob appears to be most interested in at the moment is obtaining further information about the murders of the imam and company. He reminds me what tremendous pressure there is to apprehend those responsible. However, I remind *him*, over and over again, that nothing much was discussed—other than a bit of bragging—regarding the sacrifices. I do suggest that perhaps the captives were held at the Dominion's secret location, drawing a comparison between the background noise in the Dominion's video and the humming I heard running throughout he building just a few hours ago.

Then Jacob returns to the mosque bombings and shows me more names and pictures of personnel at the Milan Army Ammunition Plant. Again, the ID of Hank Mitchell Jr. stands out. He also presents me with the names and photo IDs of key U.S. military personnel who would've had access to the C-4 production and storage facilities. That's when I spot him.

"Here," I say, almost shouting in excitement. "This guy . . . this is Zack! This has to be Zack, Nash's recruit!"

Jacob tears the copy away from my hands and studies it. "Timothy John Lester . . . 3rd Infantry Division . . . you sure that's him? He's one of the DOG?"

"I'm positive! His hair is longer now, but that's him. No doubt about it."

Jacob marks the picture and places it on top of the file. "OK. This is excellent. Do you see anyone else who you recognize?"

Again, I offer my suspicions about Hank Mitchell Jr.

"I did a little bit of digging into Mr. Mitchell," Jacob says. "Interestingly, he has a brother by the name of Ernest Mitchell who was in the U.S. military. Served two tours of duty in Iraq. He was scheduled for a third tour but he went AWOL. He was apparently under investigation for his role in the abuse of prisoners in Iraq—you remember all that kerfuffle in the media?"

"You mean about Abu Ghraib?"

"Yes. He was there. Man, what a mess that was. Anyway, he never went on trial and was cleared of all charges."

"Interesting . . ."

"It gets more interesting. Hank Mitchell Jr. here was employed as a supply management specialist at the Milan Army Ammunition Plant up until a few years ago. He simply quit his job without notice. He did this almost immediately *before* his brother went AWOL. Both men are described as being flagrant racists—especially toward Muslims and Jews. Anyway, Ernest goes AWOL and Hank quits the plant. Can you guess when the explosives are thought to have been stolen?"

"Around the same time Ernest went AWOL and Hank quit his job at the plant?"

"Bingo."

I fall back into my chair to mull this over.

"So now we have Zack . . . uh . . . I mean Timothy John Lester, who was also in the military, 3rd Infantry Division. Chances are he would've been stationed in Iraq as well. I can't help but wonder whether Mr. Mitchell and Mr. Lester were acquainted."

"So, this Mitchell character," I add, my curiosity getting the better of me, "you know, the one employed at the plant, would his position as a supply specialist have put him in a position to smuggle explosives out of the plant?"

"Yes and no," Jacob responds. "I say 'yes' in that though he was only a civilian, he had access to storage facilities, inventories, orders, shipments and so on—all the systems which would've put him in a unique position to manipulate the data. I say 'no' in that he would've needed help to smuggle it out of the compound."

"What kind of help?"

"Good question," Jacob replies, flipping through his notes. "He would've needed the help of someone to load the trucks and transport the explosives out of the compound. This would've been someone from the operator, American Ordnance. From what I've been told, Hank had many friends at AO. At this point, we don't know if the explosives were taken all in one heist or piece by piece over a longer period of time. What we do know is that whatever the U.S. military has ordered, it has received. This is true for all shipments nationwide. There have been no reports of unaccounted explosives. So, this tells us the culprits must've loaded more explosives than were ordered to God knows what destination. That's all I know. That's all the FBI is willing to tell us anyway. I'm sure they know more."

"That's all very interesting," I remark, somewhat unconvinced, "but that still doesn't connect anyone to the Dominion of God. I mean, all we have is Zack, but we haven't connected him to the ammunition plant. Neither have we connected the Mitchell brothers to the Dominion of God—"

"Not yet, but we're getting close. This is just one more piece of the puzzle. Your identification of Timothy Lester is the first connection we've been able to make to the U.S. military. This stands to be very, very significant."

"So does anyone know the whereabouts of Lester and the Mitchell brothers?" I ask even though I'm pretty confident I know the answer.

"All are MIA," Jacob replies, without a moment's hesitation. "Whereabouts unknown. The FBI thinks they may have illegally taken residence up here. So if ever you come across Zack again or spot those Mitchell brothers, you let me know ASAP."

"Will do."

We break for a few moments, with Jacob heading for the washroom. I get up to stretch my legs, and make my way to the kitchen for a glass of water. I can feel a cold draft coming from the back door leading to the fire escape. I push hard against it, ensuring it's closed properly. It becomes evident the exit hasn't been used in awhile; the door is completely jammed in its frame while the handle does nothing but turn on itself with no unbolting action. *Hope to hell there's never a fire here,* I tell myself. *So much for a quick escape . . .*

"Just to give you a head's up," Jacob says on returning from the washroom, "The Dominion will be added to the list of terrorist entities tomorrow when the Governor in Council signs it off."

"So what does that mean?" I ask, utterly clueless.

"It'll just give us broader powers of investigation. Like the seizure or forfeiture of any assets belonging to those associated with the group. It also requires any financial institution to report financial information or to freeze the group's assets, or those of any individual associated with it. It'll become an automatic offense to participate in the Dominion's activities or to contribute to its goals in any way."

I suddenly realize the implications. "Jesus, Jacob, don't you dare take further action on the E-Z businesses! I'm in enough heat here already! I swear to God—"

"OK, relax," he says, taking a seat. "I guarantee you nothing is going to be done to the E-Z businesses at this point. We don't have any proof that their transactions have anything to do with the Dominion of God. From what it appears, E-Z is just a smokescreen. All we can do now is keep a close eye on their dealings and hope they slip up."

"What about Marcus Black's accounts?"

"Same goes for him," Jacob replies. "There are no plans to freeze his assets. Not at the moment. All we have are withdrawals and transfers from his accounts to the E-Z businesses. There have been no connections between his accounts and purchases of explosive materials or weapons. Likewise, there are no connections between his accounts and any Dominion member. We need to track him down. Freezing his assets would only hinder that process."

"Somehow, this doesn't fill me with a lot of confidence," I say, sarcastically.

"I give you my word. Whatever happens from here on in, *we'll* be in ultimate control of our information." Jacob sounds remorseful. "We won't be leaving it in the hands of a foreign party again."

I try my best to probe Jacob about any progress in their investigation. Of course he can share very little, but I suspect they haven't made headway since the discovery of the bodies on Christmas morning. He doesn't have much to report on the hunt for Black Mamba either. They still think he's in the Vancouver area, possibly in Washington. For now, that's all I'm permitted to know.

Then, Jacob proposes something I wasn't expecting: to intercept communications from my cell phone and home phone line and the surveillance of my apartment complex. Even though Dominion members have only ever contacted me via pay phones or cell phones whose identity and originating numbers are blocked and whose life spans are shorter than that of a fruit fly, Jacob believes that this may be our best chance at locating some of its members and at obtaining real-time intelligence.

Skeptical, I think about it for a bit.

For whatever reason, it doesn't sit well with me. If it wasn't for a certain $50,000 that I still owe Raoul, I'd tell Jacob to take his investigation and shove it. I'm in way over my head already and I'm lucky to still be alive. But there's something else—some other motivation that's keeping me going. I can't quite put a finger on it at the moment. All I know is that deep down inside, I wish for nothing more than to see the imminent and permanent downfall of the Dominion of God and any other like-minded group out there. I've had enough of terrorists and wars and violence and hate to last me a lifetime—even more so when in the name of a God we all share in common.

In the end, I agree to Jacob's request, but under one condition: that I receive a bonus of $50,000 so I can pay off my debts. I tell him it's non-negotiable. My near-death experience is worth at least that, no matter who dropped the ball. I present him with an ultimatum: either I get that $50,000 in the next month for the danger they've put me through and for continuing to participate in their game, or I walk and cease to report.

Jacob excuses himself and makes a few phone calls to his superiors. After nearly fifty minutes' worth of deliberation and bickering, and to my complete surprise, he receives the approval. Just like that. I'm to receive the full amount within a week. I just have to check with my lenders if the payment is to be made in cash again. The intercepts will be up and running within a few days. I just hope Sarah doesn't engage in any saucy conversations that could lead to personal embarrassment. I'll have to remember this myself. As for the surveillance, it's to begin immediately.

Despite everything that's happened over the course of the last week, I now feel more optimistic about my predicament than I ever have. There's light at the end of the tunnel; I'll have rid myself of a major source of stress and anxiety. The thought of having surveillance done on my residence is also comforting should something unexpected happen again. All eyes will be on me. All we have to do now is wait for the Dominion's next move.

CHAPTER 34

Jacob is true to his word. The $50,000 is handed to me at the safe house a week following our agreement. As expected, Raoul insisted on cash, so everything is prepared and secured in a briefcase again. The delivery is to be made in person in an underground parking garage in the city's east end. Again, the exchange is to be monitored by Kipling and the municipal police.

As before, Raoul is accompanied by Omar and another man, but only Raoul steps out of the vehicle this time to greet me. He's in a pleasant mood, not surprisingly. This probably has a lot to do with the fact that his payment comes much sooner than anticipated. After all, the deadline he'd given me is still two months away. He doesn't bother counting the money this time. One quick look inside is all he needs. He warns me, however, that should anything be missing, there'll be a penalty.

"It's been a pleasure doing business," he says, grinning.

"I wish I could say the same," I reply.

He even goes so far as to offer me more loans at a lower interest rate should I require any. Says he'll outmatch the competition. I tell him thanks but no thanks and that he'll never hear from me again.

"Never say never," he says, still grinning. A quick and half-assed handshake later, Raoul and his thugs drive away and hopefully out of my life forever.

I feel a suffocating burden instantly lifted from my shoulders. The air entering and exiting my lungs feels lighter. I get so excited and am so relieved that I immediately go home and tell Sarah the good news.

Of course, she's suspicious at first. "Where did you get the money?" is the first thing she asks.

While I had planned, perhaps foolishly, to tell her I won $100,000 in the lottery, I go along and admit to her accusations of dealing drugs.

To her, it explains a lot. It explains my numerous trips across the border to Brooklyn. It explains the secretive calls I've received at all hours of the day. It explains the sudden change in my behavior, which she describes as evasive and distant. Perhaps I have been these things. No, I definitely *have* been. But not for the reasons she suspects.

Whatever the case, she's livid. Not even the news of being debt free for the first time ever can appease her. There's cursing and there's crying. I do my best to console her, to reassure her that our problems are all over and that I'll never get involved with such people again. That I'll never take part in *any* form of gambling again. That I won't start drinking again. That my trips to New York were nothing more than a means to an end, the lesser of two evils. However, this does absolutely nothing to alleviate the anger, the sadness and disappointment that consume her. This I can understand. I can sympathize. If I were her, I would've left me a long time ago. I really don't know what I've done to deserve her or what's keeping her from leaving me. But I can feel her being more distant herself these days. I just hope this isn't the straw that broke the camel's back.

CHAPTER 35

Despite the Dominion's order to meet on a monthly basis, I hear from no one, not one single call. Nearly two months of my phone line being intercepted and nothing to show for it. This is even more surprising when considering last month's decision by the courts to dismiss the case against Abdil al-Zahhari. I'm completely bewildered by this and begin to wonder whether my position has indeed been compromised. *Have they tossed me out of their circle? Are they planning something without me? Or worse, do they suspect another snitch? Has Jacob taken any action I'm not aware of?*

At this point, nothing would surprise me.

It crosses my mind that maybe some action has been taken against the E-Z businesses. Or against one of the people I've been able to identify. If that's the case, it would explain this unexpected and unprecedented silence. It would drive the Dominion further underground, if that's even possible. And if Black Mamba has finally been located and arrested, that would surely mark the end of the group.

But none of this has happened. I mean, I don't know for a fact, but I'm certain I would've heard something in the media or I'd have learned it first hand from either Jacob or Kipling, whom I've continue to meet with regularly. While they maintain that the hunt for Black Mamba and company goes on, there's nothing new to report on this front. Although there are grounds to arrest Derek, Miroslav and Conrad—or perhaps any other *senior* member of the organization—and possibly lay charges, a conviction would be next to impossible given the lack of evidence against them.

The investigation into the mosque bombings has hit a snag as the Americans continue to scramble to retrace the missing—or stolen—composition C-4 from the ammunitions plant. It's strongly believed that the culprits are from American Ordnance, or from within

U.S. military ranks. According to Jacob, the production and storage data has been so cleverly and efficiently manipulated that it'll take some time to get a clear picture as to what went wrong. The Mitchell brothers and Zack, or should I say Timothy John Lester, are still missing in action.

There's also nothing to report about the production of triacetone triperoxide a.k.a. Mother of Satan. Although it's highly unlikely to originate from the U.S., it could've been produced anywhere in North America.

With respect to the investigation into the Christmas morning murders, there's also been very little progress. The feds have been unable to identify the locations, vehicles or persons involved. Other than what I've already provided, there's hardly any evidence against members of the Dominion. Nor is there anything against the E-Z businesses or Dino & Sons Wrecking. As for Reverend Hunt and St. Andrew's, the group has obviously kept its distance to protect him and haven't held other gatherings at those locations.

Cyril's murder has also made the news—although no front page coverage—following the filing of a missing person report by his girlfriend in Saskatchewan. This is how it's being described in the media: a missing person. His body hasn't been found and his last known whereabouts are said to be in southern Ontario. This is eating me up inside. It's as though I know and don't know simultaneously, like some type of amnesia. I've even driven around a few sections of the city in hopes of finding the place of his execution—all fruitless.

Despite all the signs indicating otherwise, Jacob assures me that they *are* making progress. Every now and then, I'm presented with new information on an individual whom they suspect may have been involved in either the mosque bombings, the abduction of the imam in Toronto, the abduction of the ambassador and his son in Ottawa, or the murders of all three. I'm also presented with information on vehicles, warehouses, cathedrals, businesses, bank accounts and explosive materials. On each and every occasion, I'm asked to keep the information in mind and to be attuned to anything related.

After approximately two-and-a-half months of twenty-four hour surveillance on my home and the interception of my telephone lines, Jacob informs me that his surveillance team is being pulled out for another high priority investigation. The intercepts, however, are to remain functional.

During this time, a third round of peace talks held in Rome has come and gone. Unlike before, there appears to be skepticism and uncertainty surrounding the progress that was said to have been made during the two previous rounds. The European Union has even expressed some disappointment that no agreement has yet been reached and that it had hoped that these latest talks would have concluded with a settlement. This has prompted the EU and the League of Arab States to convene and to schedule an unprecedented fourth round in the coming weeks. It is felt that both sides are simply too close to an agreement and that not scheduling further talks would be a travesty.

It's late on a Saturday evening just two days after the surveillance team's retreat when my cell phone rings.

"Hello," I say. The line is silent. "Hello? Hello?"

Again, silence.

"Who is this?" I ask impatiently.

"I'd like to speak to the Mailman," says a deep, digitally altered voice.

"Yes, this is him."

"Remember what was discussed the last time you met with the DOG?"

"A lot of things were discussed. What in particular are you referring to?"

"Justice," the strange voice replies. "The justice that was not served."

I don't need to ask any more questions. "Yes, I remember."

"An opportunity has presented itself . . ."

"How so?"

"A contact of ours has informed us that al-Zahhari has been frequenting The Red Room on a regular basis. You've heard of this place?"

"Yes, I have."

"He's been spotted there for the past two weeks on Saturdays. He has a lady friend who works there who he's apparently madly in love with," says the strange voice, muffled by the wind. Whoever the caller is, he's calling from a pay phone. "Are you available tonight?"

"Um . . . sure."

"He may or may not be there. But let's be ready if he is. We'd like to go with option two. You OK with that?"

"I suppose," I reply, "but it seems pointless. No one will ever pay us."

"It doesn't matter. It'll give us more exposure. See it as a calling card—another warning sign that the Dominion is for real. There needs to be chaos and disorder. The world needs to know there's a resistance to the war that the enemy has waged on us. Don't you agree?"

"Of course," I reply, disingenuously.

"Good. If you can make your way to Union Station in an hour, we'll meet you there. We'll take the subway to a location that's yet to be determined. At this location, the Milkman will pick us up and we'll discuss the plan."

"In an hour?" I scoff. "These goddamn last-minute arrangements don't work for me. I need more time! I need—"

"More time for what?"

For a moment, I scramble for an answer. "Nothing . . . it's just extremely inconvenient, that's all."

"I apologize. But I'm sure you can understand it's necessary. Please, we need you. It can't work without you."

I don't respond to this, doubtful as to the sincerity behind this.

"So Union Station in one hour. We'll see you there. Goodbye."

"Goodbye." I hang up.

One hour. That barely gives me time to change and grab a bite to eat, not to mention calling Jacob and briefing him on the situation. When I do make the call, he's extremely grateful for the tip and intimates he'll try to get surveillance teams at both my residence and Union Station ASAP. Also, an undercover contingent of Kipling's men is to be deployed to The Red Room as soon as the doors open for the night. A SWAT team will be waiting outside on standby. As for Abdil al-Zahhari, Jacob tells me that he—or his father—has hired personal bodyguards following his release and the public outcry that ensued.

I spend a large part of the call begging Jacob that this information not be relayed to Abdil or his family, for if it was, it would surely get into the hands of the media one way or another. His father is just too well connected and outspoken. And should such information be leaked, there would likely be another execution of a Dominion member. And this time, I might not be so lucky.

Before we hang up, Jacob promises me they'll be on top of it, and that while they won't go to al-Zahhari or his family, they'll attempt to find him and have surveillance on him for the night and probably beyond. If there's any reason to suspect al-Zahhari's life is in danger, or if Derek, Conrad or Miroslav are spotted, Kipling's men will move in. Otherwise the undercover agents are only to observe and report—and of course, follow. Although Jacob doesn't openly admit it, I believe this strategy stems from the hope that if Abdil is abducted, we'll lead them straight to the Dominion's leadership and hideout.

With that, Jacob wishes me good luck and tells me to be very careful.

"And if everything goes according to plan," he adds, "tonight could mark the beginning of the end for the Dominion of God."

CHAPTER 36

By the time I get off at Union Station, Hal and Roch are already there waiting for me. The terminal is busy as usual and my associates blend in perfectly with the crowd. I take a quick look around to see if there are any onlookers, perhaps a lone man or woman lurking in the shadows. Or a group of two or more individuals whose occasional glances are so discreet, only a trained eye can tell. However, my eyes are not so trained and I see no one.

"Good, you're here," says Hal. "Come, let's get going . . ."

As we surface up to ground level and cross the street, Hal looks back behind him as though waiting for something. Roch is also on the lookout.

"Bastards," Hal scoffs, turning to me. "See those two guys heading up the steps? The one with the red ball cap . . . the other one with the leather jacket? They've been following us ever since we arrived at the station."

I say nothing. My eyes follow the two men as they walk past us from across the street. They appear to be engaged in a discussion, as though talking about something trivial like sports or something. If it wasn't for Hal pointing them out, I never would've noticed a few lightning quick glances made in our direction.

Hal spits to the ground. "Come on, let's get going . . ."

We walk for a few blocks until we reach a 7-Eleven parking lot where an Explorer is standing by amid other stationed vehicles. Hal takes one last look behind him and wastes no time darting for the vehicle. Roch and I immediately follow suit.

Inside, I'm taken aback by the sight of Derek sitting in the driver's seat and cleverly disguised in glasses—likely without prescription lenses—and a ball cap. While I may have been reassured by the presence of Jacob's men, nothing on earth can reassure me now—not with Derek involved.

"We're being followed," Hal declares, panting.

Derek grins. "I know."

Without another word, Derek backs out of his spot and out of the parking lot. He drives past the same two men suspected of following us. Through the rearview mirror, he keeps his eyes on them at all time.

"OK, they're looking back, one is talking on a cell phone," Derek says, his head shifting from the road to the mirror. "Do me a favor and keep your eyes open for a tail."

Derek drives at a moderate speed with no particular destination in mind. He takes a few rights, then a few lefts. It isn't long before a first vehicle—a red Civic—is noticed, then a second one—a black Pathfinder—following a few cars behind.

As though rehearsed, Derek picks up speed and attempts to lose them. We ultimately find ourselves zigzagging across highway 401, through the busy streets of North York, the 400, and back onto the freeway once again. Still, we can't seem to shake them. Like angry bees whose hive has been disturbed, they're relentless and hot on our trail.

As Derek navigates feverishly through the streets of the GTA, the rest of us watch as our followers weave their way through traffic behind us. In attempts to confuse and perhaps give the appearance of having lost them, they fall further back until they're almost out of sight. Then, they switch positions, with the Pathfinder taking the lead and the Civic falling back.

Derek just won't be outdone. Not over his dead body. Not until hell freezes over. As determined and relentless as our followers are, Derek is three times more. He knows, as we all do, that there's no shaking them on the freeway, the expressway or the parkway. If we're to lose them, it'll have to be in the busy streets of downtown Toronto, which is exactly his next move.

It's somewhere in the myriad of one-way streets in the city's downtown core that we manage to escape our predators. It takes a few daring maneuvers, including cutting off several vehicles, burning a few red lights and jumping a few curbs, to pull it off. I have to hand it to Derek, I didn't think he'd manage. But our victory has to be postponed when the sound of a helicopter overhead suddenly emerges in the distance.

Without hesitation, Derek floors the gas pedal and heads for the most direct route out of the neighborhood. As the chopper approaches, he slows down so as not to stand out from the hundreds, if not thousands, of vehicles that are likely to be on its radar. After several tense moments, his tactics appear to pay off. From my window in the back seat, I'm able to spot the helicopter circling over head. It seems to be focusing on the Moss Park area, which we're nowhere near. Perhaps it's picked up the wrong vehicle, who knows. It wouldn't surprise me. I can't imagine it being very easy to identify a vehicle in the darkness of night, even with its spotlight. In a matter of minutes, we find ourselves once again on the Don Valley Parkway.

While the rest of the crew heaves a sigh of relief, I secretly know their moment of victory will be short-lived. The Red Room will be crawling with undercover agents just waiting for our arrival. Every cop in town will also be on the lookout for an Explorer with whatever license plate adorns it. Deep down inside, I can't help but laugh at the futility of their efforts.

I watch in confusion as instead of heading west on the 401, which would've taken us to the Yonge exit where the lounge is located, Derek veers right and takes the 401 eastbound. The first thing that comes to mind is that Derek still suspects we're being followed. But as we drive further away from our destination, I sense something is terribly wrong.

"Isn't The Red Room on Bayview?" I ask.

"Yeah, it is," Derek replies in a matter-of-fact kind of way.

"So where are we going then?"

Derek's head tilts to the rearview mirror, staring me down behind those idiotic-looking glasses of his. "We're not going to The Red Room. That was just a decoy."

My world suddenly collapses. For a moment, I don't even realize I'm not breathing anymore. "We're not? Where are we going then?"

"Sapphire's in Scarborough," Derek replies "Ever heard of it?"

"No, can't say I have."

"Well, that's where we're going."

"What? Why?"

"Because that's where Abdil is going to be."

"All the way out in Scarborough?" I ask, inwardly furious. "Why such a secret?"

"Remember Cyril?" Derek responds, rhetorically. "There's obviously someone onto us . . . fuckin' choppers flying around and all. We can't be too careful."

I stay quiet for a time, pondering Derek's last statement and images of Cyril's head exploding to my right. Blood and brains splattering all over the wall. It hadn't struck me until now. Amid all these thoughts and flashbacks, I can't help but wonder if they—I mean, the Dominion—also suspect someone else. Fact is, Cyril is dead and we're still being followed. Or should I say we *were* being followed. *So much for that and so much for Kipling's undercover agents waiting for us at The Red Room*, I say to myself. *I sure as hell hope Jacob has tracked al-Zahhari . . . or else things could go very, very bad for him. And for me.*

After cruising the freeway for another twenty minutes or so, Derek takes us to a neighborhood just on the outskirts of Scarborough and into what would've been a vacant lot had it not been for a lone vehicle waiting for our arrival—a dark extended-cab pickup. From it, Mario emerges.

Derek stations the Explorer next to the pickup and tells us to get out. We each acknowledge Mario, who wishes us good luck in our mission, whatever that is.

"We were being followed," Derek informs Mario. "Take the Explorer to Dino's."

"No problem."

"Make sure he takes care of it tonight."

"Sure thing."

"There's a Caravan waiting there. Wait for us at the rendezvous point. If anything comes up, call me. Now give me a new plate."

"No problem," Mario replies, retreating to the pickup. From the cab door, he pulls out a box and carries it back to the Explorer. Whatever's inside seems fairly heavy, judging by the sound of clunking metal when he drops it to the ground.

I watch as Mario opens the box and reveals an assortment of license plates. He goes through them, showing them to Derek one by one. I simply stare in astonishment at the wide array of plates from nearly every province and territory. I even spot a few U.S. plates. Massachusetts. Maine. Pennsylvania.

In the end, Derek settles on an Ontario plate, which Mario indicates was taken just last night. After retrieving a few tools from the box,

Mario takes only a minute or two to make the switch. He then retrieves a small metal coffer and sifts through the numerous documents inside. It takes another minute or so, but he ends up finding what he's looking for: a driver's license as well as registration and insurance papers. He hands over the documents to Derek. From where I stand, it's impossible to tell whether they're genuine or counterfeit. I'm guessing the latter.

"Good," Derek says, "Now go to Dino's. Be careful, there's a chopper or two going around. There are probably cops everywhere. Lay low for a bit. Stay away from downtown, got it?"

"Gotcha," Mario replies, putting his tools away and returning the box, this time, to the Explorer. He and Derek exchange keys. "Good luck, fellas," he says. "I'll see you in a few hours."

We're then told to get into the pickup, where Derek takes the driver's seat once again. Mario disappears in the Explorer. Both vehicles exit the empty parking area and head in opposite directions. Silence reigns within our vehicle for another while, each man keeping to himself. After waiting around for someone to shed light on our rendezvous at Sapphire's, I decide to take it upon myself to get some answers.

"So . . . what's the plan anyway?" I ask out of the blue.

All eyes turn to me.

Without saying a word, Derek turns around and hands me a nine millimeter pistol.

CHAPTER 37

Hal and Roch are also handed a pistol. But Derek doesn't reveal what they'll be used for. We're just told that everything will be explained once at Sapphire's. We're assured that if everything goes according to plan, we'll never have to use them. Again, I get this *déja vu* feeling that everyone knows what's about to go down except for me. Whether things go according to whatever Derek has planned or not, I have no intention on using it.

None whatsoever.

In no time, we're at Sapphire's, which turns out to be a run-down dance club and lounge in the east end. Derek tells us that it was once a ritzy lounge frequented by an upper-middle class crowd but that it has since been taken over by some of the city's most notorious citizens. Drug dealers. Ex-cons. Pimps. Prostitutes. The usual suspects. Because of its clientele, regular folk prefer to avoid it completely. It isn't uncommon for a brawl to break out or a stabbing to take place there. The original owners sold the three-story building to a couple of Moroccan fellas a few years back and it's since become obvious they had no intention of ever maintaining the place. They've done nothing to the place since they bought it. No maintenance. No upkeep. Nothing.

The actual club itself is on the ground floor. There's also a lounge in the basement. I don't have the slightest clue as to what the upper two floors are used for. Maybe storage. Maybe nothing. I wouldn't be the least bit surprised if there's a grow-op of some kind up there, a meth lab perhaps. I couldn't care less. With most of its windows either broken or boarded up, the building looks like it should be condemned.

By the time we make our way to the front doors, it's 11:00 p.m. This is early by the standards of most night-time establishments in this city but especially for Sapphire's, whose clientele, or at least the bulk of it, won't arrive for another hour or so.

After paying our cover charge—*I can't believe they charge a fee to enter this dump*—we walk unnoticed past the coat-check area and continue down a dimly lit hallway. Instead of entering the main lounge to our right, we walk all the way past the men's and women's washrooms to a set of stairs leading to the lower level. With Derek in the lead, we descend until we find ourselves in a stuffy lounge surrounded by numerous semi-private booths. In the middle of the room is a sunken area, which I can only assume is the dance floor. Above it hangs a large and defunct disco ball. Several pin spots and sound-activated Vorma disco lights hang at the perimeter of the dance floor, filling the room with swirls of red, blue, green, purple and yellow. The rest of the area around the dance floor is sealed concrete. The walls are limestone, once grey but now blackened by years of smoke and the filth of time. Cheap electrical chandeliers hang loosely from the ceiling above the seating areas and phony lanterns adorn the walls. Except for the spinning rainbows, most of the space is very poorly lit. It feels much like a medieval dungeon with cheap lighting effects.

Some people have already gathered by the bar, others in the booths. I'd say there are already seventy to eighty clients in the lounge. But instead of going straight for the crowd, Derek hangs back and takes an unoccupied booth in the far right corner of the room. The rest of us follow suit, squeezing in. We soon realize there are no waitresses serving the floor. The only way to get a drink is to walk up to the bar. As though rehearsed, Roch rises from his seat and heads to the bar. There, he buys four beers and hands them out upon his return.

We make small talk in order not to look too suspicious. In the midst of our discussions, I notice the DJ in the opposite corner of the room on an elevated platform. He appears enthralled by the music he's playing—a mix of retro 70s and 80s. Some AC/DC, some Queen. Led Zeppelin. Abba. A little Michael Jackson. A little Madonna. I have to admit, I do like his selection. I lose myself for a few moments remembering my younger years.

Despite the tunes, the dance floor remains bare. Every now and then, a new person strolls into the room. Like a vulture waiting for the feed, Derek notices each one. He's super alert. We all know who he's waiting for. The only problem is none of us but Derek can accurately point al-Zahhari out in a crowd.

"See the bartender?" Derek asks.

The rest of us casually glance over to the bar. Behind it, a drop-dead gorgeous woman is pacing back and forth in her attempts to satisfy her thirsty customers. I wonder how on earth I hadn't spotted her before. She appears to be Lebanese or some other Middle Eastern nationality. Olive complexion. Dark hair. Piercing brown eyes. Wearing next to nothing. On her back is a tattoo of a horse of some kind—perhaps a unicorn.

"Dat's her?" Roch asks.

Derek smiles coyly. "Yeah, that's her."

"She's gorgeous! She's wearing dis perfume . . . I don't know what it is, but it must be what angels smell like. Man, I'd tap dat. What's her name again?"

"Amira."

"Amira . . ." Roch repeats, losing himself in his dirty fantasies. "She's one sexy bitch. You should see . . . when she bends over to serve drinks, you can see all da way down her shirt. No bra. Man, I'm telling ya, if dis guy doesn't show up, she's coming home wit me tonight."

This draws some laughs from the rest. All but Derek. He scowls and immediately scolds the rest of us for our lewdness and reminds us to stay focused. We keep quiet for the next several minutes, every man fearing Derek's wrath. It amazes me how the others are so easily subdued. The power and influence Derek holds over them—it really is uncanny.

As time goes by, more people flock into the room. It's now a quarter past midnight. A few have made their way to the dance floor—mostly women and a few eager men. The room becomes increasingly crowded. Soon, there's no longer a clear view to the bar. The more the night goes on, the stranger the patrons become. Some really suspicious characters lurk aimlessly. Still, our target is nowhere to be seen.

As the rest of us become restless and disinterested, Derek only becomes more alert and more obsessed. His eyes grow wider by the minute—more intense. It's like he smells his prey approaching, like the scent of blood is in the air. Several times we try to talk to him, but he doesn't answer. He doesn't even look at us. He can hear us. That we do know. But he chooses not to respond.

"Derek, how long are we supposed to wait?" Hal asks impatiently. "I thought you said he'd be here by now! He's obviously not showing up. Mario must be wondering what the hell's going on in here!"

Still, Derek doesn't respond. He doesn't even flinch.

"Fuck dis!" Roch shouts, getting to his feet. "I'm getting a—"

Derek's right arm suddenly whips Roch across the chest, guiding him back to his seat. "There he is."

I quickly look at my watch.

It's now midnight.

We all glance to Derek's twelve o'clock. After looking around wildly, we turn our attention back to Derek.

"Where?" I finally ask.

"The guy with the blue polo and black pants," Derek says. "The one making his way to the bar . . ."

Again, we look back.

"Are you sure dat's him?" Roch asks.

"That's him alright," Derek replies. "Abdil al-Zahhari . . . that fucker."

I was really hoping he wouldn't show up. I really was. Now that he has, I begin to feel weak all over. A part of me feels like running up to the kid and warning him, telling him to get the hell out of here and fast. Another part of me, the cynical one, can't help wondering if this guy truly was complicit in Black Friday. *Or was he simply a pawn, as they say? A patsy? A scapegoat?* He was only eighteen at the time, son of a successful doctor and peace activist. Could he really have been involved with Sunni Islamic terrorists? Like-minded individuals and organizations like al-Qaeda generally admit their involvement in terrorist acts. Martyrdom is their ultimate reward. But Abdil has always pleaded innocent and denies any ties to al-Qaeda or any other terrorist network. In fact, prosecutors had originally offered to dismiss the charges in exchange for a peace bond, which he adamantly refused—even if it meant his freedom. He just wouldn't do it. The courts have determined that no substantial connections could be made. It couldn't be proved that he was anything more than a casual acquaintance of some of the people involved, who happened to frequent the same mosque he did.

Had justice prevailed? I'm hoping so. I believe so. But the four men sitting next to me don't. And in their world, it really doesn't matter. They have their own brand of justice, no matter how misguided or skewed it is.

We observe Abdil for awhile. It doesn't take long before we notice he's accompanied by several individuals, including one particularly large and bulky looking fella. I'm talking about a real tough-looking brute, also of Middle Eastern origin. One thing quickly becomes apparent: he doesn't leave Abdil's side—not for one second. It's no surprise. None of us expected the recently released Abdil to venture out alone.

As soon as our target enters the lounge, he makes a beeline for the bar. The large man follows him, as does the rest of his crew. He eventually grabs the attention of the foxy bartender, who leans over the counter and gives him a big hug. She then fixes him what seems to be a non-alcoholic drink. They chat for a bit, their conversation often interrupted by the demands of other patrons. At one point, he introduces his friends. Each takes a turn giving her a kiss or two on the cheek, then go back to surveying the dance floor for women. Abdil's bodyguard, on the other hand, never smiles and has little interest in conversing with anyone.

"So what do we do about King Kong?" Hal asks.

"Leave him to me," Derek replies, unfazed. He turns his attention away from the unsuspecting targets for the first time. "We're gonna go exactly as planned. See the hallway just before the DJ booth? It leads to the washrooms. The men's washroom is around the corner to the right. Past it are stairs leading straight to the rear exit. Mario is waiting for us in the back alley."

Despite the loud music, Derek speaks softly. In order to hear, we all lean in. He goes over the plans. Plan A: Roch is to go to the bar and buy two bottled beers. Then, each one of us will take one corner on the upper level around the dance floor. Derek is to take the closest corner to the hallway leading to the washrooms. He'll be eyeing his target like a hawk. We're told to wait for his signal. If Abdil chooses to go back to the ground floor, we're to follow him up one by one. What Derek is counting on is that at some point, Abdil will make his way to the restroom. Whether or not he's followed by his juice-monkey of a friend is irrelevant. If he decides to head for the washroom, we're to wait for Derek's signal. Once the signal is given, we're all to make our way to the washroom in groups of twos. Derek and Hal. Roch and I. Roch is to be the last to enter the hallway. As he enters, he's to drop the two bottles of beer on the floor. The bouncer nearby—the one by the DJ booth—will arrive on the scene and prevent people from entering the hallway until the glass is cleaned up.

Although the rest of us have never seen this man before—the bouncer, that is—Derek assures us that he's one of us. Now that I think about it, I find it curious how the bouncers frisked those ahead of us at the club entrance for weapons but never bothered to pat us down.

Anyway, upon rounding the corner leading to the men's washroom, we're each to put on a black ski mask. By then, we'll be out of everyone's sight, except for whoever's left entering or leaving the men's washroom. Roch is to make his way directly to the exit door and warn Mario that our escape is imminent. Once he gives the OK, Derek and Hal will enter the washroom and abduct Abdil. Derek and Hal are both carrying nine millimeter pistols—Glock 17s to be precise. If anyone tries to interfere—such as Abdil's hostile-looking friend—they'll be immediately and perhaps harshly encouraged to reconsider. As for me, I'm to stand by the door and make sure no one else leaves or enters the washroom and to quickly redirect anyone who happens to get past the bouncer. Should anyone impose himself, I'm instructed not to hesitate to pull out the Glock that Derek handed to me and fire at will.

Of course, I have no intention of using it.

Derek figures that from the time they enter the washroom to the time we exit through the back it should take us no longer than thirty seconds, if everything goes according to plan. Thirty seconds—I'd put my money on that. This is something calculated. This is something the Dominion has practiced for quite some time, I'm sure. Now that I'm aware of the bouncer being in on this, I wouldn't be surprised if this has been rehearsed beforehand during off hours.

There is, of course, the possibility that al-Zahhari never makes his way to the washroom. He may simply remain downstairs the whole night until closing time. Even then, he may be allowed to remain after hours with the staff. If this happens, we execute Plan B, that is, we're to retreat outside and remain parked close by. What happens beyond this point is beyond me.

But for now, on to plan A.

CHAPTER 38

Derek and the bouncer standing by the DJ booth have already exchanged glances a few times. Every now and then, the bouncer looks over to the bar. So does Derek. It's hardly noticeable, even to the suspecting eye. But they're clearly in sync and sending each other signals.

I park myself in the opposite corner to Derek. Hal is on the corner to my left and Roch to my right. In each hand, Roch is holding a bottle of beer he just purchased at the bar. For the most part, he's out of sight, lost in the mix of drunken posers and junkies. I too, become engulfed by the crowd. A few times I'm asked if I'm either selling something or looking to buy. Marijuana. Coke. Ecstasy. Even meth. I politely decline without saying much. Roch, on the other hand, has been caught chatting and flirting with a few women. Derek notices this and I can see the anger and irritation in his eyes—even from the opposite end of the bar. Something tells me Roch's lack of control and focus won't go unpunished—or at least unaddressed.

Our target and his friends haven't moved from their position by the bar since their arrival. That was over an hour ago. I catch myself staring at them sometimes and am almost caught a few times by the would-be bodyguard.

He seems like a normal guy, Abdil does. I'd even go so far as to say he seems friendly or approachable. Clean-cut. Sharply dressed. Not the image of a stereotypical Islamic militant. He seems so young, so . . . innocent. *Could he really have been involved in Black Friday? If so, how much did he really know?* I ask myself these questions over and over again, like a broken record.

Abdil spends the entire time flirting with Amira. I can understand why. She's a knockout. Given that, plus the fact that Abdil's probably had little or no contact with women since his incarceration, one can forgive him for acting like a dog in heat. I don't know the full extent of their relationship, but they seem to be well acquainted. He appears to be practically unaware of his surroundings, his attention completely focused on the object of his desire. He barely ever takes his eyes off her, oblivious to those around him—oblivious to the four strangers and the plans they have in store for him. I pray that he doesn't head for the washrooms.

The more time goes by, the more optimistic I begin to feel. I play scenarios in my head. I think about approaching and warning him, but that would be too dangerous. I'd be a dead man. I also entertain the idea of writing him a note on a beer label or a coaster, warning him not to use the washroom. Deliver it to him in an inconspicuous way. Even better, have it delivered to him. *Delivered by who?* There are no guaranties it would ever get to him, or that it would be delivered secretively. Even then, it would still have to get past Derek and the others. So, basically, a suicide mission. Still, the thought crosses my mind several times.

I also keep my eyes open in hopes of spotting anyone who may be spying on us, hoping that either Jacob or Kipling had been able to track down Abdil before the plans got all fucked up. However, my untrained eye spots no one, leading me to believe neither Jacob nor Kipling's men have made it to Sapphire's.

The lounge is jam packed by the time the clock strikes 1:00. The DJ continues to play beats from the 70s and 80s in a mixture of rock, dance, techno and rap. Every now and then there's the odd tune from the 90s but they're few and far between. I recognized most of them, each precipitating some distant and more youthful memories.

Suddenly, al-Zahhari is on the move.

Shit.

Derek looks to each corner of the dance floor to make sure that none of us have missed it. Unfortunately, everyone has noticed and is waiting for the signal. My heart begins to pound like an African drum and it suddenly feels as though everything is happening in slow motion. Even the music appears to be playing slower in a distorted kind of way. Either that or I'm on the verge of blacking out. The tune echoing throughout the room resonates in my head; an oldie from Queen, I think.

Abdil continues to move away from the bar, weaving and squirming his way past the slew of people waiting to have their next fix. His large companion follows him but the others stay behind. The two steer left and begin to make their way toward the DJ booth. They walk right past Derek, who pretends to have his attention focused elsewhere. The bouncer by the DJ booth notices as well, and also pretends to go about his business.

Abdil eventually passes the booth and the bouncer and heads into the hallway leading to the restrooms. His bodyguard is only a few steps behind. The rest of their group continues to speak with Amira and pay no attention to the departed Abdil.

Then Derek gives us the signal.

One by one, we each abandon our posts and make our way toward Derek's end of the lounge. Roch is the first to reach him, followed by me and Hal. Derek and Hal enter the hallway first. I follow alone. Two women walk past us on their way back from the ladies room. Roch waits until they're out of the corridor before deciding to enter. On cue, he drops the two beer bottles. On hitting the floor they shatter immediately. No one hears it, the music is too loud. As planned, the bouncer—whoever he is—leaves his position and secures the area. The hallway is now sealed. I try to get a good look at this guy, but am blinded by the steady streaming and swirling of disco lights as I pass by.

Now deep in the corridor, Derek rounds the corner, as does Hal. I follow a few steps behind. Roch eventually catches up to me. We walk past the women's washroom, from which voices can be heard. Upon rounding the corner, we notice that Derek and Hal are putting on their ski masks. Abdil and his companion are nowhere to be seen. Derek signals for Roch to continue past the men's room and to make his way up the steps leading to the exit. In a quick sprint, he does so and cautiously opens the exit door. He then looks back down and gives us the OK.

By now, my heart is racing to the point where I feel I may collapse. Never have I ever thought I'd be in such a position—again. I feel so rotten, so dirty. I don't bother putting on my mask. I even contemplate pulling out my pistol and putting a bullet in the heads of my company. But that would only make me a murderer and I'd have to spend the rest of my life in prison. The only comfort I get is knowing I may be the sole chance Abdil has at making it out alive and the sole chance Jacob and Kipling have at bringing down the Dominion.

Truth is, none of us has any clue who or what we'll find behind the washroom doors. Abdil and his friend should be inside, we know that much. They should be . . . but there may be others. And more importantly, how is Derek going to handle the situation?

In one sudden movement, Derek pulls out his Glock and kicks the door open. He and Hal immediately rush in and disappear out of sight. Before the door closes shut again, I can hear Derek's voice calling out Abdil's name. Then, gunfire erupts. I can barely hear it, but it's unmistakable.

I nearly lose my senses. *Gunshots?? What the hell is happening in there?* Pulling out my pistol, I make a dash for the restroom and kick the door wide open. The moment it swivels open, both Derek and Hal reappear. Their weapons are still drawn but they then quickly tuck them away beneath their belts.

"Come on, let's go!" Derek shouts, making his way up the stairs.

As Hal also passes by, I bear witness to the carnage left behind. Blood splattered everywhere. The walls. The floor. The urinals. Lying lifeless in the middle of the room in a pool of blood is Abdil's bodyguard. In the corner by the urinals is Abdil's lifeless body, his pants still undone. His chest is marked by bullet holes, as is his forehead. I notice immediately that there's someone hiding in one of the stalls at the far end of the restroom. Not wanting to stick around for another second, I retreat back into the hallway and make my way up the stairs. I'm overcome by shock, despair, horror and anger. *I've failed him. I've failed him . . .*

It only takes me a few moments to realize that something doesn't add up. It all went by too fast. No signs of a struggle. Something tells me the plan was never to kidnap him in the first place.

And something tells me I'm the only one who didn't know about it.

I can still hear the music as I exit through the back door and join Mario and the others in the waiting pickup. I get the feeling that this tune will stick with me for a long time, like many have before, the words echoing a message that is eerily ironic considering the circumstances.

Another one bites the dust . . .

Wanting to avoid the downtown area, Derek takes us only as far as the Main Street subway station. Before parting ways, he warns us not to come into contact with one another and to lay low until further notice. That sits just fine with me. Besides, I have no way of getting in touch with anyone, not that I'd want to anyway. Derek has taken back all cell phones. We're now officially cut off from one another.

The ride home on the subway ends up being the longest ride of my life. I sit there in an utter daze, my mind numb with the horror I've just witnessed. It doesn't take long to realize I'm in big trouble. Kidnapping is one thing. Murder is a whole different ballgame. Repercussions will be inevitable. I have a sinking feeling my relationship with Jacob is about to come to an abrupt end.

CHAPTER 39

It takes me a few minutes to empty my stomach and collect myself after getting home. Despite it being nearly 3:00 a.m., Jacob returns my page promptly. He sounds alert and vibrant, as though fully refreshed. I tell him about the murder that has just taken place. To no surprise, he tells me that he already received a call informing him of the incident at Sapphire's and that he's been up for the past half hour preparing to brief his director general in the morning.

I give him as much information as I can over the phone. As I do so, I feel growing paranoia settling deep inside me. More than ever now, I'm looking over my shoulder. The thought of my apartment being bugged or my phone being tapped by someone other than Jacob's agency crosses my mind. The Dominion has already infiltrated those responsible for securing our borders. Who knows how far its web has stretched. I can't be too careful. I tell Jacob that from now on, I'll only speak to him or Kipling in person.

Before hanging up, Jacob warns me that he has no choice but to inform his superiors about my involvement at Sapphire's. He says he must also advise Kipling. He assures me that they're behind me one hundred percent and that they'll take care of me. Although he tells me he appreciates the information, the tone in his voice suggests he's disconcerted. Unless I'm grossly mistaken, his level of trust in me seems to be fading.

By sunrise, the crime has already made the front page of most newspapers across the country. It also monopolizes the early morning news on most television broadcasts. So do the murders of the remaining three alleged conspirators in the Black Friday massacre as well as all six involved in the Philadelphia attack on the U.S. side. In Canada, all four murders are reported as separate incidents, yet all are finely coordinated and executed. Unlike Abdil al-Zahhari, who was brought down execution style at Sapphire's, Mahmoud Al-Mahak, Youssef Khan and Amer Khazami were murdered while in detention at the Toronto West Detention Centre. *By God, has the Dominion even infiltrated our correctional system?*

Evidently, the Dominion now has connections on the inside. But the question remains, with who? *With inmates? Among the staff?* At this point, I wouldn't discount the group having infiltrated yet another security agency. Whatever the case, my suspicions that the Dominion is a multi-cell organism are pretty much confirmed. There's something much bigger at play than meets the eye. This diabolical little cult appears to be growing larger and stronger. The indoctrination of new members during every single gathering is further evidence of that. Hal, the newest member of our cell, has already risen high in the rankings. I wonder now how many cells are out there operating on behalf of Black Mamba.

With Sarah sleeping in the bedroom, I begin to obsessively flip through various news channels. The more I listen, the more I understand the ramifications of the killings, ramifications that will continue for quite some time. The killings are being described in the media as a major blow and insult to a country that prides itself on diversity, democracy, the rule of law, and fundamental justice. The prime minister and his cabinet are furious and embarrassed, dealing with condemnation from Saudi Arabia officials as well as from the governments of Iran, Yemen, Jordan and Pakistan. Local and federal law enforcement agencies are scrambling for answers. So too is the brass at the Toronto West Detention Centre and Corrections Canada. While no one has yet to claim responsibility for the killings, there's strong consensus that the Dominion must be behind them. Law enforcement agencies, in particular the RCMP and partnering agencies including the FBI, as well as crown attorneys, are particularly livid. There goes a year's worth of building a case and gathering evidence, witnesses and intelligence. All the money and man hours and tax dollars spent and resources put into preparing these cases. All for nothing. All the blood, sweat and tears shed in order to ensure a fair trial and the exercise of justice. To ensure human rights are preserved.

All for nothing.

Still, there are those who have expressed their support for the killings. There's a right-wing element of our society that insists Abdil and his conspirators got what they deserved. Some, in the form of graffiti or letters to the editor, are even thanking the Dominion for serving justice—a justice they insist their government can't provide for its people. I fear there's a slow wind blowing in the direction of the Dominion, sweeping along with it the more extreme elements of society—and it's gaining momentum. Quietly, slowly, more Dereks and Conrads and Miroslavs are emerging from the shadows. Anonymously but collectively, they're becoming more vocal and more passionate.

Hate groups with no affiliation to the Dominion are now expressing their support for the DOG. It doesn't matter if their ideology is racist or religious in nature. To them, it's all the same. Whites. Christians. Aryans. Whatever. On some of their websites, groups such as Stop the Islamization of Europe and Stop the Islamization of America have expressed their support for the killings. Other groups, mainly those whose foundations can be found in the writings of *The White Man's Bible*, have condoned the Dominion's actions and applauded it for its efforts in engaging in what they refer to as RaHoWa, otherwise known as a racial holy war. There are more out there. I've only begun to scratch the surface.

I'm not one of them, but I'm now an accomplice in the murder of a man. I didn't pull the trigger. I didn't provide the weapons nor did I conceive the plot. But I was there. That's all that matters. Although I've participated in the activities of the Dominion, it hasn't exactly been of my own volition. I've been guided, forced and coerced into this dark world by both the angels and the demons that are fighting for my soul. The most disconcerting thing about all this is the fact that only Jacob and Kipling—and perhaps their zombie counterparts at HQ—have any knowledge of this. As far as obtaining any sense of security and protection, the only thing I have to go on is their word.

Jacob warned me about engaging in illicit activities on behalf of the Dominion of God. To avoid them at all cost. I'd say the murder of a man is as high on the *faux-pas* scale as it can get. I figure that last night was just one of many sleepless nights to come.

CHAPTER 40

Jacob is all dressed up in a snappy grey suit when he greets me at the door of room 1212 at the Courtyard Marriott in downtown Toronto. He appears anxious. His usual laid-back demeanor is noticeably absent as he paces back to the briefcase that lies open on the bed. He quickly takes off his jacket, unbuttons his cuffs and rolls up his sleeves as though preparing to get down to business.

"Liam, what the hell is going on?" he asks, his face like stone.

In detail, I go over the night's events. I tell him about what I was told was going to happen versus what actually happened. I tell him about the change in venue, and the plan to seal the corridor to the washrooms. About the bouncer and the weapons used and who pulled the triggers. And I tell him about our getaway and the type of vehicle, along with the phony license plates. I tell him about Dino's. I tell him everything.

As usual, he takes down some notes and bombards me with questions. He makes a few calls to Kipling. We go over it again. More calls to Kipling. More notes. More questions.

After an hour or so, the room goes quiet. An uneasy silence. There's a new look on Jacob's face—a look of concern and distrust. He begins to pace around the room, thinking. I wait for him to break the silence, but he doesn't.

I can't take it anymore. "Damn it, Jacob—they did it to me again!"

"Did what?"

"Sucked me into this! I had no idea what the plan was!"

"The surveillance team informed me that the Dominion knew they were on to them almost immediately. It's like they were expecting us!"

"So what the hell are you trying to say?"

Jacob shakes his head. "Liam, we have a problem . . ."

"A problem? What problem?"

He pauses to collect his thoughts and then sifts through a stack of paper from his briefcase. "I'll just cut to the chase. My superiors are losing faith in you. The information you've been providing—"

"Now hold on just a goddamn minute," I bark, unable to believe my ears. "I've bent over backwards . . . put my ass on the line to give you everything I know! Everything I've been able to gather! Everything!"

"I know, and I believe you," Jacob replies calmly, defeated. "Believe me, I do. But not everyone involved in this file does—"

"You mean Kipling?"

"No, not Kipling," Jacob reassures me and then hands me an envelope. From it, I pull out a large black-and-white photograph that appears to have been taken from a surveillance unit. "Liam, meet Black Mamba."

A chill runs down my spine.

The more I stare at the photograph, the more I get the sense that something's terribly wrong. The man in the picture is very thin and unkempt. His hairline is receding and his face is unshaven. His pale blue eyes reflect nothing but destitution and bereavement. He appears worn and feeble, a far cry from the mental image I had of a terrorist mastermind.

"This is him? This is Black Mamba?"

Jacob doesn't flinch. "This is the man your information has led us to. This is Marcus Black, known on the street as Marco."

"He looks like a bum."

Jacob smirks. "That's because he *is* a bum."

"What?"

"He's a homeless man living in Vancouver, Downtown Eastside."

"Are you sure this is him?"

"One hundred and ten percent," Jacob replies confidently. "This is your guy, Marcus Black, born in Windsor on November fifth, 1968. This is the man whose personal information, including social insurance number and bank account, were used in the registration of the E-Z businesses and for most of their purchases and daily transactions. This is the man whose personal bank accounts have been used to move money to the E-Z bank accounts. This man is Marcus Black. No question about it. But Marcus Black isn't Black Mamba."

I let this sink in for a few moments. It doesn't make sense.

"Marcus Black has been living on the streets of Vancouver for the past eighteen months, perhaps longer," Jacob explains, in response to the dumbfounded look on my face. "He was a married man with two daughters. His wife's name was Catherine Black. They worked together for a high-tech firm in the Ottawa area, which is also where they met. Had a nice life together. On Black Friday, Catherine takes their daughters to Parliament Hill and—"

"You're shitting me . . ."

"Nope," Jacob replies, staring at the picture. "His whole family obliterated in the blink of an eye. You'd think it'd be the perfect catalyst . . . the perfect motive. We thought he was definitely our guy. But no, Marcus doesn't seek revenge or turn to terrorism. He doesn't become our little hatemonger. Instead, he becomes terribly ill. Severe depression. Despite this, he returns to work only two weeks after losing his entire family. His former employer begins to notice differences in his behavior. Pretty normal considering the circumstance, wouldn't you think?"

"Yeah, I'd say . . ."

"But we're not just talking subtle changes here," Jacob continues. "We're talking about severe mental disturbances, severe highs and lows, crying one minute, livid the next. Panic attacks. Manic-type stuff. So his boss decides to give him further time off. Indefinite leave with pay. Pretty considerate of his employer if you ask me. But Marcus never comes back. At some point, he gets arrested for causing a disturbance, uttering death threats and assault. Real neurotic behavior. He gets admitted to the Royal Ottawa Hospital where he's diagnosed with paranoid schizophrenia. He's ultimately released with meds and orders to report for periodical psych assessments. That's when Marcus Black falls off the face of the map. No one hears from him again. Not that he had much family left or anything. Parents are dead. No siblings."

"Shit . . ."

"Anyway, somewhere along the way someone must have gotten hold of his personal information. His wallet. ID cards. Bank accounts. So for the last year or so someone's been assuming his identity. We spoke to him. Hard to get a straight answer or a coherent thought out of him. He had no clue what we were talking about, even on his medication. He erupted in a fit of rage when his previous life was brought up, especially his family. Anyway, his home in Ottawa is now in possession of Catherine's sister and her husband. He pretty much became a drifter before ending up in Vancouver. Kept to himself. Picked up by local cops every now and then. We found him at the Salvation Army on Cordova Street where he often takes shelter. Workers there all know him. They say he's bearable when he's on meds. Anyway, he's not Black Mamba. Just a classic case of identity theft."

"No shit."

"But you see, that's where the problem comes in . . ."

"Which is?"

Jacob pauses for a moment. "Liam, you've been an incredible help, believe me. You've been our only source of information. You've done well. You've—"

"Get to the point, Jacob."

"The point is not everyone involved in the case seems to think so," he finally says, regret in his voice. "The powers that be—they're losing faith in you. They're unsure about continuing our relationship with you . . . my relationship with you . . . and this was *before* last night's incident."

"What?"

"Believe me," Jacob replies, scratching his head, "I'm as upset as you are. I've put a lot of work into this. But some think you're sending us on a wild goose chase—"

"A wild goose chase? Are you kidding me?" I shout angrily. "I've given you names! I've given you leads! I should be six feet under instead of Cyril! I've put my ass on the line for you bastards and you have the balls to tell me I've been lying?"

"Liam, please, just hear me out," he says, lowering his voice. "I haven't lost faith in you. I mean that. Believe me when I say I've vouched for you from the very beginning. And I'll still vouch for you. But fact of the matter is it's becoming harder to convince my superiors to continue with this relationship." He pauses again, choosing his words carefully. "Look, try to see it from our perspective. The gatherings. Wyman Hunt. The kidnappings. The Serbia fiasco. Black Mamba. And now the murders of the Toronto Four," he says, using his fingers to keep count. "Agreed, you've provided intelligence on all of these. But somehow it seems the Dominion is always one step ahead of us. Some at the agency believe we're being kept at arm's length by way of misinformation . . . that you're only telling us part of the story, giving us only what's necessary to keep us interested and occupied. And now with this Marcus Black witch hunt and our inability to link anyone you've mentioned to the Dominion of God, there are doubts as to the accuracy of the intelligence you've provided. Some involved in the file even believe the Dominion is being tipped. Take last night for instance—"

"I can't believe what I'm hearing—"

"Look, I know—"

"You've showed me photos taken from your surveillance units! Photos that I've positively identified. I've given you access to the E-Z businesses. I've given you names and locations of gatherings, of cross-border exchanges! Hell, you've tailed on a few occasions!"

"I believe you, Liam," Jacob replies, looking me straight in the eyes. "I do. But from our point of view, there's still no condemning evidence that they're involved in anything. All we have is your word. OK, so we have surveillance photos of three men in hooded robes and some of the boys at St. Andrews or at E-Z Travel. But we still don't have anything linking them to the bombings or the murders—or even to the resurgence of the Dominion of God for that matter! Nothing we have would stand in a court of law. Every time we finally have a place bugged or under surveillance, they don't ever show up again. Every time we have a telephone intercept up and running, the line goes dead or gets cancelled. Every time we're led to believe they'll be somewhere, they suddenly end up changing their plans. Every time we—"

"So what the hell are you trying to tell me?"

Jacob is obviously thinking about how to say what he has to say next. "I'm sorry, Liam. I've been ordered to suspend our relationship . . . at least for now."

Suddenly, my world collapses. A million wrathful thoughts fill my head. Among those thoughts are a million more questions and even more concerns. My mouth opens as though to speak, but nothing comes out.

"Look, this may only be temp—"

"This is bullshit!" I finally manage to say. "I want to talk to your goddamn supervisors or whoever the hell is in charge. I want to talk to Frank. He knows me better than anyone!"

Jacob shakes his head apologetically. "Frank's not available anymore. He's retired. You know that."

"I want to talk to Frank!"

"Look, I can't do that. Even if I could, I wouldn't know where he is or how to reach him. Frank is out. And when he's out, he's out. That's how it works."

I bite my lip and say no more.

"Look, I've been told that for the relationship to continue, you'd have to come in and successfully undergo a polygraph test, if you agree of course."

"You mean a lie detector?" I spit angrily. "I need to prove that I'm not a liar?"

"I'm sorry, Liam. I didn't—"

"You didn't what, Jacob?" I shout, getting out of my chair. "Lure me into this messed up game and then leave me hanging high and dry when the going gets tough?"

"You don't have to do it and I wouldn't blame you one second if you didn't."

"And if I don't?"

"Then we'll pay you what is owed and move on, or until what you've already provided can be corroborated or lead to some arrests. Those are my orders."

"That's it? Just like that?" I retort, disgusted. "What about my involvement in the kidnappings and Abdil's murder? What happens to me?"

"You have nothing to worry about. It's all under control."

"All under control, huh? Can I have that in writing?" I sneer. "I want guarantees!"

"I can't give you anything in writing, you know that," says Jacob. "Look, you have the agency and the RCMP in your corner. You acted as an agent of the Crown. You're not an accomplice. This is all documented."

"Ever heard of plausible denial?"

Jacob pauses as though stumped. "Liam, you have no idea how accountable we are to government—and to the people. This isn't the CIA. Things work differently here."

I ponder this for a while.

If I refuse the polygraph, my credibility will be further questioned. I know exactly what they're thinking. *Why would an honest man refuse?* And, if I refuse, I'll have even more heat on me and probably end up being another one of their targets. I know I've given them the truth.

But that doesn't necessarily mean I'd pass the test. I've always had my doubts about polygraphs. The way I see it, if they were one hundred percent accurate, if this was an exact science, these tests would be admissible in court. But they're not an exact science and they're not credible evidence. And if, for whatever reason, I fail the polygraph, my credibility is forever ruined and then I'm sure to become a suspect. Then what? Will Jacob and his agency stay true to their word and grant me immunity for the crimes? Or will I then be considered an accomplice, a willing party to the murders?

It goes without saying that the easiest, most sensible thing for me to do is to walk out this door and never look back. Besides, I've paid off my debts and am in no need of the money. But then I'm left fending for myself, seeking a way out of this madness—out of the Dominion, which is much easier said than done.

"You don't have to make a decision now," Jacob offers. "Think about it. You're under no obligation."

You're damn right I'm not.

Jacob waits for my reply. "I'm going to follow up with—"

"I'm out."

Jacob's arms drop to his side. "What?"

"You heard me, I'm out!"

Dead silence. Jacob lowers himself into a chair and sighs. "You don't have to give me an answer now. Take some time to think about it."

"No need. I'm through with this."

"It may only be temporary—"

"Doesn't matter. I've paid my debts—and my dues. So tell your superiors to take their polygraph and shove it up their asses. I'm done. I want out."

Jacob nods. "Alright then . . . I'll make the arrangements. I can't say I blame you." He runs a hand through his hair and sighs. "I'd probably do the same if I were you. I want you to know that your work was truly valued, Liam. You're a good person. I've really enjoyed working with you. I've enjoyed our relationship—hell, our friendship. You served your country and you should be proud."

"So what happens now?"

"Well, I'll arrange for your final pay. You'll likely receive it within the next two weeks. After that, I'll need to meet with you one more time for a final interview. This is just to tie up loose ends. It's standard procedure. It'll also give us a chance to present a plan to get you out of the Dominion—an exit strategy. After all, you're still our asset and responsibility. Despite what you think, we won't let you hang high and dry."

I nod without saying a word.

"If you change your mind, let me know," he goes on. "In the meantime, hang tight. I'll be in touch shortly. If you need anything or if something comes up, you have my number, although we won't be able to pay you for it." He stares off into the distance for a few seconds. "I'm really sorry about this. I wish things were different . . . you know, all this policy and protocol bullshit. But that's the name of the game, I guess. I have as much control over it as you do. For what it's worth, I believe you. One hundred percent. If I had my way, I'd be handing you a medal. Hopefully, everything will get cleared up real soon."

"Don't worry about it." I say, simmering down. "Even if things do get 'cleared up,' I won't be coming back. But I understand. I suppose things have happened that aren't in my favor."

We chat a bit, then shake hands and say our goodbyes. As he's pressed for time, Jacob is the first to leave the room. I remain there for a while, unsure as to where to go from here. I'm saddened, confused and bitter. Except for Sarah, Jacob has been the most consistent person in my life recently and I'd come to think of him as a good friend. Strangely, I feel as though I've just been dumped. And, like most bad breakups, we'll likely walk the earth until the day we die without ever seeing each other again—just like Frank and me.

CHAPTER 41

The period following the murders of the Toronto Four is ironically the most tranquil since the very beginning of my involvement with the Dominion. For weeks I hear nothing from them. My life returns to normal, as normal as normal can get. I've managed to resume my regular shifts at Henrique's Deli, even picking up some extra shifts along the way. More importantly, I've been able to dedicate more time to Sarah, who seems much happier of late.

Despite this lull in activity, not a day goes by without the Dominion haunting my thoughts. There's no shoving it under a rug and hoping it doesn't resurface. It's out there, watching. Recruiting. Fundraising. Scheming. Waiting. Like a deadly virus in its latent stages. Normally, I'd say it's only the calm before the storm. But something tells me I'm sitting in the dead center of the eye of the hurricane.

A week after the unofficial suspension of our relationship, Jacob calls me up. We chat on the phone for a few minutes and then decide to meet in person to finalize things. In a booth over a quiet dinner at a hotel restaurant, we end up discussing the Dominion, the renewed Israeli-Palestinian peace talks, religion and God. We also discuss less heavy things, such as sports and film.

While it's nice to talk about things other than the Dominion, an exit strategy is the order of the day. We look at a number of scenarios, including faking an accident or illness or even death. We talk about Sarah and I assuming new identities and relocating under a witness protection program. But Jacob thinks it may not be necessary. Not for the time being and not if we play our cards right. After all, the Dominion doesn't suspect me of being an informant—at least not that we're aware of. As my counter argument, I remind him that no one has ever left the Dominion of God and lived to tell about it. Cyril would attest to that if he could.

Although we explore many avenues, there's no single scenario that's foolproof and none that manages to instill much confidence in me or give me much comfort. Case in point: Jacob suggests the agency relocate Sarah and me to Pickering under the guise of caring for her mother. However, I know without a doubt the DOG would ask me to recruit and operate out of Pickering. Same goes for wherever Jacob and his geniuses have considered relocating us. Sure, I could fake an illness or an injury, but for how long? I know damn well the Dominion will do its homework and find out whatever it can about any so-called "disabilities." Even though Jacob says he could have medical reports and test results fabricated, it still doesn't sit well with me. For now, nothing more is proposed, though he assures me more discussions will be taking place at his headquarters concerning our exit strategy.

Before we part, Jacob reminds me that my final allowance will be deposited a week from now. He also does his best to coax me into taking the polygraph. But I stick to my guns and refuse. Call it integrity. Call it stubbornness. Whatever. I've made up my mind. He says once more that he understands and regrets how things turned out, and that I'll never be arrested or charged for my involvement in any of the Dominion of God crimes, because I acted at the direction of government agents. He also suggests that should any of the intelligence I've provided be corroborated or proven to be accurate, the agency would be interested in my services again.

I scoff at the idea.

We shake hands and end up saying our goodbyes once again, with Jacob promising me he'll be in touch, hopefully with a concrete exit strategy.

My work for the agency is officially done. Granted, the money was good. By being Jacob's mole, I've managed to get myself out of a terrible jam. But I've also gotten myself into a worse predicament—if that's even possible. But Jacob and Kipling will have to continue their investigation without me. It's time I got myself out of this dark world of religious extremism and fanaticism for good.

Now, all I need is an opportunity.

CHAPTER 42

That opportunity comes approximately six weeks following the murder of the Toronto Four. By this time, the frenzy of media coverage related to the killings has subsided and the Dominion is no longer monopolizing the front pages or the airwaves. Only whispers can be heard every now and then, as though the mere mention of the group has become taboo.

Despite this media hiatus, something tells me things aren't so quiet behind the scenes, either for the Dominion or for the investigation into their activities. I can only hope that Jacob, Kipling and their men are making progress—hopefully based on some of the information I've provided, so I can clear my name.

I'm underground waiting for the subway at Keele Station following my shift at Henrique's when Hal approaches me. "Hey, next Friday—expect a phone call in the late afternoon sometime. Be available. Cancel your plans, if you have any."

"Jesus, have you been following me?" I ask.

"Maybe . . . maybe not . . . What does it matter?"

"What's this about?"

"A big meeting. It's very important you be there. Orders from Black Mamba himself," he finishes, and disappears into the crowd as quickly as he emerged.

"I did have plans . . ." I mumble to myself, knowing full well there will be repercussions for cancelling the visit to Sarah's mother. She's been pretty ill with pneumonia over the past several weeks. This can actually kill seniors, or so I've heard. My skipping out on this visit will only add salt to very raw wounds.

CHAPTER 43

By the time Friday rolls around, Sarah's left for Pickering and still isn't talking to me. Stopping short of completely dumping my ass, she insists she needs time to herself to figure things out and whether she sees herself spending the rest of her life with a "a man without morals". This really, really stings. But I can't help but wonder if I am what she says. *A man without morals.* I've spent a great deal of time dwelling over this lately; whether I've done everything I've done for the right reasons.

Truth be told, I miss her already. I love her more than life itself and I want a future with this woman. In fact, I don't see a future without her. Without her, all this crap I've gone through over the past several months would be for nothing. I really want to give her everything she wants. And then some. A wedding. A family. If she only knew the intense pressure I've been under of late. Perhaps once things are settled and my life is back to normal, whatever normal is . . . perhaps . . . just perhaps.

I just hope it's not too late.

At the deli, I ask Henrique if I can leave at 2 p.m., a request he reluctantly grants. Once home, I grow restless, pacing nervously in anticipation of the dreaded phone call. I consider calling Jacob. At one point, I even pick up the receiver. But I don't dial for reasons I still can't explain. Perhaps out of spite. Perhaps out of fear of handing what may turn out to be more bogus information. Whatever the reason, I simply hang up and play the waiting game.

The call eventually comes at exactly five o'clock. The caller, who doesn't identify himself, informs me that I'll be picked up at the 7-Eleven down the street in a half-hour. I'm cautioned to come alone and not to mention this to anybody.

At the 7-Eleven, I meet Mario and Roch, who are already there waiting. We exchange pleasantries and I'm briefed on the purpose of the meeting, which is to be held in the basement of St. Andrew's Church. This comes as a shock as it isn't the Dominion's *modus operandi* to hold a gathering twice at the same location. Perhaps the Dominion is becoming complacent or overconfident, maybe even careless.

Mario tells me that a big announcement will be made and that everyone will be there. I ask whether they've heard much since our night at Sapphire's. As I expect, they deny hearing anything. When I ask if they've been up to much since our last encounter, they become curiously evasive.

We make our way to Dufferin Station and catch a train to St. Andrew's. We walk a few blocks until we reach the church. Unlike our last visit, the pews are completely empty, with no one in sight. The lights are dim. Near the altar, a few candles burn quietly.

However, my colleagues pay no attention to this, making their way to the back of the church until they reach the staircase leading to the basement. I eventually catch up to them.

At the very top of the stairs is a man sitting on a chair behind a small, makeshift desk. I immediately recognize him as one of our interrogators the day of Cyril's murder. On the desk is a laptop and some other apparatus connected to it. "Greetings," he says. "I'll need your ID card or PIN number, please."

Their membership cards already in hand, Mario and Roch take turns presenting them to the doorman, who then scans them through the device and watches the laptop to verify their authenticity. Then, with the usual portable metal detector, he scans both men from head to toe. After having passed their security checks, Roch and Mario are allowed to head downstairs.

I frantically search through my pockets, thinking I've misplaced my card. The door guy just stares at me, unimpressed until I find it buried in my wallet. I then hand it to him and watch as he scans it.

"Name?" he asks.

"Liam Sheehan."

"Alias?"

"Mailman."

"Date and place of birth?"

"October 15, 1975. New York City."

"ID, please."

"I'm sorry?"

"Can I see some matching ID. Driver's license. Health card. Anything with a picture."

"Um, sure," I respond, surprised at this rigorous security check. I hand him my driver's license.

"Thank you," he says, handing it back. He then scans me from head to toe. "You may proceed."

Before I take even one step down, I can hear the banter of the crowd below. When I reach the basement floor, I freeze at the sight before me.

The room is filled with rows of chairs facing a podium. Most of them are already occupied. I figure there are probably two, maybe three, hundred people already here—a staggering increase in numbers since my last count. Some are familiar. Some not. Some young. Some old. Some women, but mostly Caucasian men. In the crowd, I spot Mario and Roch, who are just sittting down.

"Who the hell are all these people?" I ask Mario, taking the empty seat beside him.

"What does it look like?" Mario replies. "They're members just like you and I. Haven't you recruited anyone lately?"

"No, I haven't."

"Well, some of us have . . ."

With every passing minute, the empty chairs are quickly claimed. Before long, the room is filled. Standing room only. In the crowd, I manage to spot Shane, Hal, Vladimir and Dragana from E-Z Grocery, all seated side by side. Across the room is the bouncer from Sapphire's. *Big surprise*, I tell myself. But what catches me off-guard are the men sitting next to him: Dino and his two sons, Chuck and Fred. I make a mental note.

The more I look around the room, the more convinced I become that I need to tell Jacob about this, free of charge. Whether he and his agency believe me or not, that's none of my concern. I'll have done my civic duty. I can't let this go unreported.

A few rows behind Dino and sons, I spot Zack and Nash chatting with several people, all smiles and laughs. The more I observe them, the more I realize most of those on the left side of the room are from the same contingent. Speaking loudly and boisterously, they appear to be familiar with each other. Some have a distinct Southern accent.

"Who are all those guys?" I ask Mario.

Mario looks over his shoulder. "That's our American chapter."

"Americans? All members?"

"Loud and proud. More Americans have been recruited than from anywhere else. There are more. Most aren't even here. Nash, Zack and company have done a phenomenal job. Some think Black Mamba may be American."

"What do you think?"

"I really don't know," Mario replies, poking Roch in the ribs. "Roch thinks he is. It makes sense. I betcha there are more Americans than there are of us. I betcha they're the ones who are really in charge. They probably come up here because it's easier for them to operate. Down there, they have the FBI, the CIA, U.S. marshals and then some. They have more goddamn cops than we have as total population. Coming here, it's sheer genius, if you ask me."

Sitting among the Americans and engaged in a private conversation are Wes Sanderson of the U.S. Custom Border Patrol and Brent Weiss of the Canada Border Services Agency. Both men notice me staring back at them. They send smiles, winks and nods my way. I remain collected and nod back. It's at this moment I realize fully the seriousness of the situation. Somehow, the Dominion of God has managed to reach into and infiltrate the very segment of our society that we expect will protect us—from, among other things, extremist groups like the Dominion of God.

Suddenly, there's no safety and no security. Scanning the crowd, I can't help but wonder if in fact it contains representatives from the U.S. military, Corrections, or any other security agency.

I turn away and look before me. Standing in front of the podium are Derek, Miroslav, Conrad and two other men I don't know, although one seems awfully familiar. Heads together, they appear to be finalizing some kind of presentation or speaking notes. A glass of water sits on the podium. The microphone hasn't yet been turned on.

From somewhere above, a door slams shut, followed by footsteps making their way down the staircase. The doorman with the laptop takes a seat next to the podium. He signals to those on stage. Derek motions for silence and soon the room goes quiet.

"Greetings, and welcome to the largest gathering of fellow DOG members to date! We're very pleased to see you've all answered the call. I'd like to welcome our fellow representatives from the United

States. You have come from New York, Kentucky, Tennessee, Missouri, Mississippi, Carolina, Arizona and Texas. You are strong in numbers and represent the largest chapters in our organization. You should all be proud of yourselves, and I'd like to congratulate brothers Nash and Zack on their recruitment efforts."

This draws a large ovation from the crowd.

"I'd also like to welcome our brothers who flew all the way from the U.K. just to be with us today," Derek continues, motioning to a smaller group of people on the right side of the room. "As you may or may not know, my name is Derek and I'm head of the Dominion of God in Canada. With me here are my close associates and original DOG members, brothers Miroslav and Conrad."

Derek then directs our attention to a tall, pudgy man wearing beige dress pants and a white shirt. Small rounded glasses sit on the bridge of his nose and his hair is parted to the side. Clean-cut, he resembles an academic of some type. Yet there's something eerie about this man—something not quite right.

"I'd also like to welcome brother Cleave, head of our new chapter in London."

Cleave takes a step forward and waves to the audience.

Again, the crowd applauds.

Derek points to the next man in line. "And last but not least, let's give a warm welcome to our brother Randall, Head of the U.S. DOG."

Randall steps forward and pumps a fist in the air, which draws a loud cheer from over half the room. Tall and lanky, he sports everything I'd expect a man from the south to wear. Light, tight-fitting jeans. Large silver belt buckle. Cowboy boots. Flannel shirt over a tucked-in white T-shirt. A worn red baseball cap with the Confederate flag on the front. A thick brown mustache and deep brown eyes.

The longer I stare at this Randall character, the more he looks familiar to me. I've seen him somewhere, I just can't put my finger on it. I mentally review my exploits across the border. I don't recall him being a border officer, nor do I recall his presence during any of my deliveries. *Think, Liam. Think . . .*

Then it hits me.

Oh my God, I think, images of Milan Army Ammunitions Plant photo IDs flashing through my head, *It's him . . . Hank Mitchell Jr.*

I take a quick look around the room to see if I can spot his brother Ernest, but without success.

Derek remains behind the podium. "Before we begin, I'd like to read you a letter from our leader, Black Mamba, who could not be here today. He writes: 'My dearest brothers, it's with great pleasure and pride that I greet you here tonight, united as one. You have answered the call. Whether your background is Catholic or Protestant, Baptist or Presbyterian, Anglican or United, you have pledged allegiance to a new path: the path of righteousness and the restoration of God's Kingdom. You've been summoned here tonight because you have one common bond, one common purpose. As it had been foretold by the great Prophet Roland, a war is upon us. Some of you may have once called it RaHoWa, and it is indeed such.'"

Derek flips the page. "'In the Bible, Ecclesiastes states: 'to every thing there is a season, and a time to every purpose under the heaven: a time to be born, and a time to die; a time to plant, and a time to pluck up that which is planted; a time to kill, and a time to heal; a time to break down, and a time to build up; a time to weep, and a time to laugh; a time to mourn, and a time to dance'; but, most importantly, it is stated that 'there is a time to love, and a time to hate; a time of war, and a time of peace'. My brothers, today is the dawn of the time for hate and for war. For thousands of years, dating back to the times of the crusades, the Israelites have faced great adversity and great hardships. For the most part, we have managed to quell and silence the Beast. But behold! The shadows of darkness have only grown stronger. Their campaign to annihilate God's people has only intensified. We must prepare, for the Tribulation is upon us! Each and every one of you sitting here today will be salvaged at the time of the Rapture and the Second Coming of Christ. Rest assured, there are more of you out there. It is now your duty to bring them into the fold so they too can meet the Lord in the clouds.

"'The Tribulation will bring upon dire times. Only the strong will survive. But it is inevitable. The war will bring great tribulations and suffering. We must prepare. Do not be fooled for a great Evil is upon you! It will seek to destroy you because of your devotion and because of your faith in our savior, the Lord Jesus Christ. This evil is clever! It is wicked! It will not stop until there is nothing left, until we, God's people, are gone and wiped off the face of the earth.'"

Again, Derek flips another page. "But do not fret for we will be victorious! It has been written. It has been foretold. At the end of the Tribulation, whether you are alive or dead, our Savior will come to resurrect those who have fallen and gather those who still remain. He will then lead us all into Armageddon where the Beast and his false prophets and his forces will be destroyed and thrown into the Lake of Fire."

Thunderous applause erupts. Derek pauses until it subsides.

"My fellow brothers, the war has begun. We are the chosen warriors who will lead the righteous into battle! We will stand victorious! When the war is over and the End Times are upon us, only God's people will be left standing and only then will his Dominion be fulfilled!"

Another roar from the crowd.

Derek motions for silence and continues to read.

"'You have already sacrificed much. More sacrifice will be needed. It will not be quick and it will not be easy. But together, we will ensnare the wicked and banish them forever. Good will prevail! You are the chosen. You are the blessed. Without you, the world would fall under the cloth of darkness for all of eternity. This is the dawn of a new day. The restoration of God's Dominion will be the fruits of our sacrifices and of our deeds. Let us take back what has been taken from Him! Let us take back what is God's heaven and his earth! The Lord is calling upon us! I am calling upon you! I love and bless each and every one of you.'"

Derek folds the letter and steps away from the podium. "Fellow members, those are the words of our great leader, Black Mamba," he begins, pacing back and forth on stage like some kind of evangelist. "Like the good Lord, he watches over us. He loves each and every one of you and is grateful for your allegiance. He is a great man with a great vision and has taken all of us under his wing. He is your shepherd. He is the chosen one who will lead us into battle and prepare us for the Second Coming. The Tribulation is at the horizon. We must prepare for seven years of war and suffering and hardships. This is why you've been summoned here tonight."

Conrad suddenly steps forward, taking over from Derek. "Obviously, you weren't summoned here just to have us read you a letter. No, there are much greater things to talk about. I remind you that all of you are the product of Phase I. You've been hand-picked and selected to be leaders and to be the future of the Dominion. Phase I is now complete. Now we enter Phase II. That's why you're here tonight."

Phase II? I look over at Mario, but refrain from asking.

"Our first wave of recruitment is over and we've achieved our desired numbers. Now is the time for the Dominion to blossom. But first, we require your help. What we're looking for is for each of you to bring another three members into the fold."

Conrad goes on to explain the rules of recruitment. Never identify yourself as a member of the Dominion. Canvass online and in person. Search within other religious or like-minded organizations. Never identify yourself by your real name. Refer all potential recruits to senior members. And so on.

At one point, a large and muscular man rises to his feet. "You know, down South we have organizations that'd be very interested in our kind of . . . activities," he says in a thick Southern accent. "I think y'all know which ones I'm referring to. I myself am a former member of the Hutaree. There are more like me. I've spoken to some of my associates. I can guarantee you there's a keen interest in meeting with representatives of the Dominion of God. Y'know, kinda like forming an alliance of some type . . ."

Again, Derek takes the podium. "Sonny, I think it is?"

The man nods.

"Well, Sonny, rest assure that we're already working on it. We've already tapped into some of your great organizations. In fact, there just may be some among us here tonight," he says with a smirk on his face. "But we're interested in hearing you out, Sonny. So come see us after the meeting and we'll discuss." He pauses and looks at the crowd. "Remember, there are no barriers to who may be a potential member, as long as they reject the false prophets and are not descendents of the Beast. Man or woman. Young or old. Rich or poor. It doesn't matter. Just find them. They're out there."

Sonny bows and takes his seat. Another man near the back row then stands up. "What's our goal? I mean, do you have a target number you're looking for? How many members do we need?"

Randall speaks up. "The more the merrier!"

The audience breaks into laughter, which Derek eventually interrupts. "If you don't know by now what we're aiming for, then you should question your devotion to the cause. I encourage everyone here to learn . . . to memorize . . . to incorporate the teachings and revelations of Roland our Prophet. It should be ingrained in the core of your very being! I want everyone to make it a daily practice to read, memorize and adopt."

"So what's next?" asks the unidentified man. "I mean, once we've recruited enough members?"

"Ah! I'm glad you asked!" Derek replies, looking to his associates on stage." For this, I'll let Miroslav speak, because he will be your Head of Combat Operations."

Miroslav takes the podium. "First of all, there's no end to recruitment. We'll continue to recruit indefinitely until war is over and Rapture has taken place. Conrad will continue to be Head of Recruitment. Now, as some of you may have heard, you'll be given special training in weeks and months to come. To engage our enemy, we have to use force to combat force. Sadly, it's only way. To be effective warriors, you must be trained in hand-to-hand combat, artillery and explosives as that's the method our enemy has chosen to engage. We've secured three locations where you'll be given opportunity to develop and enhance your skills—one south and one north of border, and another one overseas. Those of you who excel will be given chance to specialize in *other* areas. Although we'd rather not have to resort to violence, there will be non-believers who will use force against us in order to thwart our goals. I'm talking about cops, the military and so on. There will be those who will try to dismantle and destroy our great organization. We'll have no choice. Force will be necessary for ultimate good."

Miroslav takes a drink of water and scans the room. "In weeks to come, you'll be invited to attend one of our training camps. Training will be held over two weeks. Housing and food will be provided. Attendance is mandatory. Unless you have extenuating circumstances, you'll present yourselves at specified date and time. You'll be warned in advance of your training schedule so you can make whatever arrangements you need to in order to attend. You'll be trained in small groups and be given further assignments. You'll be provided with *Avtomat Kalashnikova* assault rifle and pistol, which will be assigned to you until you're called into action. However, your weapons will be kept and stored in safe and secure location at camps."

A flurry of chatter erupts from the crowd. I just sit there gaping, barely able to grasp the magnitude of what I've just learned. *Training camps? Artillery? Assault rifles? Explosives? What the hell for . . . ?*

Many questions are raised, which Miroslav and Derek and some of the others answer one by one. However, they refuse to give out any information on the training camps. They insist that, for security reasons, none of us will ever know the locations of the camps until the very day we're to report for duty, and we'll only be told about the one we're assigned to.

"What are we being trained for?" Mario finally asks.

"Ah! Finally! The question of the night!" Derek exclaims enthusiastically. "What are you being trained for? That, my friends, is in preparation for Phase III."

"And what's Phase III?" asks one of the few women in the room.

Derek's face breaks into a fiendish grin. "Well, my friends, in case you haven't heard, a fourth round of secret negotiations between Israel and the Palestinian National Authority have been ongoing in Rome for the past several days. The latest draft of the *Israel–Palestine Action Plan for Lasting Peace* has now been reviewed and ratified by both sides. Concessions have been made. The plan has been praised by the European Union and ratified by members of the League of Arab States. It's been reported just hours ago that a verbal agreement has been reached and that both Israel and Palestine will be recognized as sovereign states by members of the League of Arab States who will also help to ensure the peace and security of both nations. All this to say the arrangements are currently being finalized. An official signing of a peace treaty has been scheduled in Rome for the sixth of June, which is in exactly forty-five days from now."

A collective gasp ensues followed by a long, anxious period of silence. All eyes are glued to Derek and to the rest of the Dominion leadership. No one blinks. No one dares to make a sound.

"So, you ask what is Phase III?" Derek repeats, his voice echoing throughout the hall. "Phase III, my friends, is the beginning of the Tribulation and the start of a new world order."

CHAPTER 44

At the other end of the line, Jacob sounds puzzled and concerned. "So what's Phase III?"

"The hell if I know."

I decided to give Jacob a cold call from a pay phone shortly after the gathering. Whether more out of a sense of responsibility or a sense of panic, I don't really know. What I do know is that after that meeting, the stakes just got that much higher.

I tell him everything. The training camps. Phase II and whatever the hell Phase III may be. I tell him about those in attendance including Dino & Sons, the bouncer from Sapphire's, Brent Weiss and Wes Sanderson, Dragana and the rest. About the anticipated signing of an Israel-Palestine Peace Treaty and the Dominion's belief that the Tribulation is about to begin. About the group's presence in the U.K. and its large presence in the U.S., and Hank Mitchell Jr. as leader of the Dominion of God down south. About recruiting from white supremacist groups. About the true north strong and free being used as a haven and a staging ground for members and their activities.

"How many have they recruited?"

"Alot! I mean, a far cry from one hundred and forty-four thousand, but there are a lot more than I ever expected."

"Like what . . . in the hundreds?"

"Yeah, there were several hundred of them there. But not everyone was in attendance. Mario said at least half of the U.S. chapter was not in attendance. I doubt the entire U.K. delegation made it too. So I'd say the DOG likely has well over a thousand members."

"Did you see Wyman Hunt there?"

Wyman Hunt was not there, I tell him. But this isn't unusual. In fact, I've never seen the old reverend at any of the Dominion's functions. Ever. Again, I revisit the possibility of Hunt being Black Mamba.

Again, Jacob dismisses this theory. They've had their eyes and their ears on Hunt for quite some time, he says. He's still clean.

Yeah, right.

"These training camps," Jacob says. The sound of pages flipping in the background. "Did they give any indication as to their whereabouts?"

"All I know is that there are three. One in Canada. One in the U.S. One overseas."

"You mentioned earlier that some will be given specialized training . . . any idea on the type of training?"

I take a moment to reflect. "It wasn't specified."

"Perhaps bomb-making?"

"I really don't—"

"Sharpshooting?"

"I don't know!"

Jacob sighs heavily. "The Tribulation," he says, "is prophesized to begin upon the signing of a peace treaty. If all goes according to plan, the Tribulation is to begin the sixth of June, or so the Dominion believes. Has the group specified what form it will take? How will it materialize? Time frames? Location?"

"No, they haven't," I reply. "All I know is that they believe the Antichrist has arrived in the form of the Heads of the European Union and that they've used the Devil's influence and power to broker a peace treaty between Israel, the Palestinian National Authority and by proxy the League of Arab States."

"So it believes the Palestinians and the League of Arab States are the Devil's children?"

"Not just the Palestinians and the Arab League," I reply, "but Israel—or at least what it says is falsely known as Israel—as well."

I can tell Jacob is confused just by his breathing and hesitation at the other end of the line. "Sorry, I'm confused," he says, "I thought the Bible said the Antichrist would trick Israel into signing a peace treaty. Aren't the people of Israel supposed to be God's people?"

"That's what's written," I explain, "But the Dominion believes that only the Devil could bring these two nations together and that this unholy alliance, along with the backing of the League of Arab States, is the emergence of the Army of the Beast. You see, to the Dominion, this satanic union will then wage war on what it considers God's true people which it believes are those who adhere to the Dominion. The moment the treaty is signed, the Tribulation is to begin and bring about a seven-year period marked by extraordinary suffering and devastation."

"So how will this war begin? What are the Dominion's plans?"

"Your guess is as good as mine."

"Where will it take place?"

"I don't know."

"When or who will the group strike?"

"Damn it, I don't know!"

The more Jacob probes, the more cautious I become. For whatever reason, he—I mean, *they*—distrust me already. Technically, our relationship is still suspended and I'm not getting any money out of this. I need to tread very carefully.

As he has before, Jacob enquires about my interest and willingness to return to work as an informant. I tell him my position hasn't changed. I have absolutely zero interest in being a part of whatever the Dominion has planned once the treaty is signed, sealed and delivered. It will be big, I tell him, whatever it is. Derek and the rest have waited their entire adulthood for the fulfillment of this one prophecy. This is the call they've been waiting for. This is the reason for their very existence—for the Dominion's very existence. And they'll be damned if they don't respond with everything they've got.

Jacob insists that with this new information, which apparently corroborates some of Sergeant Kipling's findings, he'll likely obtain the confidence of his superiors and be able to reinstate me without the need of a polygraph. But this does nothing to deter me and my desire to distance myself from the Dominion until all ties are severed once and for all.

I then turn the tables and question Jacob about the delay relating to my exit strategy. To this date, I've seen little evidence of progress there. I'm beginning to wonder if Jacob and his agency have any intention of pulling me out of this ever-growing organization. I mean, why would they? They know that I'm a moral man, despite what Sarah now thinks of me. And I know that they know that whether they're paying me or not, I'll report any intelligence that comes my way—specially at this most critical time. I've just proven that. The more I think about this, the more convinced I become that if I'm ever to get out of the Dominion, it'll have to be on my own.

"Look," Jacob says, following a long period of silence from his end. "Kipling and I are working on something—something that could blow this whole case wide open. We've managed to obtain good intel on the Mitchell brothers. If things go our way, the Dominion will fall long before the sixth of June and you'll never have anything to worry about again. In the meantime, if what you've given me today helps our case in the least bit, I'll ensure that you get your dues."

"Damn it, Jacob! I don't want a reward. I don't want any more money! I just want out! Please—"

"I hear you, I really do," Jacob replies, sympathetically. "There's nothing I care more about than your well-being. I don't think you realize the level of responsibility and stress I feel over your predicament. Hell, I've lost a lot of sleep over it. Fact is, you're in a unique situation that could spell the Dominion's demise and potentially save an unknown number of lives. I'm trying to cut through red tape at my end and get you cleared so we can start working with you again. In the meantime, if you hear anything about those training camps or anything else that's relevant, you don't have to keep it to yourself. Any piece of information could be crucial—"

"Just get me out, Jacob!" I shout. "You'll get nothing more from me until I get something from you!" I finish by slamming the pay phone receiver back onto its base. I stew for several minutes, watching the traffic go by. Truth be told, I've always been a terrible bluffer. Hence the gambling problems I've encountered in the past.

What worries me the most is that Jacob knows this.

CHAPTER 45

A month goes by and I still haven't received an invitation to attend the Dominion's training camps. I can hear Miroslav's voice. I play it over in my head. *Expect an invitation in the weeks to come.* Well, weeks have gone by. I should've gotten my invite by now. Something doesn't seem right and I can't sit still any longer. The longer I wait for my invitation to the camps, the greater the number of those being recruited and trained in warfare by the Dominion of God. I can't help but wonder why I've yet to be called upon. After all, *I am* one of the original members in the Dominion's resurrection.

Or am I?

In a stubborn attempt to connect with the group and to obtain an explanation, I keep myself busy by scouring the various websites I've been assigned, some of which no longer exist and some whose passwords have long expired. Despite this, I've managed to identify some potential recruits and have even discovered several blogs and tweets that may be of interest to Derek and company. When I find them, I refer them *via email* to The Prophet.

Still, I hear nothing in return.

I don't hear much from Jacob either, meaning there's still no progress in my exit strategy. But there's some good news. According to my former handler, the intelligence I last provided corroborates some intelligence Sergeant Kipling was able to gather at his own end. I don't have the slightest idea where Jacob or Kipling are getting their information, but I'm guessing it's through their counterparts south of the border—likely while looking into the Mitchell brothers. Or maybe in their investigation of Wes Sanderson and Brent Weiss they've stumbled upon a gold mine of information. Who knows. Of course, this corroborating information may even stem from Jacob and Kipling's own work. I mean, they now have reason to dig a little deeper into Dino & Sons and Sapphire's, not to mention the E-Z businesses and Reverend Hunt.

What Jacob *has* been able to tell me during our last conversation is that the Canadian training camp is believed to be somewhere in northern Alberta. As for the American training camp, authorities are looking in the states of Iowa and Vermont in areas where several prominent white supremacists are known to own properties—ranches and farms or isolated areas large enough to accommodate dozens of persons and their training activities without being discovered.

As for the England connection, little is known.

And every now and then, Jacob will call begging me to undergo the polygraph. Obviously, the corroboration of my reporting wasn't enough to appease the spy gods. So I tell him again the hell with it and that I'll no longer offer him anything—not without an exit strategy put in place. I even go so far as to gamble and tell him I do have more information but that I'm withholding it.

Another bad bluff.

Eventually, this completely backfires on me. About a month following my last unofficial debriefing with Jacob and only four days removed from the bluff, he calls me up and tells me they now have full confidence in me, that he's received the OK from his superiors to recommence the relationship. Only now, they want to pay me double.

I have to admit this is tempting. Still, I remain unconvinced. This could be a bluff as well—a way to squeeze this supposed intelligence out of me. I remind him I no longer need the money. I also insist on the initialization of a concrete plan to distance me from the movement once and for all.

No plan, no intelligence. That's all there is to it.

After giving Jacob this ultimatum, I don't hear from him or Kipling for quite some time. I spend most of this time when I'm not at work twiddling my thumbs and waiting for my invitation to the camp. I do get the odd phone call from Sarah, who keeps me up to date on her mother's condition. How I miss her. This is the longest we've ever been apart. I beg her to return. I promise her things will be better. That things will change. At times, she sounds like the Sarah of old—the one madly in love with me. Other times, she sounds very cold and aloof. I never know which Sarah I'm going to get. I guess that's what they call *karma* or *irony*. For years, she never knew which Liam she was getting.

In the end, the begging pays off. I end up welcoming her back with open arms in mid-May. Still, things aren't the same. There's something missing in her eyes. In her smile. No matter how hard I try, no matter what I do, I can't seem to get it to come back, whatever it is. She tells me she feels distant, that she's confused—so much so that, most nights, we even sleep in separate beds.

Needless to say, this is very difficult on me—on us. I feel a great sadness and emptiness unlike anything I've ever felt before. It seems everything is out of my control, slipping through my fingers like sand: Sarah. My exit strategy. My identity. My life. My soul.

Finally, I decide to pick myself up and take charge of some of the things that *are* in my control. For now, that may not be Sarah's love for me. But for her to love me again, I must resolve my situation with Jacob and the Dominion of God. I can no longer sit here and wait for others to resolve this for me.

For a while now, there have been things eating me up inside. Most revolve around Reverend Hunt and the Dominion's safe house. Although Jacob has insisted that Hunt isn't Black Mamba and isn't involved in the day-to-day operations of the organization, I remain unconvinced. As for the location of Cyril's execution, it comes as a surprise to me that it has yet to be discovered. Perhaps I'd been grossly inaccurate in my sense of its location. Perhaps I did lead the agency astray after all.

The first thing I decide to do is find that abandoned office building. So on a warm Sunday morning I hop into my car and head north on the 400 en route to E-Z Travel. Once there, I begin by retracing my steps, that is, getting back onto Jane and Finch and take the ramp bringing me onto the 400 heading south. It's only a matter of minutes until I reach my first point of reference: the Sheppard Avenue overpass.

At this point, I know I'm in the right ball park, but this is where I start to get confused. While I originally suspected we remained on the 400 until it becomes Black Creek Drive, it's also possible we did in fact merge onto the 401. Another point of confusion is the remaining number of overpasses we went under. From what I remember, we passed under another two that were only seconds apart. Or were they? Whatever the case, I end up exploring the 401 and Black Creek Drive.

I explore many different paths and countless streets and neighborhoods, some more than once. Upon discovering two overpasses along Black Creek and a third train overpass before its end at Weston Road, I come to the realization I'm in the right ball park. From this point on, I can't for the life of me recall how many more overpasses there were, if any. What I do recall was the sound of a train passing overhead as we crossed one of these tunnels. But this doesn't mean anything seeing as I now find myself in an area of town notorious for its myriad of train tracks.

Despite my best efforts on this day, I simply end up getting more confused and more frustrated with every unsuccessful avenue I take beyond Black Creek. So, I decide to call it a day.

The next day, before my scheduled shift at Henrique's, I go as far as exploring the Junction, an area of the city where a set of east-west rails connect with a set of north-south rails. I swear to God, I end up exploring every single inch of every single street of the area, but to no avail. Out of desperation, I even venture in Parkdale, near my own neighborhood. Still nothing.

Finally, I decide to return to the Junction where I eventually discover another intersection of north-south and east-west rails. It's while taking a left on St. Clair Avenue off Weston Road that I find my final reference points: two train overpasses only several blocks apart. Immediately after the second overpass, I take a right onto Caledonia Park Road.

I reduce my speed to get a better glimpse of the area. To the left, nothing but a park followed by grassy knolls and trees. To my right, an empty parking lot followed by an old winery, a garden centre, a wine store, a small used auto shop and an empty lot. Just past this lot is another structure. Three stories high. Old. Decrepit. About three hundred yards past it is a hydro enclosure.

I decide to round the corner onto Davenport, which leads me under another rail overpass. I then take a quick right onto Wiltshire Road, which brings me to the other side of the tracks, giving me a rear view of the suspect building. I pull over to the side of the road next to a hydro tower and kill the engine.

I roll down the window and listen. The loud and distinct humming of electricity fills the air. At the back of the complex, just past an empty field and a parking lot separated by a chain link fence, is a set of steps leading up to a platform and a loading dock. I clear my throat.

It has to be the spot. It has to be.

I sit there for a while, pondering my next move. *Do I go back to Jacob with this?* For all I know, his people have already discovered this place on their own and have gone through it with a fine-toothed comb. Maybe I'm completely off and nowhere near my target.

Instead of wasting everyone's time and risking delivering false information that would ultimately discredit me again in their forever mistrustful eyes, I decide to explore the area on foot. But first I drive away from the scene and park my vehicle a block away and out of sight just to be prudent.

As I make my way back to the abandoned structure on foot, I scrutinize my surroundings, conducting my own counter-surveillance. At this point, I can never be too careful. Not only might the Dominion be following me, but Jacob's men might be as well. I'll be the first to admit that I've become paranoid. Thankfully, this happens to be a quiet neighborhood with very little activity.

I ultimately cut back across Wiltshire and through a grassy lot at the end of which sit several unused freight vans, flat beds and other mobile containers. I filter my way through them and cross the train tracks until coming upon the chain link fence and some bushes. Taking cover behind them, I listen for any sounds. Nothing. Only the fence, along with an empty and weed-infested parking lot, stands between me and what I hope is the Dominion's hideout.

I wait, listening, observing. Keeping a close eye the building, paying close attention to any window that hasn't yet been boarded up. Only two remain from the second floor and one at the basement level.

I continue to watch and listen.

Still nothing.

Still no one.

I quickly scale the fence and head to the structure's loading zone. After climbing the platform, I attempt to open the doors. Locked. I wasn't expecting anything less. I step off the platform and position myself directly beneath the large retracting garage door. It's about five feet from the ground, so I'm barely able to reach over the edge. Determined, I grab the bottom rubber strip and metal handle in attempt to pry it open, but it won't budge.

Desperate, I scramble around in search of something—anything—to give me better leverage. Despite my best efforts, I find nothing of use.

But suddenly it occurs to me to sprint back to the railway line, scaling the fence yet again along the way.

As with most railways, the track is littered with many discarded items, mostly debris and garbage. What I do keep my eyes peeled open for and what I'm hoping to find is the odd railway tool that can sometimes be found abandoned along the tracks. A spike. A crowbar. A shovel. Anything. If not along the rail, then perhaps at the back of the auto yard just down the road. What I do happen to stumble upon, however, is even better: an old and rusted switch alignment tool half buried beneath gravel and bushes along the tracks. Roughly six feet in length and solid steel, it should work perfectly for my needs.

I quickly liberate my new-found tool and return to the loading dock, still keeping a watchful eye. Thanks to the hydro yard to the south, a grassy knoll and a row of trees to the east across Caledonia Park Road, the used car dealership some distance away to the north, and of course the railway to the west, there's not much to worry about.

This time around, I don't mount the platform. Instead, I make my way at ground level to the garage door. Resting the switch bar on my shoulder and clutching it with both hands, I drive it beneath the large retracting door and upward toward the sky. Putting all my weight into it and using every last ounce of strength in me, I manage to finally budge the door open a few inches. I peer through the small crack and look inside.

All is dark and quiet.

I slide the switch bar further into the crevice and heave again. The door grinds and creaks open another few inches. Thankfully, it remains open, apparently jammed, the moment I release my weight beneath the switch bar. I slide the bar deeper into the crevice and push toward the open sky. It gives a few more inches before I'm at the very end of the tool and can bring it no further above my head. A gap of about one-and-a-half feet wide is the end result.

Not wasting any time, I slide the switch bar just inside the gap and attempt to slither through the opening. This proves extremely difficult, since I have to jump and slide simultaneously. Only half my body makes it through on the first try, my legs hanging outside. On my second try, I sort of jump and manage to get one leg in, which is enough to keep me over the edge. I squirm and squeeze my way under the door, tearing my jacket along the way. Once inside, I push down on the handle at the bottom of the door with all my weight until it grinds shut once again. I then pause to catch my breath.

This better be the right place . . .

Now my hearing and sight have never been my strengths. But my sense of smell has never led me astray. And the acrid smell I instantly notice upon breaking into the building confirms my suspicions. Without a doubt, I'm at the right location. I've hit the jackpot.

Adjacent to the loading dock is the exterior pedestrian door and a hallway disappearing into the basement. I cautiously tiptoe to the stairwell, forgetting completely about the switch bar. I can't see a thing at the bottom of the stairs. The only light switch I can find is for the loading area, which I opt to keep turned off for fear the lights will be noticed from the outside. I slowly make my way down, one step at a time, until I become immersed in total darkness. I take baby steps down the musty corridor, feeling my way around. I use the concrete wall for guidance and eventually stumble upon a closed door. I reach for the handle and open it without too much difficulty.

Inside the room, I blindly search for a light switch, which I eventually find just right of the door. The light flickers at a low wattage and reveals the room's contents. A tiny space, it appears to be nothing more than a storage closet. A shelf directly to my left is filled with cleaning products, dirty rags and old cans of paint. However, lying on the floor next to several empty buckets is a flashlight. I pick it up and am relieved to discover it still works. I scour the room for anything suspicious but nothing stands out. I then kill the lights, exit the room and quietly shut the door.

The light emanating from the flashlight is more than sufficient to help me find my way around. Everything is as I recall. Concrete everywhere. The floors. The walls. The ceiling. Grey metal doors with latches. The air, damp and musty, is also the same. Not to mention that acrid smell of some type of product, perhaps paint thinner.

Instead of investigating every single door along the corridor, I dart to the very last door on the right, where we had gathered a few months ago. I reach for the handle, turn it slowly and open the door. The room is completely bare. No chairs. Nothing. The walls and floor, once covered in Cyril's blood and brain matter, are completely unmarked. All evidence has obviously been washed away.

I waste no time there and return to the dark hallway. I turn immediately to the room directly across and open the door. What I discover inside stops me dead in my tracks. I direct the light in all directions, revealing even more troubling sights. The room is large and, unlike the rest of the structure, very well maintained and ventilated. In one corner sit industrial-sized drums of an suspicious chemical neatly stacked in double rows. All their labels say the same thing: "Acetone QTY 25 L," with a brief description of its properties. Below these labels are other labels—red ones—each with a fire symbol and the words "FLAMMABLE LIQUID" beneath it. I count twenty-five of these containers.

In the opposite corner are black drums of another product. Their labels read "35% Hydrogen Peroxide 55 kg." Yellow labels beneath them say "OXIDIZER," along with a symbol of a circle engulfed in flames. I count fifteen altogether.

In the center of the room is a large table with various tools—the kind of stuff mad scientists use in cheap horror movies. Beakers. Funnels. Glass cylinders. Thermometers. Large plastic tubs stacked one on top of the other. Mixing sticks. A couple of heating plates. A few more gadgets with lights—one that beeps every few seconds. I never did take chemistry in high school so everything is quite foreign to me. One thing is certain: something very sinister is going on here.

I direct the flashlight to the opposite corner of the room and discover three empty bathtubs lined up next to one another along the wall. In the other corner are three freezers and two large appliances I can't identify. Upon closer inspection, I realize they're in fact refrigerators, but not the typical kitchen appliance kind. No, these are industrial refrigerators, the kind used in research facilities, hospitals or clinics. I've seen these before. A thick glass pane at the center of each enables a view of their interiors. Inside each, numerous containers can be seen resting on their shelves. One by one, I attempt to open their doors, but they're all locked. Each has a digital thermometer reading 5 C. On each are many levers and buttons whose functions I can't begin to comprehend.

I just stand there, gaping and completely perplexed. *Bathtubs?? Refrigerators?? Are you kidding me? What's next?*

I make my way over to the freezers and open the first one. Inside, there's nothing. Same for the second one. However, upon opening the third, I notice it's filled with ice. Stacks and stacks of ice and nothing else.

Along the same wall, just below a boarded window, are a few shelving units. On one of the shelves sit a dozen 950-milliliter bottles of 98 per cent sulfuric acid. On the lower shelf there's a box of thermometers. Next to it, another box containing 5-milliliter and 10-milliliter glass syringes. A pair of protective goggles sits next to them. On the bottom shelf are boxes of salt, dirty rags and paper filters that look like coffee filters.

My first impression is that the Dominion has indeed taken on the production of narcotics to fund its operations. But, last I heard, crystal meth isn't produced out of acetone or hydrogen peroxide or sulfuric acid. Then I remember something Frank and Jacob had mentioned during our first conversations: an explosive referred to as the "Mother of Satan." Other than it being used in the mosque bombings, I struggle to remember any further details about the production of this substance. But something tells me I may have hit the jackpot.

I dare not touch anything. The way it was explained—at least from what I recall—the Mother of Satan, or whatever its scientific name is, is extremely volatile and can be detonated by the slightest perturbation in its environment. A loud sound. A sudden change in temperature. Friction. A spark. Virtually anything can set it off.

Although I fail to find any amount of the white powdery substance, my initial instinct is to get the hell out of here and contact Jacob. That would be the rational thing to do, I know. But something eggs me on. Something tells me there's more here than meets the eye.

I carefully back out of the room and close the door behind me. I then make my way over to the adjacent door and open it. Again, I freeze dead in my tracks. Directly in front of me are cases and cases of ammunition—stacked almost to the ceiling. I'm talking about ammo for AK-47s, M-16s, Uzis, cartridges for twelve-gauge shotguns and riot guns, as well as ammo for sniper rifles such as the Dragunov and the M82. Amid the cache are also hand grenades and magazines for various nine-millimeter pistols. Even more shocking, I spot a dozen or so stinger missiles resting in wooden crates at the back of the room.

I just stand there, in total shock. There's no point in even estimating the number of rounds and ammunition in the room. That's not really what concerns me. What does concern me is how they ever got here in the first place and what their ultimate use will be. Granted, Wes Sanderson and Brent Weiss likely have something to do with it. Together, they form a perfect open portal.

As I back away and turn to leave, I accidentally bump into a small table on which sit stacks of papers and a few clipboards. I shine the light on these and realize they're nothing more than inventories of the ammunition before me. Scanning the inventory, I conclude that this particular cache may only be a fraction of the Dominion's total armament. According to its inventory, forty-six stinger missiles are said to be accounted for. Even after scouring the area more attentively, I can find only twelve. This leads me to believe that Derek and the boys may have another stockpile somewhere in city—or at the very least, in the country.

Grabbing one of the clipboards, I notice a series of forms that strike me as curious. From what I can tell, they appear to be transactions and shipments between two entities. At the very top is a document with the heading *Cargo Control Document*. According to this form, a shipment destined to Dino & Sons in Toronto, Canada, arrived at the port of Montreal on March 3. The originating port is indicated as Livorno in Italy. The reported carrier is Hanjin Shipping, with a total of four containers carrying auto parts listed as engines, transmissions, radiators and carburetors of various imported vehicles. As I go through the pages, a particular invoice catches my eye. On the form, the buyer is indicated as D. Mancelli of Dino & Sons Auto Wreckers. The seller is AKJ Petrovic Inc. originating out of Serbia. The transaction amount is US $65,000.00, and there's a breakdown of the quantity of units and selling price. I find a detailed description of the goods and their weight on the next page. Not surprisingly, the order includes numerous car parts, most for European vehicles. The documents that follow include a Canada Customs invoice, a Canada Customs Coding Form and duties paid.

The next set of documents is a whole new series of identical forms for a separate shipment, only this one dated January 16. The seller this time is Marko K. Garage. After that, another package with forms dated December 27. Again, the seller is Marko K. Garage. This goes on and on and by the time I reach the final package, I've counted eight different shipments in all—each spread approximately one month apart. What doesn't add up is the cost per part, which seems to be grossly overpriced.

On another clipboard is another series of shipments and invoices. However, in these cases, the buyer has become the seller and the seller has become the buyer. What's interesting is the fact that Marko K. Garage or AKJ Petrovic appear to be buying luxury vehicles and parts, mostly imported models. Jaguars. Mercedes. BMWs. Even more curious is the fact that Dino & Sons is selling the vehicles and parts for a very moderate price. I'm talking about brand new BMWs for $15,000. They may as well be giving them away.

I remember Jacob mentioning something about a remittance system. For the life of me, I can't remember its name, but maybe that's what's going on here. Otherwise why would Dino's be purchasing vehicle parts for such outrageous prices and selling his vehicles—likely stolen, I might add—at such a discounted price?

With all the ammunition surrounding me, I begin to wonder why these documents were left sitting here among the rest. I take one good look at the skids and the crates sitting on them, the latter all labeled AKJ Petrovic Inc. Then it dawns on me: the Dominion is smuggling its weapons—or at least some of them—directly through Dino & Sons and hidden among, or in the guise of, auto parts. It makes perfect sense. It doesn't take a genius to conceal ammunition, weapons, or their components among auto parts. I'd be willing to bet that someone in the Dominion, likely Miroslav or Vladimir, has connections with someone at AKJ Petrovic or Marko K. Garage who's connected to an arms dealer in the Balkans. Jacob was right. E-Z Grocery was only a smokescreen. I'm guessing that the large withdrawals from Marcus Black's second bank account were going straight into the hands of Dino & Sons, and that if the Serbs raided Marko K. Garage or AKJ Petrovic Inc., they wouldn't come up empty-handed this time around.

I contemplate taking the clipboards and all the other documents spread out on the table. But I'm interrupted by yet another thought. So far, I've found no trace of any weapons of any kind—only ammunition. I entertain the idea that the weapons may actually be in use right now in one—or perhaps all—of the Dominion's training camps. That, or there are in fact more of these stockpiles lying around the city somewhere, or beyond. I strongly doubt that Derek and the other head honchos would put all their eggs in one basket.

As I'm about to exit the room, my hip catches the light makeshift table, sending several documents and a white Styrofoam container crashing to the ground. From the cup, a dark liquid spills across the floor. The smell of coffee fills the air. I bend down to examine the mess, using the flashlight to assess the damages. I can only stare in disbelief and pray that the heap of documents lying there weren't in any specific order.

As I quickly pick up the mess, my hands come across folded maps of some kind—at least that's my initial impression. Upon unfolding them, I realize they're not maps, but blueprints. On one of the blueprints, the various floors of a building are laid out. At the top of each page are the words CENTRE BLOCK followed by a numbered floor.

Holy mother of . . .

Everything I can imagine a blueprint to reveal is displayed: measurements, dimensions, angles, walls, doorways, windows, staircases—the whole kit and caboodle. Each room on all six floors is clearly identified. The largest rooms are identified as the House of Commons Chamber at the west end, the Senate Chamber at the east end and the Library of Parliament at the north end of the ground floor. The blueprint, evidently a copy of an original, is marked with handwritten notes and notations in red marker. All exterior exits are coded and highlighted in yellow. Some windows are also highlighted, as are several corridors. Interestingly, each and every single marker appears to be coded in a similar fashion. My best guess is that these codes are meant to indicate where a man is to be stationed, along with a specific weapon.

Sifting through the prints, I'm able to recognize two more sets identified only as the WEST BLOCK and the EAST BLOCK, which display similar color-coding.

Among the mix of sheets scattered across the floor is a floor plan for the House of Commons and Senate, each seat clearly identified with the name of a member of parliament or senator. Several red markers are indicated near the entrance to these chambers with the lettering 'Area of Execution' hand-written in red ink. Also written in ink are the words *House sitting June 4-8* and *Phase III: June 6 @ 14:00.*

"They're planning a bloody coup," I whisper quietly to myself.

I've already seen enough to know exactly what's going on. The Dominion plans on overthrowing the government—and who knows what else—the same day the peace treaty is to be signed, only a month or so away. I momentarily lose myself in my thoughts as I try to cope with the urgency and severity of the situation.

I pick up all the documents and place them back on the table. I then take a quick look around the room for anything to clean up the coffee that has pooled across the floor. Nothing. Remembering some of the items in the storage closet down the hall, I retrace my steps and retrieve an old rag and return to the affected room. The moment I lay the rag down to wipe away the coffee, I know there's something terribly wrong. Cautiously, I pick up the Styrofoam cup which still has some coffee left in it. I run my finger inside. *Still lukewarm*, I tell myself, shivers now running down my spine. *Someone was just here.*

I quickly gather all the documents and am about to leave the room when I hear a noise coming from outside. An engine. The sound of car doors slamming shut. In a panic, I drop the documents on the desk and exit, closing the door behind me. I then dart toward the stairs and make my way back up to the loading zone, turning off the flashlight and retrieving the switch bar. As I'm about to head through the back door, I hear muffled voices approaching. I quickly retreat to the lobby, hoping to make my escape through the front door. Any hopes of a clean getaway are instantly thwarted by the sight of two shadows making their way toward the main entrance. My heart races.

Desperate, I dash toward the large staircase and make my way up to the catwalk overlooking the lobby. That's when I notice the place is rigged with motion detectors. A tiny red light near the ceiling blinks as I pass by on my way to one of the vacant office rooms. I gently shut the door and listen for further noise with my ear pressed against it.

Silence.

Suddenly I hear two parties entering quietly, one through the main entrance, the other through the back door. There are no voices. At times, footsteps are heard making their way across the lobby, the sound echoing off the walls. There's no way of telling how many people there are. I take a quick look around the room for a place to hide. That's when I notice the blinking lights and the dark rectangular components from which they emanate. I count six in all, sitting atop one another on a shelving unit. Wires everywhere. Next to this unit, three computer monitors, along with their own system, keyboard and mouse, sit across a large but cheap looking table. *And there you have it,* I tell myself, *the servers for Vica.net no doubt.*

I turn my attention to the large window at the far end, quietly making my way over. A quick glance down through the dirty pane offers no reassurance. Although this is only the second floor, it's more like the third or fourth floor of most modern buildings—far too high for me to jump and land unscathed. I'd probably break a limb, or worse. While I'm thinking about this, I hear the sound of chatter.

"Go check upstairs," orders a voice as I reposition my ear at the door. I then hear two separate sets of footsteps going in opposite directions, one moving away, the other heading up the staircase.

I brace myself for an inevitable confrontation, gripping the switch bar tightly. My palms and forehead are dripping with sweat, my heart beating like a drum. I know full well that whatever happens next, it'll be do or die. There'll be no questions asked. I won't get a second chance.

Seconds seem to tick by like hours as I listen to the steps closing in. Suddenly, they cease, and I hear the sound of a door creaking open at the far end of the hall. Silence ensues. The door creaking shut. More footsteps, only closer this time. Another door creaking open and closing again. Footsteps. Another door opens and closes. The footsteps get heavier and louder until they come to a stop directly behind my door. At the bottom of the door, I spot two shadows through the crease.

I position myself against the wall, holding the switch bar like a bat and ready to strike. I wait for what seems like an eternity until the door knob slowly rotates clockwise.

The door opens slowly . . . very slowly.

I watch as a man's arm and shoulder emerge through the doorway, a Smith & Wesson pistol in hand. With every last ounce of strength, I swing the switch bar, striking the intruder across the forearm. A loud shriek ensues as the pistol falls to the ground. I immediately retrieve it and get my stalker into a head lock, dragging him into the room. The sounds of a stampede and loud voices follow, as others make their way up the balcony stairs. When I finally realize who I've struck, my whole world turns upside down and shatters into a million pieces.

CHAPTER 46

No one says a word before Derek and Mario appear at the doorway, freezing suddenly in their tracks. Both are wielding what appear to be Beretta pistols, which are pointed straight at my chest. I shield myself with their accomplice, digging the muzzle of the Smith & Wesson into his temple. Seconds go by in an awkward and confused silence, each man struggling to make sense of what's happening.

"Liam . . . listen . . . there's a good explanation for this," Kipling says, fighting to spit out his words beneath my grip. His face is already beet red and on the verge of turning blue, but I don't care. I'm not about to let go anytime soon.

Derek and Mario look on, redirecting their sights directly to my forehead. Still, they don't fire, as though waiting for a cue or instruction. I back away almost to the end of the room in order to complicate any shot they may have. "Don't fuckin' move!" I shout, as they take a step forward. "I'll blow his goddamn head off! You hear me? Stay back and don't move!"

"Liam, don't do anything stupid," Kipling begs, with one arm completely limp and dripping with blood. It appears broken, with a large lump almost breaking the darkening skin. Still, he's a strong man, even despite his age. I have no doubt he can easily take me down with one arm should I give him an inch.

I tighten my grip. Kipling struggles to breathe. "Jesus Christ, Lou! Are you him? Huh?" I say, keeping an eye on Derek and Mario. "Is this him? Your leader? Your Black Mamba?"

"Liam, put the gun down," Mario pleads, lowering his pistol.

I say nothing and hold my ground.

"Come on, Liam," Derek says, still pointing his gun at me. "Put the gun down. You don't want to do anything stupid now, do you? You're one of us, remember? You're one of God's holy warriors. You—"

"No, I'm not one of you, Derek!" I bark. "I'm not a holy warrior and neither are you! You got that? You're just a terrorist—a misguided punk and nothing more!"

"I know you don't mean that—"

"Shut the hell up, Derek. If you don't think for one second I won't shoot, you're only kidding yourself. Now, this is how it's going to work," I say, as convincingly as I can. "Both of you will drop your weapons and kick them over to me. Then, you'll back away and move to the far end of the hall. I'm bringing Kipling with me. If either of you do as much as even take a step forward before I'm out the door, I blow his brains out. You got that?"

Derek only smirks, amused. "I don't think so, my friend."

So that they know I mean business, I fire a round, taking off Kipling's right ear. Nothing but a bloody mess of loose skin remains, hanging there like ground beef.

"Drop your goddamn weapons!" I repeat.

Kipling shrieks and coughs, attempting to loosen my grip. "You heard him," he sneers, spitting through his teeth. "Drop your weapons!"

Derek and Mario glance over to one another, then back to Kipling in disbelief.

"God damn it, drop your weapons!" Kipling shouts.

Although hesitant, both men comply. Their gazes alternate between Kipling and me. Then they kick their pistols forward and back away.

I guide Kipling to the ground and retrieve the discarded weapons, stuffing the two Berettas under my belt. I then direct Kipling to move forward, one step at a time. At no point do I relinquish my grip or remove my pistol from his temple. "That's it . . . keep moving back . . ." I order, keeping a very keen eye on Derek and Mario, who are now following my instructions.

After making it out of the room, I order both men to move all the way back to the end of the walkway and to remain there until I exit the building. I remind them that if they move even an inch, Kipling loses much more than an ear.

"Liam, Kipling is one of us!" Mario shouts, as though I hadn't figured it out.

"Oh yeah? Do you know he's a cop?"

"We know that, you idiot!" Derek replies dryly.

"And that's why I'm taking him in . . ."

Derek laughs—a devious and arrogant laugh. "Taking him in? To who? The cops?"

"That's right."

"Are you sure you want to do that?"

I don't respond to this. And to be perfectly honest, I don't have the slightest clue what to do with Kipling. I mean, here I am, a Joe-nobody holding a decorated federal police officer hostage, having broken his arm and blown off his ear. And if I'm lucky enough to drag him back to my car without being seen and getting him all the way to the nearest police precinct, who knows how things would unfold then. I'd likely end up being taken into custody, and it would ultimately be my word against his. For all I know, there could be others like Kipling out there. Cops. Border officers. Prison guards. Anyone.

I really don't know what to do.

But first and foremost, I need to get the hell out of here.

Slowly, I guide Kipling back to the staircase, one step at a time. Every now and then, I take a quick look behind me, just to make certain there are no more surprises. I give Derek and Mario one last glance before we make our way down the steps. Although they're momentarily lost from view, I hear no movement coming from the gallery above. By the time Kipling and I have made it to ground level, I'm able to spot them once again. Neither has moved from their position against the wall at the far end of the gallery.

"You're making a big mistake," Kipling scoffs, panting heavily.

"Hey Liam!" Derek shouts, his voice echoing off the lobby walls. "This is your last chance! Let Kipling go . . . we'll work this out."

"Fuck you, Derek!"

"The moment you step out that door, you become one of them . . . the spawn of Satan. You'll be an enemy of the Dominion! You'll be left behind come the Rapture and you'll burn in the Lake of Fire with the other mongrels—you and that pretty little girl of yours!"

I say no more and drag Kipling to the main entrance. I push back on the crash bar, and we exit into the daylight to find ourselves on a quiet Caledonia Park Road. This is the most critical part of my dilemma. I can't possibly take Kipling around the back and get him over the fence. That leaves me with only one option: a short trek down Caledonia and under the train overpass to get around the other side of the block. From there, I'll only have two blocks to go to get to my car. What concerns me more though, is the fact I no longer have a visual on Derek and Mario. They could be up to anything at this point. Odds are they're calling others from the Dominion and planning an ambush. Maybe they're calling the cops themselves, giving an anonymous tip, telling them a member of the Dominion of God has just kidnapped a federal police officer. Whatever the case, I have to act fast.

Tightening my grip around Kipling's neck, I increase the pace as we make our way down the street. A thin trail of blood follows us, Kipling's arm now bleeding profusely. Although there are no bystanders around on this deserted street, this surely won't be the case after we round the corner and continue down a much busier Davenport Road.

Man, I wish I hadn't parked so far away . . .

By this time, Kipling has gone pretty limp, his feet simply dragging along behind him. At times, he tries to strike me with his good arm. Other times, he struggles to free himself from my grip. The more he squirms, the more pressure I apply, stopping just short of suffocating him.

Shortly after we get onto Davenport and are under the train overpass, a distant yet distinct sound is heard. It's still some ways away, but unmistakable—police sirens. It takes Kipling longer to notice it, but when he finally does, he makes one last desperate attempt to escape and a struggle ensues. We both fall to the ground, prompting me to accidentally fire my weapon into the air, the bullet ricocheting off the overpass's metal frame. Kipling's cell phone is ripped from his belt and skitters along the pavement. Unfazed, I get back to my feet and try to restrain him again. This time, however, he's ready for it. With one swift blow, he hits me right in the groin with his good arm. I collapse, releasing my grip.

The pain is unbearable and I can't do a thing except watch as Kipling races down the street back to the Dominion's safe house, holding his injured arm with his good one. The sirens become louder as he disappears around the corner. Despite the pain, I force myself back up, re-energized by a sudden, troublesome thought. At this very minute Sarah is sleeping peacefully at home, as she usually does before her night shift. The image of her face flashes before my eyes.

The sirens are closing in, perhaps just a few blocks away. I take one quick look at myself, my clothes stained with Kipling's blood. Fastened to my belt are two Berettas, not counting the Smith & Wesson in my hand. I have no idea what's been reported or by who. Covered in blood and branding three firearms, I doubt things will go in my favor. I'll definitely be arrested and taken in for questioning and likely detained indefinitely.

Derek's last words echo in my mind. It doesn't take long to realize what I have to do. I'm sure the Dominion will be coming for Sarah, and I can't afford to leave her unprotected and vulnerable. So for now, the hell with the cops.

But Sarah isn't the only one in grave danger. Kipling knows I'll be going straight to my handler to report this. I have to get to him before Kipling does or else things could get much, much worse. *I have to get to Sarah*, I finally resolve. *Jacob can wait until I know she's safe.*

I'm about to make a run for it when I spot it—Kipling's cell phone. I pick it up and stare at it for a moment. It looks exactly like the one I've been assigned to on occasion. Reeling from this stroke of luck, I stash it in my jacket, intending to explore it the moment I'm out of harm's way.

I then make a mad sprint toward my vehicle, which I can now see in the distance. The wailing sirens behind me become louder with every step. Along the way, I pass a few locals who stare at me as though witnessing a crime in progress. I pay no attention to them and increase my pace.

By the time I reach my car and leap inside, I spot four police cruisers zipping down Davenport toward the general area of the Dominion's hideaway. I immediately duck and keep my head down while reaching for my cell phone buried deep inside my pocket. Frantic, I manage to thumb my way to my frequent contacts list and dial Sarah's cell phone number. I let it ring until I reach her voicemail.

"Baby, it's me." I say frantically. "If you're home, you need to get out of the house now! I can't explain right now—there's no time. You have to get out now! Meet me at our favorite coffee shop! Please just do it!"

I hang up and try our landline.

Still no answer.

Again, I leave her the same message. I end up cursing all the curses I can possibly think of and throwing the phone on the floor. I then quickly slip the key in the ignition and make my escape, accelerating only once I've left the neighborhood.

It takes me some time to digest what's just happened and what I've just uncovered. And I know what I've become in the eyes of the Dominion: an enemy, an infidel, a spawn of Satan. And something even worse: a traitor. In the eyes of supremacists and extremists, there's no lower form of life than a person who's betrayed his own race or his own religion.

My life literally hangs on Jacob's help and loyalty. I can't imagine how he'll react to the news of Kipling's involvement in the Dominion of God, not to mention Kipling being Black Mamba. It sounds too incredible, almost impossible. But I get the feeling Jacob will believe me. At this point, he's the only person on earth who I feel I can trust. Now, if only I can get him and the agency to return that trust.

CHAPTER 47

The door is unlocked when I get home, which is strangely uncharacteristic of Sarah. She always locks the door, even when I'm there. Nervously, I step inside, keeping Kipling's pistol aimed in front of me.

"Sarah?" I call.

Nothing.

"Sarah?"

Everything looks fine—at first. When I get to the bedroom, though, my heart practically stops. It's as though a hurricane has gone through the room. The furniture is toppled over, drawers emptied and clothes thrown around everywhere. The mattress is falling off the box spring, resting partially on the floor. A few drops of blood spot the sheets and the floor. Amid the chaos, Sarah is nowhere to be found.

I frantically search the other rooms.

Still no Sarah.

It had taken me just short of twenty minutes to get home. That's how quick the Dominion must have acted. So fast, that I begin to wonder if it was indeed the Dominion. But my doubts are swiftly put to rest when I re-enter the living area and notice something I'd missed coming in: a message on the wall next to the dining table. Written in what appears to be blood, it reads:

WE KNOW WHO YOU ARE.

I freeze in complete terror, my eyes fixated on the drying blood. I shudder to think whose blood is smeared across that wall. I cringe even more to think what they've done to her, or what they might still do. My entire body begins to tremble. My legs and knees feel like jelly and I begin to hyperventilate. Collapsing to the floor, I lean back against the wall.

All rational thought has fled. It's as though time has just stopped, leaving me hanging in this eternal nightmare. It takes all I have not to weep. I know that to survive this and whatever happens from this point on, I must be strong—for my sake and for Sarah's.

I reach for my cell phone buried deep inside my pocket. I flip it open and attempt to call Jacob. In the midst of the ringing, it dies on me. For a few seconds, I just sit there in denial, staring at the blank screen. All the curses of the world spring inside my head. I then search for the receiver for our land line, which I find lying on the floor in our bedroom. The only problem is, I can't for the life of me remember Jacob's telephone number. I try several numbers, anything close to what I believe to be his number. They're all wrong. I go through my wallet hoping to find his—or should I say Jake Hartman's—business card. Nothing. In frustration, I end up throwing the receiver across the room where it crashes against the opposing wall and onto the floor.

As I'm about to break down and cry, having nearly lost all hope, the receiver lights up and begins to ring. Frozen, I wait for it to ring again, thinking I may have imagined it or that it may be acting up as a result of my outburst. More ringing.

My heart races. *It's the Dominion,* I tell myself, *likely Derek or maybe even Kipling. They're going to tell me they have Sarah. They're going to insist I turn myself in or she'll get it. They're going to insist that one of us be purified.*

I crawl to the receiver and pick it up.

"Hello?"

"Liam, it's Jacob. Did you just try calling me on your—"

"Jacob! Oh, thank God! They have Sarah . . . she's gone . . . they took her—"

"Whoa! Slow down," Jacob replies. "Who took who?"

I pause to catch my breath. "The Dominion—they took Sarah . . . there's blood everywhere! You have to help me!"

"OK, stay calm. Let me get Kipling on—"

"No—not Kipling!" I shout. "Jacob, he's in on it! He's with the Dominion!"

"What?"

"Kipling! He's one of them!" I reply, nearing delirium. "I think he's Black Mamba! I found their hideout! I found Kipling there! I—"

"That's impossible—"

"No, it's *very* possible! I'm telling you, I found this commercial space, this secret location . . . the same one where Cyril was executed. I found it! The address is 10 Caledonia Park Road. The basement is filled with ammunition and explosives. I think they may even be fabricating IEDs! Jacob, there's this lab downstairs, you should see it—there's enough shit to blow out a city block. There's also this room with computer equipment . . . servers and stuff. Probably for Vica.net. And that's not all—"

"Slow down and let me get a pen," Jacob says, "OK. 10 Caledonia Park Road . . . go on . . ."

"I think they're planning an attack of some sort, on Parliament Hill. They have these plans and blueprints and stuff. I'm telling you, something's about to go down real soon. June sixth. They're planning a coup to overthrow the government. That's Phase III! The Dominion isn't just a small cult anymore. It's now a full-fledged paramilitary organization!"

"Holy Mother of Jesus . . ." I can hear Jacob inhaling sharply. "Liam, are you absolutely sure about this? Where does Kipling fit in?"

"He was there—at their hideout," I reply, returning to the living area in order to keep an eye out the front window. "I must have triggered an alarm or something. He—Kipling, he responded. With Derek and Mario—I barely escaped."

At this point, I can barely formulate a coherent sentence. There's so much I need to tell him and all I can think of is Sarah. "Look, Kipling is one of them, trust me on this. You can't go to him. And he must know by now that we've spoken, so you're in danger—but Jesus, Jacob, they have Sarah. You have to help me!"

"OK, just stay cool," Jacob replies calmly. "I'm going to help you. But for now, you need to get out of there. They may come back for you."

He's right. I can't stay. In fact, I'm astonished no one was here waiting for me. *Why would they take off with Sarah instead of just putting a bullet in my brain? Why?* It doesn't make any sense to me. Of course, nothing makes any sense anymore.

"Where do you want me to go?" I ask.

"Can you make it to the safe house, say . . . within an hour?"

"The safe house? Does Kipling know about it?"

"No, he doesn't," Jacob says without hesitation. "Only I and my superiors know about it—and you, of course."

"Are you sure?"

"One hundred and fifty percent."

"Alright, I'll meet you there."

"Good. I'll be there waiting," Jacob says. "In the meantime, I have to get in touch with the big men upstairs. This is huge. This is going to rattle everyone involved."

"Be careful who you talk to!" I warn, my confidence in our police and security officials shaken. "Don't trust—"

"Don't worry," Jacob says. "I know exactly who to go to. That address on Caledonia Park? I'm going to get our most trusted contacts at TPS to scout the place ASAP. Just look after yourself and be careful."

I want to say more, I'm just not sure what. Maybe how desperate I am over Sarah. That I've made mistakes. That I'd do anything in the world to make sure I get her back safe and sound. That I love her. I want to tell someone how important she is to me, how much she means to me. But that's all mushy stuff and there's no time for that.

"Jacob . . ."

"Yeah?"

"Please help me find Sarah," I say, holding back tears.

"We'll find her, Liam," he replies, softly. "I promise you. We'll file a missing person report right away. As for Kipling, we'll need evidence. If we find what you say there is to find on Caledonia Park, we'll take action."

"OK."

"I'll update you at the safe house."

I hang up the phone, still staring at the message written in Sarah's blood. I take one last look around the house to be certain I haven't missed anything that could help explain what happened here just moments ago. But there's nothing.

Before leaving, I check all three pistols tucked neatly under my belt. With the exception for Kipling's Smith & Wesson, all are fully loaded. And that's when it occurs to me: Kipling's piece appears to be one issued by his agency. *How's he going to explain this to his superiors?* I ask myself, managing a slight grin. *After all, bullets were fired on Caledonia*

Park Road. That proves he was there. And I have his firearm. That may well be the evidence I need.

Keeping the two Berettas stuffed under my belt, I hide Kipling's piece inside my jacket's inner pockets. Taking a deep breath, I peer through the peephole and head out the door.

CHAPTER 48

Before knocking, I sneak up to the door and listen. I'm not sure why, I just do. Call me paranoid at this point—perhaps even clinically—and I'll accept that. I can't help but feel there's no safe place. Not even at a safe house. I wouldn't put anything past the Dominion at this point. In fact, if the group had uncovered the safe house, or if Jacob were to turn up dead, it would come as no shock to me.

I listen for any sound, any voices coming from the inside.

Nothing.

I look around and behind me to make certain I'm not being followed, as I've been doing since I stepped out of my apartment. I then rap on the door and wait while I hear footsteps approaching. The peephole goes dark for a few seconds and the door slowly opens.

"Good, glad to see you made it," Jacob says, stepping aside to let me enter. He then closes and locks the door behind us. He then reaches over and shakes my hand—a handshake that's different from all previous handshakes. Heartfelt. Sympathetic. Like the type offered at funerals. It's as though he's offering condolences.

"Ditto." I reply nervously.

We make our way down the short corridor, past the bathroom and into the dining area on the left. There, Jacob takes a seat at the table and studies some documents. I take a seat directly across from him.

"Can I get you anything?" he asks.

"No, I'm fine. Thanks."

"You sure?"

"Yeah."

"OK. Just so you know, I've briefed my supervisors. This has gone up to the highest levels," he says, taking a seat and looking at his watch. "As we speak, my DG is having an emergency teleconference with the director, the RCMP commissioner, deputy commissioner and the

National Security Criminal Investigations Unit, the TPS chief of police and the deputy chief of Specialized Operations Command."

"That's great. But how's this going to help me find Sarah?"

"There's a forensic team on its way to your apartment, along with a pair of investigators that were handpicked by the chief of police himself. Although the investigation into her abduction is just underway, we've convinced the TPS and RCMP to send out a nationwide missing person bulletin. Obviously, any connection to the Dominion of God will remain secret. Only the aforementioned are aware of this. They're aware of the whole situation."

"What about Kipling?"

"Only our side knows this at the moment. We haven't alerted the RCMP yet. It's too risky. We don't know if there are any more involved. We need to gather evidence, build a case. We need substantial proof before a warrant for his arrest is issued."

"Are you sure?" I ask, unconvinced.

"Definitely," Jacob replies with authority. "If what you say is true, then there are likely others like Kipling involved—just like our customs fellas. Before we blow the horn, we have to be sure. As for that address on Caledonia Park, a tactical unit is on the way as well as members of the bomb squad. I expect to hear from them in a matter of minutes."

I say nothing, nodding.

"The more I think about it," he continues, sifting through his notes, "the more it all makes sense to me. You know, the Dominion being so elusive, always being one step ahead of us."

"You're telling me . . ."

"It's no wonder they were so adept at eluding authorities, so security conscious. Their methods. Their techniques. They were being tipped! How can I have been so blind?" he says, shaking his head in disgust. "Funny, I often wondered why Kipling was often unavailable—why he was so evasive at times."

"He was?" I ask, perplexed.

"Yeah, he often never returns his calls or texts. Or, if he does, it's usually a conveniently delayed response. In fact, I've been trying to get a hold of him all day. He hasn't returned any of my messages."

Probably out of anxiety, I laugh. "Don't expect a response any time soon. I figure he's at the hospital as we speak."

Jacob looks at me, puzzled. "What do you mean?"

"Well . . . um . . . I may have broken his arm with a switch bar. I got a good shot in when he cornered me. I was able to get a hold of his firearm, and I kinda shot him in the ear." I retrieve the Smith & Wesson from my jacket.

Jacob's eye widen as though he's just seen a ghost.

"You have Kipling's gun?"

"I also have Derek's and Mario's," I continue, lifting my shirt to expose the Berettas. "They're fully loaded. As for Kipling's, like I said, I fired a round up on the second floor which took out his right ear. I accidentally fired another round outside while wrestling with him, just before he got away."

"You're telling me that's Kipling's firearm?"

"Yeah."

Jacob chuckles. His demeanor suddenly changes drastically. "Shit, Liam, why didn't you say this sooner? And you say you may have broken his arm? And you shot him in the ear?"

"Yeah."

"Why the ear?"

"Well," I say, slightly embarrassed. "I did it so Derek and Mario would lower their arms. So they'd disarm. They weren't exactly taking me seriously. But they sure took Kipling seriously. At his command, they dropped their weapons and backed away. That's how I was able to escape."

"This is unbelievable!" he says, clearly overjoyed. "This is exactly what we need. This is evidence! If you fired a round indoors, that means the bullet is there somewhere. This puts him at the scene of the crime! I'm going to need them . . . I'm going to have to take them in and have them properly identified and analyzed."

I slide Kipling's firearm across the table. I watch as Jacob slips on a pair of latex gloves, inspects it and seals it in a plastic bag.

"I'll also need the other two," he says, opening his palm.

I have to admit, this request leaves me slightly uncomfortable. "I know it sounds a little crazy," I say, "But can't I keep at least one of them? You know, for protection?"

Jacob shakes his head. "I'm sorry, Liam. I can't let you do that. As a government agent, it'd be irresponsible of me. I hope you understand. Besides, you won't need it. We're going to protect you. For the time being, this is going to be your home, at least until we find you somewhere more suitable."

"Fine," I say, retrieving the two Berettas from my belt.

"Thank you."

"As for this being my home," I resume, "That's just fine and dandy . . . but what about Sarah? You need to find Kipling! He would've checked in to a hospital by now. He'd know where Sarah is!"

Jacob nods. "That's right. I'll need to make a phone call. Can you excuse me for a minute?"

"Of course," I reply. "And if you'll excuse me, I need to use the washroom."

I watch as Jacob stands up and disappears down the hallway and into the bedroom. I get up and make my way to the unit's only bathroom, shutting the door behind me. I run cold water from the tap, splashing it over my face and neck. I stare emptily into the mirror, unable to come to terms with my situation. I eventually snap out of it, wiping my wet hands against my jacket and feeling a slight lump over my chest. That's when I remember Kipling's cell phone and the fact that I completely forgot to mention it to Jacob.

I reach into my jacket and pull it out of my pocket. I inspect it thoroughly this time, even though I doubt I'll find anything of use. After all, any call from a member of the Dominion from a Dominion-issued cell phone would appear as a blocked number and likely be untraceable. And strict instructions have been issued to never call from anything other than a pay phone or a Dominion-issued cell phone. However, when I turn the phone on, I notice a message on its tiny screen.

Five missed calls, caller unknown.

One new text.

How could I have missed this? The damn thing didn't ring, did it? I navigate to the main menu. After checking the phone's settings and message history, I'm able to confirm two things: the cell is set to vibrate and all messages are prior to my having possession. Other than one new voice mail, which I can't access, there are two text messages displayed in its history log. Both were sent by an unidentified party, the first one having already been read. It says:

Alarm at lab, send 3 men.

I then open the new text message. It reads:

Have not heard back from u, what is the status?

I stare at the message displayed on the screen, contemplating a response. By now, Kipling would've realized he's missing his cell phone. While I assume most of his closest associates would have been made aware of this by now, including the sender, it's unlikely each and every individual member would know. If I were to hand over the phone to Jacob, he'd simply take it back to his headquarters and have his lab analyze it. That could take days. And at this point, I'm sick of leaving my life hanging in the hands of federal agents. I want answers, and I want them now.

After silently debating the pros and cons, I decide to take a chance and respond to the text. Fingering the tiny keys, I type: *found my cell phone . . . what is happening?*

Nervous, I wait for a response. A minute passes before one eventually appears on the screen. It says: *Everything under control. Where are u now?*

I thumb my answer. *Getting fixed. My arm is busted good. Where are u?*

Much quicker this time, the response comes in. It reads: *At the rendezvous point. Will be here a while, will wait for u there.*

After thinking about my next entry, I key the following: *U got the girl?*

Yes, she's with Frenchy.

As I read this last text, the hair on the back of my neck stands erect like the bristles of a brush. My worst fears are confirmed. I tremble to think what the Dominion is doing to her, my poor Sarah. I can only pray they're simply holding her hostage until I turn myself in. If an exchange is all they want—me for her—then that's exactly what I plan on giving them. I'd give myself up. I don't care what they have in store for me. They'll do this if I'm lucky. If I'm not . . . well, I don't even want to think about that.

What about Mailman? I finally probe.

When the reply comes, my whole body stiffens as if I've been hit with a thousand volts of electricity. My head begins to spin. I drop the cell phone in the sink. Leaning over in attempt to vomit, I can only dry heave. I stand there, frozen in fear. My eyes water and soon, uncontrollable tears roll down my face. I do my best not to make a sound. I clutch the sink to try to control the trembling in my hands. I stare back into the mirror for what seems like an eternity.

Eventually, I compose myself and pick up the phone again. I look at the message displayed across the screen, hoping I've misread. As fate and the stars and God would have it, I haven't. Unmistakably, it reads:

He's with me.

CHAPTER 49

There's pounding on the door. "Everything OK in there?"

"Be out in just a sec . . ."

I collect myself and douse cold water over my face yet again to conceal any signs of distress my eyes might reveal. This time, I dry myself with a dirty white hand towel hanging on a rack. I observe myself in the mirror. My eyes are still red, but it'll have to do.

I open the bathroom door and pause momentarily. To my immediate right is the front exit—my way out. Down the hallway to my left, standing by the kitchen table, is Jacob. I want to get the hell out of there. But a part of me wants—no, *needs*—to stay. I've been betrayed in the grossest possible way. I'm disillusioned and livid and scared. Almost literally, I'm standing in the snake pit.

I think about confronting him head on. Grabbing him by the collar and torturing him until he confesses and releases Sarah from wherever the hell she's being kept. But I'm scared that any confrontation would only make matters worse. If he knew I was onto him, it wouldn't bode well for me. Better that he thinks I don't know. If he wanted me dead, I'd be dead by now. I'm still alive because he wants me to be. If Sarah is still alive, it's because he wants her to be.

Also, what's keeping me from bringing him in to the police is the fact that I simply can't trust anyone at this point. Not the police. Not the agency. No one. I feel utterly alone and helpless.

"You OK?" he asks, looking over.

"Yeah, I'm fine," I reply, calmly making my way back to the table.

Jacob takes a seat and goes through some of his files. Next to him, tucked into an open briefcase and sealed in plastic, are one Smith & Wesson and two Barettas. I fight the urge to reach over, grab one and take him hostage. But I'm afraid that if I do this, I'll never see Sarah again.

"So," he begins, "tell me more about this lab . . . and what you know about the Dominion's Phase III."

"I really don't know that much about Phase III," I say, attempting to calculate my responses wisely.

"But you mentioned you saw some blueprints, correct?"

"Yeah, I did."

"And you mentioned some dates . . . June sixth?"

"The House of Commons is sitting June fourth to the eighth," I explain, knowing full well I'm being tested. "I think the Dominion believes the Tribulation will begin June sixth at fourteen hundred that afternoon. It was written on the blueprints."

"June sixth at fourteen hundred hours," Jacob repeats, "That's the time the Israeli Prime Minister and the leader of the Palestinian National Authority are set to sign the agreement."

"No shit."

"Anything else?"

"Well, all exits were highlighted, as were all the windows. The plans were marked with dots and codes. I think to represent where the Dominion plans to station its men."

"You believe it plans on overthrowing the government?" he asks, faking curiosity.

"Yeah."

"What makes you think that?"

"On the House of Commons blueprint the words 'area of execution' was written. On a separate floor plan the names of every member of the House were indicated as per where they're seated. Same goes for the Senate."

"I see . . ."

"That's all I know."

Jacob then probes me about the ammunition and the training camps. Strangely, he asks me if I'm aware of any other place where the Dominion may be stocking weapons, which leads me to believe there are more locations. I go along and tell him what I know and what I saw. At times, he seems suspicious, as though I'm withholding something. So, he probes more, often repeating the same questions over again. The types of ammunition. The quantity. Details about the shipments. And so on.

He then inquires about the lab. The types of materials. The quantity. The equipment. Everything. Again, I go along with it and divulge what I know.

Finally, he queries me about the training camps, focusing on their location. When I tell him I don't know where they are, he becomes suspicious once again.

"You know," I say in order to gauge his reaction, "I was one of the first men the DOG called to renew its activities. I was there from the very beginning, along with Mario and Roch. Somehow, I can't help but feel I'm being left out of the loop on certain things."

Jacob stops writing notes and looks up at me. I get the sense that some wheels are beginning to spin in his head. "What do you mean by that?"

"Well, for starters, it strikes me as curious I've yet to be invited to those training camps."

"Yeah, that is strange," he says, thinking. "Have you been checking your messages?"

"Of course I have."

"You think you're purposefully being left out?"

"Perhaps."

"Well, wouldn't that be great? I mean, didn't you want to distance yourself from them? Maybe this is your chance."

"Maybe."

"But why wouldn't they invite you?"

"I don't know . . . maybe they just didn't want me to know. Maybe they suspected me. Maybe they—"

A strange sound suddenly fills the room—a chime, coming from Jacob's belt. He looks down to his waist. "Ah, that could be my boss with good news," he says, unclipping his cell. "Hold on just a sec . . ."

I watch as he opens his phone and reads his text. He then freezes momentarily. A look of uncertainty and concern crosses his face.

"Sorry, I know it's not proper etiquette, but I need to respond to this."

"By all means," I reply, curious.

Jacob thumbs a first message and waits. Then he thumbs a second one. Almost immediately, a distinct buzzing sound emanates from within my jacket. Jacob stares me in the eyes, then at my chest where the sound is coming from. Our eyes lock again. Neither of us says a word.

Another buzz.

His face goes blank and cold. At this point I know he knows. And he knows that I know. We do nothing but stare at one another, like a wild-west showdown with each man waiting for the other to make the first move.

"Well, aren't you going to answer that?" he asks coldly.

I say nothing and leap out of my chair, reaching for the briefcase. Jacob reacts and launches himself in turn, slamming the case shut. We wrestle over the table, each attempting to grab the briefcase. Our chairs go sprawling to the floor, as do Jacob's notes and documents. In the midst of our scuffle, we tumble and crash to the floor.

Having gained the upper edge, Jacob is now smothering me. In his eyes there's something different—a look I've never seen before. Not in Jacob. Not in anyone. It's as though a completely different entity has just entered his body and assumed total control. It's deeply disturbing. I only get a moment to stare the devil in the eye—the king of deception—and grasp his true nature. It's more than mere anger or rage, even more than hatred. It's nothing less than fury verging on the edge of madness.

With his hands now wrapped tightly around my neck, I begin gasping for air. I try to fend him off, but his grip is unrelenting. He grimaces, teeth barred, and groans as he applies more pressure. I can sense his desperation, but I'm just as desperate. I realize now that I'm no longer his informant—and perhaps I've never been. Whatever his game, it's now over and a new one has just begun.

In one frantic surge, I manage to shift my body, forcing Jacob onto his side. In this position, I'm eventually able to gain the upper hand and pin him under my weight. I strike him repeatedly across the face and temple, drawing blood from his nose and mouth. I don't stop pummeling him until he's no longer able to defend himself. When he finally submits, I stand up and give him two good boots to the ribs and abdomen. I then grab the briefcase and retrieve Kipling's Smith & Wesson. After unsealing it, I aim it at Jacob's forehead.

His eyes don't even look at the barrel pointing down at him. Instead, they focus on my own. "What are you going to do, Liam? Shoot me? You think you're gonna shoot me? And tell the whole world I'm with the Dominion of God? Is that your plan?" he says, spitting out blood. "I bet you think I'm Black Mamba, don't you?"

"As a matter of fact, I do," I say, unflinching.

He chuckles, spitting out more blood. "Well, I hate to tell you my friend, but you couldn't be more wrong. You couldn't be more fuckin' wrong!"

"Is that so?"

He nods, far too smug for my liking.

"The way I see it, it's either you or Kipling . . . or perhaps the both of you."

Slowly, he tries to get to his feet. "Wrong again—"

I strike him across the face with the pistol. He falls back to the floor.

"Who then?" I shout. "Who's Black Mamba?"

A sneer spreads across his face.

"Who is Black Mamba, goddamn it!"

"Why, you are."

This catches me totally off guard and robs me of any clever response. I shake my head in disbelief. *Did I hear that right? Did he say what I think he just said?*

"That's right, Liam." He wipes blood from his chin. "You're Black Mamba. You've always been Black Mamba! How do you like them apples, you fuckin' infidel . . . you fuckin' traitor!"

"What the hell are you talking about?" I sputter, taking one step back.

"You stupid, stupid man," he says. "Do you think I've been reporting what you've been telling me all this time? As far as the intelligence and law-enforcement communities are concerned, you're the leader of the biggest domestic terrorist organization this continent has ever seen!"

Speechless, I struggle to make any sense of his words. *That's impossible. He's bluffing. He's only bluffing . . .*

"You should've taken that lie detector," he finally resumes. "It would've bought you some time! It would've bought all of us some precious, precious time. No matter, we're ahead of schedule anyway . . ."

"What are you talking about?"

"Do you think the agency wanted to polygraph you because we doubted your reliability as a source? A source who's always led us astray? A source reporting on an organization that always seems to be one step ahead of us? Who continuously reports cell phone numbers that mysteriously become discontinued before we even have a chance to trace any calls? Who leads us on a wild goose chase across the country for a bum? Who refuses to be bugged and refuses to wear a GPS? Who refuses to take a polygraph? That doesn't paint a very good picture if you ask me." He pauses to spit out more blood. "No, you were to be assessed because you were being reported as a double agent—the leader of the Dominion of God pretending to be a rat. At least, that's how I've been reporting you and what my notes reflect. Ah, the art of misinformation! Go ahead, take a look for yourself . . ." he offers, pointing to a series of photos that have spilled from a folder.

Scanning the photos spread across the floor, I notice the one common denominator in them: me. I slowly crouch down, my aim locked on Jacob, my eyes alternating between the photos and my target. In one of the pictures, I'm at the club the night of Adbil's murder. The next, I'm heading out the back door moments following his execution, pistol in hand. In yet another, I'm in the van waiting in the alley just outside the imam's apartment complex. I'm also in the train yard as he's being handed over to other unidentifiable individuals. I'm also captured at St. Andrew's, several Internet cafés and at Whirlpool Bridge.

"There are also plenty of transcripts," Jacob reveals, matter-of-factly. "I had your residence line tapped almost from day one. There are some very telling moments in some of your conversations—the ones I kept, I mean. You wanna read through them?"

I'm at a complete loss for words.

"I also have every single email, discussion and exchange you've ever made," he goes on. "I have proof you've recruited for the Dominion—you remember Angelic? That was me, you idiot!" He laughs. "Boy, you should see the look on your face! Angelic, Naziboy, Crusader33 . . . those were all me. Well, actually, Kipling played the role of Naziboy. Vica.net was his brainchild. But you recruited them all. And we have proof of that."

"So who's The Prophet?"

"You again, my friend!"

"But I never sent any messages. I just received them—"

"Says who? A sender can also be a receiver. I can place you at any scene at any time I desire. Incidentally, we've been able to identify the

I.P. addresses linked to The Prophet. Guess where they've led us? That's right, those slimy Internet cafés you've been frequenting. As far as anyone can tell, you've secretly been tasking yourself low-level assignments to conceal your identities as Black Mamba and The Prophet. Clever boy, you are." he says, winking.

"You paid me," I remind him. "The government . . . the agency . . . you paid me. Directly into my bank account! How do you think you'll get around that?"

Jacob breaks out in laughter, blood running down his chin. "You kill me, Liam. You really do. You think the government was paying you? Think again. I was never given the authority to pay you. Actually, to be more precise, I never even made the request."

"But, you did pay—"

"No, the government never paid you." He smirks callously. "I've had our terrorist financing unit trace the source of your funds. This suspicious TD account you foolishly opened—do you know what they found? They found that you've been obtaining—no, transferring—funds from Marcus Black's accounts to your own . . . you know, the poor schmuck's identity you assumed. And then they found numerous withdrawals, $50,000 each. What did you do with that money, Liam?"

"You know exactly what I did with the money, you bastard!"

"I'll tell you what you did. You put it all in secure briefcases and carried them across the border to pay your arms supplier, as you always have. As far as everyone's concerned, we only recently caught on to your activities. You could have been doing this for awhile. See those pictures? That's you crossing the border. That's you handing over the loot to persons whose faces we can't see—only your face, there for everyone to see. I made sure of that."

"What about Wes Sanderson and Brent Weiss? Huh? What about them? How do they explain letting me cross the border? How do they explain finding a briefcase without ever doing anything about it? There are surveillance cameras, systems checks—"

"A lookout was placed on you, Liam," Jacob replies. "They had orders to let you through no matter what so we could keep an eye on your movements. As far as not verifying your briefcase, all record of that has been erased. I just wanted to see how well you performed under pressure."

"No . . . you're bluffing." A deep panic is growing inside me. "Where's Sarah, you sick bastard?? Where the hell is she?"

Jacob grins. "Ah. That's where it gets interesting . . ."

"Where is she??" I holler at the top of my voice.

"This is where you have no choice but to serve the Dominion of God."

I take a step forward and place the muzzle against his forehead. "Yeah, when the hell you're going to freezes over . . ."

"You don't get it, do you?" he snorts. "There's no way out of the Dominion of God! Cyril wanted out. We don't accept that. The only way out of the Dominion is by death. The ball's in my court."

I can't believe my ears. "You murdered Cyril because he wanted out?"

"You're damn right we did," he replies, defiant. "Now your time has come. You see, there are actually two balls in my court. You can either choose to serve the Dominion or perish. Either you go along pretending to be an informant of the agency until the Dominion has overthrown the government, or you'll never see Sarah alive again!"

"Are you for real? No, here's all *you* have to do. Either you hand her over to me right now or I put a bullet in your goddamn brain."

"That's not going to happen," he replies, sounding quite confident. "Because the moment you pull that trigger or step out that door and be this wannabe hero you think you are, you're going to be the most hunted man on the planet. All the information and all the evidence point to you. No one's going to believe a thing you say. If you don't do exactly what I tell you, I'll have every federal, provincial and municipal cop, every spy and every guard on both sides of the border hunting you down. I'll have you placed on Interpol. There's already a big price on your head. There are bounty hunters out there just lusting to find this elusive Black Mamba. No place will be safe for you ever again. So go ahead, pull that trigger and see what happens!"

He's bluffing . . . shoot him!

"Not only *that*, but the moment you pull the trigger or step out that door, Sarah will be Purified for the filthy whore she is." He pauses to gauge my reaction. "That's right . . . she's tied to a cross as we speak, my men waiting for the or—"

I lunge forward and give him everything I've got, my foot sinking into his abdomen. I do it again. And again. And again. By the time I'm done, Jacob is crumpled in a fetal position and gasping for precious air.

He vomits what seems to be a gallon of bile and then collects himself. "The way . . . I see it," he continues, panting heavily, "it's a mutually . . . beneficial relationship . . . just like before. I need you . . . and you need me. So . . . what will it be, *Mailman?*"

"You touch one hair on her head, and I'll purify you myself," I reply, cocking the gun. "But I'll do it my own way. Right here, right now—and it won't be as pleasant as your pathetic little ritual."

"Liam . . . it's not too late for you," he counters, recanting somewhat. "You can still join us. You can still be taken at the time of the Rapture. You can still be a part of our Savior's kingdom! One thousand years! You can still be there at the final battle where we vanquish the Beast and his spawn! All these parasites! All these false prophets and their minions! This is your last chance, you miserable little bastard! Either you're with us, the true Israelites and God's true people, or with them, the Spawn of Satan."

"You know nothing about God," I reply defiantly.

Jacob coughs but doesn't respond.

Down the hall, behind the front door, the sound of footsteps is heard making their way up the lobby stairs. The doorknob turns but doesn't open. We hear violent jerking of the door handle, followed by loud knocking.

Jacob grins. "They're here . . . just in time."

More knocking.

I keep my pistol aimed at Jacob and my sights on the door. A new surge of adrenaline courses through my veins. I glance past Jacob to the window and the fire escape beyond it.

More pounding on the door—only this time, whoever is behind it isn't waiting for an answer but is trying to break it down.

Leaping over the injured Jacob, I bolt for the window and struggle to undo the aging latches glued tight with rust and paint. Out of the corner of my eye, I spot Jacob reaching for the briefcase. At the other end of the hallway, the front door is ripped from its frame and swings wide open. Bursting through it are Derek and Mario, each wielding a revolver. They immediately spot me and begin to unload in my direction. Glass shatters all around me, exploding in countless shards.

Amid the gunfire and the downpour of glass, I manage to release the latches and raise the window sash as high as it can go. I swiftly jump through the opening, diving head first onto the fire escape. All around me bullets ricochet off the adjacent brick building, shattering some of its windows in turn. I make a mad dash down the fire escape, two, three, sometimes four steps at a time. When I reach the final ledge, I simply hop over the railing and land on solid ground.

From three stories above me, Derek peers through the open window and unloads his revolver. He then makes his way onto the fire escape, where he unloads some more.

I dart directly for the alley between two apartment complexes, knocking over garbage cans along the way. From somewhere around the corner behind me, I can hear Derek barking instructions to Mario, who's still somewhere inside the safe house.

When I finally clear the alley and find myself at the front of the building, I see that my car's been ransacked, its tires deflated and resting flat against the asphalt. I sprint past it and cross the street, my legs moving as fast as they ever have. I don't bother looking back, but I can hear the slamming of car doors followed by the screaming of wheels in hot pursuit.

I decide to cut through a small park where a few children are playing, then I make my way across another street and into another alley. The sound of screeching tires follows me relentlessly. My heart is racing and my lungs burning, but at no point do I even consider slowing down to catch my breath.

A few blocks later, I decide to head north onto a busy street in hopes of disappearing into the crowd. This, it turns out, is a brilliant move. Up ahead, the Greenwood Station awaits me. I look back and notice a vehicle rounding the corner a few blocks away, then coming to a halt in traffic. A man gets out and begins to run in my direction as the car attempts to cut through traffic.

I head toward the station entrance, taking the odd look behind me. The man chasing me turns out to be Derek, who's catching up fast. When I finally reach the escalator leading below ground, I don't just wait for it to take me down. Instead, I run and leap over numerous steps, nudging several people along the way until I'm at the platform. I notice a train heading westbound has just arrived, its doors slowly opening. I race to catch it, dodging countless people. Behind me, Derek has reached the lower level and is running along the platform.

I manage to slip through the doors as they close and seal me off from my stalker. The train begins its trek to the next stop. Through a window, I watch as Derek comes to an abrupt halt and stares me in the eyes. I can feel the wheels spinning behind them. While his revolver isn't in hand, I know it's hidden somewhere on him. I can almost feel it burning inside him, this desire to simply unload it and let fate take its course.

But he never does.

Instead, he runs alongside the train, never taking his eyes off me. He runs until he comes to the end of the platform and watches as I disappear into the tunnel. His fiendish grin is the last thing I see before being swallowed by the dark tunnel of the underground.

CHAPTER 50

By the time I resurface, I'm all the way in the west end of town. I feel lost. I feel doomed. I simply don't know what to do, who to turn to, or who to trust. I don't even know if Sarah is still alive or if Jacob was bluffing in an attempt to salvage his sick and twisted plan. I feel helpless to save the love of my life. My trust in any form of authority is gone. But I have to do something. I have to tell someone.

At the station, I walk up to the first pay phone I can find and place an anonymous call to the municipal police.

"9-1-1, what is your emergency?" answers the dispatch.

"Yes, I have credible information that the terrorist group known as the Dominion of God is storing ammunition in the basement of 10 Caledonia Park Road. There's also a makeshift lab where explosives are being fabricated."

"That's one-zero Caledonia Park Road. Ammunition stored in basement. Lab where explosives are being fabricated . . ." she repeats.

"Good. There's also a safe house located at 27 Glenside Avenue. You need to send units there right away. They're armed and very dangerous. Do you copy that?"

"Two-seven Glenside Avenue. A safe house. Armed and dangerous. How many are there? What type of ammunition and explosives are we talking about?"

"I don't know, but if you wait too long, they'll be gone. You have to send units right away. That's all I'm going to say right now. I may call back later with more information. Goodbye."

"Sir? Hello—"

I hang up but keep my hand on the receiver for a while, struggling to end an incessant trembling that has overtaken me. My whole world is crumbling before me, piece by piece. By placing that phone call, I may have just sealed Sarah's fate. I may even have sealed it back at the safe house, when I escaped. I can only hope the cops will act on this tip and find what I'm hoping they'll find. But I don't even know I can trust the cops. That's why I withheld the information about Phase III. If the cops don't act, I'll know something's up. If they do, then I'll know I can trust them.

But I can't stick around here. The cops can have pay phones traced pretty easily nowadays and could be here in a matter of minutes. I have to find somewhere to go—somewhere to lay low for a while—until I can find someone I can rely on. Someone I can count on.

But where? And who?

The answer comes to me only a short time later, after I make my way on foot to a sketchy part of town. I had actually hoped to come across a bed and breakfast or even a homeless shelter, but what I find is even better—or worse, depending how I look at it. It's arguably the shadiest accommodation in the entire city—a place where registering its guests is not a common practice.

It's called the Owl Motel. It's the place Raoul often chooses as his preferred accommodations when he and his boys are in town. I've met them here before at least twice to obtain their services. The owners are two Somalian brothers, both ex-cons. The place is a complete dive. But with the right amount of dough—a mere forty dollars up front for the night—anyone can get a room. No questions asked. If they do insist for a name, a fake one will suffice. No ID necessary. Preferable, actually. Frankly, I'd much rather stay at the Bates Motel. But this will have to do for now.

The sign in the office window says "VACANCY," the letters written in black electrical tape on a white plank. Watching an old tube television set behind a desk is a rather obese and tough-looking black man. He doesn't immediately notice my presence, too enthralled with *America's Most Wanted*—or something of that nature. On the counter is a bell on which I slam my fist. Startled, he jumps out of his chair and makes his way over to me.

"Whatcha want, brother?" he snarls, his bulging eyes digging into me.

"Just a room . . . any room," I reply.

"A room, huh? For what?"

"To spend the night."

"Just to spend the night?" he replies, eyeing me from head to toe. "Is that all?"

"Yeah."

"Nobody stays here *just to spend the night*. Who you got with ya?"

"Nobody."

"What are you then, another undercover cop? 'Cause if you another one of those, you best get the hell outa here. You ain't welcome here."

"I'm not a cop . . . just a regular joe looking for a cheap room."

"No cop, huh?"

"That's right."

"Well, I dunno . . . you seem kinda familiar to me . . ."

"That's because I've been here before," I reply, keeping my cool.

"Been here before, huh? Let me see some ID then." He turns and looks at the TV, shaking his head. He mumbles something to himself and looks back at me. "Come on, now. I ain't got all day! Let me see some goddamn ID!"

I reluctantly reach into my pocket and retrieve my wallet. I hand him my driver's license, which he inspects closely. "OK, Mr. Sheehan. You look legit. We have a few rooms left. Any preferences?"

"Nope, any room will do just fine."

He hands me back my license and picks up a clipboard. "OK, I can give you room 208. That'll be forty bucks for the night. Check out by ten tomorrow."

"Sounds good," I reply, pulling out two twenties.

"Just write and sign your name right here." He passes me the clipboard along with a pen.

So much for making up a name, I tell myself, jotting down my real name but altering my signature. He takes my cash and rings it in the register.

"You want a receipt or something?" he asks, looking back at the television set.

"No thanks."

He then goes over to a wall where a series of keys are hanging from their hooks. I wait for what seems to be an eternity before he manages to identify the proper set.

"Here you go," he says, handing me the keys. "Go back out, up the stairs, second last door at the end. Oh, and hey, if you bringing anyone here tonight, if you got a deal going on, you need to advise either myself or Maurice, you know what I mean?"

"No problem."

I leave the office and its stench behind and make my way up the metal stairs to the second-floor balcony. At the second last door, I slip the key into the keyhole of room 208 and disappear inside, locking the door behind me. The curtains are drawn, with very little light penetrating from the outside. When I open them, the room—and its condition—is revealed. The carpeted floor is filthy and stained with God-knows-what. Same for the bed sheets. In the corner next to the window, there's a torn chair with its stuffing exposed. In the opposite corner, an old twenty-inch television set sits on a cheap-looking desk. There's a smell of stagnant urine in the air, which I discover is coming from the clogged toilet in the bathroom. This is perhaps the most repulsive bathroom I've ever seen. There's hair everywhere, long and short and curly ones. In the sink. On the toilet. In the bathtub. Enough to make me sick. There are even blood stains in the tub. A thick layer of mold covers most of the shower tiles and the floor.

Just one night, Liam. It's just for one night . . .

From somewhere in another room, there's shouting. Cursing. Moans. The voices of several men and a woman apparently called Carla. Constant banging on the walls. More moans.

I shudder at the sound of this apparent gang-bang and direct my attention out the window. Across the street, there's a strip mall with a pawn shop and a store called Crazy Jay's Electronics, among others. At the very end of the strip mall, there's a small convenience store with a Canada Post office. As I watch people come and go for a while, I get an idea.

I decide to head over to the pawn shop, dodging traffic along the way. Once inside the cluttered store, I browse for several minutes until I come upon a shelf with some items of interest. A CD player. *No good.* An iPod. *No good either.* A GPS. *Nah.* A camcorder, an older model but complete with adapters and battery charger. *Bingo!*

"How much for this camcorder?" I ask the clerk, who's reading a fishing and hunting magazine behind the counter.

"That'll be fifty bucks, my friend."

Digging my wallet out of my pocket, I retrieve the only two bills I have left. "Will you take forty?"

"I dunno . . ."

"Forty's all I've got," I say, not quite true considering I do have a debit card.

He pauses to think. "OK. What the hell. It's been sitting there for a while."

"Thanks, boss," I reply, handing him the cash.

Elated, I leave the store with my purchase. After examining it more thoroughly, I notice the tiny memory card slot is empty. Not to be defeated, I decide to give the electronics store next door a try. There the clerk inspects it and finds a memory card suited to the model.

"I'll take two memory cards, please."

"Two cards?"

"Yes, please."

The clerk fetches another memory card. "Here you go, buddy."

"Thanks. Say, you wouldn't happen to sell voice recorders—you know, to record a conversation?"

"What, are you filming a movie or something?"

This makes me chuckle. "Yeah, I guess you can say that . . ."

"I think I may have what you're looking for," he says. He selects a package from a display.

"How much?" I ask.

"Nineteen ninety-nine, plus tax."

"Perfect."

He also snags a pack of AA batteries, which will be needed for the recorder. I pay with my debit card and then make my way back to my room, where the moaning and groaning can no longer be heard.

I spend the next few minutes figuring out the camcorder, then I set the unit on top of the television set. I press "Record" and back away a few feet.

"My name is Liam Sheehan," I begin, exhaling. "Otherwise known as Black Mamba, leader of the Dominion of God . . ."

CHAPTER 51

It's nearly six o'clock by the time I'm through with my recordings. I now have two separate recordings, saved on two separate memory cards. Each card contains a different account of my involvement with the Dominion. I return across the street to mail one to a recipient whose attention I'm sure to attract. The other recording I keep to myself for future reference.

I'm exhausted, both mentally and physically. I can't stop thinking about Sarah. I try to get a little sleep, but my whirling mind won't allow me such luxury. The bedbugs I find in the sheets don't make matters any better. But bedbugs are the least of my concern.

My thoughts ultimately turn to Jacob. Before today, I've never experienced betrayal and deception—at least not of this magnitude. I'd given everything I had to this man. My trust. My life. My soul. All three are now in his hands. This betrayal makes me sick to the core.

In the midst of these thoughts, I hear Kipling's cell phone vibrating. I turn my gaze over to my jacket, which I had left hanging over the chair. I had completely forgotten about it. I have to admit I'm quite shocked that I've yet to hear from Jacob—or anyone else from the Dominion for that matter.

"Who is this?" I answer brusquely.

"Liam, you sound tense," Jacob replies, his voice sounding somewhat nasal. "Perhaps you should get some rest. You'll be needing it."

"What's that supposed to mean?"

"I told you the consequences. You really should've listened. You'll need me more than ever now."

"Fuck you, Jacob. You dirty—"

"If I were you, I'd be keeping a close eye on the evening news."

Then he hangs up.

I freeze for a moment before turning on the old television set, bracing myself for the worst. Scrolling through the channels, I stop when I notice a "Breaking News" alert displayed in bright yellow on a local station. A reporter holding a microphone is speaking. Across the street behind her is my apartment complex with several police cruisers parked in front. At the bottom of the screen, the caption reads: *Breakthrough into Dominion of God investigation; leader identified.*

I turn the volume up. ". . . Authorities are not saying much at the moment, but it's suspected that Sheehan may have turned against his partner after she threatened to turn him in to the police. Sheehan is seen here in a recent photo taken by a police surveillance unit. He's described as Caucasian male, approximately 6 feet tall and 190 lbs. He's said to be in his early forties with short brown hair. Police say he's armed and extremely dangerous. They say if you spot him, do not attempt to approach him and simply call the police."

Then the news anchor says, "Now Janet, you mentioned earlier that federal authorities had uncovered a weapons cache belonging to the group. Can you tell us more about this?"

"Well, what authorities *are* saying is that a stockpile was discovered by a federal police investigator who was investigating a lead in the case. He was ambushed by Sheehan along with two unidentified males. According to Lisa Marietti of the RCMP's Media Relations Unit, the officer was beaten and shot and left in the trunk of a vehicle in a nearby parking lot for several hours before being found by a colleague also working on the case. The officer was taken to hospital where he's listed in stable condition. Now what's interesting to note here is that by the time the officer was rescued and police were able to get to the scene, the entire cache was gone, along with what's being described as a makeshift lab where IEDs were being fabricated—possibly the same type of explosive used in the mosque bombings several months ago."

They cut back to the news anchor, who asks, "And what about Sheehan's residence? Have police been able to uncover anything there? How are the neighbors reacting to this?"

The reporter nods and says, "Well, nothing's been said about what was found inside, although police were seen earlier leaving the building with firearms and what appears to be ammunition sealed in plastic. Now, I had a chance to speak with the superintendent of the building, who was shocked to hear the news. He describes Sheehan and his common-law partner as quiet but friendly—"

Having heard enough, I decide to flip through the channels. CTV. CBC. CNN. ABC. NBC. Fox. Global. All with the same headlines. I turn off the television set and stare at its blank screen for several minutes. My mind is so numb that it can hardly generate a single thought. It just jams and goes blank, like a computer freezing due to information overload. I just don't have enough RAM to deal with this. My eyes start to water and I finally break down.

I'd be lying if I said the thought of taking Kipling's pistol and putting a bullet in my brain hasn't crossed my mind. It definitely has. But the fact remains the human psyche is capable of enduring extraordinary things. I really don't know what makes some people tick, what makes them endure such hardship for indefinite periods of time. Hardships that would seem unfathomable and unbearable to most who crawl this planet. Perhaps it's hope. Hope for something better. Hope that whatever condition they're in, it's only temporary. Hope that good will ultimately prevail over evil.

Hope.

That's all I've got left.

While the odds are Sarah is already dead by now, I cling to this hope that the Dominion is keeping her alive, like a wild card waiting to be played. Maybe it's out of hope and desperation that I decide to do something I haven't done in over twenty years. And so, I get down on my knees and have a long overdue one-on-one with God.

After some spiritual reflection, I draw the curtains shut, gather my belongings and pace back and forth around the room, thinking. Out of all my discombobulated thoughts, one thing becomes certain: I can't stay in this motel room any longer. If I'm lucky, that fat and scary-looking clerk in the office is still watching *America's Most Wanted*. If he's not and has heard the news, I just pray he lacks the mental capacity to put one and one together.

Before leaving the room, I go through a mental list of those who I can turn to—those who know me too well to think I'm capable of being the leader of a terrorist organization. I have no immediate family and most of my extended family are somewhere in the U.S. or Europe. My so-called friends, or what's left of them, would likely turn me in for some type of ransom. None of Sarah's friends like me, and I'm not close enough to any co-workers to judge their loyalty, not even good ol' Henrique. Literally—and, frankly, quite pathetically—I have no one.

Still, although I feel I can't reach out to anyone, I wonder if there's anyone trying to reach out to me. So I grab Kipling's cell phone and dial my own cell number, which links me directly to my voicemail. Sure, the cops are no doubt monitoring my calls by now, but I don't care.

It turns out I have five new messages. The first four are from Sarah's mother, in a complete state of panic. She appears genuinely concerned, which is rather comforting. I even contemplate calling her back, but I'm unsure as to how she could help me. I then listen to the last message, which turns out to be nothing short of a godsend.

It's Frank.

CHAPTER 52

At first, I'm ecstatic. I never thought in a million years I'd ever again hear the voice of my former handler—perhaps the only person I ever trusted besides Sarah, of course. He had been there through thick and thin during the former days of the Dominion, in the midst of Roland's madness. He had kept every promise he had ever made and he delivered. Now, more than ever, I know I'll need him to deliver once again.

However, a dark thought consumes me. The seed's already been planted by Kipling and Jacob. *Who can I trust? Can I trust him?* It goes against everything that I feel and believe in when it comes to Frank, but this *"what if?"* will not subside.

I listen to his message once again, grabbing a pen and paper. "Liam, it's Frank," he says, his tone grave. "I've heard the news. I'm very concerned. I can't believe it. I need to talk to you. You can reach me at 416-551-0010. Please call me."

I jot down his telephone number and hang up. I consider my options and come to the realization that I really have none—none other than Frank. I acknowledge the possibility that this may be a setup, that Frank's line could be tapped. I'll have to make a leap of faith. Besides, I can't afford *not* to call him. *Frank knows me,* I assure myself; *Frank would see through this and set things right.*

Again using Kipling's cell, I dial his number.

"Hello?"

"Frank, it's Liam!"

"Liam! My God! What the hell is going on? I turn on my TV and all I see is your face everywhere! What's this all about? Please don't tell me—"

"Frank, no. Are you kidding me?" I reply, pulling the curtains just enough to peer out the window for any signs of trouble. "Listen, Frank, I've been framed . . ."

"Framed? By who?"

"By your own God damn protégé!"

"What?"

"Jacob! He's had me pegged since the very beginning! He's manipulated and fabricated intel so it would look like I'm leader of the Dominion!"

"Why the hell would he do that?"

"So he could have a decoy!" I shout, getting more upset as I recount the story. "Frank, he's with the Dominion! He may actually be the leader—he may actually be Black Mamba! He and this Sergeant Kipling from the RCMP, they're both in on it!"

There's silence at the other end of the line.

"Hello?"

"Yeah, I'm here," he finally replies.

"Frank, they have Sarah! They kidnapped her sometime today. They took her to get to me. I don't even know if she's still alive . . . her life's in danger!"

"I can't believe it. Jacob? With the Dominion? It sounds so . . . so . . ."

"So fucked up?"

"Yeah."

"Frank, I really need your help," I plead, still scanning the area below my window. "I'm the only one who knows about this. If they find me—doesn't matter if it's the cops or the Dominion—they're going to kill me."

"OK. Calm down. Where are you right now?" he asks.

I don't answer right away. My gut tells me Frank is legit, but in my shoes, there's no such thing as being too cautious. "I'm at a motel, but I won't be staying here much longer."

"OK, can you meet me somewhere? I'm going to do everything in my power to help you. But I need to get the whole story."

"Yeah, I can meet you," I say, reluctantly accepting his offer, "but where?"

"Doesn't matter. I can pick you up anywhere. We'll talk in my car. It's probably the safest bet."

"OK. I'll meet you at the Bloor-Yonge station. I can be there in about thirty minutes, assuming I even make it there."

"In the meantime," Frank replies, "I'll do a bit of digging and see what I can find on Kipling and Jacob. I'll call a few trusted contacts who—"

"No! Frank, you don't understand. It's not just about Jacob and Kipling! It goes far deeper than that. There are border guards involved, U.S. military personnel. Corrections. Who knows who else. You can't trust anyone right now!"

"OK. I won't talk to anyone before I hear you out. In the meantime, find yourself a hat or sunglasses or something to change your appearance. You're probably the most wanted man on the continent. Be careful."

"I will."

"See you in thirty minutes or so in front of Bloor-Yonge Station, northeast corner. Look for a dark grey BMW X3."

After hanging up with Frank, I take a few moments to go over our conversation. The man's never given me a reason not to trust him. Still, I prepare for the worst case scenario, that he too is with the Dominion. So, after unwrapping the AA batteries from their package and testing the voice recorder, I place the small gadget inside my jacket's interior pocket.

I'm about to step out when I hear loud pounding at the door.

I freeze and listen. There's no sound and no movement coming from the other side of the door. In fact, it takes a while before there's another knock. *It's the police,* I think. *They've found me. Or could it be Jacob or Derek?*

Finally, more pounding.

I slowly draw the Smith & Wesson from my belt and approach the door. I peer through the peephole but see nothing but darkness. I then grab the handle and turn it sharply, swinging the door wide open. Standing at the door is the large concierge wielding a sawed-off shotgun. Noticing each other's firearm, we simultaneously draw our weapons.

Everything happens so fast. In a fraction of a second, I fire and take cover behind the wall. He fires too. At first, I'm sure I've been hit. But I stand unscathed. Outside, at the door, there's no sound. I wait, holding my pistol up to my nose with both hands. Then I hear heavy breathing and groaning.

Carefully, I take a peek and notice the concierge lying on his back, his hands over his chest. Next to him is the shotgun. "You shot me, you bastard," he says, in obvious pain.

I take a step forward and aim my pistol at his head. "I'm leaving now. Make a move and I'll blow your head off. Got it?" I say, stepping around him. He doesn't respond. "Got it?"

Wincing and writhing, he nods.

Before making my way down the stairs, I pick up his shotgun and bury the shortened barrel down a pant leg, keeping the stock and trigger above my beltline. I then stuff the pistol in my belt and slip one arm out of its sleeve in order to carry the shotgun under my jacket.

In the distance, the sound of police sirens echoes across the neighborhood.

I quickly exit the motel parking lot and disappear among the people walking down the street. Somewhere along the way, six police cruisers speed by en route to the motel. I simply turn away as they speed by me before I disappear into the underground world of the TTC.

When I resurface, the smoky grey BMW is there waiting for me as promised. Its windows are slightly tinted but Frank had rolled his down so I can spot him. I limp awkwardly across to his vehicle, the shotgun slipping below my knee. In order to get into Frank's vehicle, I need to pull it out as inconspicuously as I can.

"Jesus, where did you get that?" Frank asks.

"Long story . . . Can we get the hell out of here to somewhere more private?"

"Good idea."

Frank drives the short block to Bay and turns there, heading deeper into the downtown core. He tunes into one of many local radio stations, which is reporting the breaking news. As we listen to the broadcast, we don't say much. I'm not feeling a hundred per cent trusting. And I know Frank can sense it.

We end up at the top level of the parkade at the Eaton Centre, where only a few vehicles remain. Frank parks at the lot's most northeastern corner overlooking several skyscrapers.

"The whole world's gone mad," Frank says, killing the radio.

"You're telling me . . ."

"Just so you know, I haven't spoken to anyone yet. I figure I better wait to hear it from the horse's mouth. Everything. From A to Z. The more you tell me, the better idea I'll have as to how to get you out of this mess. You understand?"

"Of course," I reply.

But before I begin my story, I secretly reach into my jacket's front pocket and thumb the voice recorder's "record" button, whose exact feel and location I've memorized. Then I tell him everything. From A to Z.

When I'm done, he just sits there, his eyes staring aimlessly through the windshield.

"I can't believe it," he finally says. "This is unbelievable . . . it's much more complex than I thought."

"You're telling me."

"Liam, I did some digging, and you won't believe what I found," he says after a bit of reflection. "Jacob's father died on 9/11. He was on a business trip in New York and was in the south tower when it collapsed. This left Jacob, his two younger brothers and his mother with a small inheritance. Now, fast forward fourteen years to Black Friday in Ottawa, where his brothers were when that truck plowed through the crowd and went off. They were killed in the blast." He pauses, his eyes intense. "A few months later, his mother, traumatized by the loss, ends up overdosing on anti-depressants and sleeping pills."

"Shit . . ."

"That's not all. I also looked into his educational background. Guess what he ends up studying?"

"What?"

"Biochemistry," Frank says, letting this sink in. "At least, that was his first degree. He does an undergrad in biochem at Waterloo, graduating with honors in the spring of 2001. With the inheritance he received from his father less than a year later, he uses the money to travel out west where he does a master's in science at the University of Alberta. While in Alberta, guess who he ends up befriending?"

"I give up."

"None other than Wyman Hunt."

"Holy shit—"

"I don't know the details as to how they met, but I went beyond the ten-year address history required for the background checks when hiring new recruits. It turns out Jacob was renting the basement of a two-story unit during his studies at U of A. Guess who was renting the other unit? You got it. Remember, this was shortly *after* 9/11. And you can bet Wyman must have smelled an angry and impressionable Jacob from a mile away."

I think about this for a minute. "Wait, don't agents go through rigorous background checks and psychological testing? Didn't you know about his history?"

"What history? A grad in biochem? Masters in science? So what? The agency hires people from all backgrounds. Law. History. Literature. Business. There are plenty with degrees in one science or another. That's totally insignificant. As for his family history, well, I'm sure the agency knew about his mother and siblings being deceased. I'm sure he was questioned about that. As far as psychological testing goes, are you kidding me? Anyone with half a brain can pass those ridiculous tests. It's no wonder some people fall through the cracks. Hell, both the CIA and FBI have found double agents among their ranks over the years. No different here. The system isn't perfect."

"What about Hunt? How was this missed?"

Frank laughs, a small, hollow laugh. "You give the agency too much credit, Liam. There are too many ways to count how we could've missed that. Whatever the case, I'd be willing to bet my left nut they kept their association very, very secret. Not many would've known about it."

"So what does he do after graduating? I mean, there are over ten years to account for before getting hired with the agency."

"He goes on to work as a technician in a lab and then as a procurement officer for Health Canada before being recruited with the agency. From one government department to another. Nothing too uncommon about that."

I try to take this all in. "I need to step outside and get some air." I finally say, opening the car door.

"Good idea."

Frank joins me outside, leaving the engine running. The air is damp and cool, the skies darkening and the sun retiring for the day. Its remaining rays reflect off the glass of the towers surrounding us. A few stories below us, the sounds of busy streets. Traffic. People. A dog barking. We stand there, looking over the ledge, momentarily lost in the commotion.

"What did I get myself into?" I ask, rhetorically.

"It's not your fault—"

"Yes, it is!" I retort. "It is my fault! If I hadn't turned out to be such a loser, I wouldn't be in this mess! I wouldn't have gotten Sarah in this mess. It was my greed and my recklessness . . . my carelessness that got us here."

"Did you really do it *just* for the money?" Frank asks, curious. "You're doing an honorable thing, you can't deny that. I admire you—look at everything you've put yourself through and the good you're trying to do. Ask yourself, would you do it all over again if there'd been no money?"

I gaze down at the people walking by, going on with their busy lives. I think about Frank's questions for a while, not knowing how to answer.

"You know," Frank says, breaking the silence, "I have to admit, this business wasn't always easy from my end of things. You end up feeling a tremendous sense of responsibility—for the life of another human being and perhaps many more. That's what made me call you today. I called because deep down inside, I feel responsible for this mess you're in." His head drops and he stares at the ground. "I remember when I started out as a new recruit. It's very hard at first, pretending to be someone you're not. But at some point, when you've befriended and taken advantage of people long enough, it becomes second nature."

"You do what you have to do, Frank." I offer, mulling over his words.

"False friendships . . . dirty liaisons . . . it becomes all in a day's work," he continues, turning his gaze away from the street below and looking me straight in the eye. "But with you, Liam, it was different. I ended up caring. Sometimes I couldn't sleep at night knowing what you were going through. This Dominion of God shit—I've never seen anything like it and thank God I never will again. I used to tell my wife I'd quit after you, when it was all over."

"Well, it's for the greater good, right?"

"I sometimes wonder . . ."

We both gaze at the city skyline and the sinking sun. "So, what next? What am I supposed to do, Frank? Sarah's out there . . ."

"I have contacts I can trust, high up in the government. I say we—"

In a split second, Frank's right temple explodes. Time stands completely still. I see everything happen in slow motion: the exit wound, the blood, Frank's pupils dilating, his eyes becoming empty and rolling back into his skull, his lifeless body crumpling to the ground.

It takes me a few moments to realize what's happened before the horror sinks in. I lean over Frank's body hoping for signs of life, but it's too late. He's gone. I look up at the office towers and high-rises surrounding me. Nothing but giant shadows and blank windows. Something travelling at light speed brushes past my ear. I don't hear it but I feel it. Behind me, a small hole opens up in the middle of the BMW's windshield.

Instinctively, I duck for cover behind the concrete ledge. I wait but no other shots are fired. I ultimately decide to make a dash for Frank's vehicle, its engine still running. Once inside, I keep my head low and put it in reverse until I'm near the exit ramp. A second bullet hole suddenly appears in the windshield next to the first, and a small cavity opens up in the headrest behind me. I lower my head even further and put the BMW in drive, pressing on the gas and swerving around to face the ramp. Another shot, this time striking the driver side door.

I speed down several ramps, from level to level, until I find myself merging into downtown traffic. My hopes, or whatever's left of them, remain up on the parkade's upper level, lying in a pool of blood.

For the next hour or so, I drive around town from neighborhood to neighborhood, wondering how to put an end to this nightmare. A dense, dark fog has taken over my mind. Nothing is clear anymore. I grieve for Frank, my only friend. I don't know much about post-traumatic-stress syndrome or shell shock or how much horror one can endure before suffering from those things, but I know that if I witness one more head being blown apart, I sure as hell will succumb to at least one of these conditions.

I'm running out of resources and out of options. I know if I keep running, I'll be found. That's just the law of probabilities. That's why I finally decide that instead of letting the Dominion of God come to me, I'll go to them. And I'll strike where it'll hurt most. They say that to kill a snake, you have to cut off its head. Thanks to Frank, I know exactly where to find the mother of all serpents.

CHAPTER 53

I study Wyman's home for nearly an hour from my vantage point a block down the street. It's now completely dark out, the street bare except for the odd vehicle passing by. I sit low in Frank's BMW, having lowered the seat back just a little. In the unit's upper level, a light is on, but I see no movement from the inside.

I begin to envision what I'd do if the old man is there. Sure, I could try and reason with him. Get him to summon Jacob and order Sarah's release. But I somehow doubt reason will get me anywhere with Hunt or the Dominion. I figure I'll need to use force. I explore the possibility of kidnapping him. Tit for tat. I even fantasize about simply barging in there and putting a bullet in the biggot's cranium for all the trouble and heartache his hateful ways have caused me and so many others. But that would be too easy. The darkest part of me would love nothing more than to see him suffer and regret he ever crossed me.

But as time ticks on, I begin to doubt whether he's the bargaining chip I need. It wouldn't be enough, I realize, to save my own hide, but maybe, just maybe, it would be enough to save Sarah's. I scour Frank's vehicle for anything that could be useful. The glove compartment holds nothing but maps, a lighter, and a driver's manual. On the backseat is a pair of gloves and a hat. On the floor behind the front passenger seat is a roll of duct tape and a bottle of windshield washer fluid.

No one has entered or left Wyman's house since the beginning of my stakeout. Not able to sit idle any longer, I stuff the camcorder in my jacket and ensure the voice recorder is still buried in my pocket. With the pistol still fastened to my waist, I grab the shotgun, duct tape and lighter and get out of the BMW.

I make my way down the darkened street until I'm standing in front of Wyman's house. I carefully approach his front steps and listen for any movement inside. All is quiet. I try to open the door but it's locked.

I then make my way to the back of the unit, where I find the back door leading to the basement level. It's also locked. However, I notice the basement window next to it isn't securely latched. Hunching over, I peer inside.

Nothing but empty darkness.

Quietly, I remove the screen and slide the window open. After slipping inside and stepping off the old leather sofa sitting beneath the window, I sneak past Wyman's bookcase—complete with hate literature—and up the stairs. On ground level, I wait and listen. A floor above me, someone is stirring. I see a shadow in the corridor amid a yellow glow.

I'm nearly halfway up the steps when Wyman steps out from the glow. When he spots me, shotgun in hand, he freezes. Our eyes meet. In his hands is a book, the cover of which I don't recognize. He's dressed in his usual grey slacks and a white, short-sleeved collar shirt.

"Oh, it's you," he says, as though expecting me.

I place a finger on my lips, motioning for silence. "Downstairs," I say softly. "Let's go."

"Who the hell do you think you are?" he asks, his voice rising.

"Shut up and don't make a sound," I warn, raising the shotgun. "If you know anything, you know I'm feeling trigger happy these days. Now let's go downstairs and chat for a bit."

I watch as he makes his way past me down to the secret location of his Church of Jesus Christ Christian. Even in the darkness, I can see all the Nazi banners and flags and posters still hanging on the walls. *I bet they were there all along,* I tell myself, realizing the magnitude of Jacob's lies. *Of course they were—Jacob and Kipling never did visit Hunt.*

I direct Hunt to his office, where there are no windows. "Take a seat," I order, looking for a light.

The old man complies, turning on the lone lamp sitting on his desk. He then lowers himself into an old armchair behind it. I take a seat directly across the room, keeping him in my sights.

"You probably know why I'm here, don't you?" I say.

He takes a moment before answering. "You're here because you're a good-for-nothing traitor. You're here because you chose to help them, the Beast and his hoards," he mutters, in his old creaky voice.

"No, that's not why I'm here. I'm here because there are people like you out there who are so terribly insecure and so terribly afraid of everything and everyone. I'm here because you're a coward, Wyman. You're nothing but a wretched, evil and manipulative coward."

"Funny, I'm not the one holding a shotgun."

"You're a coward, Wyman. You hate but you don't even know why you hate. But you're alone in your hate. That's why you seek others. That's why you prey on the weak. You plant a seed and then you watch it grow so you don't find yourself alone anymore. Misery just loves company, doesn't it?"

"I give people the power of the truth—"

"You know what makes you the biggest coward of them all?" I ask, not giving him time to reflect. "You plant that seed and then you get others to do the dirty work for you. You hide behind that illusion you created, like the coward that you are."

"I give people the truth, damn it!" he sneers, pounding his fist on the desk. "Whatever they choose to do with that truth is beyond my control!"

I can't help but laugh. "The truth? What truth? That only Israelites are God's people? That God ordered Roland and his Dominion to eradicate the "false prophets" and their followers in order to restore his Kingdom? That the Antichrist has arrived and brokered a peace treaty? That only the Dominion will be gathered into the heavens and saved at the time of the Rapture? Jesus, Wyman! Have you ever stopped to listen to yourself? Do you know how crazy you sound?"

Wyman smiles, his thin lips parting and exposing his yellow teeth. "When the time comes and when the dust settles, you'll learn of the truth I know of already. Too bad that by then, it'll be too late for you. You had your chance."

"You are one sick, misinformed and misguided person, Wyman," I retort angrily. "There's no such truth. Whatever truth you think there is, it's nothing more than a twisted and self-serving crusade to destroy what you fear."

"They're the ones who have twisted the truth!" he bellows, becoming more agitated. "Since the dawn of man they've manipulated the truth! The world has sat by and done nothing! The Jews! The Muslims! What's next? The Hindus? The Buddhists? Since World War II they've talked about a holocaust. A holocaust? Are you kidding me? Nothing but propaganda! The only holocaust there ever was and ever will be is their attempt to decimate God-fearing Christians from the earth!

Hitler and the Nazis stood up against this uprising! Call it whatever you want, but there's no denying we've been targeted for economical, political and spiritual cleansing!"

"Do you honestly believe man knows anything about God, Wyman?"

"Of course I do, damn it!"

"I feel sorry for you, Wyman," I say, standing up. "I can't imagine living the way you do. So miserable. So fearful. Spiritually and morally crippled. Rotting from the inside out. But, I'm not here to debate with you."

"Then what the hell *do* you want from me?" he barks.

"Either you tell me where the Dominion is holding Sarah, or I expedite your ticket to hell," I reply, raising the shotgun to his head.

"I have no idea where she is," he snarls, looking away. "Even if I did, I'd never tell you. Now get the hell out of my house!"

I stand up and step toward him. "Whether you know or don't, I don't care. If you don't know, find out. If you don't find out or don't tell me, I'm going to do to you whatever it is they're doing to her—and then some."

The old man responds by spitting on me. Enraged, I strike him across the temple with the stock of the gun. He falls from his chair and remains dazed for several moments.

"Where is she, Wyman?" I shout.

"Go to hell, you friggin' mongrel-lover!! You damn traitor to your own kind! You'll burn in the fires of—"

Furious, I belt him across the head once again and grab him by the collar. Dragging his modest frame across the concrete floor, I head to his workshop at the other end of the basement. He squirms and cusses and cries out along the way, but I remain unmoved. I'm through messing around.

"They're going to find you!" he screams, blood running from his nose. "There's no hiding from them! They'll find you and they'll purify your mongrel-lovin' carcass till you bleed no more! And they'll do the same to that filthy whore of yours!"

I scan the workshop, hoping to find something that would serve the purpose I have in mind. All around us are tools and paint cans and cleaners. But it's the gasoline tank sitting on the work table that catches my eye. Still holding on to Wyman by the collar, I deposit the rifle on the tabletop and retrieve the gas tank.

"What the hell are you doing?" he bellows, his tone coming down a notch.

I don't reply and unscrew the cap from the tank.

His eyes grow wide as though he's witnessing the devil himself. There's something new in them. He kicks and thrashes and attempts to crawl away, but I pull him back. I then douse his entire body with gasoline, the fumes quickly filling the air.

"Stop! Please, stop!" he begs, spitting fuel from his mouth. "What do you want from me? You want me to call them and tell them to give up the girl? Are you kidding me? I don't control the Dominion!"

I reach for Kipling's cell phone and toss it over. "Call them!"

"What?"

"Call them now or by God you'll burn alive!"

"Call who?"

"Your guess is as good as mine," I reply. "Call whoever's in charge. Jacob, Kipling, Derek—I don't care. Tell them to deliver Sarah to the nearest police precinct and have her call me from there. Tell them they have thirty minutes to deliver or you're going up in flames."

He looks up to me, trembling. "I—I don't have their numbers . . ."

From my pocket, I pull out Frank's lighter. "I'm giving you one last chance before lighting this place up."

"Do you actually think you can cut a deal with the Dominion? You think they'll just give her back and let you ride away on your high horse?"

I try to get a flame from the lighter, but can only manage a few sparks.

"OK! OK! Stop!" he whimpers, shielding himself with his hands. "I'll call Jacob! You happy now? I'll call him!"

His hands tremble as he grabs the cell phone and dials a number. Ringing.

"There's no answer."

"Try again."

He dials another number, again to no avail.

"Try another number!"

Again, he dials. More ringing. Still no answer.

"Well, I guess you're shit out of luck!" I sneer, spinning the roller once again to produce a few sparks.

"Damn it, stop!" he begs, "just stop! I . . . I think I know where they are . . . I'll tell you. But I'm warning you, you're not coming out of this alive."

"I don't care how I come out of it." I grab the shotgun. "But however Sarah comes of it, so will you. That, I promise you. Now where is she?"

I listen carefully as Wyman describes a secluded farm and a distant field on the southwestern tip of Lake Simcoe near the town of Innisfil. He tells me this is where the Dominion has performed some of its rituals. On this night, there's to be a Purification, though he insists he doesn't know the identity of the sufferer. The ceremony is to begin at midnight. It's now 10:30 p.m. and Innisfil is at least an hour away, more if traffic's bad.

When he's through explaining, I pull out the roll of duct tape from my pocket and begin wrapping it around the barrel of the shotgun, all the way to the end.

"What the hell are you doing?" he demands.

"I'm taking you with me," I explain, triple-wrapping the end of the barrel.

"The hell you are!"

"You've got no choice."

"What's with the tape?"

"Let me show you." I grab him and place the end of the double-barrel firmly against the back of his neck, just at the base of his skull. I wrap the duct tape several times around his neck, only loose enough to allow him to breathe. I fasten more tape around the barrel to reinforce the link. Then I force his hands behind his back and tie them together using the rest of the roll.

"Now," I say, "Lead me to this ritual."

CHAPTER 54

I have to say it's been an uncomfortable and awkward ride so far. For over an hour, I've been sitting next to the country's most hate-filled man and he reeks of gasoline. Not even the wind whistling through the bullet holes in the windshield and side window can alleviate the stench. I want nothing more than to set him ablaze, I truly do. I want that exterior shell to burn and expose the demons lurking deep within his flesh, his bones and his soul.

Steering wheel in one hand, sawed-off shotgun in the other, I speed down Highway 400, sometimes at thirty, forty or fifty over the limit. I'm concerned about being clocked by a traffic cop, but I doubt they have speed traps at this time of night. Even if they did, I have a pretty good alibi buried deep inside my jacket pocket, recording our every word.

But our exchanges have been few and far between since we hit the road. Every now and then, when I pay close enough attention, I notice Wyman's eyes rolling in my direction, his neck unable to rotate. He just stares at me, emanating this unworldly rage as though attempting to harm me in some kind of supernatural way. Like some kind of voodoo doctor trying to cast a curse.

"Why do you do it?" he asks, eventually breaking the lengthy silence. "Why do you help the filth of this world?"

I think long and hard before answering. "Why do you think of them as filth, Wyman? Why do you think of anyone as filth? Where does all this hate come from? What good has it done you?"

"Because they *are* filth! They're mongrels! Lower than Negroes and faggots! Take a good look at them! They want noting but to destroy us! Are you blind? Why are you closing your eyes to the evil truth? Open up and look around you!"

"My eyes are perfectly open," I reply, keeping my eyes on the dark road ahead. "You know what's funny? The problem starts because there are too many people like you in the world, Wyman—on all sides. Those extremists . . . those terrorists you speak of . . . you're no different, Wyman. You're just like them . . . all carved from the same mold. I hope for the sake of the good people of the world that all you hate-mongers—all you extremists—on all sides end up killing each other off and leave the rest of us here in peace."

Infuriated, he attempts to turn to me, but I jam the barrel of the shotgun back into his neck. "You cock-sucking little faggot! You're just like all the other hypocrites out there! You go around pretending everything is OK, but deep down inside you think exactly like I do. The only difference between you and me is that I have the balls to stand up to foreign aggression!"

I can't help but laugh. "You and I ain't nothing alike, Wyman."

"Oh yes we are," he replies, "You're just too stupid to know it!"

"Wyman, you really are one simple and primitive son-of-a-gun. I feel sorry for you. You have the world's worst case of tunnel-vision—you can't see the big picture."

"What big picture?"

"That you're doing what you consider "your own kind" more harm than good. It's a shame we humans haven't yet learned that responding to violence with more violence doesn't work. It just adds more fuel to the fire. And then people retaliate with even more violence . . . it's a vicious cycle, Wyman, one that'll just keep getting more vicious."

"So what's your point?"

"My point is, how do you stop the cycle? How do you stop the fire?"

"'Easy—you extinguish their flame."

"No, you talk to them," I reply, knowing full well the old man isn't buying this one bit. "Through dialogue, compromise and respect, you try to understand each other . . . understand each other's needs, wants, motives, fears and joys. By treating someone how you'd like to be treated. "Do onto others" and all that. Are we that primitive a species that we have to respond in such primitive ways? If that's the case, we're no more evolved than the lowest life form on the planet. Even animals don't even treat their own kind with such heartlessness."

"Talking doesn't work with animals—"

"We're all flesh and blood, Wyman. Everyone you hate is flesh and blood, just like you, with their own fears, they're own feelings, their own pain. All born from a mother and a father. All once a small child longing to be loved, longing to live a happy life and in peace. See, I don't believe anyone's born evil, Wyman. Maybe we're born with the *potential* to be evil, but we're taught to be evil . . . taught to be evil by people like you."

"I don't believe that," he scoffs. "We're all born in Original Sin. It's written in the Bible! Some cannot be salvaged! Some are born from mongrels and—"

"That's where I think you're wrong, Wyman," I reply, looking over to the old man sitting next me. "I don't believe in Original Sin. I don't buy that. A child isn't born out of hate or evil. A child doesn't come out of its mother's womb and naturally hates Christians, Jews, Muslims, *Negroes* or *faggots*, as you'd say."

"What the hell is your point?"

"My point is, if a child isn't born to hate, where does it come from? Where does all this anger . . . this animosity . . . this hate come from, Wyman?"

The old man looks away and doesn't respond.

"Do you know what xenophobia is, Wyman?"

Again, silence.

"I'll tell you what it is. It's a fear—a phobia, actually—of all that's strange or foreign, including people. That's where your hate comes from. Fear. And what causes fear? Any real or perceived threat. The key word here is *perceived*, Wyman. People like you, Wyman, can't tell what the hell is real and what the hell you think is real. Like a collective form of paranoid schizophrenia. Everything and everyone that is different becomes a threat to you."

"Foreign filth is a real threat! Look at 9/11! Look at—"

"No, you just think they are in that messed-up, narrow-minded little brain of yours. But what goes around comes around. And I guarantee you one thing—karma will not be on your side."

"The hell with karma," he responds, unflinching. "I have God Almighty in my corner. That's all that matters to me."

"Speaking of God Almighty, didn't he say 'Do not judge lest ye be judged'?" I offer, not giving him a chance to answer. "Who the hell are you to judge who's good and who's evil? Who are you to judge who should live and who should die? Who are you to judge anything?"

"Fuck you."

"Are you God, Wyman? Is that what you're saying? Because you sure like to go around acting like you're God. And I guarantee you when the time comes to stand before Him, when it's your turn to be judged, He sure won't appreciate you impersonating him over the course of your miserable life."

He turns away as far as he possibly can, looking out the side window.

I abandon my debate with Wyman, knowing far too well I can't teach an old dog new tricks. There's no point. No argument or conversation would ever break him. The roots are simply too deep. There's nothing anyone could ever say or do to change him. It'd take an act of extraordinary kindness and compassion and love to even begin to peel the old man's layers of prejudice and hate.

But that's not my problem, or my mission.

What *is* my business for the night, however, is to get Sarah back—and obtain more evidence to support my innocence. "Wyman, how long have you known Jacob Hoffman?" I ask.

"We've known each other for a long time, that's all you need to know."

"I have to say, playing me like that was pretty brilliant. You know, setting me up to be Black Mamba and all . . . who's brainchild was that? Yours or his? Or maybe Kipling's?"

"Kipling? Hell, no. That was all Jacob," he replies, smiling. "He does me proud. He's a smart boy. He's a warrior. So are Miroslav and Conrad. They'll lead the charge against Satan and his army. They've been training the recruits for months, you know. Months! Right under your ratty little nose. Jacob . . . he's a genius, I tell you. I sure wish there were more out there like him. You're not half the man he is."

"The mosque bombings, the imam and the ambassador, the murder of the Toronto Four . . . I'm assuming that was all Jacob as well?"

"You bet your ass it was!"

"Clever bastard."

"He's going to kill you, you know," he says, still staring out the side window. "He'll have you hanged to a cross and bleed you to death, just like the dirty pig you are. There's no greater pleasure he'd rather have than to see you bleed and to see you burn."

Up ahead, there's a road sign: Innisfil 17 km.

"Take a right up ahead," Wyman says.

We soon find ourselves on a dark gravel road. On all sides are nothing but corn fields—empty spaces filled only with darkness. I roll the window down and stick my head out the window to listen for any sounds. The only thing audible is the sound of the wheels spinning against the gravel, spitting dirt and rock into a trail of dust behind us.

I glance frequently at the digital clock below the dashboard. With only ten minutes to go before midnight, time is running out. "We almost there?" I ask, becoming more anxious by the minute.

"I think so," Wyman answers. "Slow down a little or you'll pass it . . ."

"Pass what?"

"See that barn up ahead? There's a trail on the left just past it. Turn there."

I would've missed it if it wasn't for Wyman. I never even would've noticed it, but there it is: a set of muddy tire tracks cutting through the field. Up ahead, nothing but cropland. If it weren't for the moon's ghastly silver glow, I would've sworn there was nothing but endless pasture. But, somewhere in the distance, a dark mass looms just below the glow at the horizon. Trees. A woodlot. The closer we get, the more distinct they become. I kill the headlights hoping to avoid early detection. It isn't until reaching the very edge of the woodlot itself that I notice several vehicles parked at its perimeter.

"This is it," Wyman announces, smirking. "We'll have to make our way on foot from here. You sure you don't want to turn back now? It's not too late for you."

I open the door. "Shut up and get out of the car," I say, pulling on the shotgun and dragging him by the collar. Wyman carefully gets out through the driver side door, stumbling a little. "Now lead the way."

CHAPTER 55

In the woods, all is eerily dark, the moon's dim glow now engulfed by the growing foliage above us. Only faint specks of light manage to break through, just enough to warn of any shadows ahead of us.

At my command, we trek slowly, quietly. Somewhere along the way, and without Wyman's knowledge, I reach into my jacket pocket and stop the audio recording. Then, choosing a random spot, I lob the device into the darkness, where it's swallowed by the thick underbrush to my left.

We walk for a short distance until we notice a faint glow visible through the brush. Distant voices are heard, singing some type of hymn or chorus. As the glow grows stronger with every step we take, I see a clearing up ahead. Some three hundred yards beyond, at the far end of this clearing, several torches burn brightly, illuminating a formation—a circle—consisting of a large number of people. It's only after stepping out into the clearing and edging my way toward them that I notice something standing erect at the center of the formation.

A cross.

And bound to it, hanging by her limbs, is Sarah.

Terrified I may be too late, I feel my heart leap in my chest. I stare as she hangs loosely from the ropes that bind her, her head drooping forward, her mouth gagged. Desperate, I shove Wyman forward, ordering him to quicken his pace. We trudge another hundred yards or so when I decide to stop abruptly.

It's difficult to tell how many are present, but my best guess would be in the dozens. All are dressed in dark and hooded robes. Even from a distance, I'm able to spot the shiny silver masks worn by each member, the soft metallic moldings glowing brightly like ghosts hovering in the darkness. That's when I realize my worst nightmares—every image that's haunted my dreams for the past twenty years—are materializing before my very eyes.

The chorus suddenly ceases. Only the rustling of leaves and the blowing wind can be heard. From the formation, a lone man steps forward and addresses the group, his dialogue muffled. In his hands he holds a book.

Not wanting to waste another second, I force Wyman to continue forward. "Let her go!" I shout, following behind him with my finger pressed firmly against the trigger.

Almost instantly, all heads shift and gaze in our direction. With their faces concealed behind those ghastly masks, I can't tell one man from another.

"Let her go, or Wyman is a dead man!"

There's no reaction, just blank, empty stares.

"Tell them to stop their little ritual and let her go, Wyman," I whisper, shielding myself behind his thin and feeble frame. "Tell them or by God I'll light you up."

Indignant, Wyman stalls for a moment. "Let the girl go!" he finally shouts. "I'm dripping with gasoline here—"

"Let her go or Wyman goes up in flames!" I finish.

From the group, a figure steps into the darkness and slowly makes his way over. About a dozen feet before us he stops dead in his tracks. "We weren't expecting you, I have to admit," he says calmly in a voice I don't recognize, "But now that you're here, I'm sure we can arrange something."

"Get her down, now!" I bark, reaching into my jacket pocket for the camcorder. "I have everything you want! It's all on here. My confession to being Black Mamba. My involvement in the bombings. The kidnappings and murders. Everything. Take a look for yourself," I offer, lobbing the device to this mystery spokesperson, who easily catches it in midair.

The masked man takes a look at the camcorder and flips open the tiny screen. He then plays the video and watches attentively, listening. Behind him, an army of ghosts wait patiently for his word.

After he's viewed it, he looks up at me. "Do you think we'll give up the girl for this?"

"That, and Wyman's life . . ." I reiterate.

"What makes you think we give a damn about the old man's life?"

"I don't care whether you care or not," I retort, flashing the pistol strapped to my belt. "If you don't set her free right this minute, I'm sending Wyman straight to hell and you along with him."

"You don't have enough rounds for all of us."

"I don't care."

A long, nervous silence ensues. The eyes behind the mask remain fixated on my own. Behind them, there's nothing but a cold and calculating emptiness.

"Jacob? Is that you? By God, if that's you—"

He raises his hand as though summoning silence. "I'm sorry, but Black Mamba is not available at this time. Allow me to consult with the council."

"Sorry, but I can't let that happen," I reply, standing my ground. "You really have no decision to make. Either you let her go or both you and Wyman are dead. I'm a wanted man now. I've got nothing to lose so don't think for one second I won't blow your goddamn head off—because at the end of the day, it really won't make a difference for me now, will it?"

The eyes behind the mask glance down to the camcorder then back into my own. There's a moment of hesitation, of uncertainty. What I wouldn't give to know what he's thinking—what they're all thinking.

After a short silence, he turns to his posse and signals with his hand. Almost immediately, two members break from their formation and head for the cross. Each taking a side, they free Sarah from her bindings and help her down. She appears weak, barely able to stand. Supported by the two members, she's led away from the formation and into the dark, empty field.

The man in the mask turns to face me. "Now, before we hand her over, there's something we want from you."

"And what's that?" I ask, keeping an eye on the approaching trio.

"We want you, of course."

"What?"

"We want you," he repeats in the same tone. "We always wanted you."

"I don't think so, pal."

Unfazed, he shakes his head. "I'm afraid there's no other way."

The men escorting Sarah come to a halt behind their speaker. Up close she appears exhausted and dazed, but alert nonetheless. Her mouth is still gagged. A blindfold covers her eyes. She tries to speak, but can't manage anything audible through the gag.

"Sarah, it's me!" I cry out. "Baby, it's me. Everything's going to be OK. You hear me? I'm going to get you out of here."

"You in exchange for her," the man says, turning to Sarah and removing the blindfold from her eyes. "I think that's a fair trade, don't you?"

I look her right in the eyes. Terrified, tears begin to roll down her cheeks. Now more than ever, I'm determined to get her to safety, no matter what the cost. "Let her go, and I'll do whatever you want. But unless I see her walk out of these woods and drive away safely, you'll get nothing from me but a hole in your head."

"First, let Wyman go. You let him go, and we let the girl go. Consider it an exchange, if you will."

"No dice."

"Then we have no choice but to complete the ritual," he says, and motions for his minions to escort Sarah back to the formation. "You see, unfortunately for you, loss of life is a price we're all willing to pay for the greater good. So, if you're willing to take my life and Wyman's life, then it's God's will."

I watch helplessly as Sarah is led back to the formation. I quickly come to terms with the fact that if I'm to get Sarah back, I'll have to make some dire concessions. Perhaps naively, I've suddenly come across an element I hadn't considered: the fact that the threat of death won't sway the Dominion. As much as any kamikaze, they're willing to die for the cause.

I wrestle with the thought of pulling the trigger and watching Wyman's neck explode and then putting whatever bullets are left in the pistol into the man before me. However, considering the legion of onlookers waiting to be summoned, I know that neither Sarah nor I would make it out of here alive if I pull such a stunt.

"Wait," I say, removing the duct tape from the barrel of the shotgun. "You can have Wyman—but only if you let her go."

The mysterious man signals to the trio and they return. The shotgun no longer attached to Wyman, I keep it pressed firmly between his shoulder blades anyway. There's a moment of uncertainty, of hesitation, but Sarah is released. I shove Wyman forward and release him too.

The detainees cross paths until they're safely in the company of their liberators.

Sarah falls into my arms and I immediately remove the gag from her mouth. Without ever taking my aim away from either Wyman or the speaker, I hand her the keys to the BMW and order her to leave immediately and drive to the South Simcoe Police detachment in Innisfil. I tell her to tell the cops everything—and that I've been set up by key federal authorities involved in the investigation of the Dominion of God. I tell her I'll explain everything later, but that for now she needs to get out of these woods alive.

But, despite my insistence, she refuses to leave without me.

"We're leaving now," I announce. "The first to make a move gets his head blown off. Don't follow us, I'm warning you . . ."

Despite my warning, the moment we begin to step back toward the edge of the clearing, the leader signals to the rest of the group to abandon the formation and pursue us. In unison, they march into the darkness like an army being called into battle.

"I'm sorry, but only one of you can go," the leader announces, signaling for his clan to halt. "If you both try to escape, we'll chase you down and offer the good Lord the blood of two sufferers tonight."

I turn to Sarah. "Sarah, baby, you have to get out of here," I whisper, pushing her away from me. "See that trail? There are vehicles parked at the end of it. Take the grey BMW—it's an SUV. Go to the police. You hear me?"

"Liam, I'm scared," she replies, tears still flowing from her eyes. "I'm not leaving you here alone with . . . with these monsters. What do they want from you?"

"I'll explain later, we don't have time right now! Just go! Please!"

"I'm not leaving you . . ."

"Listen to me," I repeat. "If we both try to leave, they'll hunt us down and they'll kill us. Do you understand? Baby, I need you to be strong right now! You have to leave without me. Don't worry about me, I'll catch up with you later."

I watch her face and I can tell she's struggling, fighting every single impulse in her body. Finally she kisses me on the cheek, tells me she loves me and makes a mad dash into the woods. Several minutes go by before the start of an engine is heard in the distance. A few seconds later, the legion of silver faces resumes its advance and I'm swiftly surrounded by a sea of metallic masks, the eyes behind them hollow and devoid of humanity. Like conscienceless robots, they follow their leader's every command.

"We can either do this the easy way, or the hard way," he says, ordering his clan to halt. "Either way, there's only one outcome."

I stand my ground with a pistol in one hand and shotgun in the other, my arms extended and pointing outward. In an instant, I see my life flash before my eyes. My time is up, I figure, and I'm not going to make this easy for them. I'm not going down without a fight.

"OK, you win," I concede, slowly lowering the pistol. "You can resume your sick and demented ritual . . . I give up."

As they begin to approach, I quickly reach into my pocket and retrieve the lighter. Again, I attempt to set it alight but manage only to get a few sparks. The hoard around me immediately reacts and closes in on me. With one last flick, I set it alight and toss it to Wyman, who instantly goes up in flames. His shrieks and wails fill the air as the group turns their attention to their figurehead, who's now lighting up the sky. Someone throws him to the ground and numerous members begin to roll him over and cover him with dirt.

Amid the commotion and the panic, I dart into the forest. I run like I've never run before, plowing through brush and thicket along the way. The screaming and howling ultimately subsides, but is replaced by the sound of a stampede somewhere behind me intermixed with angry voices describing my location and direction. Up ahead, I manage to spot the vehicles stationed at the edge of the woodlot.

I'm nearly at the edge of the field when I see a large truck coming to a screeching halt, blocking my path. Two silver masked figures climb out. I freeze momentarily, contemplating another route. In that split second, I'm struck on the back of the head with some blunt object, which instantly sends me to a realm filled with nothing but silence and darkness.

CHAPTER 56

My eyes open slowly, revealing a kaleidoscope of color and light. Everything is hazy and undefined, like in a dream, or as if I'm on some kind of mind-altering drug. It's all so unreal and strange that I begin to think I might be no longer on earth and my soul is passing on to . . . well, hopefully to something better. I'm aware, but not quite sure I'm awake.

At times, I see faces and hear voices—or at least I think I do. They come randomly and unexpectedly only to disappear as quickly as they appear. Sometimes, they are distinct, recognizable, even. Most times, however, I can't tell whether I'm in the presence of a fellow man or God himself.

It takes an immeasurable amount of time before I'm able to confirm I'm both awake and aware. At times, the world around me becomes defined, only to quickly fade away to near total obscurity and darkness once again. I can feel myself slipping in and out, as though succumbing to some type of anesthetic or extreme fatigue or delirium.

At the back of my head, there's a pounding ache, like a beating drum. I'm also aware of a hunger and a thirst unlike anything I've ever felt before. My muscles are weak and unresponsive, the signals I try to send them apparently inhibited by an unknown and invisible force.

I remain in this state for quite some time, slipping in and out of consciousness.

In.

And out.

Slowly, I begin to put the pieces together as images strobe through my mind. Fire. A cross. Sarah. Silver ghosts hovering in the dark. It seems like it all just happened, yet, it also feels so long ago. Although I manage to recall—at least vaguely—most of the night's events, I'm baffled as to how it ended.

My hearing is the first sense to fully return. My eyes still unfocused, I listen. At first, what I hear sounds like nothing more than countless kernels of corn popping somewhere in the distance. But with every passing second, the tiny explosions become louder and more distinct until their nature becomes unmistakable. Somewhere close by, a fierce battle is taking place in the form of armed warfare.

I try to get to my feet, but after several failed attempts, I flop back down into a heavy leather chair to which I'm handcuffed. As my vision improves, my surroundings begin to materialize. Before me is a large, majestic desk made of some type of fine wood—oak, I think. On it, documents and blueprints are spread about. Just past the desk, several more leather chairs are scattered about. It soon becomes evident that I'm in the office of someone rather important—a lawyer, judge or perhaps even a Senator or minister of Parliament. Whatever the case, I can't recall ever being inside such an impressive room before.

Everything around me is made of solid wood. The floors. The walls. The window frames and blinds. The doors. All the desks, chairs and lamps also have fancy wood components. At the far end of the room, in the left-hand corner and just in front of the door, is a sofa surrounded by a coffee table and two end tables. At the right of the door is a small desk with a chair at each end. Displayed in the center of the room is a fancy Persian rug. To my right and left, two of our national flags hang loosely from their staffs.

The lighting in the room is quite dim, with little natural light seeping through the blinds and shutters. Closed on purpose, I assume. My eyes become transfixed by the warm glow of a desk lamp, the main source of light in the room. Despite the darkness, I freeze at the sight of several dark shadows standing just a few feet past the desk, the glare of their lenses staring down on me. Various blinking lights, some red and some green, float around them in the semi-darkness. A sea of cables rests on the floor at their feet, each snaking all the way to an electrical outlet somewhere in the room.

Somewhere below me, a thundering blast occurs. The floor beneath my feet trembles, rattling every piece of furniture in the room, including the mammoth desk. Not a tiny tremor. My best guess, a perfect ten on the Richter scale.

Again, I attempt to break away from the handcuffs. No luck. To make matters worse, I'm also unable to roll away, because the chair's tightly chained to the heavy desk. For the next several minutes, I just sit there, trying to figure out a way to escape. All around me, gunfire continues.

In the midst of my struggles, a new, troubling detail of my predicament emerges. It's the wide-open sleeves that hang loosely around my wrists that I notice first. Distraught, I scan my body all the way up to my shoulders and back down to my feet, and I realize I'm clad in one of the Dominion's trademark robes, the hood hanging loosely between my shoulder blades.

What the f . . . ?

Somewhere beyond the heavy wooden door at the end of the room, just past the blinking lights, shouting erupts. The sound of someone in distress. I listen and wait nervously as the source of all the hollering approaches the door.

More gunfire, only louder this time.

Something—or someone—heavy crashes into the wall and collapses on the floor just behind the door. Then, the door opens and closes shut. Heavy panting ensues.

"You . . . son-of-a-bitch . . ." yells an irate voice, it's shadow branding a pistol or revolver. "What did you do? Where is everyone? Where's all the staff? All the MPs? The PM?? We're getting annihilated out there!"

Utterly clueless as to what's happening, I remain silent.

Somewhere at the far end of the room just past the blinking lights, the gunman crashes to the ground. "You're going to pay for this—you're going to pay for what you've done!"

I stay quiet and watch as the shadow gets back to its feet. I hear a click and suddenly I'm flooded with blinding light. I can't do anything but squint or close my eyes completely as I become engulfed in heat emanating from the powerful bulbs.

When I'm finally able to focus, I notice a lone man directing and operating one of several television cameras in the room. A small pool of blood has already collected at his feet. His clothing's stained dark red. He's hunching and favoring his right side, his forearm encased in a blood-stained cast. In his left hand he holds a pistol.

"Look at me!" he orders, toying with the equipment.

Kipling? Can it be—

I stop in mid-thought as I notice several brick-sized packages fastened to the walls and to the ceiling above me. Except it quickly occurs to me these aren't any ordinary switch boxes or camera equipment. I've seen these before. Blocks of M112. Plastic explosives. All bound to the wall and wired to one another. It seems I'm sitting in the middle of a suicide chamber.

"Look at me you goddamn piece of shit," Kipling snarls, abandoning his post and limping over to the desk before me. He's wearing dark military fatigues and a bulletproof vest. Despite his armor, he's got a deep wound to his abdomen, blood and other bodily fluids oozing from it. Blood trickles from his mouth. Strapped to his right ear are several layers of gauze.

From his belt hangs a two-way radio crackling with frantic transmissions: "Kilo . . . India . . . come in. Kilo . . . India . . . do you read me?"

"This is Kilo-India, copy," Kipling replies.

"What's your twenty?"

"I'm at home base."

"Frenchy and his team are down . . . I repeat, Frenchy and Alpha team are down. We've lost Frenchy—they've captured the House and Senate . . . we still hold the library . . . we're pulling back and heading your way."

"Ten four. I can't find Miroslav . . . he's not answering on Channel 2."

"Is Black Mamba with you?"

Kipling turns to me and smirks. "He's good and ready to go, but . . ."

"But what?"

"I'm afraid I'm not doing so well, Captain. I've been hit."

"Hang tight, we're on our way!"

"Godspeed."

Making no attempt to clip it back to his belt, Kipling drops the radio to the floor. He then reaches into his military vest pocket and pulls out a single handcuff key. Stumbling to my side, he unlocks one cuff, liberating my left hand.

"Now, unlock the other!" he orders, leaving the key on the desk within my reach. Confused, I simply watch as he slowly backs away, aiming his pistol between my eyes. "You know, if it was up to me, I'd be cutting off your balls right now and stuffing them down your throat.

But lucky for you, the boss has bigger plans. Now unlock the goddamn cuff!"

Hesitantly, I do as I'm told.

"Good. Now see that yellow document there?" he says, pointing his pistol at the desk. "When I give you the signal, you look at the camera and read it out loud. And try to be convincing or by God I'll make you wish you were never born!"

Kipling spits out more blood and limps over to the far end table by the sofa, where a fancy-looking antique telephone is sitting. He picks up the receiver and dials a number. "This is the Dominion of God, We're giving you the feed now. Stand by . . ."

My eyes scan the document. It looks to be some kind of speech, a proclamation of the beginning of the Tribulation. It's also a letter inciting all like-minded citizens of the world to renounce their faiths and take up arms against the false prophets, and all else that consists the Army of the Beast. It's an invitation to partake in a new order that is the Dominion of God and to engage in warfare and genocide against the Beast and his people in order to prepare for the Rapture and the Second Coming of Christ and to restore God's kingdom.

Its gruesomely explicit nature makes my stomach churn and sickens my soul. It's quite possibly the most repugnant piece of literature I've ever read or that's ever been written.

"You ready?" Kipling asks, taking a position behind the cameras.

"I refuse to read this . . . this filth!" I snarl, discarding the paper.

"You pick that up right now and read the damn thing or by God I'll skin you alive from head to toe!"

"The hell I will!"

Kipling storms out from behind the camera, blood trailing behind him. Clutching his abdomen and ribs, he appears woozy and delirious. His eyes are as hollow as they've ever been, staring madly down on me. From his belt, he retracts a hunting knife with a six-inch blade. "Pick up that sheet and read it now or I start gutting you like a fish!"

"OK, you win." I pick up the document.

Kipling wobbles his way back to the camera. "Look at the camera, you no-good mongrel . . . on three, two, one . . . Go!"

Suddenly, a massive explosion rocks the foundation of the entire building. Behind me, the sound of helicopter blades accompanied by the rapid fire of miniguns or other Gatling-style weaponry roars past the shuttered windows. Another blast, only smaller this time. Frantic screams coming from levels below and above us. The sound of high-powered rifles. A rocket being launched. More hollering. More gunfire.

I stall.

Kipling becomes irate. "Go! Go, Goddamn it!"

"Ladies and gentlemen, great citizens of the world," I begin, pretending to read and quoting a passage I had once memorized from the Bible. "Today is the beginning of a new world, of a new order. I've come to warn you that false prophets are among you just as there are false teachers among you. They introduce destructive heresies. Many, sadly, follow their shameful ways and will bring the way of truth into disrepute, as has the Dominion of God—"

"You son of a bitch!" Kipling roars, pulling out his pistol.

But I remain focused.

"These teachers will exploit you with stories they've altered or fabricated. Beloved, believe not every spirit! The Dominion of God is a false prophet and has been defeated! The Dominion of God is—"

With every last ounce of strength left in him, Kipling launches himself at me, striking me across the head with his pistol and knocking me out of my chair. Dazed, I topple to the floor, Kipling falling with me. He continues to unleash his fury, landing heavy blows. Something warm begins to run down from my forehead and into my eyes.

Kipling eventually moves away, laboring to get back to his feet. He teeters for a few seconds above me, as though about to collapse once again. Unable to maintain a steady footing, he leans back against the big desk and cocks his pistol.

"Should've done this a long time ago," he grimaces. "See you in hell . . ."

I close my eyes and await my liberation.

Click!

Reopening them, I see Kipling struggling with his firearm.

Click!

Click!

Click!

"Empty? That's impossible!" he cries, scrutinizing the pistol and checking his clip. Again, he pulls the trigger. And again. And again. Still, nothing. Unable to hold himself upright any longer, he collapses backward onto the desk, arms spread out and gun and knife sprawling to the floor. His chest rises and collapses at longer and longer intervals.

After wiping away the blood running down into my eyes, I crawl to the discarded pistol and grab it. Slowly gathering strength, I'm able to get to my hands and knees and ultimately to my feet using the chair and then the desk as leverage. Despite the aching and the swelling resulting from Kipling's blows, I remain determined to confront whatever life remains in his body.

"God will punish you for this," he says, his voice weak and fading. "I hope you're proud of yourself. At least *I'll* be taken at the Rapture. I *will* be resurrected. I'll see you at Armageddon . . . you Goddamn traitor . . . you . . ."

Kipling takes his last breath, his eyes rolling back in their sockets. I watch as all the hate and the prejudice desert his now lifeless body, like a tire that's sprung a leak. For the first time in a very long time, his body is pure and sinless. Where the evil has gone, God only knows.

CHAPTER 57

Time passes following Kipling's demise. Not much, but enough to allow me to collect myself and ponder my next move. My main goal is to get the hell out of this office before the explosives go off. I don't see a timer anywhere, which leads me to believe the detonation device isn't time-activated. That probably means the detonator, wherever it is, will have to be activated manually.

Needless to say, I don't have much time to spare. The roaring of automatic rifles, the helicopter blades, the random blast, the miniguns and other heavy artillery and the pandemonium that surrounds me remind me of that fact. I contemplate opening the blinds or the shutters and calling out for help. I also consider bolting out of the office with guns ablaze. However, I figure either the Dominion or a well-meaning military sniper will shoot me dead on the spot.

But I can't think of another alternative.

I inspect Kipling's pistol, releasing the magazine. To my astonishment, it turns out to be fully loaded. Not one single bullet is missing. I slide the magazine back into place and pull the trigger. Oddly, it goes off without a hitch, opening a small hole in the ceiling. I stare at the muzzle and the thin trail of smoke escaping the chamber. For a second I'm paralyzed, knowing full well my brains *should* be all over the floor. *Was it a malfunction? Or was it divine intervention?* Time not on my hands, I don't ponder this any further. I simply count my blessings and move on.

I consider taking Kipling's radio. Transmissions continue to flood the airwaves, some seeking orders, others seeking backup, many seeking terms of surrender. In every voice, there's panic and desperation.

Almost instinctively, I pick up the device. "Black Mamba to all units. Attention all units. This is your leader. We've lost key positions and are on the verge of defeat. We are surrounded. Many have already perished. I've negotiated the terms of surrender. I've been advised that those who lay down their arms will be treated accordingly. As your leader, I order you all to lay down your arms."

It's only after completing my transmission that I notice the large television cameras are still filming. Somewhere in the city or across the country or perhaps even across the world, I'm being broadcast. I don't know to who or to where. But somewhere, I figure, someone is watching. For a split second, the thought crosses my mind to spill the beans, from start to finish, and plead my innocence. But I've done that already and I can only hope that the mayhem around me is a direct result of it. Besides, any plea at this point in the game would only be interpreted as a terrorist mastermind's pathetic and desperate attempt to save his hide.

As I'm about to step away from the desk and from Kipling's body, the door swings open and I find myself face to face with Derek and Jacob, who immediately notice me and Kipling's corpse. In his right hand Derek is wielding an Uzi. Jacob is brandishing a revolver. Both are dressed in military fatigues, complete with boots and bulletproof vests. They halt suddenly, obviously caught off guard.

We exchange glances for a few short breaths.

Then, all hell breaks loose.

I'm the first to raise my pistol and open fire, striking Derek in the lower abdomen just below the vest. As he's falling, he unloads the Uzi in my direction. I take cover behind the desk and watch as the leather chair is ripped apart by gunfire.

"It's over, Liam!" Jacob shouts, followed by the sound of heavy doors slamming shut. "Come out, wherever you are!"

"You're goddamn right it's over! Over for you! Over for the Dominion and your sick and pathetic little plan . . ."

From somewhere at the end of the room, Derek winces in pain. He curses and unloads again, the bullets incapable of penetrating the thickness of the wood that shields me. Despite Jacob yelling to him to hold his fire, Derek fires his weapon until he's out of ammo.

"Give it up, Liam!" Jacob continues. "The treaty has been signed. There's no turning back. Will you just give up this pointless crusade? What is it you're trying to accomplish? Who is it you're trying to help? The foreign scum-sucking parasites that infests the planet? You think you're their saviour? Like some kind of crusader riding in on his big white horse?"

"No, Jacob, I don't think I can save anyone . . ."

"That's right, you can't save—"

"But I refuse to judge or condemn anyone either! My legacy in this world will not be one of hate and violence. If I'm going to die trying to make the world a better place, then so be it!"

"What do you think *we're* trying to do?" Derek snarls.

"Liam, I sure hope for your sake you're comfortable with that . . . because you *are* going to die, right here and right now," Jacob says, pausing. "Go ahead, look around the room. You'll realize you aren't getting out of here alive. None of us are."

I take a peek around the corner of the desk and spot Derek sitting up. In his hands is a small device that resembles a typical remote control. He notices me and smirks, waving the device to be sure I've spotted it. Finally, the detonator I've been looking for.

"Unless . . . unless . . ." Jacob continues, obviously desperately scheming. "Unless you get back up into that chair and tell the world you've killed Kipling and that you're now holding a federal agent hostage."

"What about Derek?" I ask, still peering around the corner.

Jacob suddenly appears in my field of vision at the other end of the room behind the glaring spotlights. He pauses for a moment and turns to Derek, who's looking up uncertainly at his leader. Before Derek can even muster a word, Jacob raises his arm and empties a round right between his eyes. Blood sprays from the back of Derek's skull as his lifeless body collapses to the floor, sending the detonator shooting past the cameras at the center of the room.

"That's none of our concern now," Jacob says. "It's just you and me."

I catch a glimpse of Jacob sprinting for the device and I fire two rounds, both missing. Still, it sends him bolting in the opposite direction to take cover behind a sofa that he pulls away from the wall. His head then pops back up and he fires several rounds in my direction, tearing the corner of the desk apart.

For a short while, we remain still. But I'm sure we're both thinking the same thing: to be the first to get his hands on the detonator without getting killed. The only difference is, we want it for opposing reasons.

We continue to wait, neither one of us daring to make the first move. All around us, fighting continues but less intensely now. The sound of a helicopter circling the building continues, minus the miniguns.

"Liam, we can both get out of this alive," Jacob finally says. "All you need to do is get in front of those cameras and tell the world you've kidnapped me and that you're now surrendering. Do that and you'll spare both our lives."

I can't help but laugh. "Yeah, sounds like a great bargain!"

More silence.

"How's Wyman by the way?" I ask, not because I care.

"Not looking so good . . ."

Another long silence ensues.

"Why do you do it?" Jacob asks, exasperated. "We had a good plan, you know. A plan where no one would ever again suffer the pain and heartache I felt the day my father was taken from me and the day I lost everyone I had left. My brothers, obliterated in the blink of an eye. I later watched my mother take her last breath. But although I've lost my family, I've found a new one. We were going to restore God's Kingdom! A Kingdom free of these sinners . . . these imposters . . . and of the Devil's abominations!"

"And you think this is how they'd want you to go on?"

"Yes, I do," he replies with conviction. "You don't know, Liam. You don't know what a tragedy like this does to the heart of a man. Until you've been through it, you'll never know. You'll always be there, forever in a position of ignorance . . ."

"You say you want a world where no one would suffer the pain you have, yet you're willing to inflict pain. Your actions have resulted in the same pain and loss you felt—and are still feeling. Is this what you want? For others to feel the same pain?"

"Those of the Beast don't feel pain like you and I."

I don't bother answering to this. There's just no point and no merit. I think about it for awhile. "Do you remember the Tower of Babel, Jacob? Book of Genesis, 11:1?"

"Yeah, so?"

"Then you'll recall that after the Great Flood, the people of the world had only one language. They were one people—" The sound of a small blast followed by gunfire makes me pause briefly. "They decided to build a city and a tower that would reach the heavens. But when

God saw this, he came down to earth and confused their language so they wouldn't understand one another. He messed up their plans and scattered the people of the city all over the face of the earth."

"So what's your point, Liam?"

"Do you know why God did this?"

"Indulge me . . ."

"For two reasons," I continue. "One, because he knew of their intentions. The people of Babel became arrogant in their unity. And in their arrogance, they were building a monument to themselves, to express their own achievements and abilities instead of paying glory to God. God knew that man thought himself so high and powerful that he'd build a stairway to heaven and proclaim himself God. God knew that in a force so united, man was capable of many great and terrible things. By building this stairway to heaven, man wasn't getting closer to God, but further and further away."

"I see where you're going with this, and I—"

"Two, and what people like you don't understand, is that God did this to teach mankind humility, compassion, understanding, tolerance and love. It was a test. A challenge. How hard could it be if everyone was the same? What would we learn? It's all a test, Jacob—a test to weed out the pure of heart from the wretched. To see who's capable of loving his fellow man despite differences in skin color and language and religion and culture. You—and all your associates—have failed that test. And you ask me why I do it? It's because I'm not arrogant like you, Jacob. I don't think myself any better than anyone else . . . I don't go around pretending to be God."

"Think what you want," he finally replies. "It's all a matter of interpretation . . ."

"Yeah, it is, isn't it? Perhaps that's the real test."

"All I know is that in God's own words, he's summoned his people. He's calling us into battle in preparation of the Second Coming of his son—his own flesh and blood. Haven't you read the Bible?"

"Not your version of it, no."

"Not my version, God's version . . ."

"So I take it you're ready to die, then?"

"I am, Liam. Are you?"

"I'm ready to die for what's good," I reply. "But I'm not ready to kill for what's good. So if dying today means I'll have done something good for the world—not just for me or a certain people, but the *whole* world and everyone and everything in it—then yeah, I'm ready to die."

"I wonder if this is how Roland and the others felt when they were deceived . . . when they were betrayed and went down in flames inside that farmhouse. You fuckin' traitor. Once a traitor, always a traitor. That's all you'll ever be . . . and nothing more."

A few small explosions rock a distant target. Somewhere above us, gunfire erupts. Voices shouting. A helicopter is still circling, its miniguns becoming active once again. A rocket is launched but apparently misses its target. More gunfire. More shouting.

"You know, I'm going to have a son . . ." Jacob says.

"I thought you said you didn't want to know the sex."

"I changed my mind."

"Don't you care what's going to happen to him? Is it really worth it? Don't you want to be his father? See him grow up?"

"I'm creating a better world for him. He'll live through me. He'll come to understand. He'll follow in my footsteps. He'll be my legacy. I'll always be his father . . ."

"No, your death will be his salvation!" I shout. "It's the only chance he'll ever get!"

I release the clip from my pistol and realize there's only one bullet left. I have no clue what Jacob's ammunition status is, but I know I now have to make this one bullet count, or else it could be all over for me and whatever life I might have left.

Suddenly, I hear footsteps racing across the room. Peering over the desk, I spot Jacob making a run for the detonator. Without hesitating, I raise the Smith & Wesson and fire my last bullet, striking him just above the groin. He goes down like rock in front of the row of cameras and a few feet from the detonator. His revolver goes flying across the floor and out of his reach. For the longest time, he remains there, writhing in pain.

My magazine's now empty. But Jacob doesn't know that. *This is my chance, it's now or never,* I tell myself, and slowly creep out from behind the desk. For a moment, I think about getting the hell out of there, leaving Jacob behind with his detonator so he can blow himself to pieces. But I could be shot the moment I step out that door. Besides, letting Jacob kill himself would be an easy way out. And I have no intention of making it easy for him.

I quietly ease my way to the revolver and retrieve it. Two bullets remain in their chambers. Jacob lifts his head and winces in pain. His eyes lock onto the revolver in my hands, then the detonator. Then back onto me.

"Make one move," I say, pointing the revolver, "And I'll blow your goddamn brains out."

Despite my warning, Jacobs rolls toward the detonator. I fire a round that buries itself in his shoulder. "Stop it—you win, Liam! You got me!" he screams, dropping flat to the floor.

From somewhere behind the door, voices are heard approaching. Then silence. Slowly the handle turns, but the door doesn't open. A loud voice orders us to come out with our hands in the air. "This is your last chance," says the deep voice. "Open this door immediately or we break it down!"

Jacob and I exchange glances. I keep steady aim at his head. His arm is now extended toward the detonator, a move I somehow missed. Then he does something I should've expected.

"Help me!" he cries at the top of his lungs. "This is Agent Jacob Hoffman of the Canadian Security Intelligence Service! I've been kidnapped along with Sergeant Louis Kipling of the RCMP. I'm being held hostage by this lunatic! He killed Kipling. He's got the place rigged with plastic explosives—get me out of here!"

There is murmuring now on the other side of the door. The sound of a two-way radio going on and off. Silence. Seconds tick by like hours. I think about going to the door, but I know that the moment I take my eye off Jacob, he'll send us all to oblivion. Instead, I take a few steps closer. Jacob extends his arm, stretching it as far as he can go toward the detonator.

The door suddenly bursts wide open. Numerous Special Forces personnel come flooding in armed with laser-guided automatic rifles. With a revolver in hand, I immediately become the target, with numerous red dots pointed directly at my chest.

"Drop you weapon!" commands the lead officer. "Drop your weapon now and get down on the ground! Do it now!"

"If I do that, he'll blow us all to hell!" I plead, keeping my aim on Jacob.

"Drop your damn weapon or we open fire!"

"Shoot him!" Jacob shouts, still inching his way to the detonator.

"Look to the floor!" I yell, easing myself—and my weapon—down to the floor while keeping my aim on Jacob. "That's the detonator! Shoot me if you want, but don't let him get his hands on it!"

A few of the officers redirect their aim to Jacob. One of the officers, a large black man believed to be the commanding officer, reaches for his two-way radio and requests the assistance of a bomb squad.

"Shoot him!" Jacob barks at the officers. "Shoot him you, idiots! What are you waiting for? He's the leader! He's Black Mamba!"

All lasers are now pointed at Jacob, who for the first time appears defeated. His eyes roll back, looking up to the ceiling. His lips move slightly, as though saying a prayer.

"Move away from the detonator!" shouts the commanding officer, slowly advancing on Jacob. "Do it now! This is your final warning!!"

Completely ignoring the commander's orders, Jacob closes his eyes briefly and then makes one last dash for it. This time, he's successful. But before he can activate it, he's literally torn apart by a barrage of bullets.

I drop the revolver and let the Special Forces swarm me. I offer no resistance. I know this is protocol and that I'm not going to receive any special treatment. The commanding officer announces my capture over the radio and escorts me out of the room. Before rounding the corner, I take one last look at the mangled and lifeless body of the man who turned my life and soul into something I can no longer recognize.

CHAPTER 58

A lot of things are revealed to me during my time in detention. I'm interrogated by countless individuals, including high-ranking RCMP officials and intelligence officers as well as their American counterparts. They tell me that uprisings also occurred in Washington D.C. and London on that very same day, where the Dominion had also stormed the White House and the Parliament in those respective countries.

Thankfully, those too were quelled.

Altogether, 656 members of the Dominion of God perished in its failed coup in Canada, with another 111 having surrendered. In the U.S., over 400 were rounded up, with another 310 killed in action. In England, a total of 277 members were killed and 126 surrendered.

The package containing the second video recording I produced at the Owl Motel had been received—and just in time too. The package was to be delivered to the office of the prime minister in the early afternoon of June sixth, just under an hour before the Dominion's 14:00 arrival on the Hill. I arranged for this to catch the Dominion off guard and to give whoever was on the Hill that day enough time to evacuate. It also provided sufficient time for the city's SWAT team to mobilize until the arrival of the Armed Forces. Everything was done covertly and silently.

The problem was, I had no idea who to have the package delivered to and who I could trust. With the Dominion planning a coup on Parliament Hill and the execution of all members of government, I finally figured it was best to send the recording directly to those targeted for assassination. And so I sent it directly to the Office of the Prime Minister.

The recording, however, was not a duplicate of what I gave the Dominion on the night of their ritual. It wasn't a confession of my involvement in the Dominion of God. Instead, it was a far different account of a deeply rooted right-wing conspiracy in the heart of the country's security apparatuses and perhaps even its government. Like Frank would say, I laid it all out on the table, from A to Z.

Fortunately, the recording was taken seriously. A full evacuation was ordered as the city police dispatched its SWAT team and awaited the arrival of both the Dominion of God and the military. What no one knew was exactly *how* the Dominion was planning to storm Parliament Hill or what modes of transportation it would employ to get there.

As it turned out, the Dominion and its gear arrived in five rusty school buses and ten separate moving trucks—some from Montreal but most from Toronto. Two of these were filled with shock-proof and temperature-regulated containers of TATP—the Mother of Satan. While it hasn't been established exactly what the group intended to use the explosives for, it's believed they were meant to wipe out the entire Hill along with security forces in the eventuality of a defeat. Thankfully, the explosives were never detonated.

The group easily broke through the SWAT team's defense lines, which were completely outnumbered. The DOG then penetrated and captured the Centre Block while the East and the West Blocks were captured shortly after. Within twenty minutes of the siege, the military's ground forces were mobilized and took over command of the operation.

It turned out I was the Dominion's captive for nearly three weeks, from the night of the ritual to the failed coup. Blood tests have revealed high levels of a sedative called dexmedetomidine and traces of an anesthetic known as Propofol that were likely administered after my capture. Doctors have said it's a miracle I'm still alive.

Despite this, my innocence wasn't immediately assumed. While the video recording was key in thwarting the Dominion's plans, it didn't guarantee my freedom. It took weeks of investigation to corroborate my story and put the pieces together. What did help, though, was the voice recording I discarded in the woods on the night of the ritual. It was discovered the day after the attack on Parliament and revealed convincing testimony from the very lips of an irate Reverend Hunt. However, perhaps the most conclusive evidence was the live footage—complete with audio—that was broadcast over the Internet from the office of the prime minister. Jacob had no idea we were being broadcast.

I have Kipling to thank for that.

I was told that Miroslav and Vladimir and a few others had escaped sometime shortly after the beginning of the siege, likely after realizing their coup had already been foiled. It's believed they had a boat waiting for them on the river behind Parliament Hill. Even before the coup, they had purchased plane tickets destined for Montenegro in case the Dominion wasn't successful in its coup. Miroslav and his associates were eventually tracked down thanks to a piece of intelligence I provided during my interrogation. In the end, Miroslav and the others were found in Montenegro in hiding. While Vladimir and the others were returned back to Canada, Miroslav was extradited to Serbia where he was placed in detention where he was to await his trial for the crimes he committed during the Bosnian War. That, unfortunately, will never happen. Miroslav committed suicide by slicing his own jugular a week following his arrest and detention. In Cyrillic, and his own blood, he wrote "God will be my judge" on the wall inside his cell.

Indeed, He will.

As for Dino & Sons, they all perished on the Hill, along with Wes Sanderson and Brent Weiss, the bouncer from Sapphire's and pretty much everyone else I had come in contact with.

South of the border, numerous arrests were made in relation to the theft of plastic explosives from the Milan Army Ammunition Plant. Six American Ordnance employees, four contractors, and another seven civilian employees of the U.S. Army have been taken into custody and are awaiting trial.

In a speech the day following the attacks, the prime minister declared June sixth both a day of mourning and a day of celebration. Although numerous law enforcement and military personnel perished that day, their efforts were not in vain. The most significant threat to national security in the country's history had been averted and neutralized. The PM thanked all the men and women who participated in the operation for their courage, dedication and loyalty. He also thanked those in the intelligence community and promised the public that something like this would never happen again. He went even as far as offering an apology on behalf of the government for its failure to detect extremist elements within its ranks and for failing to assure the safety and security of all residents. As for me, I wasn't mentioned by name, but a special thanks went out to, and I quote, "an individual whose dedication and loyalty not only to his country, but to his fellow man, cannot be underestimated and will never be forgotten."

On another note, the peace treaty between Israel, the Palestinian National Authority and the League of Arab States was signed and delivered without a hitch. There were protests worldwide, some of which are still ongoing, but they are dwindling in strength and numbers. As far as I can tell, life on earth remains the same. No Antichrist. No Tribulation. Nothing. And it doesn't look like anything is going to change anytime soon which, for once, is fine with me.

I was released two weeks following the events of June sixth. I was offered a witness protection program and twenty-four-hour surveillance until the rest of those involved with the Dominion are found. I knew it wouldn't be necessary, but I accepted anyway. A few weeks following my release, I attended a private ceremony where I was a recipient of the Order of Canada. Although it was the proudest moment of my life, it wasn't the greatest one. No, that day was soon to come. But first, there's someone who I was dying to see.

CHAPTER 59

Wyman Hunt has been a resident of room 1201 at the Toronto East General Hospital since that fateful night in the field. Nearly eighty percent of his body, including his hands, feet and face, suffers from second or third-degree burns. His doctor, a funny-looking man by the name of Dr. Gerald Moss, insists that it's a medical miracle that Wyman did not go into hypovolemic shock and succumb to his injuries. He has undergone several reconstructive surgeries, the healthy skin from his back and legs having been used as grafts for the severely affected areas.

Standing in the doorway to his room, I realize I would never have recognized him if I hadn't already known who he was. Most of his face and body is either bandaged or covered in a cast. The parts that are left exposed, such as his left eye and parts of his mouth, resemble melted wax. He's connected to various pieces of equipment, including numerous intravenous drip bags and a heart monitor. I almost feel sorry for the old man—almost.

To be honest, I'm not quite sure why I'm here. It's surely not out of pity. It's not to rub salt in his wounds or add insult to injury either. Maybe it's for closure; I really don't know. But now that I'm here, I don't know how to feel. A flurry of emotions is rushing through me, like giant waves in a perfect storm: anger, sadness, and everything in between. I just want to save the old man. Save him from himself. But I don't know how to do it, or if it's even possible. Perhaps there is no saving him. Perhaps it isn't my responsibility either.

He doesn't notice me as I enter the room—at least I don't think he does. He just lies there like a corpse, his exposed eye staring out the window. When I catch my own reflection in the window pane, I know he's spotted me.

"Why . . . did you . . . come . . . here?" he asks softly and painfully.

"Hello, Wyman."

"You . . . should leave."

"I won't be too long," I reply, stepping forward.

Wyman doesn't turn to me. He just keeps staring at my reflection in the window and maybe to the garden beyond, where several beds of flowers and exquisite shrubs and trees grow.

"Do you ever have any regrets, Wyman?" I ask.

He doesn't respond.

"I don't hate you, Wyman," I say, gauging his reaction. "Although I dislike and disagree with what you stand for, and I'm bitter for everything that it's put me through, I don't hate you. I want you to know that, Wyman. I don't hate you. You can hate me all you want. You can hate whoever you want. I don't care. It's not going to stop me from loving. It's not going to stop anyone from loving anyone."

Finally he turns his head, as painful as the movement appears to be. His eye simply stares back at me, his cracked lips slightly parted and his breathing loud and forceful. After a few moments, he turns back to the window without saying a word.

"I know you don't understand," I say. "I don't think it's in your blood to understand. But I just hope you realize, for whatever time you have left on this planet, that it wasn't worth it. All this misery and violence and death your hate has caused. I hope you realize that and that you ask God for forgiveness. May He have mercy on your soul."

Wyman turns again to me. "God . . . will be . . . my judge."

"Indeed He will," I say, leaving a small bouquet of flowers at the foot of his bed.

A nurse walks in, dressed in the usual nurse's outfit along with a hijab covering her hair. Her eyes are dark and deep, her skin a healthy shade of olive. She smiles at me, revealing a set of perfect white teeth. She's strikingly beautiful, with a tall and slender build. In her hands are a clipboard and a clear plastic bag containing several plastic bottles.

"I'm sorry, sir," she says politely, "but I'm afraid I'll need some time alone with Mr. Hunt. It's time for his medication and he needs his rest."

"No problem at all," I reply, smiling. "I was just leaving."

She smiles as I walk past her. She tends to Wyman, administering some kind of oral medication. So much care and kindness in her actions, like an angel from heaven. I wonder whether she's aware of the dark history of her patient. I fight the urge to ask her. I fight the urge to tell her. I figure there's no real reason to do it. That it wouldn't—or shouldn't—make a difference.

"Nurse," I say before leaving.

"Yes?"

"Please take good care of him."

She smiles again, lighting up the room. She nods and turns to Wyman. Then something outside catches her attention—something in the garden. She stares long and hard. Wyman does so as well. Whatever it is appears to captivate them both, but with an opposite effect. While the nurse appears to be at peace, the old man seems like he's witnessing the Devil himself. I don't bother finding out what it is. I simply walk out of the room, knowing I'll never see either of them again.

Sarah is waiting patiently for me in the hospital lobby. She refused to accompany me to Wyman's ward. It's still beyond her why I insisted on coming here in the first place. I couldn't explain it to her. I still can't. I told her I simply needed to go. I told her everything. Not just my involvement with the Dominion this time around, but also my dealings with the group twenty years ago. It was a very difficult pill for her to swallow. It still is. All the lies. The deceptions. This double identity I had assumed. It may take awhile to get her to trust me again and to get over the events leading up to June sixth. But I'm willing to wait an eternity if that's how long it'll take.

On the way back from the hospital, we stop at Mount Hope Cemetery, where Frank was buried just a few weeks ago. The earth is still fresh from the burial. Several bouquets of flowers and cards and notes from loved ones decorate his grave. We stay for a while so I can pay tribute to my former handler. For years to come, he'll be in my thoughts and my prayers. I also vow to fulfill a promise I made to him many moons ago.

A few days later, I decide to take Sarah to Niagara Falls for a much needed escape. We do the usual touristy stuff by the falls and the surrounding gardens. A few weddings are taking place during this time, with bridal parties posing for pictures by the falls and in the gardens. Our first night there, standing just a short distance away from the beautifully spot-lit cascades, I get down on one knee and finally ask her to marry me. I vow to love, honor and protect her for as long as we both live, and beyond, as God as my witness.

Without hesitation, she accepts my proposal.

I feel like the luckiest man alive.

I later learn that Jacob's wife—or widow—gave birth to a healthy baby boy. Weighed 8 pounds, 5 ounces. She named him Nathaniel. While I feel sad for her and for this child who's now fatherless, I also feel relief. Relief that the bond is broken, that this pattern of hatred won't be passed on. At least this child will have a chance, unlike many others who don't, never did and never will. For that reason alone, I feel content.

Since the failed coup and the fall of the Dominion, I end up spending a lot of time thinking about things I'd never really put much thought into before. I think a lot about fate, chance, divine intervention, and of course, the Father of all creations. While at one point in time I would've attributed Kipling's pistol misfiring to mechanical malfunction, I'm now convinced I had a hand from someone—or something—beyond my realm of understanding.

I believe that now.

My mother often said to me as a boy "the Lord works in mysterious ways". I think she was both right and wrong. I've come to know that, if I open my mind and my heart wide enough, things aren't so mysterious after all.

EPILOGUE

Despite the intense heat and my skin burning to a crisp, I don't step into the fountain. Instead, I stand my ground and cast whatever energy remaining within me back onto the silver faces. I give the demons all I've got until there is nothing left for them to harm. I'm no longer afraid.

Furious, they howl and shriek and try to grasp my soul. But it is not within their reach. The flames grow bigger and stronger, the heat more intense. But I don't feel the heat any longer.

I stand before them, an army of things that never were. Their faces—their masks—reflect not what is real, but what I choose to believe is real. And so as I stare deep into the mirrors that are their existence, the raging fires reflecting from them begin to dwindle. But my spirit alone is not enough to cast the army back into the shadows and the nothingness from which they came.

At first, I can't see it or hear it or even feel it. It comes gradually, a growing wave of energy. A life force. A source. Something. Slowly, I feel invigorated, reenergized and omnipotent. I know now that I'm not alone.

I can see them now. I can feel them. Standing right next to me, surrounding me, and a part of me, is a multiplying army of souls. From all ages and from all corners of the earth, they've come. With them, they bring the consciousness that was the goodness and righteousness of their lives; all their memories, all their energy, all their love. Perhaps in our past lives and in our past forms, we weren't the same. We may have held different views, different opinions and different beliefs. We may have possessed different strengths, different values, different morals and different feelings. But that's all irrelevant now. What matters is that we were once the shepherds of good rather than evil, of love rather than hate, and together, we brought love into the universe. Together, we always were and always will be one.

The forces of evil become no match for our own. The Beast is fading, as is his army. The silver masks reflect fire and death no more. The steeds on which they ride crumble to the ground, the fire in their eyes extinguished forever. They turn to dust. Still, the silvers masks resist. They attempt one final onslaught, unleashing their fury and hatred upon us. The assault is strong, but united as one we do not falter. We're able to shield ourselves with a force the demons will never have. Before us, they wither and weaken until their faces reflect the garden as it once was. The surrounding flames are extinguished. Amid their dying howls and woeful shrieks, the army is vanquished forever.

All around me, life begins to regenerate. Shrubs, vineyards, orchards, flowers, trees and meadows spring into bloom. The endless forms of life return to the peace that is now restored. And all the loving beings from all the ages and four corners of the earth remain.

Today, in my dreams or perhaps even in my reality, I roam endlessly in the garden. The ghostly images of the silver faces do not return; they haunt me no more.